# IN THE EARTH'S EMBRACE

## KOTAHI BAY 2

IRIS BEAGLEHIKE

NOVA BLAKE

# CHAPTER 1

A cascade of tiny bells announced Alyssa's arrival as she pushed open the door to Sage & Salt. The sound mingled with the shop's usual gentle tinkle of wind chimes and the crystals shimmered, nestled in their displays.

The familiar scent of Sam's shop washed over Alyssa – sandalwood and sage, beeswax candles and old books – undercut by something green and vital that reminded Alyssa of soil after rain. It was comforting, that smell. It reminded her of Gran's house during her childhood, but without the weight of expectation or legacy. No ancient grudges or family obligations attached.

Samantha's shop was busier than Alyssa had expected for a weekday morning. Two older women huddled near a shelf of herb bundles, and a couple examined a display of polished pounamu pendants. None of them looked up as Alyssa slipped in with her cloth bag clutched protectively against her chest.

Sam emerged from behind a beaded curtain that separated the shop floor from the back room. Her blonde hair was piled atop her head in a messy bun, secured with a carved wooden stick. Her flowing turquoise dress caught the light as she moved, rippling like water.

"Alyssa!" Sam called out, her face lighting up. "I was just thinking about you this morning." She gestured towards the small brass teapot steaming near the register. "Kawakawa tea?"

"That depends. Will it tell me my future or just soothe my nerves?" Alyssa smiled, relaxing slightly. She'd been in town for weeks now, and this friendship still felt new, tentative.

Sam laughed, the sound bright and effortless. "Both, if you're paying attention." She poured the earthy toned liquid into a brown pottery mug. "How are things at the house?"

"Quieter," Alyssa admitted, accepting the tea. "No more Magnus, just the occasional flickering light when I'm particularly emotional." She took a sip, feeling a pang of something—sadness? She let the peppery tang of the tea coat her tongue. "I think the house is settling. Or I am."

Sam nodded knowingly. "The land remembers. It takes time to truly become part of a place like Kotahi Bay. You're doing well."

Alyssa felt a flush of pride at those words, though she tried not to show how much they meant to her.

"I brought some things, like I said," she gestured to her bag. "Some of Gran's stuff I'm ready to let go of. And a few... experiments of my own."

Sam's eyes lit with interest. "May I?" she asked, reaching for the bag.

Alyssa hesitated only a moment before handing it over. She'd been working on these pieces for weeks, letting her fingers remember what Gran had taught her so long ago. It felt both familiar and new, this deliberate channeling of energy into physical form.

Sam carefully emptied the contents onto the counter, unwrapping the delicate objects from their scrunched newspaper. Gran's old silver hand mirror with the tarnished edges. A collection of antique medicine bottles in amber and cobalt blue. A deck of weathered old tarot cards that Alyssa couldn't bring herself to use but couldn't bear to keep, either. And nestled among these remnants of her grandmother's life – Alyssa's creations.

Simple jewelry at first glance: copper wire wrapped around sea glass and crystals, leather cords strung with carved wooden beads she'd reclaimed from the tassels on an old coat, silver chains holding carefully arranged dried herbs encased in glass baubles she'd sourced online. Alyssa knew that each piece hummed with subtle energy, with intention woven into every twist and knot. She just didn't know if it was good enough to sell.

Sam picked up a pendant – a smooth river stone wrapped in an intricate pattern of copper wire that formed a tree of life. "This is yours?" she asked, holding it up to the light streaming through the shop's front window.

Alyssa nodded, suddenly nervous. "Just playing around with some techniques Gran taught me. Nothing special."

"Nothing special?" Sam scoffed, turning the pendant over in her hands. "Alyssa, this is..." She paused, closing her eyes briefly as she held the piece. "There's protection in this. And clarity. Did you intend that?"

Alyssa shifted her weight from one foot to the other. "Maybe? I was thinking about...paths. Choices. How to see the way forward when everything feels uncertain."

Sam opened her eyes and smiled. "Your magic sings, Alyssa Whenua. You have a gift."

"It's just crafting," Alyssa insisted, though a warmth bloomed in her chest at Sam's words.

"Crafting with intention is magic," Sam replied simply. She gestured around her shop. "Why do you think people come here? They're seeking connection, protection, meaning – even if they don't have the words for it." She began examining each piece, murmuring appreciatively.

The tourist couple approached the counter, breaking the moment. As Sam turned to help them, Alyssa wandered towards the window, tea in hand, and gazed out at Kotahi Bay's main street. There were quite a few people around for this time of the day, couples sitting at the outdoor tables of the cafe, families strolling the sidewalk, windowshopping like they were on the high street of a big city and not a small seaside town. The wind was picking up, bringing with it an energy of change and making the pōhutukawa trees sway, their crimson blossoms bright against the deep green leaves.

She could smell the salt air even here, five minutes' walk from the actual ocean. This place was in her blood, whether she wanted to admit it or not. A month ago, she'd been ready to pack up and flee back to the city. Now, the thought of leaving made her chest tighten.

Sam returned after ringing up the tourists' purchases. "The magical fair starts setting up tonight for this weekend," she said, returning to the items Alyssa had brought. "With more visitors coming to town, I could put these in my stall. They'll sell fast." She glanced up. "If you're willing to part with them."

Alyssa shrugged, blushing slightly. "Sure. I suppose selling them is the point. That's why I brought them to you." She felt an odd sensation creeping over her at the thought of strangers wearing her creations. Carrying her magic.

"I'll pay you, of course," Sam added, misreading her hesitation. "These are quality pieces, Alyssa."

"I don't know what they're worth," Alyssa admitted. "I didn't make them with a price tag in mind."

"That's usually when the best magic happens." Sam's smile was warm. "Trust me, I've been doing this a long time."

Alyssa found herself smiling back, wanting to trust this woman, to let her in. "Alright. Whatever you think is fair."

Sam nodded, then became businesslike as she began sorting the items into categories, occasionally pausing to examine a particular piece more closely. "You know," she said without looking up, "if you wanted to make more pieces, I could set up a permanent display for you here. Your grandmother's charms were always popular, but these..." She held up one of the wire-wrapped crystals. "These have your energy. Different, but just as powerful."

"I don't know," Alyssa said, running a finger along the edge of a display case filled with polished stones. Despite the fact that she didn't want to leave, she still had a hard time thinking about making this permanent. The offer of a permanent display at Sage & Salt felt heavy in her stomach. Too much like commitment. "I'm not sure how long I'm staying. Still feels like I'm just..."

"Housesitting?" Sam suggested with a raised eyebrow.

Alyssa laughed despite herself. "Something like that. Gran left some big shoes to fill. I'm not sure I'm the right fit."

"Those shoes were made for you," Sam said, her voice gentle but firm. "But you don't have to wear them the same way she did."

"Is that cryptic witch talk for 'find your own path'?" Alyssa joked, deflecting the weight of Sam's words.

Sam's eyes crinkled with amusement. "Something like that." She finished sorting the items and made a quick calculation on a notepad. "How does this sound?" she asked, sliding the pad towards Alyssa.

Alyssa's eyes widened at the figure. "That's way too much."

"It's what they're worth," Sam insisted. "More, if you

consider the magic imbued in them. I might be all sunshine and light, but I'm also a businesswoman, Alyssa – I don't overpay."

Alyssa wanted to protest further but recognized the stubborn set of Sam's jaw. "Thank you," she said instead, genuine gratitude warming her voice.

Sam leaned across the counter, her blue eyes suddenly serious. "The fair brings in all sorts of people. Those with magic, those seeking it. It changes the energy of the Bay." She paused. "Your grandmother used to help keep the balance during these times."

And there it was. The expectation Alyssa had been avoiding thinking about. "Sam..."

"I'm not saying you have to do what she did," Sam said quickly. "But if you're sensing changes, feeling the energy shift... just know it's normal. The boundary thins when so many magical folk gather in one place."

"Boundary?" Alyssa asked, her throat suddenly dry.

Sam hesitated. "The barrier around the town. You know this place is magical... It's why Kotahi Bay has always attracted certain... visitors."

The memory of Magnus flickered through Alyssa's mind – his ancient eyes, the cold power that had flowed through her when they'd made their pact. "Like Viking ghosts?"

"Among others." Sam straightened up and stared Alyssa in the eyes. "You miss him, don't you?"

Alyssa nodded. "I hope he's found peace, wherever he's gone off to. It wasn't his fault he was trapped here for so long. He deserves his freedom."

"That's right." Sam's smile returned as she reached for her cash box. "Now, let me pay you for these beautiful pieces, and you can tell me all about how that cat ghost of yours is doing."

As Sam counted out the money, Alyssa found herself glancing back out the window. The sky was darkening with gathering clouds, the wind picking up speed. Change was coming to Kotahi Bay – she could feel it in her bones, in the way the earth seemed to hum beneath her feet.

Alyssa tried to shake that feeling off as she took the money Sam proffered. A nice wad of cash in the hand felt better than so many things, Alyssa thought to herself as she stuffed the money into her bag. There was too much to go into her wallet, which made her grin. The scent of sandalwood followed her out onto the street and she walked away from Sage & Salt feeling a lot like the kererū that got the ripest berries.

While she still wasn't sure if Kotahi Bay was where she would settle for good, there was something to be said for having her own home with no mortgage, and being able to walk just about anywhere she needed to. And among the wreckage that June had left behind, Alyssa had been able to cobble together what looked like a future.

This was only the first of what could be many payments from Samantha, who'd agreed to sell Sylvie's things on consignment, along with the jewelry Alyssa was making. She still had a lot to learn, but had been surprised by just how quickly the knots and twists that Gran had taught her came back; as though her fingers knew exactly what they were meant to be doing.

And it was fun.

Her old life had rarely been fun, especially in the lead up to Grant breaking her heart; and here she could basically do as she pleased with no one to frown on her. That said, if she could bring herself to tell her mother that she was still in the Bay, there would be a whole lot of frowning.

Her stomach rumbled as she approached the cafe, and

obviously, that meant she should treat herself as a reward for selling her first pieces. She walked through the open door, inhaling the scent of... was that an almond croissant? Whatever it was, it smelled amazing, and the coffee as always, divine.

Alyssa approached the counter and the same poster caught her eye as it did every time she came in here, but this time she realised the date was, well, today. Sam had said that the magical fair was setting up that night, so it couldn't be long before the house trucks and buses that populated these events rolled into town. It felt strange to think of outsiders coming here. The Bay was out of the way, and didn't seem to get many visitors; which was some of the appeal, Alyssa realised. It felt safe.

Now that she'd had time to adjust to the reality of the town, it hit her that this magical fair might be truly magical. Tingles ran down her arms at that thought; new people, strange new things. Were all tarot readers and healers actually working with magic? How could one tell a charlatan from a true magical being?

Alyssa's brain sparked at the reminder that there was a hidden world; one she could have been part of her whole life but had actively avoided connecting with. Now that she'd dipped her toes into the well of power, it was hard not to see it rippling everywhere, though, in the trees, the hills, the abundant growth of plants on her property.

She was trying to ignore it.

"What will it be today, love?" the kind woman behind the counter asked her. Alyssa thought her name was Lynn, but she wasn't confident enough to start calling the locals by name.

"I'll have a flat white with a shot of hazelnut, please." She could treat herself to something a little special on a day like today.

"Have here, or takeaway?" The woman raised an eyebrow, and it was as though she was asking a deeper question, maybe whether Alyssa was staying in the Bay or not.

"To go," she said. Then added, "I've got some work to do in the garden today. Get Gran's place back in shape."

That seemed to appease the other woman, whose face softened at the mention of Sylvie.

"Glad to see someone taking care of the place, love." She nodded in approval and moved to the coffee machine.

"Has this fair come to town before?" Alyssa asked, curious to know more.

"Oh yes, they come every year. They're a bit like this place, but then, you'd know that." The woman winked at Alyssa and a shiver ran down her spine. This woman was apparently in on the secret magic of this place. But was it really a secret?

Alyssa took her cue to step back and glanced over the other pamphlets dotting the noticeboard while other customers left or entered the store, attempting to dull the feeling that was flowing through her body. There was one notice for a lawnmower person, and maybe that was what she needed. The grass was getting very long.

"Alyssa," the barista called to her and she spun to collect the proffered cup, inhaling the warm hazelnut and coffee scent. Loving the way it grounded her in the here and now. Just a normal day, in a normal town.

"Thank you," she called as she headed for the door. While she was inside, Constance had taken up her regular spot at an outdoor table. The older woman's eyes seemed to drill into her, a hopeful look that Alyssa refused to acknowledge. As if dealing with the ghost hadn't been enough; there was clearly more that this town wanted from her.

How many letters and phone calls had she ignored from Mrs Nolan now? She was losing count. Refused to count.

She kept walking, past the beauty salon, past the corner store. She was just hitting the end of town when a loud horn blared and she jumped, spilling coffee down her shirt.

Someone wolf whistled, and Alyssa spun to see a car slowing to a crawl, a familiar face leering out the window.

"Kelly!!!"

# CHAPTER 2

"Oh my god, your hair!" Kelly squealed, jumping out of the car and throwing her arms around Alyssa in a bone-crushing hug. "You look absolutely gorgeous! Who did this? Please tell me there's a decent hairdresser in this place because I need their number immediately."

Alyssa felt her cheeks warm at the compliment, touching the ends of her new haircut self-consciously. "Thanks, Kels. There's actually this amazing – "

"Get in!" Kelly interrupted, bouncing on her toes like an excited puppy. Her dark hair was in its usual messy bun, wisps escaping to frame her face, and she wore her standard uniform of expensive jeans and a black tank top that showed off her CrossFit-toned arms. "I have a surprise for you!"

Kelly practically shoved her into the passenger seat and was racing around to the driver's side. The car still smelled like Kelly – her vanilla perfume mixed with the faint aroma of old wine.

"How did you even find me?" Alyssa asked as Kelly pulled away from the curb with characteristic enthusiasm.

"Small town, babe. I just arrived and there you were." Kelly shot her a look.

"It sure is, and you only have to turn the corner and drive three blocks to get me home." She navigated the short distance. When they pulled into the driveway, Kelly let out a low whistle.

"Well isn't this cute!" She got out and exhaled deeply, taking in the garden beds Alyssa had been tending. "Look at those flowers! Since when do you garden?"

Alyssa felt a flush of pride as she surveyed her handiwork. The dahlias were blooming in riots of orange and pink, and she'd managed to tame the overgrown lavender into something resembling intentional landscaping. "Since I inherited a house with an established garden. Turns out I don't have a black thumb after all."

"Must be nice," Kelly said, heading to the back of the car, "inheriting a whole house. Too bad it's in the middle of Nowheresville!" She pulled out a large box that clinked and sloshed ominously.

"Now, I got you a gift, but no peeking."

"Is it alcoholic?" Alyssa asked. So much of their time together was wrapped in a warm, buzzed state, and while part of her missed that, she'd barely touched a drop since Magnus had disappeared. She wasn't sure how she felt about her old life and her new one colliding.

"No, well, yes, I did bring alcohol, but this one is a little... You'll see." Kelly reached in for another box as she spoke.

"This seems suspiciously like the dregs of our alcohol cabinet," Alyssa said, raising an eyebrow as she looked at the box. She tried to keep a playful tone but Magnus's voice still echoed in her head – something about her drinking habits that had hit a little too close to home. Had she been trying to escape instead of be present in her life?

Kelly grinned, bumping the car door closed with her hip. "Yup! I can't drink it all on my own, and if you're staying put then we need to warm your new house appropriately."

Alyssa forced a grin that felt like plastic on her face, but Kelly didn't seem to notice. She was too busy admiring the villa's weatherboard exterior and the porch swing Alyssa had repaired last week.

"What, no key?" Kelly called out as Alyssa pushed open the front door.

"It's the Bay, Kels. No keys necessary." She didn't mention that in her case it had more to do with the fact that her grandmother had performed decades of magic within these walls and the house was carefully warded.

The house itself seemed to recognize her now, welcoming her home each time she approached. Alyssa was pretty sure that Kelly wasn't ready for that level of intel.

"If you say so," Kelly said, skepticism replaced by glee. "Now, close your eyes."

Alyssa raised an eyebrow at her friend but did as she was told, trying not to feel hurt that Kelly didn't seem to notice the inside of the house she'd worked so hard on. The walls were freshly painted, the horrible yellow banished in favour of crisp white that made the whole space feel bigger and brighter.

"Put your hands out."

"I'm not sure I like this, Kels. If you're giving me something slimy, I will kill you."

"Oh no, this is something far better."

Alyssa closed her eyes and something small, soft and warm slid into her hands. Tiny claws pricked her palms and she heard the tiniest mew. Her eyes shot open to see a small grey kitten with white paws, squirming in her grip. She got such a fright that she almost dropped it.

"Kelly!"

"I know, I know, you're going to tell me you can't have pets or you're allergic or something, but hear me out." Kelly held up her hands. "This little guy just appeared, mewling at my doorstep. I was on my way here and I wondered if maybe you could take him, you know avoid him having to go to a shelter..."

Alyssa's eyes darted between the kitten and Kelly, who was cradling her hands under Alyssa's, ready to catch the kitten if needed.

"He just showed up on your doorstep, so maybe it was meant to be." Alyssa lifted the little guy to her face and rubbed her cheek against his impossibly soft fur. Kelly's story was a total fabrication, but in this case, she'd let it slide. "Thank you for rescuing him from certain death. I'm sure I can find a spot for him here."

"A spot? Don't tell me you've gone all crazy cat lady already. I told you, you have to be at least forty five to claim that title!"

"We'll be there in no time, and I was thinking that seeing as I can't have kids, I could start early on the cats. No?" The words came out lighter than she felt them.

Kelly's face softened, the manic energy dimming for a moment. "Babe..." She reached out and squeezed Alyssa's shoulder. There was so much water under the bridge of Alyssa's infertility leading to her break up with Grant. Kelly knew too much about that already. Alyssa wanted to forget.

"Let's not," Alyssa said quickly, cuddling the kitten closer. "What's his name?"

"I like Socks," said Kelly.

"Socks? Socks?!"

Kelly blushed and reached out to stroke the kitten's ears. "Yeah, you know, because of his little white paws."

Alyssa swallowed a laugh. "Socks it is then."

She set Socks down in the hallway and watched him assess his new domain, taking a few tentative steps on the wooden floor before his back legs slipped out from under him. "Oh yeah, we're going to be great together."

There was a discontented feeling from behind her and she turned to see the ghostly form of Buttons materialize in the living room doorway, glaring at the living kitten with spectral fury. Alyssa's heart skipped and she almost gave herself away. She'd gotten so used to the ghost cat that she'd forgotten Kelly couldn't see them.

"So this is the living room," she said quickly, steering Kelly past the irritated ghost feline and into the freshly painted space. "I painted it myself."

"Very nice," Kelly said. "Though I can't believe you did manual labor voluntarily. Remember when we tried to assemble that IKEA bookshelf?"

"That was different. That was Swedish torture disguised as furniture." Alyssa led her through to the kitchen, proud of the way the afternoon light streamed through the windows she'd finally gotten around to cleaning properly.

"And this is where the magic happens?"

Alyssa's eyebrows shot up.

"Cooking magic," Kelly clarified. "You know, the kind where you burn toast."

They both laughed. "Some things never change. So, show me the rest of this place! I want to see where you've been hiding out."

They continued through the house, Alyssa carefully avoiding the basement door and the room where she'd been storing Gran's more obviously magical items. Kelly made appropriate noises of appreciation, though Alyssa could see her trying to understand why anyone would choose this quiet existence over city life.

"Okay, house tour's over," Kelly announced, reaching out to grip Alyssa's hand. "Now you need to show me this town. I want to see what's so special about Kotahi Bay that you don't want to live with me anymore."

"How's it going with your new flatmate?" Alyssa asked, feeling a pang of guilt that she'd both abandoned her friend, and neglected to check in as much as she should have.

Kelly shrugged and looked away. "Let's go!"

"Are you sure? There's not much to see," Alyssa said, though part of her wanted to show Kelly the places that had become important to her.

"Yes, and Socks needs supplies anyway." Kelly was already heading for the door, energy crackling around her like electricity. "Plus, I'm starving. Please tell me there's somewhere to eat that isn't a gas station."

Alyssa grabbed her bag, making sure Socks was secure inside before they headed out. "There's actually a really nice café, and a bakery that does the most amazing – "

"Lead the way, tour guide!"

Minutes later, they walked down the main street. "Oh my goodness, babe. Is this the entire town?"

"It's not about size," Alyssa protested, feeling oddly defensive. "Look, there's the café. They do incredible flat whites and their almond croissants are life-changing."

Kelly peered through the window skeptically. "It's cute, I guess. Very... rustic."

They passed the bakery next, where the smell of fresh bread wafted out onto the street. Mrs Wren was arranging cupcakes in the window display – today's special was lavender honey with lemon and thyme cream cheese topping.

"Wait," Kelly said, stopping abruptly. "We can't just walk past that smell. I need whatever's making it immediately."

Before Alyssa could protest, Kelly had dragged her into the

bakery. They ended up with today's cupcake special and two kumara and sage scones still warm from the oven, the earthy sweetness of the kumara balanced perfectly with the subtle herb flavour and a generous swipe of butter that melted instantly into the fluffy interior. Kelly made an obscene noise at her first bite.

"Okay, fine," she said, crumbs flying as she spoke with her mouth full. "Your nowhere town has one thing going for it. This is better than that fancy place we used to go to – what was it called? The one with the outrageously expensive croissants?"

"Told you," Alyssa said smugly, savouring her own scone. The butter was definitely local – she could taste the richness of grass-fed cream, probably from the farm just outside town. Mrs Wren winked at her as they left.

"Okay, that was amazing," Kelly conceded. "But where's the wine bar? Is anything open after 9pm?"

"We have a pub," Alyssa offered weakly.

"A pub. Singular." Kelly laughed, linking her arm through Alyssa's. "You've really embraced the simple life, haven't you?"

They turned the corner and the view opened up – the bay spreading out before them in shades of blue and green, the pōhutukawa trees lining the shore with their crimson blooms blazing in the afternoon sun. Even Kelly stopped talking for a moment.

"Okay," she said quietly. "That's beautiful."

"Right?" Alyssa felt a surge of pride. "And you can walk here from anywhere in town. The beach is amazing for swimming, and there are walking trails all through the bush, and –"

"And that's it? Beach and bush?" Kelly was back to her teasing tone. "What do you do for fun? Besides making friends with all five residents?"

Alyssa was about to respond when she spotted a familiar poster taped to a lamppost. The Magical Fair – tonight through the weekend. Her stomach dropped. How was she going to keep Kelly away from that?

"What's this?" Kelly had noticed it too, moving closer to read. "'Magical Fair'? Oh my god, Alyssa, is this like a hippie craft fair? With crystals and dream catchers?"

"I think so," Alyssa said carefully.

"We have to go! It'll be hilarious. We can get our auras read and buy some healing stones." Kelly was practically bouncing again. "When does it start?"

"Tonight, but – "

"Perfect! We'll get dinner and wine and then check out the magical mysteries of Kotahi Bay." Kelly's grin was wicked. "Maybe I'll find out what's really keeping you here. Got yourself a local wizard boyfriend?"

"Definitely not," Alyssa said firmly. The last thing she needed was Kelly exposed to actual magic, but she knew her friend, and there was no way she'd be able to keep Kelly away from the fair all weekend.

They continued walking, passing Tricks and Tresses where Alyssa pointed out Quinn's salon ("They did my hair!"), the corner store ("Bigger than it looks from outside"), and Sage & Salt, where a handwritten sign in the window read "Back in 5 minutes!"

"Sam's probably just grabbing coffee. She sells some of my jewelry."

"You've mentioned her before, right? Your new friend's shop?" Kelly asked, peering through the window at the crystals and incense displays. "Wait...You're making jewelry now?" Kelly's voice held a note of surprise. "When did you become crafty?"

"Gran taught me when I was young. I'm just... remembering." Alyssa didn't mention that each piece hummed with protective magic, that her fingers seemed to know exactly how to weave intention into wire and stone.

They ended up at the small general store, where Kelly proceeded to buy what seemed like half the shop's supply of kitten food, cat toys, and "essential accessories" that Socks definitely didn't need.

"A bow tie collar? Really?" Alyssa held up the offending item.

"He needs to look distinguished!" Kelly protested. "Besides, what else am I going to spend money on in this town?"

The dismissal stung more than Alyssa expected. "There's plenty here. It's just... different."

"Different is one word for it," Kelly said, not unkindly but not exactly supportive either. "I mean, it's pretty and all, but don't you miss civilization?"

"Not really – " Alyssa sputtered.

"I'm kidding!" Kelly bumped her hip against Alyssa's. "I just don't get it. You had a life in the city. Friends, a job, options. I understand the appeal of pretty views and free rent, but..."

Alyssa shook her head. "It's not for you, I get that. But let me enjoy it. I like it here."

"Fair enough," said Kelly.

"After everything with Grant, I needed – "

"To run away?" Kelly's voice was gentle but pointed.

"To start over." Alyssa lifted her chin. "And yeah, it's good here. The people are kind, the air is clean, and I can actually hear myself think."

Kelly studied her for a long moment, her eyes softening, shoulders sagging a little. "You really like it here."

"I really do."

Kelly let out a huff and rolled her eyes, grinning in that way she did to blow off her real emotions. "I hope it gets more interesting..."

Alyssa let out a surprised laugh. *More interesting?* It had already been far too interesting! If only Kelly knew how not-boring Kotahi Bay really was. Ghost cats, inherited witch powers, ancient spirits locked in basements – boring was the last thing her life had been lately. Alyssa wanted to tell her the truth. About Magnus and Buttons, about the magic humming in her veins, about the way the earth here seemed to sing to her. About June's attack and Mrs Nolan's demands and the weight of a family legacy she was still trying to understand.

Instead, she said, "It's peaceful here," linking her arm through Kelly's again. "Come on, let's get home."

As they walked back, Kelly chattering about everything and nothing, Alyssa found herself thinking about the fair starting tonight. She'd have to find a way to keep Kelly distracted from any real magic. In her experience it was all far too dangerous!

# CHAPTER 3

Constance Mōhio traced the rim of her teacup with a gnarled finger, its iridescent paua blue-green surface catching the morning light. From her cottage window, she could see the forest edge where native birds flitted between branches – pīwakawaka with their fan-like tails, the occasional flash of a kererū's purple-green plumage.

Her joints ached more than usual this morning. Weather coming, certainly, but something else too. A pressure in the air, a sense of something vast and ancient stirring beneath the seemingly tranquil surface of the Bay.

The barrier was thinning.

Constance sighed, her breath disturbing the steam that rose from her kumerahou tea. The timing of that blasted magical fair couldn't be worse – and yet, perhaps it couldn't be better. All those visitors with their various energies would disrupt the delicate balance she and the others had maintained for decades. But that same influx of power could be channeled, directed into strengthening the town's protections.

If they were careful. If they were prepared.

She glanced at the calendar hanging beside her stove, marked with phases of the moon and tide times. The fair would fully open for three days. Vehicles were already arriving, colourful house trucks and buses parking in the designated field at the edge of town.

A tūī called from the pōhutukawa tree outside her window, its song rising and falling like an alarm. Constance smiled; her messenger, bringing news from the edges of the Bay. The song shifted, taking on an urgent tone.

"I hear you," she murmured, rising slowly from her chair.

Time to go.

She gathered her walking stick, carved with protection symbols that spiraled along its length. Her pounamu pendant hummed against her chest as she stepped outside, its energy resonating with the land beneath her feet. The path from her cottage wound through a small garden of medicinal herbs and native plants – horopito with its pepper-sharp leaves, mānuka heaving with tiny white flowers, kawakawa with its heart-shaped foliage.

Constance paused, letting her awareness spread through the soil, feeling the ancient roots that connected all living things in Kotahi Bay. The vibration was stronger today, almost discordant – like a guitar string tuned too tight, ready to snap.

She had just reached the garden gate when she spotted Matai approaching, his tall figure unmistakable even at a distance. His tattoos seemed especially vivid today, the protection runes flowing across his forearms shifting slightly in the diffused light.

"I was coming to see you," he said with concern.

"I know." Constance nodded, unsurprised. "Walk with me. We need to find Samantha."

They fell into step together, Matai unconsciously slowing

his pace to match hers. The gravel path crunched beneath their feet as they headed towards the centre of the Bay.

"The barrier weakened again last night," Matai said, keeping his voice low though there was no one else around. "I felt it from my place. Like something pressing from the other side."

"Yes." Constance tapped her walking stick against the ground for emphasis. "My time is running short, Matai. There's work to be done if the next generation is to take up the task."

Matai's expression darkened. "You still have years ahead of you."

"Perhaps," she conceded with a small smile. "But certainly not enough time to delay what must be done. Tū grows stronger by the day."

They passed from the wooded outskirts into the village proper. The scent of the forest gave way to more human smells – fresh bread from the bakery, coffee from the café, salt from the distant ocean. Voices carried on the wind, growing louder as they approached the main street where there seemed to be twice as many people as normal. The air buzzed with antic-ipation.

Sam herself was arranging a display table near the front of her store, carefully setting out crystals and small fabric pouches of herbs.

"Any progress with Alyssa?" Constance asked without preamble as they approached.

Sam looked up, her face brightening at the sight of them. "Perfect timing! I was just about to message you both." She gestured towards the display. "Look what Alyssa dropped off this morning."

On a velvet cloth lay several pieces of jewelry – simple yet elegant designs of wire-wrapped stones, carved wooden beads on leather cords, and pendants containing herbs suspended in clear resin. Even from a distance, Constance could sense the energy woven into each charm.

Matai picked up a bracelet, its copper wire forming intricate knots around a smooth river stone. "She made these?"

"Every one," Sam confirmed proudly. "I've never seen someone with untrained abilities create such powerful protective charms. It's like she instinctively knows how to channel her energy."

Constance leaned forward, examining a pendant containing what appeared to be dried kawakawa and mānuka leaves. The materials themselves held power, but it was the intention behind their arrangement that made the piece sing with protective energy.

"Her grandmother taught her the basics long ago," Constance said. "The knowledge has been dormant, not absent." She set the pendant down carefully. "But making trinkets is one thing. Taking responsibility for the Bay's protection is quite another."

Sam's expression sobered. "She's powerful, I can feel it. But she's not yet committed to staying. This place... it still carries painful memories for her."

"And she doesn't understand the challenges ahead," Matai added. "Nor is she ready to."

"No," agreed Constance. The breeze shifted, carrying the scent of coming rain and something else – something older, wilder. She turned her face towards it briefly, then looked back at Sam and Matai. "Be on the lookout for the others."

Sam frowned. "Others?"

"We need all of the new generation guardians to take up the mantle," Constance explained, her voice dropping. "The pattern has already begun to form. Alyssa is just one thread in the weaving."

"The barrier won't stand a chance without them. All the

power here, all the magic accumulated over generations, will be at risk."

Sam's voice dropped. "You mean Tūmatauenga."

Constance's walking stick struck the ground sharply. "Do not speak his full name so freely. Tū is the god of war. The god of domination. Names have power, and his attention is the last thing we need."

The breeze died suddenly, as if the air itself was holding its breath. Sam shivered despite the warmth.

"He's already watching, isn't he?" Matai said quietly.

Constance didn't answer. She didn't need to.

A distant rumble of thunder punctuated her words, rolling over the hills that cradled Kotahi Bay. The wind picked up, carrying the subtle scent of iron and ash.

"The fair begins soon," Constance said, turning to look across at the field of colourful tents. "With it will come opportunities... and dangers. Keep watch, both of you."

She didn't need to elaborate. They knew as well as she did that power attracted power, that the thinning of the barrier would draw all manner of beings to Kotahi Bay – some benign, some decidedly not.

# CHAPTER 4

The fair had transformed the empty field at the edge of Kotahi Bay overnight, as if it had been conjured up. House trucks and jewel-toned tents created a meandering pattern, fabric billowing softly in the early evening breeze as visitors wandered between the stalls. The air was thick with the scent of woodsmoke, incense, and caramelized sugar.

"This looks amazing!" Kelly said, squeezing Alyssa's arm in excitement. "Like real magic..."

Alyssa felt the unmistakable tingle of magic humming in the air – a subtle vibration that most people would dismiss as excitement or atmosphere. But she knew better. This wasn't just any traveling fair; real magic flowed through it, hidden in plain sight from non-magical people like Kelly.

She could only hope that it stayed that way.

"It's just good stagecraft," Alyssa said with studied casualness, watching as a nearby vendor lit a bundle of herbs that released silver smoke into the air. "They know how to make everything look mystical."

Kelly rolled her eyes. "You're always so practical. Can't you just enjoy the mystery of it all?"

Before Alyssa could respond, Kelly grabbed her hand and pulled her towards a crimson bell tent set slightly apart from the others. A hand-painted wooden sign hung from its entrance: *Tarot Reader & Intuitive Guide.*

"Come on," Kelly urged, "we have to get our cards read!"

Alyssa's stomach dropped. She had heard about Mia by reputation – a genuine witch with serious talent, not someone who put on a show for tourists. "I don't think that's – "

"Please?" Kelly's eyes lit up with enthusiasm. "We go to these fairs every year and never do it. I want the full experience!" The unspoken words 'this time' hung in the air for Alyssa, and she wondered if Kelly felt them too.

As they approached, the tent flap parted and a woman with dark hair tied back in a colourful scarf emerged, bidding farewell to her previous client. A small wooden sign listed prices, and a single chair sat empty beside the entrance.

"Perfect timing," Kelly whispered. "No line!"

The woman – Mia – turned towards them, and Alyssa felt a jolt of recognition pass between them. Mia's eyes widened slightly before her face settled into a knowing smile.

"Welcome," she said, her voice warm but carrying a hint of something deeper. "Are you interested in a reading?"

"Yes!" Kelly answered eagerly. Then she nudged Alyssa forward. "You go first though. I want to see how it works."

Inside the tent, the air was thick with the scent of vanilla and dried herbs. A small round table covered in deep crimson velvet stood in the centre, surrounded by cushioned stools. Crystals caught the light from small lanterns hanging from the tent's frame, casting prismatic patterns across the canvas walls.

A magpie perched on a wooden stand in the corner, its eyes

unnervingly intelligent as it tracked Alyssa's movements. It was smaller than most, and Alyssa had heard that Mia had rescued him when he was just a baby.

"Whoa..." said Kelly, eyeing the bird.

"Please, sit," Mia gestured to one of the stools. "I'm Mia, and this is Rufus."

The bird made a soft chattering sound that sounded almost like a greeting.

"I'm Alyssa," she replied, sinking onto the stool. From the corner of her eye, she could see Kelly hovering near the tent's entrance, watching with fascination.

Mia began shuffling a tarot deck with practiced hands, the soft whispering of card against card filling the small space. "Your friend," Mia said quietly, her voice barely audible, "she doesn't know about you, does she?"

Alyssa's breath caught but fortunately Kelly was distracted by Rufus, cooing at him. "No," she whispered. "She's my best friend, but she has no idea."

Mia nodded, then laid three cards face down on the table. "A simple past-present-future spread," she explained, louder now for Kelly's benefit. "We'll start with your past."

She turned over the first card. The painted figure of a woman sitting amid lush vegetation gazed up at them.

"The Empress," Mia said. "Creation, abundance, nurturing. A deep connection to the natural world." Her dark eyes met Alyssa's. "Our mother earth has always responded to you, hasn't she?"

Alyssa shrugged. "I've been getting into gardening lately."

The second card showed a winged figure pouring water between chalices. "Temperance – finding balance, moderation, patience. You're currently working to harmonize different aspects of your life." She glanced briefly towards Kelly, who had come closer now. "Different worlds, perhaps."

Alyssa's skin prickled with awareness. She could feel Kelly shifting her weight from foot to foot behind her, and she desperately wished that her friend wasn't here right now. That she wasn't here either.

Mia's fingers hovered over the third card before turning it over. A skeletal figure astride a white horse gazed up at them, its empty eye sockets somehow compelling.

"Death," Mia said softly.

Kelly gasped. "That can't be good."

"The Death card is often misunderstood," Mia explained reassuringly, though her eyes remained fixed on Alyssa. "It represents transformation, change, the ending of one cycle so another can begin." Her fingertip traced the outline of the card, leaving a trail of goosebumps on Alyssa's arms. "Something significant is shifting in your life. Old patterns falling away to make room for new growth."

The air in the tent seemed to thicken, making it harder to breathe. Alyssa could feel each beat of her heart, loud in her ears.

"Is that... good?" she managed to ask.

"Change is rarely comfortable," Mia replied, her voice gentle yet firm. "But it's necessary. The card doesn't specify whether the transformation will be easy or difficult – only that it's coming." Her gaze softened slightly. "Be ready."

Alyssa stepped outside the tent, scrambling for fresh air. She blinked, trying to clear her head of Mia's warning.

"Well?" Kelly prompted. "What do you think?"

"It's all pretty vague, stuff about change coming," Alyssa replied, forcing her voice to sound casual. "You know how these things are."

"My turn then!" Kelly declared, but as she stepped towards the tent entrance, she hesitated. Through the open flap, they could see Mia watching them, Rufus now perched on her shoulder. The bird's black eyes gleamed in the shadows.

Kelly took a step back. "Actually... I think I'll pass."

"What? Why?" Alyssa asked, genuinely surprised. "You were so excited to do this."

"I don't know," Kelly rubbed her arms as if suddenly cold. "Something about it just feels... off. Like she could see right through me."

"That's a bit strange," Alyssa said, frowning. "You're the one who dragged me over here."

"I changed my mind, okay?" Kelly's tone was defensive. "Besides, I spotted a stall selling the fancy candyfloss – you know, the one with like six different flavours? Let's get some instead."

Before Alyssa could argue, Kelly was already moving towards the food section. "I need to find Sam's stall anyway," Alyssa called after her. "She said she'd be over this way."

"Perfect! I'll get the candyfloss and meet you there," Kelly replied, already joining the queue at a stall where a vendor was spinning colourful clouds of sugar onto paper cones. "Which way is that again?"

Alyssa pointed towards a row of stalls near the edge of the fairground. "Over there, under the big oak tree. Find the green banner with the leaf design."

As Kelly waited in line, Alyssa made her way through the crowd. Lanterns were being lit, transforming the atmosphere from festive to enchanted as tiny lights winked on one by one.

She found Sam's stall easily – a beautiful display of hand-crafted charms, dried herbs hanging from the frame, and bottles of tinctures arranged in a rainbow gradient. Sam looked up as Alyssa approached, her face brightening.

"You made it!" Sam exclaimed, coming around the table to

give Alyssa a quick hug that smelled of lavender and cloves. "How's the fair treating you?"

"It's wonderful," Alyssa admitted. "Though I'm here with my friend Kelly who just happened to surprise me with a visit... so I've been pretending none of the magic is real."

Sam's mouth quirked into a sympathetic smile. "Quite the charade," she muttered, her smile crinkled into a frown. "I wonder how she got through the town's barrier."

Before Alyssa could respond, she noticed someone else behind the stall – a woman with dark hair and thoughtful eyes, wearing a deep red garnet ring that pulsed with energy.

Sam followed her gaze. "Oh! Alyssa, this is Ursula. She's just been travelling in Cornwall - staying in another entirely magical village called Myrtlewood - can you believe it? I'm selling some of their goods as well."

When Alyssa smiled at Ursula a current of energy passed between them – like touching a live wire, but pleasant rather than shocking. Ursula's eyes widened in recognition.

"The earth magic in you is incredibly strong," she said softly, still holding Alyssa's hand. "It's practically radiating from you."

Alyssa blushed. "I'm still learning to harness it, honestly."

Two more people approached from behind the stall – a tall man with long, wavy dark hair and striking green eyes, and a woman with bright purple hair wearing what looked like a vintage dress from another era.

"These are my partners, Rowan and Hazel," Ursula introduced them.

Alyssa noticed that half of Sam's table was covered with their wares – delicate glass pendants and small terrariums. Each contained miniature plants that looked impossibly vibrant and alive despite their enclosed spaces.

"Hazel was just admiring your charms," Sam said, nodding

towards the jewellery Alyssa had brought her earlier, which dangled from a hanging shelf above her stall.

"Oh yes. Did you make them yourself?" Hazel asked.

"It was just a first attempt," Alyssa admitted, self-consciously. "I was just messing around."

Rowan leaned closer, his voice low and melodic. "They're quite powerful. Whoever taught you knows what they're doing."

Alyssa glanced over at their side of the stall, and moved towards it, drawn in by shimmering pendants. She picked one up, marveling at the tiny ecosystem inside – a perfect miniature fern unfurling amid moss and small crystals. It felt warm to the touch, alive in a way that ordinary glass shouldn't be.

"These are beautiful," she said. "And...real! How do you keep the plants alive in there?"

"They're enchanted to connect with the wearer's vital life force," Hazel explained, her eyes sparkling with enthusiasm.

"We sell them to non-magical people too," Ursula added with a wink. "They just think we've found some clever terrarium trick."

The conversation paused as Kelly approached, balancing two enormous clouds of candyfloss – one pink, one blue. The sticky sweet scent preceded her arrival.

"Sorry, that took forever!" Kelly exclaimed, handing the pink candyfloss to Alyssa. "The line was ridiculous, but totally worth it. Try it – it's strawberry and rose water."

Alyssa introduced Kelly to everyone, watching carefully as they exchanged greetings. Something odd flickered across Sam's face when she shook Kelly's hand – a moment of tension that was there and gone so quickly Alyssa almost missed it.

While Kelly chatted animatedly with Ursula about the glass pendants, Sam pulled Alyssa slightly aside.

"Be careful," she warned in a whisper, her eyes serious. "I'm getting weird vibes from your friend there."

Alyssa blinked in surprise. Sam's eyes darted towards Kelly, then back to Alyssa.

"She is a bit odd," Alyssa said, quietly. "But..." She opened her mouth to say more but stopped as Kelly turned back towards them.

"These are gorgeous!" Kelly exclaimed, pointing to the pendants. "We should get matching ones, Alyssa." Then she grabbed Alyssa's arm, sticky fingers leaving traces of sugar on her skin. "But we should see the rest of the fair first. There's still so much to explore!"

As Kelly pulled her away from the stall, Alyssa looked back at Sam, questions burning in her mind. Was it just that Kelly wasn't magical and everyone else here was? She made a note to follow up at a better time, but something in her gut knew Sam was onto something. Kelly was acting strangely, even more erratic than usual. Something was up and Alyssa was going to find out what it was, one way or another.

# CHAPTER 5

The strings of fairy lights crisscrossed overhead lit up as dusk settled over Kotahi Bay. Brendan moved between the stalls with deliberate nonchalance, careful not to let desperation show on his face. Scents from the food stalls mingled with the salt breeze rolling in from the nearby ocean.

Magic hummed beneath the surface of everything here – not the parlour tricks sold to tourists, but real power. He could feel it brushing against his senses, familiar and strange at the same time.

His phone vibrated in his pocket. *Michael had another bad night.*

Brendan shoved the phone away without replying. He couldn't think about that now – not if he wanted to keep his composure. Not if he wanted to find what he came for.

Focus on the task at hand. Ignore the message, ignore the threads of spirit that lingered here, roaming the field along with all the living patrons.

A collection of crystals gleamed under lantern light. A woman with dreadlocks wrapped in colourful fabric talked animatedly about cleansing energies and alien harmonic frequencies to a rapt audience. Brendan moved past without slowing. New age mumbo jumbo wouldn't help. Not now.

He paused at a stall displaying handcrafted jewelry. Not the mass-produced stuff, but items made with intent. His attention caught on a pendant – simple copper wire wrapped around beach glass that reminded him of summer storms. Something about it called to him, the way it caught the light, fractured it, transformed it.

"That piece speaks to you?"

The blonde woman behind the counter was familiar – from the crystal shop in town.

"I'm just browsing," he said, voice carefully neutral.

"It's good protection," she said, eyes thoughtful as she studied him.

Brendan's chest tightened. It wouldn't solve his problem entirely, but maybe it would help. At this point, he'd try anything. "How much?"

She gestured to the price tag.

"Seems a small price to pay for protection," he muttered.

She nodded. "Though I didn't make this one – it's special." She tilted her head. "A local artist. She has a gift."

He handed over the cash, watched as she wrapped the pendant in tissue paper with surprising care.

"You're new in town," she said. Not a question.

"Just passing through."

She smiled like she knew better. "No one just passes through Kotahi Bay."

Something in her gaze made him uncomfortable – too perceptive, too knowing. Like she could see the tangled mess of desperation and determination that drove him. He took the pendant and nodded his thanks, backing away before she could ask more questions.

The tarot reader's tent stood slightly apart from the other stalls, its deep crimson fabric glowing like a wound in the twilight. Brendan hesitated, hand unconsciously closing around the pendant in his pocket.

Professional fortune-tellers could be frauds, but sometimes... sometimes the real ones hid in plain sight. And he needed information – any edge he could get.

"I wouldn't waste your time."

Mrs Nolan's voice cut through his thoughts, sharp as a blade. She wore her usual severe black pantsuit, looking absurdly formal among the dreadlocked hippies and flowing dresses of the fair patrons.

"I gave you a task," she continued, voice pitched low. "June's house contains magical items that could be of actual assistance. You won't find answers at carnival sideshows."

"I'm covering all bases," Brendan replied, jaw tight. "And I haven't found anything useful in that house yet."

"Keep looking." Her smile didn't reach her eyes. "Time is precious, isn't it? For your situation..."

The casual mention of his "situation" made his skin crawl. Mrs Nolan wielded information like a weapon, reminding him of exactly what he stood to lose if he didn't play along.

"I'll handle it," he said, the words tasting bitter.

Mrs Nolan's gaze shifted suddenly, her expression souring. "Speaking of problems."

Brendan followed her line of sight across the fairground. A woman stood by a house truck, laughing with the vendor. Her hair caught the light, her profile striking even at a distance. Something about her pulled at him – a current of energy that rippled through the evening air. He'd seen her around town. Noticed her.

"That's her? Sylvie's granddaughter?" he asked, unable to keep the interest from his voice.

"Alyssa," Mrs Nolan confirmed, lips pinched. "Still in town, despite my best efforts. She should have sold her grandmother's house and moved on by now."

The woman – Alyssa – turned slightly and Brendan could see her face properly. There was an openness to her expression, a warmth that contrasted sharply with Mrs Nolan's calculating presence beside him.

"She could become a problem for your plans," Mrs Nolan continued, her voice dropping further. "If she starts poking around, asking questions... we might need to get rid of her. One way or another."

Brendan's stomach twisted. He understood what that implied.

"Is that really necessary?" he asked carefully.

Mrs Nolan's tone was ice. "Some sacrifices are unavoidable."

Alyssa was just living her life. She hadn't asked to be caught up in whatever game Mrs Nolan was playing. And yet here he was, contemplating her fate as casually as checking the weather. But then he thought of Michael.

"Let me deal with her," Brendan said. "I'll make sure she doesn't interfere." And he could ensure there was no need to go as far as his employer had implied.

Mrs Nolan studied him, suspicious. "And how will you manage that?"

He shrugged, forcing a casual smile. "Charm has its uses."

"Just remember where your loyalties lie," she warned, but her attention was already shifting to someone else in the crowd. With a final pointed look, she moved away, melting into the throng of festival-goers.

Brendan exhaled slowly, unclenching his fists. The pendant pressed against his palm, edges biting into his skin.

Across the fairground, Alyssa laughed at something. The

sound was musical. Enticing. He turned away, forcing himself to focus. Whatever this witch was doing, whatever power she had, Michael was more important. He had to remember that.

Even if it meant becoming the villain in someone else's story.

# CHAPTER 6

Something shifted in the air around Alyssa, like the moment before lightning strikes. The hairs on her arms stood up beneath her cardigan, and the candyfloss Kelly was waving at her suddenly tasted too sweet, cloying.

Then she heard it – bright, genuine laughter cutting through the ambient noise of the fair. Her magic recognized the voice before her mind did, a familiar vibration that made her chest tighten with dread.

*No. Not here. Not now.*

Alyssa's head snapped up, and there she was. Twenty meters away, standing beside a pottery stall.

Miri.

Could it be her? The woman's dark hair was shorter, framing her face in a way that made her appear so confident. She was laughing at something one of her friends had said – two women Alyssa didn't recognize, both holding steaming paper cups. Completely at ease.

The memory hit without warning: *"Just a little fire, Lysie. Show me how you make those coloured flames you told me about!"*

Alyssa's stomach lurched. The acrid smell of burning hair flooded her nostrils as if it were happening all over again. The sound of screaming. The sight of angry red burns spreading across pale skin like spilled paint. Miri's face, twisted in agony, staring at her as if she'd become something monstrous.

*I did that. I hurt her.*

Her heart hammered against her ribs so hard she was sure everyone could hear it. The fairy lights strung between the stalls began to flicker, responding to her distress. She needed to leave. Right now. But her feet might as well have been set in concrete.

"Alyssa?" Kelly's voice seemed to drift from somewhere far away. "You right? You look like you've seen a ghost or something."

"Alyssa Whenua!"

The sharp voice sliced through the moment. Mrs Nolan appeared beside them as if she'd been waiting in the shadows, her smile predatory and far too pleased. "How delightful to see you embracing the community spirit. And this must be your friend from the city."

"I – " Alyssa's voice cracked. The panic was rising, making it hard to breathe. She looked desperately back towards the pottery stall, searching for Miri's face in the crowd, but the space where she'd been standing was empty.

*Gone.*

"Since I've caught you, dear," Mrs Nolan continued, her tone dripping with false concern. "Perhaps this would be the perfect time for that chat about your responsibilities – "

"No." The word came out strangled. Alyssa backed away. "I can't – I need to – "

She spun around, searching desperately for any sign of Miri's dark hair, any chance to...what? Apologise? How could words possibly be enough?

But Miri had vanished into the crowd as completely as if she'd never existed.

"Alyssa, what the actual hell – " Kelly grabbed her arm, genuine worry creasing her features.

Mrs Nolan stepped closer, eyes gleaming with opportunity. "As I was saying, there are urgent matters that simply cannot – "

The string of lights above them exploded in a shower of sparks.

# CHAPTER 7

**B**rendan's death-sense thrummed like a struck tuning fork. Usually he could push them back, create boundaries, but in Kotahi Bay's spirits were different. Hungry.

Through the darkness, the drowned woman's hair floated around her face like kelp in an invisible current. She walked towards him on the narrow footpath. Two more spirits crowded close – an elderly man with his head at the wrong angle, a young man with an old fashioned cap and vacant eyes.

The salt in his pockets that usually warded away ghosts felt as powerful as a handful of sand against an incoming tide.

He turned onto June's street and the spirits surged forward, then slowed.

The wards around June's house smelled of sour milk and old copper. Brendan pressed his palm against the gate, feeling for the shape of the protection. There – a gap where the magic had worn thin. He pushed through with his mind, and the ward split like overripe fruit.

The spirits stayed stuck at the rusted gate like moths against a window, mouths opening and closing in silent pleas.

He ignored them. Poor lost souls. He couldn't do anything to help them. Not now. He had work to do and time was running out.

The front door opened at his touch. Inside, lavender potpourri couldn't mask what his Kaipō senses picked up – layers of dark magic, each one leaving its stain. The ceramic cats on the mantel seemed to watch him pass. Every surface cluttered with doilies and dust, pill bottles and figurines, like an old woman's life compressed into these rooms.

*Objects of power*, Mrs Nolan had said. *June collected them.* Her smile had been sharp as glass when she'd given him the address. *Unless you'd prefer to handle things alone? Time is running out for your... situation.*

Brendan hated how she wielded his desperation like a weapon. But she might be his only chance, and that made him hate her more.

His phone buzzed. Esther: *It's getting worse. Please hurry.*

He shoved the phone away and focused on the pull of his Kaipō powers. In the living room, it led him to a brass compass on the coffee table. When he picked it up, phantom frost spread across his palm. The needle spun wildly, not seeking north but something else entirely. He pocketed it.

The wooden box beside it made his teeth ache. Symbols carved into its surface seemed to writhe when he wasn't looking directly at them. Inside, a tarnished silver ring that reeked of stolen years. His magic recoiled from it – whatever this ring had done, it had torn holes in the natural order. He wrapped it in his handkerchief before touching it.

The kitchen yielded a bell that rang in frequencies only the dead could hear. The bathroom, a mirror that reflected rooms that didn't exist in this house. Each object pulled at him differently – some ice-cold with death energy, others fever-hot with trapped life force.

In the back bedroom, he found the worst of it. A leather-bound journal that made his fingernails bleed just from lifting it. Pages filled with June's cramped handwriting, documenting things that shouldn't be documented. Names. Dates. Methods. The dark energy here was so thick it felt like breathing syrup.

Brendan gathered the objects, wrapping the worst pieces in kitchen towels. These were instruments of cruelty. No wonder Mrs Nolan hadn't wanted to touch them herself.

He was her puppet now, dancing on strings made of his own desperation. But puppets could learn their master's secrets. And June's journal might tell him exactly what kind of monster he was working for. He wanted to leave this place, to run. But running wasn't an option. Not anymore.

# CHAPTER 8

The pub was exactly as Alyssa had promised – nothing fancy, but the shepherd's pie was rich and hearty, the mashed potato top golden-brown and crispy at the edges. It was so comforting, and yet she still couldn't get her head away from Miri's face.

Or the way all those lights had exploded. Had that been her, or someone else?

Kelly had commandeered a corner booth. "Okay, I take it back," Kelly said, digging her fork through the fluffy potato into the savoury meat below. "This is actually really good. Like, suspiciously good for a town with one pub."

"The cook's Irish," Alyssa said, savouring a bite of the perfectly seasoned lamb and vegetables. "He uses his mother's recipe. Won't tell anyone what's in the gravy."

Kelly took a long pull from her beer – some local craft brew that she'd ordered with theatrical suspicion but was now on her second pint of. "So, are we going to talk about that absolute snack who was staring at you at the fair?"

Alyssa nearly choked on her peas. "What? Who?"

"Oh, come on." Kelly's grin was wicked. "Tall, dark, brooding? Looked like he wanted to either paint your portrait or ravish you in the fortune teller's tent?"

"I have no idea what you're talking about." Alyssa concentrated very hard on her meal, trying not to think about any of the people they'd encountered at the fair. Miri, the exploding lights, Mrs Nolan's predatory smile, the death card – it all felt like something from another lifetime, not just an hour ago.

"Sure you don't." Kelly waggled her eyebrows. "He had that whole mysterious stranger vibe going on. Very Heathcliff on the moors, except, you know, at a magical hippie fair instead of Yorkshire."

"Can we please talk about literally anything else?" Alyssa knew exactly who Kelly was talking about. She didn't know anything about him, but she'd noticed him. How could she not?

"Fine, but I'm filing this away for later interrogation," Kelly muttered. "This place is growing on me. In a Stockholm syndrome kind of way."

They walked home under the warm glow of the town's old-fashioned looking lamp-posts, as the darkness settled over Kotahi Bay. The summer air was heavy with the scent of mānuka blossoms and wild jasmine, undercut with salt from the bay.

"Smell that?" Kelly breathed deeply. "That's what money can't buy in the city."

"I thought you hated it here," Alyssa said, linking their arms to keep Kelly from veering into someone's lavender hedge.

"I hate that you're here without me," Kelly corrected. "There's a difference."

Alyssa couldn't imagine Kelly trading in the city for anything though, and, she realised, she didn't know whether she would want to share this place with Kelly. What did that say about their friendship? She shivered, despite the warmth, and nudged Kelly onward. Her friend was too tipsy to pick up on Alyssa's vibe though.

By the time they made it back to the house, Alyssa was feeling almost ready for bed, but Kelly opened a bottle of wine and set up Amélie on the TV with the subtitles off – their tradition since university, pretending they understood French while making up increasingly ridiculous dialogue.

"She's definitely telling him about her secret cheese addiction," Kelly slurred, gesturing at the screen with her glass.

"Obviously. And he's confessing his fear of accordions." Alyssa was curled in her corner of the couch, Socks purring on her lap while Buttons glared from his perch on the mantle. The living kitten hadn't noticed the dead one yet, but Alyssa caught herself holding her breath whenever they got too close. People always said that cats could sense spirits, but so far Socks seemed oblivious to his rival.

"So," Kelly said during a quiet moment in the film, "are we going to talk about the elephant in the room?"

Alyssa's heart stuttered. Had Kelly seen something magical? The ghost cat? "What elephant?"

"The fact that you haven't asked about Grant once."

Relief and guilt warred in Alyssa's chest. They had all been friends once, and of course Kelly had stayed true to Alyssa, but she barely thought of the man these days, and she definitely didn't want to bring him into her house like this. "There's nothing to ask. We're done."

"Good." Kelly's voice was fierce. "Because he's already seeing someone else and I didn't want to tell you but also I did want to tell you because secrets are stupid and – "

"Kels." Alyssa reached over and squeezed her friend's hand. "It's okay. Really."

Kelly squeezed back, then suddenly brightened. "Oh! Did you hear Spanna got pregnant?"

The words hit like a physical blow, but Alyssa kept her smile steady. "Wow, she's the least maternal person I know. Is she happy about it?"

"Ecstatic. Turned her whole life upside down but she's glowing like one of those fertility goddess statues." Kelly must have caught something in Alyssa's expression because she quickly added, "But who needs kids when you have cats, right? Look at this little angel!"

She scooped up Socks, who mewed in protest before settling against Kelly's chest. It was such a transparent attempt at comfort that Alyssa felt tears prick her eyes.

"Speaking of major life changes," Alyssa said, desperate to shift focus, "you mentioned a new flatmate?"

Kelly's whole body stiffened. "Did I?"

"Come on, spill. You can't just drop that bomb and not give details."

"It's nothing. Just some guy." Kelly wouldn't meet her eyes, suddenly fascinated by Socks' paws.

"Some guy? Are you into him, Kels?"

"Can we just watch the movie?" Kelly grabbed the remote, blushing, fumbling with the buttons. "I don't want to jinx it by talking about it too much."

It was so unlike Kelly – who usually overshared about every date – that Alyssa felt a chill despite the warm night. But she recognized the stubborn set of her friend's jaw.

"Fine, keep your secrets. But I want photos at least."

"He doesn't like photos." The words came out too fast, too defensive.

"Fine." Alyssa couldn't help but think back to the warning Sam had given her. What was Kelly hiding?

"Where do I put the empty bottle?" Kelly asked.

Alyssa groaned. "You've just reminded me that tomorrow is rubbish day, and we're never going to be up in time to put the bins out."

"We could pull an all-nighter? Like old times?" Kelly's grin was hopeful but her eyes were already drooping.

"We are way too old for that." Alyssa hauled herself off the couch, the room spinning gently. "I'll just do it now. Come help?"

"I'll just rest my eyes for one second..." Kelly was already horizontal again.

"Lazy bones!" Alyssa grabbed the recycling bag and headed for the door. "Fresh air will do you good!"

She stepped out into the cooling night, breathing deeply. A ruru called from the trees behind the house, its cry mournful and wild. The street was silent, dark except for –

Alyssa froze. June's house, three doors down, was lit up like a lava lamp. Every window glowed as if lit from within by something more than electricity. She'd been so sure the house was empty, had been since...

"What are you staring at?" Kelly stumbled out beside her, clutching the recycling.

"That house. Do you see – "

"See what?" Kelly squinted into the night. "God, it's creepy out here. No traffic, just... nature." She shivered dramatically. "How do you sleep?"

"You get used to it," Alyssa said, still staring at June's windows.

They hauled the bins to the curb, Kelly humming something off-key. But as they turned back to the house, Alyssa caught a flicker of movement in June's garden. Just for a moment, a shadow that didn't match the trees.

Her skin prickled and the alcohol fog in her brain evaporated, replaced by the chill of fear.

"What's up?" Kelly asked as she looked suspiciously at Alyssa.

"I need to check something," Alyssa said, her voice carefully controlled. "Why don't you go wait inside?"

"What? No way." Kelly swayed slightly but her eyes were bright with mischief. "What's wrong? You look like you've seen a ghost."

*If only she knew.* Alyssa's magic stirred uneasily beneath her skin, a warning tingle that something wasn't right. June's house had been empty for weeks, sealed up after... everything.

"That house should be empty," Alyssa said, already moving down the footpath. Her bare feet were silent on the cool concrete. "Just some neighbourhood watch stuff."

"neighbourhood watch?" Kelly giggled, stumbling after her. "Since when do you – oh my god, are we doing detective work? This is the most exciting thing that's happened all night!"

"Shh!" Alyssa hissed, but Kelly just grinned wider.

As they approached the house, the light flickered and died, plunging the property back into darkness. Alyssa's magical senses flared – there was definitely someone inside. The air around the house felt charged, like the moment before lightning strikes.

Whatever magical wards June had left in place seemed to be broken, now. Or had they just faded with time?

Alyssa crept to the house with Kelly close behind. She pressed herself against the weatherboard, the paint rough beneath her palms. Kelly followed, far less gracefully, her shoulder bumping Alyssa's.

"Ow," Kelly whispered loudly. "Your stalking skills need work."

Alyssa ignored her, creeping to the first window and peering inside. The bedroom beyond was empty, but something felt off. The shadows seemed too deep, too dark. The next window revealed the living room where she knew a horrible yellow-brown dominated the space.

Kelly tripped over a garden hose, cursing colourfully.

"Could you be any louder?" Alyssa whispered.

"Could you be any more paranoid?" Kelly shot back, but she was grinning. "This is like that time we snuck into the dean's office, except with more potential for arrest."

They rounded the corner to the back of the house. Through the kitchen window, Alyssa caught a glimpse of light – a flashlight beam sweeping across the room perhaps. Her heart hammered. Whoever was in there was searching for something.

"Stay here," she ordered Kelly.

"Like hell – "

"I mean it." She added some force to her words. Alyssa was already climbing onto the deck, the wood creaking softly under her weight. She crept to the kitchen window and peered inside. The flashlight had vanished, leaving only darkness and her own reflection staring back.

She moved to the door, fingers closing around the handle. Just as she began to turn it, the handle twisted in the opposite direction. The door swung open and she stumbled forward, her palm connecting with a solid, warm chest.

"What the – " a deep voice growled.

Alyssa jerked back with a strangled yelp. A hand shot out and caught her wrist – large, strong, definitely male.

*Not June.*

The realization hit her like cold water. Of course it wasn't June. This was –

"What the hell – "

The flashlight beam swung up into her face and she squinted, trying to see past the glare. Her heart hammered against her ribs as her eyes adjusted. Tall. Much taller than her. Broad shoulders in a white t-shirt. Dark hair.

"I – you – this house – " Words tumbled out incoherently as her brain tried to catch up with the situation. He still had hold of her wrist. Grip firm, but not painful.

"Breaking and entering?" His voice was gravelly, tinged with a lilt she couldn't place through her panic. He lowered the flashlight enough that she could finally see his face properly – stubbled jaw, dark eyes that looked either amused or annoyed. Maybe both. She recognised him then. The guy from the market who Kelly was teasing her about. The one she'd seen around town, who she'd noticed, who had stared at her.

The light swept down briefly, taking in her bare feet and wine-stained shirt, before returning to her face. "That's a bold choice..." he stated.

Heat flooded her face. "I wasn't breaking in. The door was opening – you opened it – and this house is supposed to be empty!"

"Is it?" He stepped out onto the deck, forcing her to move back. He was even taller than she'd thought, and he smelled like cedar and something darker, more dangerous. There was magic in him, no doubt about that, but she couldn't interpret the energy coming off him. "Because I have a key. Which is more than I can say for you."

"You live here?" The words came out higher pitched than intended. "Since when?"

"Since today, I suppose." He lowered the flashlight, and in the ambient streetlight, she could see the sharp cut of his jaw, the way his t-shirt clung to his chest. "The power went out. I was looking for the fuse box. Not that I need to explain myself to someone skulking around my backyard at midnight."

"I wasn't skulking! I was – " She stopped, realizing how ridiculous she'd sound. *I thought my possessed ex-neighbour might have returned from whatever supernatural banishment she'd suffered* wasn't exactly a reasonable explanation.

"You were?" he prompted, and now there was definitely amusement in his voice. He still hadn't let go of her wrist, and her skin tingled where his fingers pressed against her pulse point.

"I was concerned," she finished lamely. "The previous tenant left... suddenly. When I saw the lights..."

"You decided to investigate. Alone. Barefoot. At midnight." His thumb moved slightly against her wrist, and she wasn't sure if it was intentional. "Very brave. Or very foolish."

"I'm not alone," she said, then immediately wished she hadn't as Kelly chose that moment to appear.

"Oh hello," Kelly said, her eyes going wide as she took in the scene – Alyssa backed against the deck railing, the stranger's hand on her wrist, the charged air between them. "Don't mind me. Please, continue whatever this is." Kelly waved a hand at the two of them.

The man released Alyssa's wrist slowly, his fingers trailing across her skin. "Friend of yours?"

"Unfortunately," Alyssa muttered.

He laughed – a low, rich sound that did things to her insides. "Well, as entertaining as this has been, I really do need to find that fuse box. Unless one of you happens to know where it is?"

"Basement," Alyssa said without thinking. "Northeast corner, behind the water heater."

His eyebrows rose. "You seem very familiar with the house for someone who doesn't live here."

"I – June and I were – it's complicated." She pressed her lips together, afraid she had given away too much with just those few words.

"Most interesting things are." He studied her for a moment

longer, then stepped back. "I'm Brendan, by the way. Since we're apparently neighbours."

"Alyssa," she managed.

"Alyssa." He tested the name, and she shivered despite the warm night. "Next time you want to check on my wellbeing, maybe try knocking. During daylight hours?"

"Next time, don't blow all your fuses at midnight," she shot back.

"No promises. Try not to assault any other new neighbours tonight." He stepped back into the doorway, pausing. His eyes held hers for a moment longer than necessary. "Sleep well."

The door closed with a soft click, leaving her standing on the deck in the dark. Through the kitchen window, she could see the flashlight beam moving away, heading towards the basement stairs. Her wrist still tingled where he'd held it, and she found herself absently rubbing the spot.

"Um, hello?" Kelly's stage whisper broke through her daze. "Are we going to stand here all night, or can we go back and discuss what just happened? Because that was..."

"Don't," Alyssa warned, but she was already walking back towards the street on unsteady legs.

"I'm just saying, the chemistry – "

"Kelly, I swear – " she muttered as she walked home.

"Oh. My. God." Kelly grabbed her arm the moment they were back on the street. "That was the guy from the fair! The one who was staring at you!"

Alyssa blushed.

"That was the hottest thing I've ever seen," Kelly continued, practically bouncing. "The tension! The hand-holding! The smoldering looks! When's the wedding?"

"Shut up," Alyssa groaned, but her face was burning. "That was mortifying."

"That was a meet-cute if ever I saw one," Kelly corrected.

"You clearly haven't read enough romance novels. Did you see how he looked at you? Like he wanted to – "

"Kelly!"

"What? I'm just saying, if you don't climb that man like a tree, I'm revoking your friendship card."

They reached the house and Alyssa locked the door firmly behind them, trying to ignore the way her hands shook slightly. That man - Brendan - in June's house. Looking at her like...

"I need more wine," Alyssa announced.

"You need a cold shower," Kelly laughed, collapsing on the couch. "Or a hot neighbour. Oh wait, you already have one of those!"

Alyssa buried her face in a cushion, but she couldn't stop thinking about those stormy eyes and the way he'd said her name. Whatever had brought Brendan to Kotahi Bay, she had a feeling her life was about to get a lot more complicated.

# CHAPTER 9

Alyssa's head felt like someone had taken up residence inside it with a jackhammer. She groaned, rolling over to check her phone. 7 AM. Why had she set an alarm?

Oh. Right. The midnight assault on her new neighbour.

"Kill me," she muttered into her pillow, memories of the night flooding back. His hand on her wrist. The lingering look in those storm-grey eyes...

From downstairs came the sound of Kelly's snoring – an impressive chainsaw symphony that could probably be heard from the street.

At least one of them had slept well.

Alyssa dragged herself vertical and stumbled to the bathroom, avoiding her reflection. She didn't need to see the wine-stained evidence of last night's poor decisions. After brushing her teeth twice and downing two glasses of water, she felt marginally human.

A plan. She needed a plan. Something neighbourly and normal that said "Sorry I tried to break into your house at midnight" without actually saying it.

Pikelets. Perfect. Nothing said small-town apology like homemade baked goods.

She crept downstairs, poking her head into the lounge to see Kelly's sprawled form on the couch. Her friend had one arm flung over her face, mouth open, still fully dressed from the night before. Even the morning sun streaming through the windows didn't stir her.

Alyssa put on some quiet music and got to work, muscle memory taking over. Gran had taught her to make pikelets when she was seven, standing on a stool to reach the counter. "Food is love," Gran had said. "But it's also excellent for apologizing when you've been a right fool."

Prophetic, really.

The familiar rhythm of mixing the batter and then pouring and flipping the pikelets soothed her hangover and her nerves. She made a double batch – half for the apology, half for Kelly's inevitable hunger when she finally surfaced. By the time they were cooling on the rack, Alyssa felt almost brave enough for what came next.

She showered quickly, then stood in front of her closet in a towel, paralyzed. What did one wear to apologize to an unfairly attractive neighbour? Not the wine-stained shirt from last night, obviously. She settled on her nicest jeans and a soft blue top that Kelly always said brought out her eyes. Casual but put-together. Definitely not trying too hard.

The pikelets went onto her second-best plate (the best one seemed too eager), arranged with her homemade plum jam and a dollop of whipped cream in the centre. She checked her reflection one more time, smoothed her hair, and headed out before she could lose her nerve.

June's house – Brendan's house, she corrected herself – looked different in daylight. Less ominous, more... normal. The curtains were drawn, and for a moment she panicked. What if he was still asleep? What if she woke him up twice in twelve hours?

Then she heard it: the distinctive roar of a lawnmower starting up around back.

Relief flooded through her. She followed the sound, her bare feet quiet on the grass, plate balanced carefully in both hands. As she rounded the corner of the house, she stopped dead.

Brendan had his back to her, pushing an ancient mower through the overgrown grass. The morning sun was already warm enough that he'd stripped off his tee, which was currently tucked into the back pocket of his jeans. Muscles moved under tanned skin as he wrestled the mower around a particularly stubborn patch of kikuyu grass.

Kelly had been right. So very, very right.

He wore protective earmuffs, bright orange things that should have looked ridiculous but somehow didn't. She stood frozen, plate in hand, suddenly aware that she was essentially stalking him. Again.

*Just tap him on the shoulder,* she told herself. *Like a normal person.*

She approached carefully, mindful of the plate, and reached out to tap his shoulder. The moment her fingers made contact, he spun around with surprising speed. His elbow caught the edge of the plate, sending it flying up and directly into her chest.

Time slowed. Pikelets launched into the air. Cream and jam created an abstract masterpiece across her carefully chosen blue top. One particularly ambitious pikelet made it all the way to her hair.

"Jesus!" Brendan yanked off his earmuffs, his expression cycling through alarm, recognition, and then – damn him – amusement. "You have got to stop sneaking up on me."

Alyssa stood frozen, arms still extended, processing the disaster. A glob of cream slid slowly down her chest. "I brought you pikelets," she said stupidly.

His lips twitched. "I can see that. You're wearing most of them."

"This was supposed to be my apology for last night." She looked down at the devastation. A pikelet was somehow stuck to her shoulder. "I was trying to be neighbourly."

"Mission accomplished." His eyes danced with suppressed laughter. "Very... thorough neighbourhood relations."

"Don't laugh," she warned, but she could feel her own lips betraying her. "This is mortifying."

"Which part? The midnight breaking and entering, or the breakfast food assault?" He reached out and plucked a pikelet from her collarbone, examining it critically before taking a bite. His eyes widened. "Oh, these are good."

"You're not serious – " But he was already reaching for another one, this time from just above her hip. His fingers brushed the sticky fabric of her shirt as he retrieved it.

"Waste not, want not." He grinned, and she noticed he had a dimple on his left cheek. Of course he did. "Besides, I haven't had breakfast yet."

"There are some on the plate that haven't been on my person," she pointed out, gesturing weakly at the few survivors clinging to the ceramic.

"But these come with a story." He stepped closer, ostensibly reaching for another pikelet near her shoulder, and suddenly she could smell him – grass clippings and soap and that cedar scent from last night. "May I?"

She nodded, not trusting her voice. He peeled the pikelet off carefully, his fingers barely grazing her shoulder, but even that light touch sent heat racing down her arm.

"So," he said conversationally, as if he wasn't standing

shirtless in front of her, eating food off her clothes, "you were apologizing?"

"Yes." She found her voice. "For last night. The attempted breaking and entering. And the general... everything."

"Apology accepted." He licked jam off his thumb, and her brain short-circuited. "Though I notice you're developing a pattern of violent encounters. Should I be worried?"

"Only if you keep startling me." She was proud of how steady her voice sounded. "Or moving into houses that are supposed to be empty."

"Ah." His expression grew more serious. "You knew June well?"

The name hit her like cold water. June's house. June's kitchen where she'd drunk cursed tea. June's eyes when Magnus had –

"We were... acquainted." She took a step back, needing distance. "She left town suddenly."

Something flickered across his face. "So I heard. The rental agent mentioned it. Said the house had been empty for weeks."

"Yeah." Alyssa became very interested in wiping jam off her hands. "Anyway, I should go. Let you get back to your mowing. And I need to..." She gestured at her destroyed shirt.

"Wait." He disappeared around the side of the house and returned with a damp rag. "Least I can do."

She accepted it gratefully, dabbing at the worst of the damage. "Thanks. And sorry again. For everything."

"Alyssa." The way he said her name made her look up. "Thank you."

Heat flooded her cheeks. "Right. Well. I'll just..." She backed away, still clutching the rag and the mostly empty plate. "Bye."

"The rag?" he called as she fled.

"I'll wash it!" she called back, practically running now.

She heard his laughter follow her around the house, warm and rich and entirely too appealing.

Kelly was awake when she burst through the door, sitting at the kitchen table with her head in her hands.

"Coffee," her friend croaked. "Need coffee."

"In a minute." Alyssa collapsed into the opposite chair. "I just need to process my complete humiliation."

Kelly looked up, took in the state of Alyssa's clothes, and perked up considerably. "Oh my god. What happened? Did you guys – "

"No! God, no. I tried to apologize with pikelets and ended up wearing them instead."

"And he was okay with that?"

"He..." Alyssa buried her face in her hands. "He ate them. Off me. Like it was completely normal."

Kelly's shriek of delight could probably be heard three houses away. "I KNEW IT! I knew there was chemistry! This is better than – ow, my head. Worth it though. Tell me everything."

"Coffee first," Alyssa bargained, getting up to put the kettle on. "And I need to change. Again."

"And have a cold shower?"

Alyssa's silence was answer enough.

"I'm extending my stay," Kelly announced. "I need to see how this plays out. Also, we still need to talk about those letters."

"Kelly – "

"No, listen." Her friend's voice turned serious. "I know you. You avoid things until they blow up in your face. Like Grant – you knew things were bad for months before you finally confronted him. And your mom, you still haven't told her you're living here permanently."

"I haven't decided if it's permanent," Alyssa protested weakly.

"Bullshit. You're making magical jewelry, you're apologizing to neighbours with baked goods, you've got a cat. You're nesting, Alyssa. But you're still pretending like you might leave any day."

Alyssa focused on making coffee, uncomfortable with how accurately Kelly had pinpointed her patterns. "It's complicated."

"It always is with you." Kelly's voice softened. "Look, I get it. After everything with Grant, you don't want to commit. But ignoring that Nolan woman isn't going to make her go away. And whatever happened with June – yeah, I noticed how you freaked when lover boy mentioned her – you can't just pretend it didn't happen."

"I'm not pretending anything." But even as she said it, Alyssa knew it was a lie. She was pretending she could make jewelry without acknowledging the magic she wove into each piece. Pretending the town didn't expect things from her. Pretending that living in June's shadow – literally, with Brendan next door – wasn't going to be a problem.

"Right." Kelly accepted her coffee gratefully. "So we're going to the beach today, and you're going to tell me what's really going on. And then I'm going to march over to this Preservation Society and find out what the deal is with those letters."

"Kelly, no – "

"Someone has to be the adult here, and clearly it's not going to be the woman wearing breakfast food." Kelly's grin took the sting out of her words. "Now, go change. And maybe keep that shirt. Seems like Brendan enjoyed it."

Alyssa fled upstairs, her friend's laughter following her. In her room, she caught sight of herself in the mirror – jam in her hair, cream on her shirt, face flushed with embarrassment and something else. Something that had sparked when Brendan's fingers brushed her skin.

Living in Kotahi Bay was definitely getting more complicated. And her old pattern of running away was no longer an option.

Not if she wanted to stay here. Not with Kelly here to call her on her patterns. Not with Sam waiting to hear about her latest creations. Not with a grey-eyed neighbour who ate pikelets off her clothes like it was the most natural thing in the world.

She was in so much trouble.

# CHAPTER 10

The black sand was still cool beneath Brendan's bare feet as he made his way to the largest pōhutukawa tree at the far end of the beach. The ancient tree's massive trunk twisted upward, its canopy of dark green leaves and crimson flowers creating a natural cathedral against the clear blue sky.

The spirits pressed close as soon as he knelt in the sand. The drowned woman's hair floated around her face in invisible currents, droplets of phantom seawater eternally dripping from her blue lips. The elderly man stood with his head at that terrible angle, his Sunday-best suit faded to grey after decades of wandering. The young man in his flat cap clutched at something invisible - fishing nets, perhaps, or the steering wheel of a long-lost boat.

Brendan withdrew the ritual items from his pockets. Simple things - a piece of driftwood worn smooth as silk, its grain following patterns that reminded him of souls in flight. A shell that sang with the memory of tides, their inner surface catching the light like a pearl. A vial of seawater he'd collected at high tide on a full moon.

"Sarah," he whispered to the drowned woman, the name coming to him as names sometimes did when he opened himself to the dead. "Thomas." The elderly man's eyes flickered with recognition. "Hemi." The young fisherman turned towards him with desperate hope.

The salt spray from the waves mixed with the honey and gorse blossom as Brendan pressed his palms to the sand. The earth pulsed beneath his touch as if speaking to him. He could sense the tree's ancient roots ran beneath him, a network of life and death intertwined. Where they touched the bones of the earth, doorways opened.

"You've been lost so long," he murmured, his voice barely audible above the rhythm of the waves. "Be soothed now."

He didn't need elaborate rituals or commanding words. Brendan simply opened the door that was there, hidden beneath the pōhutukawa's guardian presence.

The spirits, now soothed, began to pass through the gateway. For a moment, Brendan felt the crushing weight of water in his lungs, the terror of that last wave. Then warmth flooded through the connection - her gratitude, her release, her joy at finally, finally being able to let go.

"Thank you," the woman's lips formed silently before she dissolved into morning mist that sparkled briefly in the sunlight before vanishing.

Brendan remained kneeling, his whole body trembling from the effort.

The beach felt different now - cleaner, lighter, as if a weight had been lifted from the very air. He gathered his ritual items slowly, his fingers stiff and cold despite the warming day.

The walk back towards the village felt like surfacing from deep water. But his heart was light in a way it hadn't been for a while. This was what his gift was meant for - not the dark dealings others tried to force on him, but this. Release. Peace. Healing.

As he approached the fairground, he caught the scent of woodsmoke. The fair hadn't opened for the day yet, but smoke rose from a campfire near the edge where several figures sat around like they were having their own private festival. He could hear laughter and the clink of bowls.

He hesitated, not wanting to intrude, but Matai called out, "Plenty of kai here, bro. You look like you need it."

He sized up the gathering, he knew Samantha in passing, Matai was an old friend, and the others he recognised from some of the stalls the night before. He decided to approach. The warmth of the fire was welcome after the chill of working with spirits. Sam handed him a wooden bowl filled with porridge that smelled of cinnamon and cardamom, topped with fresh berries that burst tart and sweet on his tongue.

"Thanks," he said, sinking gratefully onto an empty spot on one of the logs. It was a second breakfast, but he was hungry and the pikelets from earlier were more...fun...than substantial.

"Everyone, this is Brendan," Matai said. "Brendan, this is Ursula, Hazel, and Rowan - they run that beautiful glass pendant stall. And Mia, who does the tarot readings."

"Nice to properly meet you," Ursula said, her garnet ring catching the firelight. "I saw you wandering the fair last night."

"Yeah," Brendan admitted between spoonfuls of the warming porridge. "Quite an experience."

"You should see the ones in Europe," Hazel said, her purple hair bright in the morning sun. "We just got back from Cornwall - spent a few months in this tiny village called Myrtlewood. It was incredible - full of shenanigans I'd never have imagined in my wildest dreams."

"I've heard so much about Myrtlewood," Samantha said.

"Apparently it's the sister-village to Kotahi Bay. I'd love to visit someday."

"Myrtlewood was something else," Rowan agreed. "Remember the night the Morri – "

"We agreed never to speak of that," Ursula cut him off with a laugh. "Some things are better left in Cornwall."

"Speaking of last night," Hazel leaned forward conspiratorially, "did anyone else see that weird thing that happened with the lights? For a moment there, it looked like the whole sky was shimmering."

"I thought I was imagining it," Mia admitted. A magpie peeked out from the hood of her jersey, directing its beady eyes at him. She reached up to give the bird a scritch. "But several of my clients mentioned seeing strange lights."

Brendan caught the quick glance between Sam and Matai, but the others were focused on their food. Alyssa was there when the lights flickered. Was it something to do with her? He felt a hum through his chest that he didn't quite understand.

"Could have been the moon phase," Mia suggested. "Or just the collective excitement setting things off. Fairs create their own kind of magic."

As the sun climbed higher, the group began to disperse. The fair would be opening soon, and there were stalls to prepare. Brendan helped bank the fire, moving carefully as his body still felt drained from the morning's work.

"It was lovely meeting you properly," Ursula said as they gathered their things.

After they left, Brendan found himself alone with Sam and Matai for a moment.

"Interesting people," he commented.

"Good people," Sam corrected. "The kind who see the world as it really is, not just as they're told it should be."

"Speaking of which," Matai said casually, "you should really get to know Alyssa better."

Brendan's gut tightened. "What do you mean?"

"Just that she's new in town too. Could probably use a friend who understands what it's like to be finding your feet here." Matai's expression was innocent, but something in his tone...

"She seems...nice," Brendan said carefully.

"She's more than nice," Sam said. "She's – " She caught herself, glancing at Matai. "She's been through a lot. Losing her grandmother, inheriting that house, all the pressure to..."

"To what?" Brendan asked when she trailed off.

"To adjust to being here," Sam finished, but Brendan could tell that wasn't what she'd meant to say.

"Anyway," Matai stood, stretching. "I'm sure you'll run into each other again. Kotahi Bay's not that big. Walk with me a bit, bro?"

Brendan nodded, falling into step beside him. They'd known each other for years now, ever since that summer when they'd both been teenagers struggling to understand why they'd been cursed with gifts that belonged in horror stories rather than real life.

"You did something down at the beach this morning," Matai said. It wasn't a question.

"Yeah." Brendan didn't bother denying it. Matai could sense magic like others could smell coffee brewing. "Some souls needed sending on."

"That's good work." Matai kicked at a stone. "Using it to help instead of harm - that's my philosophy. You can't escape what you are, but you can learn to master the power so it doesn't destroy."

They'd learned, through trial and painful error, that running from what you were only made it worse.

"Remember what you told me that first summer?" Brendan asked. "About tools?"

Matai smiled slightly. "Was is something super wise like: All power is a tool. Tools can be used to hurt or help. It's the hand that wields them that matters."

"Still the smartest thing anyone's ever said to me."

"Gift." Matai snorted. "Took us both long enough to see it that way. But look at us now - you helping souls find peace, me keeping the magical balance in check. Not bad for two guys who should by all rights be cursed."

They walked in comfortable silence for a moment. Then Matai said, almost too casually, "Speaking of balance, you should know something about Alyssa."

Brendan's shoulders tensed. "What about her?"

"She's a powerful witch, bro. More powerful than she knows."

The words hit Brendan like cold water. A chill of suspicion crept down his spine as he thought about their encounters - her fumbling attempt to break into his house, the apologetic pikelets, the way she'd blushed and stammered. Those delight-fully random moments...

The unexpected feelings that were brewing within him even before he met her...could that be part of her magic?


Alyssa parked the car in front of Sage & Salt. "Stay here for a minute, I just want to check something, okay?" she said, already reaching for the door handle.

Kelly barely looked up from her phone, thumb scrolling. "Mmm-hmm," she murmured, waving Alyssa away with her free hand.

The shop's wooden door chimes sang their familiar greeting as she pushed inside. Light fractured into a thousand tiny rainbows through Sam's window display. The scent of lavender and sage and something earthier, hit her. It worked its magic as always, her shoulders dropping from their defensive hunch.

Sam looked up from the counter where she'd been sorting rough amethyst points. Her smile was warm until she caught sight of Alyssa's expression.

"What's up?"

Alyssa let out a sigh that seemed to come from her toes. "I need to talk to you."

Sam's eyes narrowed, that careful assessment Alyssa had seen her use on difficult customers. "What about?"

The words tumbled out in a rush. "I've been getting letters from Mrs Nolan. She keeps writing about me taking over Gran's position in the town, about consequences if I don't."

Sam shook her head. "Mrs Nolan is...challenging."

The door chimes interrupted her, as Kelly pushed inside. She'd tucked her phone away and now stood in the doorway, city confidence radiating from her designer jeans.

"Got tired of waiting in the car, and wanted to check out the crystals," Kelly announced, but her eyes were assessing, taking in Alyssa's tense posture and Sam's guarded expression. "Everything okay?"

"Fine!" Alyssa said too quickly.

"So you're Alyssa's new bestie, I guess," Kelly's eyebrow arched. "Funny how that works, isn't it? Almost like she's living a double life down here." The words were light, joking, but there was an edge underneath.

Sam covered her mouth with her hand, but the amused smile leaked through anyway. "You make this place out to be a lot more exciting than it really is. It's pretty quiet here. Hopefully you'll enjoy your visit. How long are you staying?"

"A few days. We'll see how things go." Kelly's glance at

Alyssa was loaded with meaning, and guilt twisted in Alyssa's gut like a living thing.

She was being a terrible friend. Kelly might not have been there when Gran died – too busy with work, always too busy – but she'd held Alyssa through the brutal end of her relationship, through the fertility treatments that led nowhere, through every small heartbreak of their twenties. And in return, Alyssa had fled to this town and all but vanished from Kelly's life.

"Hey," Alyssa reached out and grabbed Kelly's hand, squeezing it the way they used to in university when one of them needed courage. "Why don't you take a look around? Pick something to take home with you, a little piece of the Bay. From me."

Kelly's expression softened slightly. "Never look a gift horse in the mouth." She squeezed back before releasing Alyssa's hand and wandering deeper into the shop.

The moment Kelly was out of earshot, examining a display of locally-made jewelry, Alyssa leaned closer to Sam. "I feel awful. I'm a terrible friend."

"You haven't told her anything, have you?" Sam's voice was low, urgent. "About what you are? What this place is?"

"I told her that you all thought Gran was a witch, but she doesn't believe in witches." Alyssa watched Kelly pick up a pendant, hold it to the light. "I know she knows there's more going on here. I just... I don't know what to say to her. I can't explain any of this. She's got it in her head that she needs to go and see Mrs Nolan to find out what kind of trouble I'm in – "

Sam's frown deepened. "Mrs Nolan really shouldn't be harassing you. Look, I need to go see Constance and sort this out. Nolan has overstepped her role."

A phone buzzed – Sam's, not Alyssa's. Sam glanced at the screen and her face went pale beneath her summer tan. "I really need to go," she said, then raised her voice. "Did you find something you like?"

Kelly turned from the jewelry display, shaking her head. "Not yet, there's so much stuff here, I don't know how to pick."

"That's okay. Maybe you can come back later. Something's cropped up and I need to go deal with it, but come back before you leave town to pick something." Sam was already grabbing her bag and keys, movements sharp with urgency. She paused just long enough to pull Alyssa into a quick hug that smelled of sage and secrets. "Be careful," she whispered. "And call me later. This is important."

"It happens," Alyssa said aloud, trying to keep her voice light as Sam all but fled the shop.

As Alyssa guided Kelly back to the car, her mind raced. Sam knew Mrs Nolan, and the casual way she'd said "she's overstepped her role" like there was a hierarchy Alyssa knew nothing of...

"What was that about?" Kelly asked as they climbed back in the car.

"Oh, she got a text. She does some volunteering I think. We're not that close." The lie tasted bitter, but it was also partly true. She'd thought Sam was her friend here, her anchor, but really, what did she know about Samantha beyond the shop and their casual conversations? The woman had always wanted Alyssa to lean into her witchy heritage... There were layers to this town she'd barely scratched.

"Right," Kelly said, her tone making it clear she didn't buy it for a second. "So, beach?"

"Beach," Alyssa agreed.

Just as they pulled away, Alyssa spotted a familiar figure. Constance moved with that peculiar walk of hers, her grey dress seeming to float around her ankles despite the still morning air. As their car approached, the older woman turned, her gaze finding Alyssa's through the windshield.

Constance raised one hand in a slow wave, and Alyssa felt the gesture like a cool finger trailing down her spine. There was knowing in that look, assessment, and something that might have been a warning.

"Who's the witchy-looking lady?" Kelly asked, craning to look back as they passed.

"Constance. She's... a local character." Alyssa's hands tightened on the steering wheel. "Lots of interesting people in small towns."

"Interesting is one word for it," Kelly muttered, but she was already distracted by the view as they crested the hill and the ocean spread before them, dark blue touched with gold where the sun hit the waves.

The beach parking lot was nearly empty – just a few surfers' vans.

Someone vaguely familiar emerged from behind one of the vans, wetsuit half-peeled down to reveal a sports bra underneath, her dark hair dripping saltwater onto the gravel.

"Hey, you're the new resident, aren't you? I'm Jade," she extended a hand.

Alyssa shook it. "You're friends with Sam and Matai, right?"

"That's right!" Jade's grin was bright and uncomplicated. "Are you going to get into the water? Perfect morning for it. The waves are *choice*!"

"Not sure we're swimming just yet," Alyssa said. "This is my friend Kelly, visiting from the city."

"Sweet as." Jade gave Kelly a friendly nod. "You surf?"

"I've tried a few times," Kelly said, and Alyssa could see her responding to Jade's easy energy. "Not very successfully."

"We all start somewhere. I'm heading back out if you want

to borrow a board later. Got a spare softie that's perfect for learning." Jade was so at ease in her body, in this space, and Alyssa felt a pang of jealousy.

"Maybe," Kelly said, actually looking tempted.

As Jade jogged back towards the waves, board under her arm, Kelly turned to Alyssa. "She seems cool."

"Yeah," Alyssa agreed, not sure if Kelly meant it as a compliment or a comparison to the morning's earlier interactions.

The beach was almost empty, just a few distant figures and surfers' silhouettes carving through the waves. The black sand was warm between Alyssa's toes as she stepped down from the bank, the familiar scent of salt spray wrapping around her.

"Wow. Okay, maybe I get why you like this place." Kelly inhaled deeply, turning in a slow circle to take it all in. "This is kind of beautiful."

"It is. Something magical about this place, Kels. I tell you. It gets under your skin."

"Well, hopefully not too far under because I have work in a few days." Kelly's grin was wry as she shook out her beach blanket with practiced efficiency, claiming their spot on the sand.

"Don't want to go for a walk first?"

"Nah, we can walk later. Right now, I want to crack open a beer and enjoy the peace and tranquillity."

Alyssa settled beside her, the sand conforming to her body like a warm embrace. She opened the cooler, condensation dripping from the bottles as she passed one to Kelly. The glass was blissfully cold against her palm.

"Here's to good friends, and great views," she said, raising her bottle.

"And hot men," Kelly added with a wicked grin. "And beer, and wine. And forgiveness."

The last word hit Alyssa like a small wave, cold and unexpected. She knew that tone, knew Kelly hadn't let go of the morning's strangeness or the months of distance between them.

"Forgiveness?" she asked, though she knew what was coming.

"Yeah, you know, because that's a vital part of friendship right?" Kelly pushed her sunglasses up onto her head, revealing those sharp brown eyes that had seen through every one of Alyssa's bullshit excuses over the years.

"It is." Alyssa sipped her beer, the bitterness appropriate for the conversation. "I'm sorry for not being a better friend. I kind of abandoned you and I didn't realise it until you came down here. I just left."

"You did just leave. But I forgive you." Kelly's voice was gentle now, understanding. "I know things were pretty shitty, with you and Grant and the whole infertility thing, and then your Gran dying. I get why you wanted to escape. I'm not mad, just...sad, you know?"

"I do know. I'm sad too," she admitted, though for such different reasons, and her life was still in flux, forces exerting on her decisions that she couldn't even begin to explain to Kelly. "Life is so different now. I guess I needed to run away for a bit."

"But it's not for a bit, is it..." It wasn't a question. Kelly turned to face her fully, and Alyssa could see the hurt there, carefully controlled but present. "You're staying, right? You're not coming back to the city. Ever."

This conversation felt like a breakup, and maybe it was, in its own way. They couldn't be the friends they'd been when they lived together, when their biggest worry was which wine bar to try on Friday night.

"No, I don't think I am." The words came out steady,

certain. More certain than she actually was, but she couldn't let Kelly stay hopeful for any longer. It was better this way. "I'm sorry."

Kelly's smile was sad but real. "You don't have to be. Really, it's okay. You're finally doing what you need to do. You're growing up. I'm so proud, my little chicken has left the nest." She reached out to chuck Alyssa on the chin, a gesture from their younger days.

Kelly's laugh was bright, clearing the air like a fresh breeze. "Come on, enough serious talk, let's finish this beer and then have a swim before we get so drunk we drown."

"Good thinking, Mum."

Kelly's snort of laughter sent beer foam up her nose. She shook her head, sputtering, and downed the rest of her bottle in mock defiance before stripping down to reveal a sleek black bikini. "Last one to the sea cooks dinner!"

"Cheat! You had a head start." Alyssa was reaching for her sundress when her phone rang, the electronic trill jarring against the natural sounds of wind and waves. "I'll catch up," she called.

Kelly waved acknowledgment before sprinting towards the water, her city-pale skin almost glowing in the sunshine.

"Hello?"

"Hey, it's Sam." The voice was tight with controlled urgency.

"Oh, hi. I wasn't expecting a call. Everything okay?"

"No, not really. I don't think we should talk about this over the phone though. Can you come back to the shop?"

Alyssa watched Kelly dive into a wave, emerging with a whoop of shock at the cold. "I can't right now. I promised Kelly we'd spend the afternoon at the beach."

The words were true, but Alyssa knew there was more to it. She wasn't ready to face whatever Sam had discovered, wasn't ready to juggle another crisis when she'd just finished patching things with Kelly. And deeper than that – she didn't want Kelly anywhere near the magical complications of Kotahi Bay. Some worlds weren't meant to mix.

"Are you sure? It's important." Sam's insistence was unusual, worry leaking through despite her attempt at control.

"I'll call you when we're home, okay? I'm sorry, Sam. I just can't right now."

There was a pause, then a sigh. "Okay, call me as soon as you get back. And Alyssa? Be careful."

The line went dead, leaving Alyssa staring at her phone. Be careful of what? Mrs Nolan? The town politics she barely understood? Or something else entirely?

She dropped her phone onto the sand beside the empty bottles and shed her sundress in one quick motion. Whatever was waiting for her in Sam's warnings, it could wait a few more hours.

Kelly was waving from the water, calling something the wind stole away. Alyssa fixed a grin on her face and ran towards the waves, leaving her phone and all its complications behind on the warm black sand. The ocean rushed up to meet her, shockingly cold and wonderfully simple. But even as she dove beneath the surface, salt water washing away the morning's tensions, she could feel the weight of Sam's words pulling at her like an undertow. *Be careful.*

# CHAPTER 11

The sand on Alyssa's toes had dried to a fine crust by the time they got home, and her skin felt tight with salt and sun. Five missed calls from Sam glowed on her phone screen like accusations. She switched it to silent and shoved it deep in her beach bag.

"Dibs on first shower," Kelly announced, already halfway out of the car. "I've got sand in places sand should never be."

"Guest privilege," Alyssa agreed, grateful for the reprieve. She needed a moment to think, to figure out how to handle Sam without dragging Kelly into Bay business.

Inside, the house felt cooler, dimmer, as if it had been holding its breath while they were gone. Kelly thundered up the stairs, and soon the pipes groaned to life overhead. Alyssa dropped the beach gear by the door and padded into the kitchen, where Socks was curled in his bed looking thoroughly neglected.

"Sorry, baby," she murmured, scooping him up. He mewed pitifully and buried his face in her neck, his purr vibrating against her collarbone. "Kelly's been monopolizing my time."

A chill brushed her ankle – Buttons, manifesting just enough to be felt. The ghost cat had been in a mood since Kelly arrived, and Socks' presence only made it worse. Alyssa watched, fascinated despite herself, as Socks suddenly stiffened in her arms, his tiny body going rigid as he stared at what Kelly would see as empty air. She put him down before he freaked out and scratched her.

Buttons materialized more fully, his translucent form stalking closer with spectral dignity. Socks hissed, batting at the ghost with one small paw that passed right through. Buttons, affronted, swatted back – and somehow, impossibly, his ghostly paw connected just enough to send Socks tumbling.

"What the hell?" she breathed, watching as the kitten landed on his feet and immediately pounced at Buttons' tail. The ghost cat's expression shifted from annoyance to something like amusement. Within moments, they were chasing each other around the kitchen – one solid, one spectral, in a game that defied every law of physics Alyssa thought she understood.

The shower shut off upstairs. Kelly would be down soon and Alyssa couldn't think of any explanation for the kitten's strange behaviour. Cat nip?

"Okay, you two, that's enough supernatural playtime," Alyssa said firmly. Buttons gave her a look that clearly said he'd stop when he was ready and not a moment before, but he faded from view. Socks sat in the middle of the kitchen, looking bewildered, his head swiveling as he searched for his playmate.

"Right," Alyssa said to herself. "Dinner. Normal dinner. Nothing weird about dinner."

Kelly slid into the room and put some music on low. They worked together in the kitchen like old times, Kelly chatting about work drama while Alyssa chopped vegetables for a stir-fry. The wine bottle emptied steadily between them, and Alyssa felt the familiar warmth of their friendship settling back into place. Almost like nothing had changed.

Almost.

"I still can't believe you gave up everything for this," Kelly said, gesturing with her wine glass at the kitchen, the house, the quiet evening beyond the windows. "No nightlife, no decent restaurants, no..." She trailed off, catching Alyssa's expression. "Sorry. I know you love it here. I'm trying to understand."

"It's okay," Alyssa said, though the words stung more than she expected. "It's not for everyone." Had she really changed that much? Perhaps the Bay, and its occupants, had lulled her into the quieter life, and if she just returned to the city she'd remember how much she'd loved the vibe.

They ate on the back porch, watching the sun paint the sky in shades of peach and purple. Socks wound between their legs, begging for scraps, while somewhere in the shadows Alyssa could sense Buttons watching. The ghost cat's presence had become as familiar as breathing, but tonight it felt heavier, more expectant.

Kelly yawned as they finished the last of the wine. "God, I'm exhausted. Sun and sand really take it out of you." She stood, stretching. "I think I'm going to crash early, if you don't mind?"

"Of course," Alyssa said, though something in Kelly's tone seemed off. Too casual, too bright. "Sweet dreams."

Kelly paused at the door, looking back. "You know I love you, right? Even if I don't get this whole small-town thing."

"I know," Alyssa said softly. "Love you too."

Kelly's footsteps faded into the house, and Alyssa imagined she could hear the creak of the guest bed. On the porch, the night sounds serenaded her – crickets, the distant crash of waves, the rustle of something in the garden that might have been a hedgehog or might have been something else entirely.

She was washing the dishes a short while, hands deep in soapy water, when the temperature plummeted.

The kitchen window fogged with her suddenly visible breath. Ice crystals formed on the tap, spreading across the metal like frozen spiderwebs. Alyssa's hands went numb in the water, but she couldn't seem to move, couldn't seem to –

"You need to stop ignoring what's happening."

She spun, heart hammering. Magnus stood by the kitchen table, more solid than she'd ever seen him. The overhead light flickered, casting strange shadows that seemed to move independently of his form. He looked... tired, she realised. Ancient and tired and worried.

"Gosh," she breathed deeply, trying to slow her heart rate, struggling to contain the range of emotions that flooded through her upon seeing him again. She'd thought he was gone for good. "A little warning next time?"

"There may not be a next time." His voice carried the weight of centuries, the accent she could never quite place more pronounced. "Things are moving faster than anticipated. The fair has accelerated everything."

Alyssa dried her hands on a tea towel, needing something normal to do while her Viking ghost loomed in her kitchen. "Sam's been calling. I know I should – "

"Samantha Kereama is the least of your concerns right now." Magnus moved closer, and the air grew colder still. Frost spread across the windows, obscuring the night beyond. "You need to understand what's truly at stake here."

"Then tell me," Alyssa snapped, fear sharpening her voice. "Everyone keeps hinting at dire consequences but no one actually explains anything. Gran left me with ghosts and a house and a legacy I don't understand. So if you know something, just tell me."

Magnus smiled, but it was a sad thing. "Your grandmother was one of the last of the old guardians. She held the compact, maintained the balance. But she grew tired, and in her tiredness, she ignored things, let them slide."

"What kind of things?"

"The kind that opened doors that should have stayed closed." He gestured, and the frost on the windows formed patterns – symbols that hurt to look at directly. "Mrs Nolan isn't working alone, Alyssa. There's a faction in this town, has been for decades, who believe the barrier is a prison rather than a protection."

Alyssa's stomach turned. "They want to bring it down?"

"They want to control it. To use it." Magnus's form flickered, solidified. "The fair has drawn attention from beyond Kotahi Bay. Old powers are stirring, drawn by the weakening boundary. And your friend – " He paused, gaze flicking upward towards Kelly's room. "Her presence here complicates things. She has no protection, no understanding. She's vulnerable."

"Kelly's got nothing to do with this," Alyssa said firmly. "She's just visiting."

"There are no coincidences in Kotahi Bay." Magnus moved to the window, staring out at the frost-obscured night. "Why do you think she couldn't find the town before? The barrier recognizes blood, recognizes those who belong. But now, with it weakening, outsiders can enter. And once they're here..."

"What?" Alyssa demanded when he trailed off. "Once they're here, what?"

"They become part of the weave. Connected. Vulnerable to those who would use that connection." He turned back to her, and for a moment she could see through him to the window beyond. "The old compact – "

His form wavered, like a TV with bad reception.

"Magnus?" Alyssa stepped forward, reaching out instinctively.

" – must be renewed or – " Static filled the air, a sound like breaking glass and screaming wind. Magnus's mouth moved but no words came. His eyes widened in what looked like alarm, and then –

He vanished.

The frost melted instantly, water running down the windows in rivulets. The kitchen felt suddenly too warm, too normal, as if the last few minutes had been a dream. A nightmare.

Alyssa stood frozen, mind racing. The old compact? Renewed or what? And Kelly – vulnerable how? To whom?

A floorboard creaked overhead.

Alyssa's blood chilled in a way that had nothing to do with ghostly presences. The guest room was directly above the kitchen. The creaking came again, deliberate footsteps moving towards the stairs.

Kelly hadn't been asleep at all.

And depending on how much she'd heard, Alyssa's carefully maintained separation between her two worlds was about to come crashing down.

She held her breath, waiting, but the footsteps moved past the stairs to the bathroom and Alyssa exhaled, though she couldn't find much relief. Magnus's warnings echoed in her mind – dark factions, old compacts, Kelly being vulnerable just by being here.

# CHAPTER 12

Brendan pulled the door open, the morning air still carrying the salt-sweet scent of pōhutukawa blossoms. Mrs Nolan stood on his doorstep, her grey suit as severe as her expression, looking like she'd stepped out of a council meeting rather than walked the quiet streets of Kotahi Bay.

"Mr. Cartwright." Her voice could have frosted windows. "We need to talk about your progress."

His stomach clenched. He'd known this confrontation was coming – had been dodging her calls for days while he tried to figure out what the hell he was actually doing here. "I thought we agreed on Friday?"

"Some things cannot wait." She pursed her lips, examining him like he was a disappointing specimen. "Well? Are you going to invite me in?"

As much as he'd tried to tidy things up, the house still smelled of June – lavender potpourri and something darker underneath, like old copper. Mrs Nolan swept past him into the lounge, claiming Gran's favourite chair as if she owned the place. Maybe she thought she did.

"I trust you're settling in?" Her tone suggested she didn't care. "Though the place still reeks of June."

"Leave her out of this." The words came out harsher than intended. Whatever June had become, whatever darkness had claimed her in the end, she'd still been family. "You want to discuss business? Fine. But I won't listen to you speak ill of the dead."

Mrs Nolan's smile was thin as paper. "How... principled. And a strange choice in your line of work. Very well. Let's discuss why you're here."

She folded her hands in her lap, but Brendan caught the tremor in her fingers. Whatever hold she thought she had over him, she was nervous too. Good.

"The Bay requires certain safeguards," she continued. "At present, those needs are not being met. Your particular skill set could help restore the balance. Don't tell me you're afraid of dirty work. You're a necromancer, after all."

"Kaipō," he corrected. "We call ourselves Kaipō. Eaters of darkness."

Mrs Nolan's smile was thin. "Whatever you prefer to call it, Mr Cartwright. The effect can be the same, when properly motivated."

The threat was clear enough. He let it pass - for now.

"You need me?"

"Yes." The word came out clipped, distasteful.

"So who do you want raised?" He kept his voice casual, though his palms had started to sweat. Every raising cost him – shortened his life, darkened his soul a little more. But for Michael...

"Ideally, no one. If you can convince the Whenua girl to take her grandmother's place, your darker services won't be required." She peered over her glasses. "I'm told that would be in everyone's best interest. Including your nephew's."

The casual mention of Michael made his blood run cold. Of course she knew. She'd known from the beginning – it's why she'd chosen him.

"You're talking about Alyssa." It wasn't a question. The pretty woman with the terrible breaking-and-entering skills and excellent pikelets. The one that Mrs Nolan had told him to stay away from, back when he'd last visited June.

"You're acquainted?" Mrs Nolan's eyebrows rose. "How convenient."

"We've met." He thought of Alyssa's flustered smile, the way she'd blushed when their hands touched. The way magic seemed to swirl around her even as she denied having any. "She seems nice enough. Why does she need convincing?"

"Her grandmother was a powerful witch. It's the duty of their line to maintain the Bay's boundaries. Alyssa is... reluctant to embrace her heritage."

Brendan scrubbed a hand over his jaw, buying time. This was worse than he'd thought. Convincing someone to use magic they were comfortable with was one thing. Forcing someone into power they didn't want? That was how you created monsters.

"So you want me to manipulate her into becoming something she doesn't want to be. Or raise her grandmother to do it instead."

"Precisely."

"No deal." He stood, using his height advantage. "Find another Kaipō. I'm done."

But Mrs Nolan didn't move, didn't even blink. "No, Mr. Cartwright. You're not. We have an agreement."

"The agreement was that I'd come to the Bay and help with your boundary problem. In exchange, I'd get access to June's artifacts and that cure you promised." His voice dropped. "The one that might save a dying child."

"And you'll get all of that. Once the job is done." She finally stood, barely reaching his shoulder but somehow filling the room. "The Whenua girl must take her place, one way or another. The boundary weakens daily. Soon, things will start getting through. Things that will make your nephew's illness look like a blessing."

The threat hung between them, cold and clear.

"Have you even tried talking to her?" Brendan asked. Genuinely confused as this strange power move the woman was making. "Or did you just start with threats and demands?"

"I don't have time for hand-holding. She has a duty." Mrs Nolan moved towards the door. "You have one week, Mr. Cartwright. Convince her, or I'll require you to use your other talents. And if you try to leave town..." She smiled, and it was terrible. "Well. Let's hope it doesn't come to that."

The door clicked shut behind her, leaving Brendan alone with the scent of lavender and copper and his own rising anger.

"Damn!" He slammed his fist into the wall, leaving a dent in June's carefully maintained plaster.

He couldn't do this. Wouldn't do this. Alyssa deserved better than manipulation and lies. He'd pack up, leave town, find another way to help Michael –

His phone buzzed. Esther's number.

"Brendan?" His sister's voice was thick with tears. "We might only have days...maybe a week. He's asking for you."

The world tilted. Brendan sank onto June's couch, the floral cushions releasing the scent of dust and old perfume. "I'm trying, Es. I'm so close to finding something that might help."

"Just... hurry. Please."

The line went dead. Brendan stared at the phone, his hands shaking. Days. Michael had days.

Outside, a car door slammed. Through the window, he saw

Alyssa climbing out of her vehicle, a beach towel wrapped around her shoulders, her hair still damp and curling from the salt water. She moved with casual grace, unaware of the power that radiated from her like heat from sun-warmed stone. Her friend followed, but she didn't hold even a moment of his attention.

Alyssa paused at her mailbox, checking for letters, and the light caught in her hair. For a moment, she looked towards his house, and their eyes met through the glass. She smiled – quick, surprised, genuine – before disappearing inside.

His gut twisted. He couldn't trust what he felt around her, not with her unconscious magic pulling at him like a tide. But something deeper than attraction, deeper than magic, told him to stay.

Michael needed him to stay.

Brendan picked up his phone again, scrolling to Mrs Nolan's number. His thumb hovered over it for a long moment before he set it aside.

One week to find another way. One week to save his nephew without destroying an innocent woman.

One week to figure out if what he felt for Alyssa was real, or just another trap in a town full of them.

He stood, muscles aching with tension, and headed for the kitchen. If he was staying, he'd need coffee. And a plan that didn't involve betraying the first person in years who'd made him feel like he might be more than just death walking.

# CHAPTER 13

Alyssa's phone sat silent on the kitchen counter, Sam's name flashing across the screen for the seventh time that day. "Aren't you going to answer that?" Kelly asked from her spot on the couch.

"Nope." Alyssa took another sip. "Today is about us. No drama, no complications, just – "

The angry buzz of a lawnmower shattered the lazy afternoon peace, drowning out whatever lie she'd been about to tell. The sound was jarring in sleepy Kotahi Bay, where even the waves seemed to whisper rather than roar.

"Is that...?" Kelly scrambled to the window, pressing her nose against the glass like a child at a candy store.

Alyssa joined her, and her glass of cola nearly slipped from her fingers. Brendan was pushing a mower across her disaster of a lawn, shirtless in the afternoon sun. Grass clippings clung to his tanned skin like green confetti, and sweat traced rivers down the muscles of his back already. A pīwakawaka – a fantail – danced around him, catching the insects disturbed by the mower, its tail fanning out in delicate displays.

Kelly leaned against Alyssa's shoulder, warm and giggling. "If I wasn't seeing someone... I'd tap that. You better get in fast girl before some other lonely lady in town gets her claws into him."

"Kels!" Alyssa pushed her off and scowled, but heat flooded her cheeks. After everything Magnus had said about power and attraction, about earth magic drawing people like moths to flame... She shook the thought away, but her fingers tingled where they gripped the glass. The pīwakawaka chirped, a sound like tiny bells that she shouldn't have been able to hear over the mower, and it seemed to look right at her before flitting away.

"I need to use the ladies," Kelly said in a mock whisper that was anything but quiet. "I'll leave you two alone." She waggled her eyebrows suggestively and headed for the front door, her steps only slightly unsteady.

Alyssa watched Brendan work for another moment, memorizing the play of sunlight on skin, before stepping outside. The afternoon heat hit her like a wall after the cool dimness of the house. The air smelled of cut grass and the sea, with an undertone of mānuka honey from the trees that bordered her property.

Brendan killed the motor and pulled off the catcher, grass clippings falling like green snow. He looked around, clearly searching for somewhere to empty it, and she called out before he could wander off.

"Hi. Over here." Alyssa gave a little wave and tried to stand up straight despite nerves making the world tilt gently, like being on a boat. "Thought it safer not to approach. Who knows what might have happened."

He turned, and his face broke into that devastating grin. "Oh hey, I wondered where you were."

"Just chilling out with Kelly. We were talking about maybe

having a barbeque tonight." She heard herself and winced internally – way to commit to a plan on the fly.

"And you didn't think to invite me?" He raised his eyebrows, mock-hurt playing across his features. "Where do you want these?" He hefted the catcher, biceps flexing with the movement, and Alyssa's mouth went dry despite the wine.

She exhaled slowly, trying to focus on anything other than the bead of sweat trailing down his chest. "Ah, there's a compost heap out back. I'll show you."

He followed her around the house, and she was hyper-aware of him behind her – the soft pad of his bare feet on grass, the way his presence seemed to charge the air between them. The garden beds were thriving despite her lack of actual knowledge, Gran's hardy natives blooming in defiance of her sporadic watering. Purple harakeke flowers stood tall, and the scent of rosemary drifted from the herb garden, mixing with the earthier smell of the compost.

"This is a great spot," Brendan said as he emptied the clippings. "Good sun exposure, sheltered from the wind. Your gran knew what she was doing."

The casual mention of Gran made something twist in Alyssa's chest. Would she ever get used to the fact the woman was gone? "What brought you to the Bay?" she asked, deflecting.

"Work... of a sort." His answer was as vague as morning mist.

"And yet you have time to mow a stranger's lawn?" Alyssa quipped, leaning against the weathered garden shed. The wood was warm against her back, grounding her.

"A rather pretty stranger, who happens to make excellent pikelets and has a noble concern for neighbourhood safety." His eyes met hers and the intensity of his gaze sent heat flooding through her that had nothing to do with the after-noon sun.

"Well, I mean, it's not anything out of the ordinary." She stumbled over the words, attraction making her tongue clumsy. A tūī called from the kōwhai tree, its bell-like notes mixing with her nervous laughter. She felt drunk, though she'd not had anything alcoholic today. Magnus's warnings kept circling in her mind like sharks. *Power calls to power*, he'd said. Was that what this was?

Before she could second-guess herself, she blurted, "Do you want to come over for the barbeque? It's the least I can do to thank you for helping out with this." She waved at the half-mown lawn, then laid her hand on his forearm. His skin was warm beneath her palm, and she swore she felt something spark between them – static electricity, surely. "Gran would roll over in her grave if she knew how out of hand I'd let it get."

He glanced down at her hand, and she watched his throat work as he swallowed. When he looked back up, his smile was softer, more genuine. "Sounds great. What should I bring?"

"Something to drink. I'm not going to give you any tips, but you will be judged on your choice." Emboldened by his response to her, she leaned in and pressed her lips to his cheek. He smelled of summer – cut grass and clean sweat and some-thing uniquely him that made her want to bury her face in his neck. "Thank you."

She turned and walked back to the house on legs that felt only slightly unsteady, aware of his eyes on her the whole way. Behind her, the mower roared back to life, and she smiled despite herself.

She had work to do. Like scrounging up enough food for a hungry man. And figuring out how to get through an evening with Kelly and Brendan without mentioning magic, or Viking ghosts who appeared in kitchens with dire warnings.

Alyssa pushed through the back door and called, "Kelly! I need help!"

Footsteps thundered down the hallway. "What? What's wrong?" Kelly appeared in the doorway, eyes wide with concern.

"So, I kind of just invited Brendan to a barbeque we're having tonight."

"We're having a barbeque?" Kelly raised an eyebrow, but her lips were already curving into a knowing smile.

"We are now." Alyssa yanked open both fridge and freezer doors, cool air washing over her flushed face. Thank god she'd stocked up on meat. "Here, chuck these in the sink with some hot water." She passed Kelly packages wrapped in butcher paper – mince, steak, and chicken breasts.

Kelly groaned as she juggled the frozen packages. "How badly do you want to impress him?"

"I don't want to impress him! I just had to take control, you know? He – "

"Does things to your girly bits." Kelly's grin was wicked.

"Shut up! It's not like that, okay it is like that, but... Shut up." Alyssa shook her head, hair escaping from her messy bun. "Hook me up with some music, Kels. I need to get sorted."

"On it!" Kelly danced out of the room, returning moments later to plug her phone into the speaker. Soon, something deep and bassy throbbed through the kitchen, the kind of music that made you want to move your hips while cooking.

"Can you clear out all the wine bottles? Stash them in the laundry and hopefully he won't think we're total alcoholics."

"Yes Ma'am." Kelly saluted, then paused mid-bottle-gathering. "Alyssa... about earlier... We should probably – "

"Later," Alyssa said firmly, running hot water over the frozen meat. Steam rose, carrying the metallic scent of defrosting beef. "After dinner. When it's just us."

Kelly nodded slowly, something unreadable in her eyes. "Yeah. Okay. But we are going to talk about it."

"I know." Alyssa turned back to the sink, letting the hot water numb her fingers. Outside, the lawnmower droned on, an oddly domestic soundtrack to her racing thoughts.

Three hours later, the meat sizzled on the grill, filling the air with the smell of charcoal and caramelizing fat. The garlic naan was keeping warm in the oven, and the potato salad – Gran's recipe, heavy on the mayo and fresh dill – chilled in the fridge. The sun had begun its descent towards the sea, painting the sky in shades of peach and gold that only Kotahi Bay seemed to manage.

And Brendan still hadn't shown up.

"Pour me another, wench," Kelly declared from her sprawl on the outdoor chair, holding out her glass like a queen demanding tribute.

"When did I become your drink-bitch?" Alyssa asked in mock offense, though she was already reaching for the bottle. The afternoon of drinks had mellowed into evening tipsiness, edges softened and tongues loosened. They'd carefully avoided any mention of the previous night, dancing around it like it was a sleeping taniwha.

"Oh hon, since I got here. Didn't you realise?" Kelly took a generous sip and leaned back, the chair creaking ominously. "Do you think he's actually going to show?"

"Who else are you expecting?"

Brendan's voice, warm as aged whiskey, made Alyssa's heart skip. She turned with a grin that she hoped looked more confident than giddy. He stood at the corner of the house, mercifully clothed now in jeans and a grey t-shirt that did nothing to hide what she'd seen earlier.

"Only you. We're keeping it low key. Kotahi Bay couldn't withstand the full force of our party prowess." She looked him up and down with theatrical disappointment. "So, what did you bring?"

He pulled a bottle from the satchel slung over his shoulder, presenting it like a wine sommelier.

"Kahlua, huh? Yeah, I guess I approve." She pretended to consider. "I certainly hope that you provided something to drink it with though because I do not have a lot of milk."

"Oh, I always provide." He set the bag on the weathered outdoor table and pulled out his supplies like a magician – vodka, milk, and a tub of vanilla ice cream that was already starting to sweat in the evening warmth.

"Okay, you totally pass the test." Alyssa grabbed the ice cream before it could melt completely. "I'll grab some clean glasses. Kelly, check the steak." She escaped inside, needing a moment to compose herself.

In the relative safety of the kitchen, she hummed to herself – some pop song Kelly had been playing earlier. Thank god Brendan hadn't arrived until she'd downed a decent glass of Dutch courage. It had been so long since she'd navigated the waters of a new attraction. With Grant, everything had been comfortable, predictable. This felt like standing at the edge of a cliff, wondering if the water below was deep enough to dive.

She returned with glasses and ice, pausing in the doorway to admire the view. Brendan had taken over the grill, moving with easy confidence. The evening light caught the highlights in his hair, turning it to burnished gold.

"White Russian, anyone? Who am I kidding, you're all getting one." Her hands trembled slightly as she built the drinks, aware of Brendan's eyes on her. She was generous with the vodka – liquid courage seemed like a good idea right about now.

Kelly accepted hers with a conspiratorial wink. "He's even hot when I'm sober," she stage-whispered. "Maybe more so."

"Real subtle, Kels. Besides, I'm not sure you're as sober as you think you are" Alyssa rolled her eyes, then turned to hand Brendan his glass. Their fingers brushed in the exchange, and that spark was there again – electricity that had nothing to do with static and everything to do with chemistry.

He took a sip and winced. "I see you like them strong."

"Yes, but also it's been a few years. You can make the next round."

He chuckled, taking another sip with determined bravery. "No, this is fine. At least I don't have to drive home. How long does it take to stumble to my place?"

"I wasn't that drunk the other night." The words came out more defensive than she'd intended.

"No, but you weren't that sober." His grin took any sting out of the words. "How do you like your steak?"

She peered at the grill where the meat had definitely seen better days. "By now I think it's all well done, so that'll have to do. Let's eat, I'm ravenous."

They settled around the outdoor table as the first stars began to appear in the darkening sky. The fairy lights Alyssa had strung up last week cast everything in a warm glow, and somewhere in the distance, a morepork called its haunting song.

"I think we can call this your official welcome to the Bay," Alyssa said, raising her glass. "Here's to new friends, and new towns. Cheers."

"Cheers," Kelly and Brendan echoed.

"Thanks for this, Alyssa. You really didn't have to invite me over." Brendan's gaze lingered on her face, intense enough to make her cheeks warm.

"I wanted to." The admission came out softer than intended.

"Yes, she really did," Kelly chimed in, her grin sharp as

broken glass. "Alyssa's been a little lonely since she came to the Bay. So I think it's great that she's making new... friends."

"Shut up," Alyssa hissed, but Kelly was on a roll, wine loosening her tongue and sharpening her edges.

"No, no, please, enlighten me." Brendan leaned forward, clearly enjoying the show.

"Well, Alyssa here hasn't exactly been Little Miss Social since she ran away from the city. Hiding out in her grandmother's house, avoiding everyone who tries to help her..." Kelly's tone was light, teasing, but there was something underneath it – frustration that had been building since she'd arrived. Alyssa's wide eyed look, begging her friend to shut up was doing nothing, and she knew a kick under the table wasn't going to help the situation.

Brendan laughed, then started coughing as his drink went down the wrong way.

"Shit, don't die on us!" Kelly declared, thumping him on the back with more force than necessary.

"I'm fine, really," he wheezed. "Could I use your bathroom though?"

"Sure, it's down the end of the hall, on the right." Alyssa waited until he disappeared inside before rounding on Kelly. "I don't know what you think you're trying to do, but quit it. I don't need your help."

"Are you sure?" Kelly set down her glass with a sharp click. "Hon, you've been out of the game so long, I just wanted to make sure he knew you were into him. You're not making that very clear. Same as always – holding back, keeping people at arm's length."

"I need to do this my way. I'm not you." The words came out sharper than intended.

"What does that mean?" Kelly's playful mask slipped, revealing hurt underneath.

"It means that I don't just throw myself at men and use my womanly charms to lure them into bed." The moment the words left her mouth, Alyssa wanted to snatch them back.

"Low blow, Lysie. Low blow." Kelly's voice had gone dangerously quiet. She knocked back the rest of her drink in one swallow.

"I'm sorry, Kelly. I didn't mean it like that!" Alyssa stood, reaching for her friend. "You know I love you to bits, but I'm not as forward as you. Not as confident. I never have been."

"Well maybe you should be." Kelly's eyes glittered with wine and something meaner. "Maybe that lack of confidence is partly why things with you and Grant fell apart."

The words hung in the air like a curse. Alyssa felt them land like a physical blow, stealing her breath. Kelly knew – *knew* – how much Grant's rejection had gutted her, how she'd blamed herself for not being enough. And now...

Kelly's face crumpled as she realised what she'd said, reaching out, but Alyssa was already backing away.

"I'm going for a walk. I'll be back soon. You can tell Brendan... I don't know, tell him whatever the hell you want."

She fled into the gathering dusk, leaving behind the warmth of fairy lights and the weight of words that couldn't be taken back. Behind her, she heard Kelly call her name, but she didn't stop. She couldn't. Not when the hurt was this fresh, this raw.

The streets of Kotahi Bay were quiet, most people inside having their own dinners, living their own uncomplicated lives. Alyssa walked without direction, just needing distance between herself and the disaster she'd left behind. The air had cooled with the setting sun, carrying the salt-sweet scent of the sea and the sound of waves against the shore.

She'd made it to the end of the street when she heard footsteps pounding behind her.

# CHAPTER 14

The sound of footsteps made her heart race – sharp slaps against pavement, too heavy to be Kelly's. After Magnus's warnings about factions and danger, being followed in the dark sent ice through her veins. Her fingers curled into fists, magic prickling beneath her skin like static before a storm.

"Hey, wait up," Brendan called. "Don't you know it's not very hostess-like to take off on a guest?"

Relief flooded through her at his familiar voice, warm honey over the cold fear. "Oh shut up," Alyssa said, her voice sharp, abrupt. She couldn't find it in her to apologise for snapping, didn't even know if she wanted to, so she just kept walking, even picked up her pace a little. Her sandals clicked against the concrete, a staccato rhythm that couldn't quite drown out the sound of his longer strides catching up. The night air tasted of salt and approaching rain, and somewhere a dog barked, the sound echoing off the quiet houses.

"I'm sorry, I was just trying to lighten the mood. What's going on? Kelly said she'd upset you." He came up alongside her, and she couldn't help but *feel* him there, his presence a balm even when she didn't want it to be.

"Well, she did." The words came out sharper than intended, edged with hurt that sat like broken glass in her throat.

Brendan huffed out a little laugh. "Is this like, regular girl fighting, or something more?"

"Something more. I think. I'm not sure." She finally stopped walking and turned towards him. The streetlight caught his face, throwing half of it into shadow, turning his eyes dark as the ocean at night. For a moment she wondered if she could trust him. Magnus had warned her about everyone having their own agenda, and here was this man who'd appeared in her life at exactly the wrong – or right – moment. The shadows seemed to shift around him, and she couldn't tell if it was her imagination or something more. "I am sorry for walking off. I just needed to get some space. Things have been a little weird with Kelly and I don't know why. It's not your fault." She pressed her palms into her eyes until she saw stars. It was easier than looking at his kind, handsome face.

"But my presence is making things a little more tense?"

The question hung between them like morning mist. Alyssa sighed, dropped her hands, tasting Kahlua and regret on her tongue. A moth fluttered past, drawn to the streetlight, and she envied its simple purpose. "She seems desperate for me to hook up with you. I have no idea why. That's not her normal M.O."

Brendan paused a beat, assessing her before he spoke. She could almost see him weighing his words, trying to choose carefully. "And what about you?"

Her stomach flipped. "What do you mean? Am I desperate to hook up with you? No, I am not desperate, but I'm curious. You're good to look at and I like your sense of humour. You feel..." She shrugged, grimacing. The admission made her cheeks burn despite the cool night air.

"Okay then." He nodded slowly, and she caught a flash of something in his expression – satisfaction? Relief? "I can work with that. Do you want me to back off until she goes?"

"What the hell is wrong with you?" Alyssa declared, throwing her hands up in the air. The reasonable response was so unexpected, so unlike what Grant would have done. Grant would have pushed, would have made it about his ego, would have – "Why the hell are you being so bloody rational? I take it back. I'm not interested – "

He cut her off with his lips.

The kiss was nothing like their polite interactions, nothing like the careful dance they'd been doing around each other. It was hunger and heat and the taste of Kahlua still sweet on his tongue. She wrapped her arms around his neck, fingers tangling in his hair, pressing herself against him and giving in to the desire that had been simmering since she'd first seen him. Every warning Magnus had given her evaporated like morning dew. The jasmine hedge beside them released its perfume into the night, mixing with his scent – soap and grass and something indefinably male that made her head spin.

She didn't care what the neighbours thought. Didn't care that this was just what Kelly wanted, because it was what she wanted too. And clearly, what Brendan wanted. His lips were divine, moving against hers with a skill that spoke of experience and desire in equal measure. His hands roamed down, cupping her butt and drawing her further in, until there was no space between them, just heat and want and the solid presence of him anchoring her to the earth. She could feel him, hard against her belly, and a sound escaped her throat that she'd deny making later.

This was definitely more than just attraction. The air

around them seemed to hum with energy, crackling like the moment before lightning strikes. She could feel it in her bones, in the marrow-deep magic that had awakened since she'd come to Kotahi Bay. Was this what Magnus meant about power calling to power? But then Brendan's tongue swept against hers and she stopped thinking altogether, lost in sensation, in the way her body remembered this dance even after months of loneliness.

When they finally broke apart, she was breathless, her lips swollen and tingling. Alyssa extracted herself from the kiss, pushing him lightly away before she did something truly stupid like drag him into the nearest garden.

"Wow." She exhaled the words, watching them mist in the cool air between them. "You sure know how to stop an argument."

"You're kind of cute when you're irate." He reached for her hand and brought her fingers to his lips. The gesture was oddly old-fashioned, courtly even, like something from another era entirely. His lips were warm against her knuckles, and she wondered not for the first time if there was more to Brendan than he let on. There had to be; she just wasn't sure what. The streetlight flickered above them, casting strange shadows that seemed to dance independently of their bodies. "Still need a walk, or do you think we could go back? I'm a little hungry." Lust flared in his eyes, pupils blown wide in the dim light, and while she was half sure he wasn't talking about the food kind of hunger, her belly chose that moment to growl, reminding her she'd barely touched her dinner.

"Yeah, I'm hungry too. Come on."

Brendan held her hand all the way back to the house, his thumb tracing small circles on her palm that sent shivers up her arm like tiny lightning strikes. The night air brought with it the scent of the ocean – salt and seaweed and that indefinable smell of deep water – mixed with blooming jasmine. Normal scents, grounding her in the real world even as her lips still tingled from his kiss and the magic hummed beneath her skin like a live wire.

Kelly was nowhere to be found when they got back, though her car still sat in the driveway like a patient animal. The porch light cast long shadows across the yard, and the abandoned plates on the table looked like props from a play that had ended badly. Which, Alyssa supposed, it had.

"Do you want me to go and look for her?" Brendan asked, slipping his arm around her shoulder and drawing her in for a hug. God, it had been so long since she'd been held by a guy like this, warm and solid and safe. His chest was firm against her cheek, his heartbeat steady and calming. She could stay here forever, pretending the world was simple, that she was just a woman being held by a man she was attracted to. Even if nobody in Kotahi Bay was really safe.

"No, she gets like this sometimes. She'll come back soon enough, and we'll apologise and get over it." The words were automatic, a script they'd played out before, though never with quite this much weight behind it. "We fight sometimes, and since I left the city things have been a bit odd. We just need time to figure out what our friendship is going to look like now."

"Yeah, I get it. Do you want me to wait with you?" He looked hopeful, though not expectant, and she loved him a little for that – for not pushing, for not making this about him.

"I do, but you can't. I need to sort this out and if you're here when she gets back it's going to be awkward. Sorry." Alyssa grimaced, hating herself for being practical when all she wanted was to drag him inside and forget about everything else.

"Well, you know where to find me if you need me. Just,

knock on the front door this time, hey?" His lips curved into that grin that did dangerous things to her insides, and he gave her a soft kiss that tasted like promises. Then he picked up his plate with the half-eaten steak. "I'm going to take this with me, but I promise I'll return it. Washed even."

Alyssa rolled her eyes and laughed, the sound surprising her with its genuineness. "Sure. That's totally fine."

Brendan gave her a little salute and headed back around to the front of the house. She watched him go, admiring the view one last time before reality crashed back in. She plopped herself down on her chair with a sigh that seemed to come all the way from her toes. "Well, I guess that wasn't a complete failure," she said to the empty yard.

The night sounds seemed louder now that she was alone – crickets chirping their endless song, the distant crash of waves against the shore, the rustle of something in the bushes that might have been a hedgehog or might have been something else entirely. She kind of wished that Magnus was here to talk to. He could be a pain in the ass, but he always had good advice. Though he'd prob- ably have opinions about her kissing strangers in the street. *Not strangers,* she corrected herself. *neighbours. Mysterious neighbours who show up to mow lawns and kiss like they're trying to steal souls.*

She reached for her plate and picked at the cold steak and potato salad for a few minutes before giving up. The meat tasted like cardboard now, all flavour leached away by drama and time. Thinking of Kelly wandering around the streets of the Bay made her feel ill, anxiety curdled in her stomach like sour milk. After what Magnus had said about outsiders being vulnerable, about dark factions hunting for power...

But Kelly was smart. She'd stick to the main streets, wouldn't go anywhere dangerous. Wouldn't wander down to the beach where the barrier was thinnest.

Would she?

Alyssa stood abruptly, needing to move, to do something with the nervous energy crackling through her veins. She picked up the dishes and dumped them on the kitchen bench with more force than necessary, the plates clattering like bones. The hot water steamed as she filled a bucket, the scent of dish soap sharp and lemony. She grabbed the steel scrubbing brush and attacked the grill, using her anger and hurt to scour away every trace of char and grease. At least if something happened while she was cleaning, she'd have a weapon handy. The thought was only half-joking.

"Hey."

Alyssa froze upon hearing Kelly's voice, her knuckles white around the brush handle. She placed it carefully in the bucket of water, watching the suds swirl like tiny galaxies, and smoothed her hands down her jeans. The denim was rough under her palms, grounding. She could do this. She could have this conversation without mentioning ghosts or magic or the way the very air in Kotahi Bay seemed alive with possibility and danger.

"Hi," she replied, turning slowly.

Kelly's face crumpled in three seconds flat, mascara already smudged beneath her eyes like bruises. She shuffled towards Alyssa, her usual confidence stripped away, reaching out hands that trembled slightly. "I'm so sorry. That was such a cruel thing to say. I don't know why I said it. I..."

The words hung between them like a blade. Alyssa could still feel the sting of them, the way they'd sliced through all her carefully constructed defenses. But looking at Kelly's devastated face, she couldn't hold onto the anger. It slipped through her fingers like water.

"It's okay," Alyssa said, and meant it. Sort of.

"It's not. I'm sorry." Tears were streaming down Kelly's face now, catching the porch light like tiny crystals.

"No, it's not, but I don't want you to feel bad." Alyssa started to cry too, the tears hot and sudden, tasting of salt and wine and the bitterness of change. She pulled Kelly close, and they clung to each other like survivors of a shipwreck. Kelly's hair smelled of coconut shampoo and the beach, familiar scents that made Alyssa's heart ache for simpler times. "I forgive you. I don't know why things are weird now. I was a bad friend, and so this is my fault too. I'm sorry. We just need to figure out a way through this."

"Thank you," Kelly whispered into her hair, the words warm and damp with tears. She sniffed loudly as she pulled away, wiping her nose with her sleeve in a gesture so ungraceful and so purely Kelly that Alyssa couldn't help but smile. "Now, you need to give me the gossip. What happened with Brendan?"

Alyssa snorted with laughter, the sound bubbling up from somewhere deep and slightly hysterical. "Some things never change huh?"

"Yup, so spill. Did he kiss you? Did he storm off? Is it on, or off?" Kelly sat down and picked up her glass, apparently unbothered by the fact it had been sitting out for an hour. Alyssa did the same, the wine warm but still alcoholic enough to take the edge off. At least they had pushed past the issues for now, even if it felt like putting a bandaid on a bullet wound.

"He came after me, and we talked a little. He did kiss me, and it was amazing. My word. It's been a long time since someone kissed me like that." Alyssa sighed in contentment, her lips still tingling with sense memory. She could still taste him, still feel the press of his body against hers. "He gave me some space when we came back so it wouldn't be weird when you got home."

"Hot and considerate. He sounds perfect. When's the wedding?" Kelly's grin was wicked, but there was something else in her eyes – worry? Knowledge? It was gone before Alyssa could be sure.

"Kelly!"

"Oh come on, you know I'm joking. I'm happy for ya chook, it's about time you met a decent man."

"I hope he is. Not like I know a whole lot about him at this point." And that was the problem, wasn't it? In a town full of secrets, where a Viking ghost appeared in the kitchen, how could she know who to trust? Brendan could be anyone, anything. The thought should have scared her more than it did.

"Plenty of time for that. First you need to get him in the sack so that you can tell if he's a keeper." Kelly grinned lasciviously, waggling her eyebrows in a way that was both ridiculous and endearing.

"Might wait until you've left town for that to happen. I'd hate to keep you up all night." Alyssa poked her tongue out and Kelly dissolved into laughter, the sound bright and sharp in the quiet night.

But even as they joked and gossipped like old times, even as they fell back into their familiar rhythms, Alyssa couldn't shake the feeling that everything was about to change. The air felt heavy with more than just the approaching rain, charged with potential like the moment before a spell is cast.

The wine glass was empty in her hand, but she didn't refill it. She wanted to remember this – Kelly's laughter, the warmth of reconciliation, the taste of possibility still sweet on her lips. Because tomorrow would come soon enough, bringing with it truths that couldn't be untold and choices that couldn't be unmade.

In the distance, thunder rumbled like an old god clearing its throat. A storm was coming.

# CHAPTER 15

The morning air carried the scent of salt and something heavy – dense like molasses. Sam's fingers drummed against the steering wheel as she pulled up outside Constance's cottage, her warning from years ago echoing in her mind: *When the barrier trembles, the guardians must stand together.*

Constance was already waiting on her porch, white plaits gleaming in the sun, her carved walking stick planted firmly on the weathered boards. Despite her age, there was something timeless about her – as if the earth itself had taken human form and decided to wear sensible shoes and a floral dress.

"You felt it too," Constance said as Sam approached. Not a question.

"The whole shop hummed with it this morning." Sam helped Constance into the passenger seat, noting how the older woman's fingers trembled slightly as she buckled in. Time was catching up even to Constance, the last of the old guard. "The crystals were singing, and not in a good way."

"Mrs Nolan has overstepped." Constance's voice carried

the weight of mountains. "Threatening Alyssa, pushing where she has no right to push. The council was meant to support the guardians, not command them."

Sam started the engine, stealing glances at Constance as they drove towards the council building. How many times had this woman faced down threats to Kotahi Bay? How many secrets did she carry in those deep-lined hands?

And how much of that would be lost forever when Constance passed from this world?

"Tell me about the early days," Sam said softly. "When you and Sylvie first took up the mantle."

A smile ghosted across Constance's weathered face. "Ah, we were so young then. So certain we knew everything." She gazed out the window at the passing pōhutukawa trees. "Sylvie could make the very air sing with power. I was always more grounded - but there were others too, a whole circle of guardians with divine powers handed down from the gods - Kuraatua."

"You told me about Rose," Sam recalled.

"Rose saw patterns none of us could. Past, present, future – all woven together in her mind like the most intricate korowai." Constance's voice grew heavy with loss. "When she passed, we felt the threads begin to loosen. Now with Sylvie gone..."

"We have Alyssa." Sam tried to inject confidence into her voice.

"Yes. Raw power without training, fear without understanding." Constance shifted in her seat, and Sam caught the slight wince of pain. "But she has something we didn't have at her age – she's already faced some of her demons and won. That ghost could have consumed her, but she found another way."

They pulled into the council parking lot, the building

looming like a concrete monument to bureaucracy. Sam helped Constance out, feeling the tremor in the older woman's grip.

"How much time do we have?" Sam asked quietly. "Really?"

Constance's eyes, still sharp as polished greenstone, met hers. "Less than we need. More than we fear." She patted Sam's hand. "You and the others – you're ready, even if you don't feel it. The new guardians will be different from the old. They must be."

Inside, the building's fluorescent lights flickered overhead, casting sickly shadows that made Sam's skin crawl. The reception area smelled of stale coffee and fear – the particular brand of anxiety that clung to government buildings like mold.

"Excuse me!" Janine, the secretary half-rose from her desk, her voice pitched high with alarm. "You can't just – Mrs Nolan is in a meeting! You need an appointment!"

Constance didn't even slow. Her walking stick struck the linoleum with measured beats – tap, tap, tap – each impact somehow louder than it should be, resonating through the floor like a judge's gavel. The fluorescent light directly above her flickered and died.

"Ms Mohio! I said you need – " Janine's protest died in her throat as Constance turned her head, just slightly, those ancient eyes catching the harsh light.

The younger woman sank back into her chair, hand trembling as it reached for the phone. But she didn't dial. Couldn't, maybe. The authority radiating from Constance was older than any bureaucracy, more absolute than any policy manual.

Sam followed in the elder's wake, catching the secretary's wide-eyed stare. "Don't worry," she murmured as they passed. "We won't be long."

The hallway stretched before them, each footfall of Constance's stick marking their progression like a countdown.

Other office doors remained firmly shut, as if the building itself recognized who walked its halls and chose to stay out of her way.

Mrs Nolan's office door was closed. Constance didn't knock.

The councillor sat behind her desk like a spider in an expensive suit, phone pressed to her ear. Her eyes widened as they entered, something flickering across her face – fear? Anger?

"I'll call you back," she said quickly, setting the phone down. "Miss Mohio, and Miss Clarke. To what do I owe – "

"You know perfectly well why we're here." Constance lowered herself into a chair without invitation, and Sam took position behind her, one hand resting protectively on the older woman's shoulder. "Threatening newcomers? Trying to force Alyssa's hand? That's not how we do things in Kotahi Bay."

Mrs Nolan's fingers tightened on her pen. "The barrier is weakening. We need – "

"What we need," Constance interrupted, her voice carrying the rumble of distant earthquakes, "is for you to remember your place. The council serves the guardians, not the other way around. Your mother understood this. Your grandmother certainly did."

"Times change." Mrs Nolan's jaw set stubbornly. "The old ways aren't enough anymore. We need structure, control – "

"Control?" Sam couldn't keep quiet any longer. "Alyssa just banished a thousand-year-old ghost without any training. She's making protective charms by instinct. And you want to control that?"

Mrs Nolan's gaze snapped to her. "Miss Clarke, you're still young. You don't understand the forces at play here."

"She understands perfectly." Constance's walking stick tapped once against the floor, and Sam felt the pulse of power ripple through the room. The fluorescent lights flickered. "As do I. There are rules older than this building, older than this town. Laws written in the very bones of the earth."

The councillor paled. "You wouldn't dare – "

"I've protected this bay for longer than you've been alive, Vivica Nolan." Constance leaned forward, and suddenly she seemed to fill the room, ancient and implacable as the hills. "I've stood against forces that would turn your hair white just to know their names. And I will not let petty politics and power games destroy what generations have built."

Sam watched Mrs Nolan shrink back in her chair, the woman's carefully constructed authority crumbling under Constance's quiet fury.

"The girl needs time," Constance continued, settling back. "She needs teaching, yes. Support, certainly. But not threats. Not manipulation." She studied Mrs Nolan with those knowing eyes. "What has he promised you, Vivica? What price did you agree to pay?"

Mrs Nolan's face went white, then red. "I don't know what you mean."

"Don't you?" Constance's smile was sad. "I can smell the binding on you, child. Subtle work, but sloppy. Someone's pulling your strings, and you're letting them. Why?"

For a moment, Sam thought Mrs Nolan might break, might confess whatever deal she'd made. But then the woman's face hardened again.

"The Bay must stand. By any means necessary."

"And there it is." Constance sighed, suddenly looking every one of her many years. "The ends justifying the means. That's how it always starts." She pushed herself to her feet, Sam quickly moving to steady her. "Very well. But know this – if you move against Alyssa again, you'll answer to me. And I may be old, Vivica, but I am far from powerless."

They left Mrs Nolan sitting frozen at her desk, the weight of Constance's warning hanging in the air like ozone after lightning.

In the hallway, Constance sagged against Sam's arm. "She's more compromised than I thought."

"What do we do?"

"We protect Alyssa. We teach her what we can." Constance's fingers found Sam's, squeezing with surprising strength. "And we prepare for what's coming. The fair brings challenges, but also opportunities. The other new guardians will be drawn here – I can feel it in the earth's song."

As they made their way back to the car, Sam caught Constance gazing at the horizon, where dark clouds gathered despite the morning sun.

"What do you see?" Sam asked softly.

"Change," Constance murmured. "The turning of ages. The old guard passes, the new rises." She looked at Sam with those ancient eyes, full of love and sorrow and fierce pride. "You're ready, my dear. All of you. Even if you can't see it yet."

Sam helped her into the car, memorizing every line of Constance's beloved face, every word of wisdom. Constance looked so tired. Sam would have to go and track Alyssa down herself, but first she'd get the old woman home and into her comfy chair with a cup of kawakawa tea. Time was short, she could feel it in her bones. Soon, too soon, they would lose their last anchor to the old ways. Sam would soak up every precious moment she had left.

# CHAPTER 16

The pounding on the door felt like hammers against Alyssa's skull, each knock reverberating through the house's old bones. Her mouth tasted of copper and Kahlua, remnants of last night still clinging to her tongue. The harsh words, that kiss. A faultline in her friendship with Kelly.

"I'm coming!" she called out, her voice raw. "For the love of all things holy, will you stop making that noise?"

The floorboards were cold under her bare feet, each step sending shivers up her spine. The house felt different this morning – or was it her? She could feel the protective wards humming in the walls, responding to her distress. When had she become so attuned to them?

She swung the door open, squinting against the assault of morning sunlight. Sam stood on the doorstep, her usually serene face tight with worry, blonde hair escaping from her messy bun in agitated wisps.

"You know I don't lock the door, why didn't you just come in?" Alyssa covered a yawn and nodded towards the kitchen, trying to ignore how Sam's magical aura made her skin prickle. "Shut the door, would you? There's a kitten around here somewhere."

"Where the hell have you been?" Sam demanded, following her inside. The scent of sage and power clung to her like perfume. "I've been calling your cell non-stop."

"Yeah, I must have left it on silent." The lie tasted bitter, mixing unpleasantly with the residue of last night in her mouth. She could tell by Sam's expression – those too-knowing blue eyes – that she wasn't buying it. "Okay, fine. I just wanted to clock out for a bit. I know you have something important to tell me, but I just... Well, I didn't want to know. Kelly is here, and..."

Alyssa busied herself with the morning ritual of coffee, the familiar actions grounding her. The kettle's whistle felt too shrill, the bread slamming into the toaster too violent. Every-thing felt heightened, raw. Socks entered the kitchen, his tiny bell chiming like a fairy's laugh. She reached down to pat him, his fur soft and real under her fingers, purposefully avoiding Sam's gaze.

"You've been doing a lot of not wanting to know since you got here, and it's time that stopped." Sam placed a hand on one hip, her silver rings catching the light. Each one held its own enchantment, Alyssa realised with a start. When had she begun seeing such things?

"Look, before we get into it – I'm sorry about Mrs Nolan." Sam's expression softened as she slid into a seat at the table. "The way she's been harassing you... it's not right. Constance and I paid her a visit this morning. Gave her a proper talking to."

Alyssa blinked, surprised by the apology. "You did?"

"Of course. You're one of us, Alyssa. We protect our own."

Sam glanced towards the hallway. "Where is Kelly, by the way?"

"Still sleeping probably. Nothing wakes her until she's well and ready." The thought of Kelly – normal, safe, wonderfully oblivious Kelly – made Alyssa's chest tighten. Just like Miri had been, before –

No. She wouldn't think about that.

"Okay. Good." Sam nodded, then took a deep breath that seemed to draw in more than just air. "You make coffee, I'll talk."

"Sounds good to me." It didn't, not really. Her hands shook slightly as she poured water into the mugs, the steam rising like tiny ghosts.

"You know Sylvie was a witch."

"Yup," Alyssa said, the mention of her grandmother making her throat tight. Behind Sam, she caught a glimpse of movement in the glass cabinet – Magnus's face materializing in the reflection, watching with those ancient eyes.

"Well, she, and other women from your blood line have played an important role in the Bay, helping to keep it safe from those outside, who... well, who want to see things change around here."

The words 'blood line' made Alyssa's stomach clench. Blood line. The same blood that had enslaved Magnus, that had twisted power into chains. In the cabinet's reflection, Magnus nodded gravely, his expression dark with memory.

"The Bay is a quiet, safe little town. It's got a beautiful seaside location, and you know, change might not be such a bad thing. A little tourism goes a long way, right?" She placed the coffee mugs on the table with too much force, coffee sloshing dangerously close to the rim.

Sam's eyes flashed dangerously. "You have no idea, do you?

No idea what this place really is. How catastrophic it would be if the barrier fell."

The vehemence in Sam's voice made Alyssa step back. Behind Sam, Magnus raised an approving eyebrow, clearly pleased someone was finally being direct.

Maybe she didn't want him to return after all.

"So tell me then!" Alyssa threw up her hands. "Why all the secrets? Why the cryptic warnings and half-truths?"

Sam took a deep breath, her fingers white-knuckled around her coffee mug. "Kotahi Bay is the birthplace of the gods, Alyssa. Where the atua first touched this land. The power here... it's ancient, primal. Too vital to fall into the wrong hands."

The words hung in the air like a physical presence. In the cabinet, Magnus's expression had gone deadly serious, all trace of his usual sardonic humor vanished.

"You are so good at avoiding things," Sam continued more gently. "You avoid grief, you avoid responsibility, and you avoid living the life you were meant to live. What happened that made you so afraid?"

The question hit like a physical blow. Miri's face flashed behind her eyelids – laughing, trusting, then terrified as the magic Alyssa couldn't control had –

"Just because I don't want Kelly dragged into this, it doesn't make me afraid," Alyssa said. "I came here, and I dealt with the ghost. I've been making protective charms, I've met some more people in town. I was starting to – " Her voice cracked.

"Starting to accept it," Sam finished softly. "Until Kelly arrived."

Magnus made a face in the cabinet that was so comically knowing, Alyssa had to bite back an inappropriate laugh. Sam noticed her fighting the smile and frowned in confusion.

"Don't think I don't know how you dealt with the ghost, Alyssa." Sam's knowing look made her squirm. Behind her, Magnus waggled his eyebrows suggestively, and this time Alyssa couldn't stop the snort of laughter.

"What's so funny?" Sam demanded.

"Nothing, sorry. Nervous energy." Alyssa shot Magnus a warning look. He smirked and made a zipping motion across his lips.

"Seriously, does nothing go unnoticed around here? Why can't you people just back off and let me do my thing?" Alyssa shot up from the table, the chair scraping against the floor. She paced the kitchen floor, scooping up Socks for comfort. "All I want is to keep Kelly safe. To keep everyone safe from – from me."

"From what happened with Miri?" Sam asked gently.

Alyssa froze. In the cabinet, Magnus's expression had gone sympathetic, understanding in a way that made her eyes burn.

"How do you – "

"Sylvie told Constance, years ago. She was worried about you, about why you ran from your gifts."

"Gifts?" Alyssa's laugh was bitter. "I nearly killed my best friend, Sam. The magic just... exploded out of me. I couldn't control it. I couldn't – " Her voice broke. "The look on her face..."

"You were fourteen," Sam said firmly. "Untrained, unguided, not to mention struggling with puberty and hormones. That wasn't your fault."

"Tell that to Miri." Alyssa sat back down heavily, letting Socks knead his tiny claws into her shirt.

"I think you should talk to her. Eventually, but right now, the Bay is more important than personal grievances," Sam said, not unkindly. "You have a connection to this place, I know you feel it. These past weeks, you've been blooming, Alyssa.

Your charms are already some of the strongest I've seen. Can you be honest about that?"

Magnus nodded enthusiastically in the reflection, giving her two thumbs up. Despite everything, Alyssa felt her lips twitch.

"I am honest, generally. But yes, I do feel it. The Bay's been... waking something in me."

"It is your home," Sam said, that word holding more meaning to Alyssa than it ever had before. "You're meant to be here. The barrier needs you, Alyssa. We all do."

"Only if you promise to stop with the cryptic speak. Kelly's going to be up any minute now and I'd kind of like for you to be gone by then." She reached across the table to grab Sam's hand. The contact sparked with power, making them both gasp. "I'm not saying no, Sam. I'm just... I need to keep Kelly away from this. I can't watch someone else I care about get hurt because of what I am."

"The barrier is weakening," Sam said urgently, her blue eyes huge, sparkling like stars. "Constance felt it, I felt it, and I know you feel it too. Without the protection your family has maintained – "

"My family." The words tasted like ash. "The same family that enslaved Magnus for centuries? That used his power like a battery?"

Magnus's reflection shifted, and suddenly he was standing beside the cabinet rather than in it, translucent but visible. Sam couldn't see him, but his presence was oddly comforting.

"They were wrong," Magnus said, his voice only Alyssa could hear. "But you are not them. You freed me. You chose differently."

"Like I was saying before," Sam continued, unaware of the ghostly commentary, "your family has a connection to this land that goes back to the beginning. Your ancestor – "

"I know what my ancestors did," Alyssa interrupted. "And that's exactly why I want nothing to do with their legacy."

Magnus rolled his eyes dramatically. "Oh for the love of – tell her you'll think about it so she'll leave before your mundane friend wakes up and complicates everything further."

Despite the situation, Alyssa had to fight another inappropriate smile at his practicality.

"Just, think about it," Sam said, misreading Alyssa's expression as softening. "Constance... she won't be with us much longer. And when she goes, if the barrier isn't strengthened..."

From down the hall came the sound of a door opening, Kelly's sleepy voice calling out.

"You better go," Alyssa said quickly. Sam squeezed her hand once more.

"We're not our ancestors, Alyssa," Sam said softly. "We can choose to be better. And for what it's worth? I think you already have."

Then she was gone, the door closing gently behind her. Magnus lingered a moment longer.

"She's not wrong, you know," he said. "Though her delivery could use work." He studied her with those ancient eyes. "You're nothing like them, little witch. Stop punishing yourself for their sins."

"Lys?" Kelly's voice came from the hallway. "Who were you talking to?"

Magnus faded with a knowing wink, leaving Alyssa alone with her racing heart and the taste of destiny thick on her tongue.

"Just the neighbour," she called back, forcing brightness into her voice. "Ready to attack that garden?"

But even as she said it, she could feel the magic inside her stirring, responding to the Bay's call. She just prayed she could keep it contained long enough to keep Kelly safe. There had to be a subtle way she could get her friend to head back to the city, sooner rather than later.

# CHAPTER 17

The first light of dawn crept through the curtains of June's spare room, painting shadows across the walls that looked too much like reaching fingers. Brendan hadn't slept. Couldn't. His mind kept replaying the kiss, the way Alyssa had tasted of wine and possibility, the way the world had suddenly felt lighter, full of promise.

For one perfect moment, he'd forgotten.

Forgotten the ticking clock, the desperation that had driven him to this godforsaken town. Forgotten that he was drowning in quicksand, and every move only pulled him deeper.

That a woman he couldn't stand was trying to force him to harm Alyssa, who didn't deserve it. Had done nothing but be… her slightly chaotic, lovely self.

He sat up, running his hands through his hair. The kiss had been a mistake. A beautiful, intoxicating mistake that made him want things he couldn't have.

Brendan dressed mechanically, his body moving on autopilot while his mind churned. Mrs Nolan had promised –

sworn – that coming here would lead to answers. That she could save Michael where modern medicine had failed. Matai couldn't help. Samantha couldn't help. And Alyssa...

Gods, Alyssa. So new to her power, so resistant to embracing it. How could he put the burden of Michael's life on her shoulders? It wouldn't be fair. It wouldn't be right. And after what he'd found out family had done – what June had done – he had no right to ask anything of her.

He'd finish mowing her lawn. One last gesture of kindness before he left. Something to remember him by that didn't taste of desperation and lies. Though perhaps he was the only one whose tongue was swollen by those things.

The morning air was thick with humidity as he retrieved the mower from June's shed. The machine sputtered to life, drowning out his thoughts as he pushed it across to Alyssa's yard. The grass was longer in the back, neglected, and he found a strange peace in creating neat lines, bringing order to chaos.

He was halfway through when he heard the front door slam and peered around to the front to see Sam leaving Alyssa's house, her face tight with worry. She spotted him and paused, something flickering in her eyes – recognition, concern, maybe even pity.

"Brendan," she said, having to raise her voice over the mower. He killed the engine.

"Sam." He wiped sweat from his forehead. "Everything okay?"

She glanced back at the house. "That depends on your definition of okay." She studied him for a moment. "You're June's family, aren't you? The one Mrs Nolan brought in?"

No point in denying it. "Yeah."

"Be careful," Sam said softly. "This town..." She shook her head, mouth working as though she wasn't entirely sure what she wanted to say. "You might not be the bad guy here, but it's very easy to cross that line." With that, she walked away before he could ask what she meant. Her words left a heavy stone in his stomach though, confirming his decision to get out of town now, before he crossed that line that she'd alluded to.

He finished the lawn in record time, the physical labor doing nothing to quiet his mind. Inside June's house, he showered, packed his few belongings, and tried not to think about how Alyssa's lips had felt against his.

Michael needed him. That was all that mattered right now.

But as he loaded his car, he kept glancing over to Alyssa's place. He couldn't just leave. Not without some kind of goodbye. Not after last night. He found paper and a pen, his hand hovering over the blank page. What could he possibly say? *Sorry I kissed you and ran? Sorry my family is cursed and my nephew is dying and I'm too much of a coward to tell you the truth?*

In the end, he kept it simple: *Had to go. Family emergency. Take care of yourself. – B*

He walked to her letterbox, the note feeling heavier than it should. This was for the best. Clean break. No messy entanglements. No dragging her into his personal nightmare; she had her own to deal with.

The drive out of town should have taken five minutes. Ten at most. But somehow, twenty minutes later, he found himself passing the same café, the same shops, the same bloody pōhutukawa tree for the third time.

"What the hell?" He pulled over, checking his GPS. According to the screen, he was on the main road heading north. According to his eyes, he was back in the town centre.

He tried again. This time he paid attention to every turn, every landmark. The edge of town appeared ahead – he could see the sign, "Thank you for visiting Kotahi Bay" – but as he crossed what should have been the boundary, the world seemed to fold in on itself. One moment he was leaving, the next he was driving past the council building.

Again.

And again.

By the fifth attempt, his hands were shaking. By the tenth, he was sweating despite the air conditioning. The town wouldn't let him leave. Couldn't let him leave.

He pulled over, his chest tight with something between rage and panic. Michael was dying, and he was trapped in this damn town like a rat in a maze. His phone rang. Mrs Nolan's number.

"What the hell have you done?" The words came out as a snarl, all pretense of civility gone.

"You made an agreement, Mr. Cartwright, and we intend for you to keep it." Her voice was calm, controlled, infuriating.

"My nephew is dying!"

"Then you'd better work faster." The line went dead.

He hurled the phone onto the passenger seat, a stream of curses in multiple languages pouring from his lips – English, Māori, Portuguese, even some Russian June had taught him in one of her rare generous moods. His vision blurred red at the edges. The rage that lived deep in his bones, the family curse that went beyond seeing the dead, threatened to break free. He could feel spirits gathering, drawn to the extreme emotions coursing through him. Tempted to just let go, to unleash it all.

He gripped the steering wheel until his knuckles went white, breathing through his nose. *One. Two. Three.* He couldn't lose control. Not here. Not now.

The note. Damn, the note.

He spun the car around, tires squealing, and raced back to Alyssa's street. But he was too late. She stood at her letterbox, his pathetic goodbye in her hand, her face a mixture of hurt and confusion that made his chest ache.

He pulled up to the curb, and before he could even turn off the engine, she was yanking open the passenger door and leaning in.

"I thought you were skipping town?" Her voice was steady, but he could see the tremor in her hands, the way she clutched the note like evidence of a crime. She wouldn't even look at him.

"I changed my mind." The lie tasted like ash. "You made me want to stick around."

"Bullshit." Her eyes were bright with unshed tears. "You were going to leave. Just like – " She cut herself off, but he could fill in the blanks. *Just like everyone else had left her.*

"Alyssa – "

"No." She shook her head, anger replacing hurt. "You kissed me last night. You kissed me like it meant something, and then you were just going to disappear? Leave a bloody note like some coward? You didn't even put your number on it."

The words hit harder than any physical blow. Because she was right. He was a coward.

"It's complicated," he said weakly.

"It's always complicated." Her laugh was bitter. "God, I'm such an idiot. I actually thought – " Her voice cracked and she stood up, slamming the passenger door closed.

He was out of the car before he could think better of it, pulling her into his arms. She resisted for a moment, then collapsed against his chest, her shoulders shaking. He wasn't sure if she actually wanted comfort from him, or whether she just needed it so badly right now that any warm body would do.

"I'm sorry," he murmured into her hair. "I'm so sorry. I didn't want to leave. I have family stuff that's... Christ, Alyssa, it's bad. Really bad. And I didn't want to drag you into it."

"How would you drag me into it?" she demanded, forcing a

little space between them. "Like I said, we barely know each other, and it was just one kiss."

"One very good kiss, and the start of a connection that I was really hoping to explore more..." He hoped so badly that she could see the sincerity in his eyes, that he could see the truth of them, even if it wasn't the whole truth.

Gods, he wished he could just tell her the whole truth, but it was too complicated and it would only drive her further away. Her reaction to his potential abandonment made his chest ache; he couldn't do that to her right now. Not when she was clearly feeling so vulnerable.

"This is ridiculous," she said, dragging her palms across her face to wipe up the few stray tears. "I hardly know you. I shouldn't be reacting like this."

He reached out slowly, waiting to see if she would pull away, but she didn't, he cupped her cheeks gently. "Hey. You've been hurt before. Abandoned. It makes sense that this would –
"

"How do you know that?" She pulled away again, arms folding over her chest like roots that could protect her. Her magic seemed to hum around her now too, fired up by her suspicion.

He thought of June's files, Mrs Nolan's briefing, all the things he knew about her that he shouldn't. "Call it intuition. Plus... What Kelly said, and..." He managed a weak smile. "We have a connection, you and I. You feel it too, don't you?" His brow furrowed and he held his breath. He didn't deserve to have any confirmation of that, but he needed it.

She nodded slowly, searching his face. "So why were you leaving?"

The truth burned in his throat and he wanted to vomit it all out. Michael. The family curse. Mrs Nolan's trap. Instead, he said, "My nephew. He's... he's very sick. I needed to get back to him, but..." He gestured helplessly at the town around them. "Seems the Bay has other ideas. I tried to get out of town so many times and found myself right back where I started."

"You can't leave?" Her frown deepened. "What do you mean?"

"I mean I literally can't leave." He threw his hands up in the air. "I've tried ten times. The road just... loops back."

Her eyes widened. "That's not possible."

"Welcome to Kotahi Bay," he said dryly.

She wrapped her arms around herself tighter and swallowed hard, as if she was trying to consume a difficult realization. "Mrs Nolan?"

He nodded and he found it hard to swallow too. Because he knew she was putting the pieces together. Knew it was only a matter of time before she'd turn away and never look back.

Alyssa grimaced, lips pursed, poised, and then she asked the question he had hoped that she wouldn't. "Are you trapped here because of me?"

"Not because of you," he said firmly, raising a hand to try and reassure her, but when she flinched a little, he dropped it. "Because of them. Because of people who think they can control others, manipulate them into doing what they want. Manipulate you. And me."

She looked at him for a long moment, then displayed the crumpled note. "Next time you need to leave, talk to me first. Don't just... don't just disappear." Her eyes were glassy, and he hated that this time, her unshed tears were his fault.

"I promise." He shook his head. "I'll be here for a bit longer anyway. Got work to do, apparently."

"Your boss is still a cow?"

Mrs Nolan was a cow. They both knew it. But for some reason Alyssa was giving him a reprieve. Pretending that she didn't know.

Despite everything, he found himself smiling. "The worst. But..." He reached out, tucking a strand of hair behind her ear. "There are compensations."

She leaned into his touch for the briefest moment, then stepped back. "I should go. Kelly's probably wondering where I am."

"Alyssa?" He called as she turned away. "I really am sorry. About the note. About all of it."

"I know." She gave him a sad smile. "That's what makes this whole thing worse."

He watched her walk back to the house, the morning sun painting gold highlights in her hair. His phone buzzed. Another text from his sister. Another update on Michael's declining condition.

He was trapped in a town that wouldn't let him leave, bound by a deal with a woman he didn't trust, falling for someone he had no right to want. And somewhere, a little boy was running out of time.

The rage simmered under his skin, but now it had a different flavour. Not just anger, but determination. If he couldn't leave, if he was stuck playing this game, then he'd play it his way. He'd find another path, one that didn't require sacrificing Alyssa on the altar of his family's sins.

He just prayed he could find it before it was too late.

# CHAPTER 18

"I just had the weirdest run-in with Brendan," Alyssa said as she dropped the note on the kitchen table. The paper made a soft whisper against the worn wood, joining the morning symphony of creaking floorboards and the distant cry of seagulls through the open window.

Kelly reached for it, her movements too quick, too eager to change the subject. The way she held the note – fingers trembling slightly, eyes darting across the words without really reading them – sent a cold thread of unease through Alyssa's chest.

"He's leaving?" Kelly's voice pitched higher than usual, a false brightness that reminded Alyssa of cheap tin bells.

"No. He changed his mind about that." Alyssa watched her friend's face, cataloguing the micro-expressions – relief, confusion, something else flickering too fast to catch. "Don't you think it's a bit weird though? He gets into town, meets a girl he apparently likes, and then he tries to leave?"

She frowned, her fingers unconsciously tracing patterns on the table's surface, following the grain of the wood like reading braille for answers. The morning light streaming through Gran's lace curtains cast intricate shadows across her hands, reminding her of the complexity of human connections – how what seemed solid could be full of holes.

Kelly's laugh came out brittle, like ice cracking underfoot. "Men are weird." She shrugged, but the gesture was too stiff, a marionette's movement. "And we need to go to the grocers."

The abrupt change of subject hung in the air between them like fog off the bay. Alyssa studied her oldest friend – the way Kelly wouldn't quite meet her eyes, how her hands kept moving, straightening already-straight items on the counter, picking at a nonexistent thread on her sleeve. When had Kelly become a stranger wearing familiar skin?

"Why don't you go? I really can't be bothered. And I need to get some stuff done around the house." The words came out harder than Alyssa intended, but she suddenly, desperately needed space to breathe, to think without Kelly's nervous energy crackling through the room like static electricity before a storm.

Brendan had all but admitted he was involved in whatever was going on in the Bay, and even if she didn't know the specifics, it unsettled her.

"Alright, but no complaining about my purchases." Kelly's attempt at their usual banter fell flat, a deflated balloon of normalcy.

"Come on, you know me better than anyone." The lie tasted bitter on Alyssa's tongue. Did Kelly know her at all? Did she know Kelly? Why was everything so hard right now? Was Mercury in retrograde and she just hadn't noticed? "I trust you." Another lie, this one sharper, cutting her throat on the way out. "Actually, you could stop in and see Sam. Pick out a souvenir while you're in town."

"That sounds like an excellent idea." Kelly grabbed her

purse with obvious relief, the keys jangling like alarm bells. The door closed behind her with a soft click that echoed in Alyssa's chest like a coffin nail.

Finally alone, Alyssa sighed and looked around Gran's kitchen – her kitchen now. The morning sun had shifted, painting golden rectangles across the linoleum floor that Gran had laid herself forty years ago. Each scuff mark told a story, each worn patch a memory of meals prepared, conversations had, lives lived. She pressed her palms flat against the table, feeling the solid reality of wood grain beneath her skin, anchoring herself in the present even as her thoughts spiraled.

She was into Brendan, that much was clear. The realization sat in her stomach like honey and hornets – sweet but dangerous. His erratic behaviour this morning, the way he'd shifted from leaving to staying, the fact that he was living in June's house, involved with Mrs Nolan, was stuck here in this town... Warning bells chimed in her head, a discordant carillon she couldn't ignore.

She hadn't asked him about June. Why hadn't she? The question burrowed under her skin like a splinter. Was she trying not to pry, respecting boundaries like a good neighbour? Or was she too scared to find out anything else that might shatter this fragile new thing before it had a chance to bloom?

The word 'bloom' made her think of the garden, of things growing in darkness before pushing towards the light. Some plants were weeds disguised as flowers until it was too late, until they'd already choked out everything good. Was Brendan a weed in disguise? A threat to her burgeoning peace?

And what the heck was going on with Kelly this morning? Such erratic behaviour.

Erratic behaviour.... The phrase triggered muscle memory, her body recalling things before her mind caught up. Grant had acted that way in the last months of their relationship. Just a little odd at first – missed dinner dates explained by work emergencies, strange charges on credit cards dismissed as gifts for his mother, phone calls taken in the other room because of 'bad reception.'

Each explanation had been a stone added to the wall between them, and she'd been too trusting, too desperate to believe in their future to see the wall for what it was – a fortress hiding betrayal.

She needed to remind herself that Brendan was not Grant, though. Or maybe she was just desperate to believe that they weren't the same. The mantra played in her head like a scratched record. Not only that, but Brendan didn't owe her anything. They'd only met the other day. A few conversations, some charged looks, a moment that felt like standing at the edge of possibility – none of it added up to obligation or expectation.

But still.

Gardening would help. It always did. Connecting with the earth felt like communion, like prayer without words. Even weeding became meditation, each unwanted plant she pulled a metaphor for the thoughts and fears choking her mental landscape. She could almost hear Gran's voice on the salt-tinged breeze: "Gardens and hearts need the same things, love. Patience, care, and the courage to pull out what doesn't belong, even when it hurts."

Outside, the morning had ripened into something glorious. The Bay stretched out like hammered silver, and the air carried the complex perfume of the coast – salt and seaweed, the green smell of beach grass, the faint sweetness of climbing roses three houses down. She breathed it in, filling her lungs with home, with possibility, with the promise that life continued despite heartbreak. The innate magic of life vibrated all around her; it was impossible to ignore.

Socks followed her outside, his grey fur ruffled by the breeze, his yellow eyes tracking invisible things in the garden. He kept close to her feet, occasionally batting at stray leaves with the focused intensity of a tiny predator. When she knelt by the flower bed, he settled beside her, purring a rumbling soundtrack to her work.

The soil was cool and damp beneath her fingers, rich with the promise of growth. She found the first weed – chickweed, its delicate white flowers deceptive in their beauty – and grasped it firmly at the base. The key was to get the whole root system, to not leave anything behind that could regrow, resurface, reclaim the space she was trying to clear.

As she pulled, she thought about roots, about how deep they could go, how they could tangle with other plants until you couldn't tell where one ended and another began. Like her friendship with Kelly. Twenty years of shared history, roots so intertwined she couldn't imagine her life's garden without that presence.

The chickweed came free with a satisfying release, trailing pale roots like exposed nerves. She tossed it into her garden bucket and reached for the next invader – bindweed this time, its vines already trying to strangle her grandmother's peonies.

Hopefully she'd feel an immediate sense of achievement and that would spur her on. That would be the advice Gran gave her, if she were still here. "Start small, love. One weed, one dish, one phone call. The mountain only looks impossible from the bottom."

God, she wished Gran was here. The ache of it hit fresh, a wave that threatened to pull her under. This week alone had proven, again, that she didn't know Gran as well as she thought she did. The basement full of journals, the history with June, the weight of being the family record keeper – so many secrets buried like bulbs, waiting for the right conditions to sprout into understanding.

She almost wanted to call her mother, to see if she knew some of the history of their family. The thought was a shock of cold water. When was the last time she'd actually wanted to talk to her mother? Their relationship had been a casualty of distance and misunderstanding, each conversation a minefield of unspoken resentments and carefully avoided topics.

Was Alyssa strong enough to willfully defy family duty? The question tangled with the bindweed in her hands. At times she'd been frustrated and sad that her mother had stopped her from seeing Gran, that she'd denied Alyssa of knowing about the family heritage. She'd painted her mother as the villain in that story, the keeper of gates that should have been open.

But after talking with Sam this morning, seeing the weight of knowledge in her eyes, understanding dawned like a slow sunrise... Her mother hadn't been the villain. She'd been the protector, the one who chose exile over expectation, freedom over the crushing weight of being the keeper of everyone else's truth.

It wasn't fear that had kept her mother away from the Bay, or maybe not just fear, but also the drive to protect those she loved. To save her daughter from inheriting a burden she hadn't chosen, a role that could consume a life if you let it.

The realization was a thorn through her heart. And here Alyssa was, keeping her mother shut out. Ignoring her calls, rejecting her attempts to reconnect, building her own walls out of hurt and stubbornness. The parallels were too clear to ignore – her mother fleeing the Bay to protect Alyssa, and Alyssa fleeing to the Bay to protect herself. Both of them running, both of them building walls, both of them choosing isolation over the messy, painful work of connection.

She dropped the weeds into the bucket and stood up, her

knees protesting the sudden movement. Dirt clung to her hands, embedded under her nails, marking her as someone who dug deep, who wasn't afraid to get messy in search of truth. If she wanted to. She needed to call her mother. Right now, before she lost her courage, before the walls rebuilt themselves.

Dusting her hands on her pants, she headed inside, purpose quickening her steps. The screen door squeaked its familiar protest, a sound that had probably echoed through decades of women coming in from this same garden, carrying their own burdens and revelations.

The sound of a ringing phone hit her ears as she crossed the threshold, jarring in its urgency. But her phone was still flat, abandoned on the counter where she'd left it this morning in her distraction. Kelly's then, the ringtone some pop song Alyssa didn't recognize, all synthesized beats and auto-tuned longing.

She found it beneath a newspaper on the table, the screen lit up with hope or doom – she couldn't tell which anymore. The caller ID made her pause: 'Babe'.

Since when did Kelly have someone saved as 'Babe'? The new boyfriend she supposedly had no photos of? Another secret in a friendship that apparently was built on them?

"Hello, Kelly's phone," she answered, curiosity overcoming courtesy.

There was a pause on the other end, the kind of silence that preceded bad news, that gathered itself like a wave before crashing down. And then the voice that spoke turned her blood to ice, froze her heart mid-beat, stopped the world on its axis.

"Um, Alyssa?"

Grant. Grant's voice through Kelly's phone, under the contact name 'Babe', casual as a knife between the ribs.

"Grant? What the hell are you doing calling Kelly? Why

does it say Babe?" The words came out in a rush, her voice climbing octaves she didn't know she possessed. She felt like all the air had escaped her lungs, like she was drowning in her grandmother's kitchen, the solid ground suddenly quicksand.

She collapsed into a chair, her legs unable to support the weight of this revelation. The phone tumbled from nerveless fingers, clattering on the table like bones thrown for divination, telling a fortune she didn't want to hear.

"Oh my god. Oh my god." Her breath came in short gasps, each one a struggle against the crushing weight on her chest. The room spun, Gran's carefully hung plates becoming a carousel of betrayal, the lace curtains shrouds for a friendship that had apparently died without her knowing.

She could hear Grant talking still, his voice tinny and distant through the phone's speaker, explaining, justifying, doing what he did best – making excuses. But she couldn't process the words, couldn't let them past the roaring in her ears, the sound of twenty years of friendship collapsing like a house of cards.

With shaking fingers, she found the end button and pressed it, cutting off his voice mid-sentence. Then she pushed the phone back under the newspaper, as if hiding it could hide the truth, could undo the last two minutes, could rewind to a time when Kelly was her best friend and not another loss to add to the collection.

Kelly hadn't been acting weird because Alyssa had moved to the Bay. The truth was a puzzle piece clicking into place, the picture suddenly, horribly clear. Kelly was acting weird because she'd shacked up with Grant. With Grant. The words played on repeat in her head, each iteration driving the knife deeper.

Time passed – minutes or hours, she couldn't tell. She sat at Gran's table, in Gran's kitchen, in Gran's house that was supposed to be her sanctuary, her fresh start, her escape from the wreckage Grant had made of her life. But the wreckage had followed her here, carried in the pocket of someone she'd trusted with everything.

The front door opened and closed, the sound echoing through the house like a gunshot. Through the doorway, Alyssa could see Kelly entering, arms full of shopping bags, face bright with false normalcy. She'd been waiting – how long? An hour? A lifetime? – unable to do anything but sit and try to piece together the shattered fragments of her world.

There were a million questions brewing inside her, a witch's cauldron of hurt and confusion and rage. When had the affair begun? How many times had Kelly comforted her about the breakup while secretly celebrating? How many lies had been told, how many betrayals disguised as girl's nights and supportive phone calls?

But foremost among these was the only one that really mattered, the one that would determine if this friendship could survive even as a memory worth keeping: Had this started before Grant broke it off with Alyssa? She could, maybe, forgive the rest of it. One day, when the wound scarred over, when she could think Kelly's name without tasting ashes. But not if this had started when he'd still been Alyssa's boyfriend. Not if every hug had been Judas's kiss, every word of comfort a lie wrapped in friendship's clothing.

Kelly spotted her, cocked her head to one side and frowned, the picture of innocent concern. "What's up chook? Everything okay?"

The pet name, used since they were fifteen and thought Australian slang was the height of sophistication, cut like glass. Alyssa choked out a bitter laugh, the sound scraping her throat raw. "No, Kelly. Everything is not okay."

"What's wrong honey? What happened?" Kelly put her

bags down on the floor and crossed to Alyssa, kneeling before her in supplication, reaching out for the hug that had always fixed everything before – failed tests, family fights, bad dates, broken hearts.

Alyssa pulled back, her body recoiling from the touch that now felt like contamination. She shook her head, and a few tears slipped free despite her best efforts. She brushed them off roughly, angry at the betrayal of her own eyes. She wouldn't cry for this. For them.

"Your boyfriend called while you were gone." She said the words softly, each one a stone thrown into still water, watching the ripples of impact spread across Kelly's face. The way the colour drained, leaving her pale as driftwood. The way her mouth opened and closed, a fish gasping on the deck. "How could you?"

"Lysie, I promise. I never meant to hurt you." Kelly reached for her again, desperate now, the facade crumbling like sand-castles at high tide.

But Alyssa was already moving, standing and walking around to the other side of the table with deliberate steps, putting furniture between them like a barricade. She kept her arms folded over her chest, trying to contain the hurt that wanted to explode outward, to destroy everything in reach. Her magic trembled through her veins, rising with her anger, and it was all she could do to keep it contained.

Miri's expression crashed through her mind.

Alyssa would get through this without drawing from her witchy heritage. She focused on the pain, and struggled desperately to draw energy from the earth beneath the house, from the roots of her ancestors.

"Then how could you? Him, of all people. Grant." Her voice broke on his name, a crack in the dam she was desperately trying to maintain. She didn't love him anymore, not like that.

He'd broken her heart thoroughly, efficiently, with the casual cruelty of someone who'd never really seen her as more than a placeholder.

Things hadn't been perfect, no, but what kind of callous asshole breaks up with a girl when she finds out she can't have babies? The memory of that doctor's appointment, the devastating diagnosis, Grant's slow withdrawal disguised as support – it all came flooding back.

"We'd been planning a life together, and what, now he's carrying out those plans with you?" The irony was acid on her tongue. "If it wasn't for all the boozing you've been doing since you got here, I'd think you were already knocked up."

The words were cruel, designed to wound, and she saw them hit their target. Kelly flinched as if slapped, her hand going unconsciously to her stomach.

"Don't be like that, Lysie."

"Don't call me Lysie!" The nickname exploded out of her, twenty years of friendship weaponized into rejection. "If you were really my friend, you wouldn't be with him. What is wrong with you?"

"It wasn't meant to come out like this." Kelly's voice was pleading now, tears streaming down her face. "I've been trying to find the right time to talk with you about it – "

"Don't worry, it all makes sense now." The pieces were falling into place with sickening clarity. "You came here to tell me you've shacked up with my ex, and you thought pushing me at some hot guy down the street would help soften the blow."

Alyssa cradled her head in her hands, her fingers shaking like autumn leaves. She wasn't thinking straight, she knew that. The hurt was too fresh, too raw, her thoughts scattered like startled gulls. She took a deep breath, tasting salt and sorrow, and looked up, dropping her arms to her sides in surrender or defiance – she wasn't sure which.

"I think you should go. Okay? I know now, and you're free to get on with your life." The words came out calmer than she felt, each one carefully measured, carefully controlled. "But can you tell me one thing?"

"Don't make me leave it like this." Kelly was openly sobbing now, mascara running in black rivers down her cheeks. "Alyssa, you're my best friend."

Alyssa shook her head slowly, finally understanding the past tense that sentence required. "Did this start before I left? Before we'd broken up?"

The question hung in the air between them, the last test of a friendship already failed. Kelly pressed her lips together, trying to hold in the truth, but her eyes gave her away. The pain pooling there, the guilt swimming in tears – it was all the answer Alyssa needed.

The last thread holding them together snapped, audible as a breaking guitar string.

"Get your stuff sorted, but leave Socks. He's mine now." One thing she could keep from this devastating visit, the smallest, furriest of comforts. "When I come back I want you gone."

Alyssa walked out, leaving Kelly crying in Gran's kitchen, leaving twenty years of friendship bleeding out on the floor, leaving another life behind.

Outside, the sun still shone with obscene brightness, the Bay still glittered like scattered diamonds, the world still turned despite her personal apocalypse. She walked without direction, her feet finding their own path down towards the water, towards the eternal rhythm of waves that didn't care about human betrayal, that had been washing clean the shores of grief for millennia.

Behind her, she left the sound of Kelly's sobs, the weight of shared history, and the last of her illusions about the safety of trust. Ahead lay the ocean sprawled out endlessly from the Bay with all its mysteries, along with the terrifying possibility of starting over with nothing but herself and the truth.

The garden would have to wait. Some weeds, she was learning, had roots too deep to pull without destroying everything around them. Sometimes the only choice was to walk away and let the whole garden grow wild.

# CHAPTER 19

She didn't know where to go, or what to do, so she just walked. Walked, and walked, and walked. Her feet found their own rhythm on the pavement, a metronome marking time between who she'd been this morning – a woman with a best friend, a fresh start, a tentative new romance blooming – and who she was now. Someone utterly alone.

The betrayal sat in her chest like a stone, heavy and jagged, scraping against her ribs with every breath. Twenty years. Twenty years of sleepovers and shared secrets, of being each other's emergency contact, of planning to be each other's maid of honour. How many of those years had been lies? How many times had Kelly looked at her and thought about Grant, wanted him, maybe even –

No. She couldn't follow that thought to its conclusion. Not yet.

She needed something else to pour her energy into. Her eyes moved towards the town, where Sage & Salt sat, looking sunny and inviting.

But Alyssa couldn't face Sam right now, not after blowing

up at her this morning about the pressure she felt to become the town witch. God, she'd been worried about old family duties when her best friend was sleeping with her ex. The irony tasted like copper pennies. And Brendan had said he was going to work, probably at the boat shop, smelling of varnish and possibility. Or something more nefarious that she couldn't even begin to think about yet. That left her with a big fat nothing.

This whole thing was a sham. Nothing was real. She had no place here in this town where everyone knew her family's history better than she did, no place in the city now that her former best friend was currently packing up to go live her happily ever after with the man who'd shattered Alyssa's future.

It wasn't until that moment when Kelly's face revealed the truth – the guilt swimming in her eyes like fish in a too-small bowl – that she realised she really had no one to turn to. The loneliness of it threatened to swallow her whole, a sinkhole opening beneath her feet.

But that wasn't quite true. She veered across the road, barely checking for traffic, and turned onto another street, her body knowing the way even as her mind reeled. The cemetery. She was heading for the cemetery, because the only person she wanted to talk to was six feet under and couldn't betray her, couldn't reveal they'd been sleeping with her ex, couldn't add another crack to her already shattered heart. Couldn't say a damn thing that would make this day any worse.

It had been a few weeks since she'd gone to see Gran. There was still so much of the woman in the house – her lavender sachets in the linen closet, her handwriting on jam jar labels, her presence in every creak of the floorboards – that Alyssa hadn't felt the need to visit a tombstone. But now, with Kelly's belongings contaminating that sacred space, she needed somewhere else, somewhere Kelly had never been.

The Kotahi Bay graveyard was actually fairly big considering the relatively small size of the town, sprawling across a hillside that overlooked the water. The older section held stones so weathered the names had worn away, leaving only the faintest impressions of lives lived and lost. But Alyssa got the feeling that people who came here didn't move away too much. Roots, again. Always roots, growing deep, holding fast, binding generations to this soil.

Was she destined to end up in a plot with Gran as well? The thought should have been morbid, but instead it felt almost comforting. At least then she'd belong somewhere, have a place that was definitively hers, that no one else could ruin, even if she had to be dead to claim it.

The iron gate squealed as she pushed through, the sound like fingernails on the chalkboard of her nerves. Within a few minutes she'd reached the newer section, abandoning the neat gravel path to walk among the graves, her feet finding their way between the headstones like she was navigating a familiar room in the dark. Gran was in the far left corner, along with other relatives – great aunts and second cousins, a whole family tree planted in reverse, growing down instead of up.

None of whom she'd actually met, but who she felt like she was getting to know from the not-so-pleasant things she'd been learning. The record keepers, the duty-bound, the ones who'd made choices that echoed through generations. Had any of them been happy? Had any of them chosen love over obligation, freedom over tradition?

She plonked herself down on Gran's grave, the granite cool through her jeans despite the sun. Then, in a move that would have horrified her mother, she lay flat on top of the stone, spreading herself across it like she was trying to sink through marble and earth to wherever Gran had gone. No one else was here to judge her, and the sun on her face was just what she needed – warm and constant, unlike everything else in her life.

She trailed her fingers over the engraving on the headstone, feeling the grooves of letters that spelled out a life reduced to dates and a name. "Sylvia Mary Whenua. Beloved Grandmother. Keeper of Stories." That last bit had been Alyssa's addition, paid for with her paycheck from the job she no longer had.

"So, I wish you were still around, Gran. I need your gentle assurances." She laughed, the sound bitter as burnt coffee. Gran was not really that gentle – she'd had a spine of steel and a tongue that could flay when necessary – but she'd at least tell Alyssa to get her shit together. "Though it's not really my shit that's the problem right now, is it? It's everyone else's shit landing on my doorstep like flaming paper bags."

The image made her laugh again, a little less bitter this time. Gran would have appreciated the metaphor.

"I wish Mum had never found out that you were training me. About the magic, the duties, all of it. That you'd been able to teach me everything the way you taught me to garden, to bake, to read the weather in cloud formations. At least then I might not feel so out of my depth. These people keep asking me to do things I know nothing about. They keep expecting me to be you, but I'm not."

Did she want to be? That was really the question, wasn't it? Did she know Gran as well as she thought she had? Or was she making assumptions based on the personal memories she had. This woman who'd made bread every Sunday and kept a garden that was the envy of the neighbourhood – she had also wielded power she'd never spoken of. Or was her grandmother really a verging-on-psychopathic witch like the others – June with her games, the ancestor who'd trapped Magnus, the one who'd created a child from earth itself? Was Alyssa doomed to follow in their footsteps, her DNA a roadmap to moral compromise?

And hell, did it even matter now? It wasn't like she had anything else going for her. No job, no best friend, no life in the city to return to. Just a house full of ghosts and a town full of expectations and a heart so broken she could hear the pieces rattling around in her chest when she breathed.

Alyssa sighed and rolled over onto her belly, folding her hands under her cheek like a child settling for a nap. The stone was warm now, heated by her body and the sun.

"Maybe there's something at the house that could tell me about the family. I don't want to be like June, or the woman who trapped Magnus, or the one that you wrote about who created a child for herself from the earth around here." She paused, really thinking about that story for the first time. A woman so lonely, so desperate for connection, that she'd shaped it from dirt and desperation. "God, is that what I'm doing? Creating something from nothing because I can't bear to be alone?"

She pushed herself up and dangled her legs over the edge of the tombstone, kicking her shoes off so that she could feel the grass on her feet. The blades tickled, cool and slightly damp despite the sunshine. Warmth radiated from the ground below, pulsing like a heartbeat, and she found herself thinking again about the earth baby story.

Seriously, who did that? What kind of power did it take to breathe life into soil? And yet... and yet she'd always felt it, hadn't she? That connection, that awareness of the earth's rhythms that went beyond mere gardening knowledge. She knew when rain was coming not by the clouds but by the way the ground seemed to hold its breath. She could feel the seasons turning in her bones, could sense the moment seeds decided to sprout before they'd show any visible signs.

If the story was true, then it was literally in her blood. Part of her magical heritage stemmed from a connection to Papatūānuku – the earth mother in Māori mythology. Despite the dubious ethics of how that had come about – creating life to serve your own loneliness – she felt grateful for the connection. It was the one thing in this whole mess that felt genuinely hers, not inherited or imposed but simply part of her being.

The thought comforted her. Kind of. And she'd take any small comfort she could get right now, even if it came from a story about reproductive magic and earthen children.

"What did you do, Gran?" she asked the stone, the earth, the sky. "Was there something you did that I didn't know about? Some choice you made that changed everything? Did you ever feel this lost, this betrayed, this alone?"

The cemetery held its silence, but the earth beneath her feet seemed to pulse in sympathy. Or maybe that was just her imagination, her desperate need for connection making metaphors into reality. Either way, the visit had helped clear some turmoil from her mind, like sediment settling in disturbed water.

She had a plan now, or at least the beginning of one. All things going well, Kelly would be gone when she got home, taking with her the contamination of betrayal and the cat who'd never really liked Alyssa anyway. And Alyssa was making it her top priority to search the house for remnants of family history. Those journals in the basement were a start, but there had to be more. In a house that old, with a family that deep-rooted, secrets would be layered like sedimentary rock.

In fact, there was a library in town. If her family had been here since the beginning, there would be records, newspaper clippings, something more objective than June's manipulations or Sam's careful warnings. Maybe that was a better way to go about it – approaching her history like a researcher instead of a grieving granddaughter.

She didn't dare ask Sam, who might actually know something, not after the way Alyssa had blown up at her earlier. The memory made her cringe. She'd accused Sam of trying to manipulate her, of being part of June's games, when really Sam had just been trying to navigate an impossible situation with grace.

Seriously, what else could go wrong? At least she hadn't alienated Brendan. Yet. Only a matter of time though, wasn't it? If her track record was anything to go by, she'd find a way to destroy that tentative connection too. Maybe he had been secretly married to June. Maybe he collected ceramic dolphins. Maybe he was perfectly wonderful and she'd ruin it anyway because that's what she did – pushed people away before they could leave, rejected before she could be rejected.

Alyssa cringed as she grabbed her shoes, not bothering to put them on, letting the grass tickle her bare feet as she stood. "Catch ya later, Gran. Love you."

At least that was still true. No matter what her grandmother might have done, the Gran she'd known was loving and kind, and would have done anything for Alyssa. That was all that mattered. Love was actions, not secrets. Love was Sunday bread and patient gardening lessons and a house left to a granddaughter who needed a safe place to land.

The walk to the library was shorter than she'd expected, her bare feet finding their own rhythm on the warm pavement. She'd passed the building before – a sturdy brick structure that looked like it had been built in the 1950s and hadn't been updated since. The kind of place that still had a card catalog alongside its computers, where the librarian knew every patron by name and their reading preferences by heart.

She paused on the steps to slip her shoes back on, grass clippings falling from her feet like green confetti. Through the glass doors, she could see stacks of books creating a maze of knowledge, and her heart rate slowed for the first time since answering Kelly's phone. Libraries had always been her safe spaces, places where you could be alone without being lonely, where silence was companionable instead of oppressive.

She pushed open the door, the familiar smell of old books hitting her nose like a welcome home – that particular mixture of aging paper, binding glue, and the faint must of decades of knowledge settling into itself. Despite the fact she'd never set foot in this particular building before, her body relaxed into the familiarity of it.

A small, wiry man looked up from the desk, blinking behind wire-rimmed glasses as if surprised to see anyone there. He had the look of someone who'd been pressed and dried between the pages of a book – thin, preserved, slightly yellowed around the edges. His cardigan had leather patches on the elbows, because of course it did.

"Can I help you?" he asked, shuffling papers to the side with the careful movements of someone who treated every-thing as precious. His voice had a gentle rasp to it, like pages turning.

"I'm looking for the local history section, old newspaper clippings and stuff. Do you have one here?" Alyssa approached the desk as he got up, noting the way he moved – quick, bird-like, eager.

"Of course! Wouldn't be much of a library if we didn't keep that stuff. Our history section is my pride and joy, actually. Anything in particular you're interested in?" His eyes lit up behind his glasses, and she recognized the look of someone about to share their passion. "I'm a bit of a history buff. Well, more than a bit. It passes the time, and this town... oh, this town has stories."

He headed for the back without waiting for her answer, clearly assuming she'd follow. She did, weaving between stacks that smelled of time and secrets. In the far corner, there was a section lined with local history books, filing cabinets that looked like they'd been there since the town's inception, and a desk with both a microfiche system and a newer computer that was still probably a decade old.

"Everything you need is here," he said, gesturing proudly like a game show host revealing prizes. "We've got newspapers going back to 1895, property records, birth and death certificates — well, copies anyway — oral histories, photographic collections. I've been digitizing what I can, but there's something about the originals, you know? Do you want a hand?"

Alyssa steeled herself, half afraid that if she was straight with him he'd leap into some kind of speech about her family and their duty to the town. Everyone else seemed to have opinions about what she owed this place. But she didn't want to be here too long — the walls of her grandmother's house were calling her, promising secrets — so she might as well get this over with.

"I'm looking for some family history. My grandmother was Syvia Whenua, and our family has been here for a long time." She watched his face carefully, waiting for the recognition, the shift in demeanor that would tell her he knew exactly who she was and what that meant.

His face did light up, but with the pure joy of a historian who'd found a fellow enthusiast. "Since the town's inception, actually! Your ancestors were fundamental to setting this place up. Oh, you've come to the right person. I'm Del, by the way. Del Morrison. My family's been here almost as long as yours, though in a much less..." he paused, seeming to search for the right word, "significant capacity."

"Alyssa," she said, relaxing slightly at his enthusiasm. It was more about the history than the present, and that felt like such a relief. "I had no idea about that, about us helping start the town."

"Well, it was a long while back, and you're pretty new to town, right? I'd heard Sylvie's granddaughter had moved into the old Whenua place. That house – magnificent example of colonial architecture. Original timber throughout, I believe?"

"You could say that." She thought of the basement, wondered if Del knew about spaces that didn't appear on any architectural plans.

He switched on the microfiche machine, the fan whirring to life with a sound like tired bees, and turned to the filing cabinets, fishing around in several drawers with the confidence of someone who knew exactly where everything lived. "The Whenua women have always been... notable. Strong tradition of community service, midwifery, herbalism. Your great-great-grandmother, Pare Whenua, was particularly remarkable."

"Pare?" The name was new to her, another gap in her family knowledge.

"Mmm, yes. Fascinating woman. She appeared in town in the 1890s, seemingly from nowhere, though there were rumors..." He drew out several collections of film and laid them on the table with reverent care. "Well, you'll see for yourself. If you start looking in here there should be some retrospectives of the town, anniversary editions and such. You'll come across snippets of the family throughout. Anything in particular you're hoping to find?"

Alyssa hesitated. How could she say she was looking for evidence of magic, for stories of earth babies and trapped spirits and the weight of inherited duty? "I guess... I want to understand the women in my family. Who they really were, not just the stories that got passed down. And maybe..." she took a breath, "maybe understand why my mother left and never came back."

Del's expression softened with understanding. "Ah. Yes, I remember when Sarah left. Quite the scandal at the time – the Whenua heir abandoning her birthright. Though between you and me," he leaned in conspiratorially, his voice dropping to a library whisper that was somehow even quieter than his normal tone, "I never blamed her. The expectations placed on the Whenua women... well. Let's just say your grandmother bore them with more grace than most would have managed."

"What kind of expectations?" Alyssa tried to keep her voice casual, but her heart was racing.

"Oh, you know how small towns are. Everyone expecting the old families to maintain traditions, keep up appearances, be the backbone of the community. And the Whenua women, well..." He adjusted his glasses, seeming to choose his words carefully. "There have always been stories. About their connection to the land, their way with growing things, how they always seemed to know when storms were coming or when someone was about to pass. Nonsense, of course, but in a town like this, stories have power."

It felt like he was a balm to the others she had met, as if despite living in a magical place, he didn't give much credence to it all. Maybe that was its own kind of magic.

He turned back to the microfiche, loading the first reel with practiced movements. "This is from 1918, the town's 25th anniversary edition. Good place to start. I'll leave you to it, but please, don't hesitate to ask if you need anything. Oh, and if you're interested in the really old stories, the ones that didn't make it into newspapers..." He gestured to a locked cabinet in the corner. "The oral history project. Recordings from the

1960s, interviewing the old-timers about the founding families. Your gran actually contributed to it."

"She did?"

"Indeed. Fascinating stuff about the early days, the relationships between the founding families, the – well, I'll let you discover it yourself. Just let me know if you want access to those recordings." He gave her a small smile and started to walk away, then paused. "Oh, and Alyssa? If you're looking for information about the house itself, you might want to check the architectural surveys from 1924. There were some... interesting findings about the foundation."

Before she could ask what he meant, he'd glided away, disappearing into the stacks like a ghost returning to his haunt. Alyssa stared after him for a moment, then turned to the microfiche machine.

"Okay then..." She sat down on the little wooden chair, the vinyl seat cracked with age and mended with duct tape. It felt a lot like she was back in high school – which was probably the last time she'd used a microfiche, come to think of it. The machine hummed expectantly, waiting for her to discover what it held.

She looked through the dates Del had pulled and decided to start with the oldest, slotting it in and adjusting the focus. The machine thunked as she clicked through each image on the film, the sound rhythmic and oddly soothing. She scanned headlines about crop yields and church socials, advertisements for tonics and farm equipment, the everyday life of a town finding its feet.

It was an image that stopped her in her tracks.

The photograph was grainy, black and white aged to sepia at the edges, but the face staring back at her was shockingly familiar. God, she looked a lot like her relatives. Alyssa had always known their family resemblance was strong – she looked like her mother, who was a spitting image of Gran – but she'd never met her great-grandmother, and photos had been sparse.

This woman, despite being frozen in a century-old image, could have been her mother. Or herself, dressed in period costume. The same sharp cheekbones, the same stubborn chin, the same eyes that seemed to see through the camera to something beyond. Her belly was swollen with pregnancy, her hand resting on it protectively, and she looked on as a house was built behind her.

Her house. Alyssa's house. She leaned closer, studying the background. It was definitely the same structure, though younger, rawer, the timber fresh-cut and pale. Workers swarmed over it like ants, but the pregnant woman – Pare, it must be – stood apart, watching with an expression that was hard to read. Satisfaction? Sorrow? Calculation?

The caption read: "Miss Pare Whenua oversees construction of the Whenua family home, 1895. The house, built to her exact specifications, will stand as a testament to Whenua ingenuity and community spirit."

Exact specifications. Alyssa thought of the basement, of the room that shouldn't exist, of the journals hidden in spaces between spaces. What kind of specifications had Pare Whenua insisted upon?

She clicked to the next image, then the next, finding more pieces of her history. Here was Pare again, older now, standing in what was clearly her garden, plants towering around her in impossible abundance. Another showed her at what looked like a town meeting, the only woman in a room full of men, her expression serene and implacable. And another, this one making Alyssa's breath catch – Pare with a young girl who must have been Alyssa's great-grandmother, both of them kneeling in the garden, their hands pressed to the earth as if listening to something beneath.

Was it really that old? Over 125 years of Whenua women living in those rooms, tending that garden, carrying whatever burden Mrs Nolan seemed to think was Alyssa's birthright.

She thought of Del's mention of the 1924 architectural survey, of "interesting findings about the foundation." What had they found? Evidence of the basement room? Or something else, something that might explain why the house felt so alive sometimes, why the gardens grew so well, why she could feel the earth's pulse through the floorboards?

"Find what you were looking for?" Del's voice made her jump. He'd materialized beside her as quietly as he'd left, holding two cups of tea.

"Sorry, didn't mean to startle you. Thought you might like some tea. Gets a bit intense, diving into family history. Like archaeology of the self, isn't it?" He set one cup beside her, the steam carrying the scent of peppermint.

"Thank you." She accepted the tea gratefully, wrapping her hands around the warm ceramic. "I found... a lot. My great-great-grandmother, Pare. The house being built. But I have more questions now than when I started."

"That's the nature of history, I'm afraid. Every answer spawns three new questions." He sipped his own tea, looking at the image on the screen. "Pare Whenua. Now there was a woman with secrets. She appeared in 1894, claiming to be a widow, though no one ever found record of a marriage. Had enough money to buy the land and build that house, though no one knew where it came from. And then there were the stories..."

"What kind of stories?"

Del glanced around, though they were clearly alone in this corner of the library. "The Māori workers on the house, they said things. About how she insisted on certain rituals during the construction. Foundation stones laid at specific times, aligned with... well, they said it was about the seasons, but there were whispers of other alignments. Older ones."

He adjusted his glasses again, a nervous habit. "And then there was the child."

"My great-grandmother?"

"Yes, but also... no. There were stories about another child. Before the one in the records. A daughter who was there one day and gone the next, though no one could say where she'd gone or even agree on what she looked like. Like she'd been a dream the whole town shared and then forgot."

Alyssa's hands tightened on the tea cup.

"Of course, these are just stories," Del continued, but his tone suggested he wasn't entirely convinced of that himself. "Small towns breed tall tales. But the Whenua women have always been... different. Connected to something the rest of us can't quite see or understand. Your grandmother, she had it too. That quality of being both completely present and somehow elsewhere, like she was listening to music no one else could hear."

"Did you know her well?"

"As well as anyone knew Sylvie Whenua, which is to say, not very. She was kind, generous with her time and her garden's bounty, but there was always a part of her held in reserve. Like she was guarding something. Or guarding against something." He paused, studying Alyssa's face. "You have it too, you know. That quality. Like you're standing at a threshold the rest of us can't even see."

Alyssa didn't know what to say to that, so she sipped her tea and changed the subject. "You mentioned recordings? Of my gran?"

"Ah yes. 1967, I believe. Part of an oral history project the historical society did for the town's 75th anniversary. Would you like to hear them?"

"Please."

He led her to the locked cabinet, producing a key from his cardigan pocket. Inside were rows of cassette tapes, each carefully labeled and stored. He ran his finger along them until he found what he was looking for.

"Here we are. Sylvia Whenua, interviewed by Margaret Thompson, July 15th, 1967." He handed her the tape and pointed to an ancient cassette player on a nearby desk. "Still works, surprisingly. Mechanical things last when you take care of them."

Alyssa took the tape with hands that trembled slightly. This was Gran's voice, preserved in magnetic particles and plastic, waiting to speak across the decades. She inserted it carefully and pressed play.

Static, then a clearing of throats, and then a voice she'd thought she'd never hear again filled the small space:

"My name is Sylvia Mary Whenua, and I was born in this house in 1939. My ancestor was Pare, who built this house with her own specifications and her own will..."

Alyssa closed her eyes, letting Gran's younger voice wash over her. She sounded different – not just younger but less careful, as if the weight of years hadn't yet taught her to guard every word.

The interview covered the basics at first – family history, the house, the garden. But then the interviewer asked about the stories, about the Whenua women's reputation, and Gran's voice took on a different quality:

"Every place has its stories, Margaret. Some are true, some are wishes, some are warnings. The Whenua women... we've always understood that the line between those categories isn't as clear as people like to think. My mother taught me, as her mother taught her, that our duty is to tend things. The garden, yes, but also the stories. The boundaries. The spaces between..."

There was a pause on the tape, then the interviewer's nervous laugh. "I'm not sure I understand what you mean, Sylvie."

"No," Gran's voice was gentle but firm. "I don't suppose you do. But my granddaughter will, when the time comes. We always understand, we Whenua women. It's in our blood and bones, deeper than knowing. Deep as roots, patient as seeds."

The tape continued, but Alyssa found herself stuck on those words. My granddaughter will. Had Gran meant her mother who was just a baby at the time? Or had she somehow known, even before her birth, that Alyssa would be the one to inherit this duty?

"Powerful stuff," Del said quietly. He'd been so still she'd almost forgotten he was there. "There are more tapes if you want them. Other interviews, other perspectives on the family. Mrs Patterson from next door had some particularly interesting things to say about your grandmother's garden during the drought of '63."

Alyssa removed the tape carefully, holding it like the treasure it was. "I think... I think I need to go home first. Process this. But I'll be back."

"Of course. Take your time. History isn't going anywhere." He smiled kindly. "And Alyssa? If you find things in that house, things that don't make sense according to what we think we know about the world... well. Sometimes the world is bigger than our understanding of it. Your grandmother knew that. I think you do too."

She looked at him sharply, but his expression was innocent, helpful librarian written in every line. Still, there was something in his eyes...

"Thank you, Del. For everything." She couldn't quite figure him out, but perhaps he was playing it safe while he determined what she did and did not know.

"My pleasure. And do come back. I have a feeling you're going to have questions, and I do so enjoy a good historical mystery."

Alyssa gathered her things, her mind already racing ahead to the house, to the basement, to the secrets waiting in the walls her great-great-grandmother had built to her "exact specifications." As she walked towards the door, a thought struck her with sudden clarity.

She wasn't going to search randomly through the house, hoping to stumble upon answers. She wasn't going to rely on Mrs Nolan's manipulations or Sam's careful hints. She was going to go directly to the source.

She was going to hold a séance.

Not because she was some kind of medium or because she thought it would be spooky fun. But because she was apparently a witch, whether she liked it or not, and witches throughout history had claimed to speak with the dead. If there was even a chance she could talk to Gran, could ask her directly about the duties and the choices and the secrets, wasn't it worth trying?

The idea solidified as she stepped out of the library into the afternoon sun. She had a house built on mysterious foundations, a basement that existed outside of architectural logic, and a heritage of women who'd understood things others couldn't see.

What she needed now was a plan. Séances didn't just happen; they required preparation, intention, the right conditions. She thought of the basement room with its journals and its strange atmosphere. If she was going to pierce the veil between worlds, that seemed like the place to do it. A room that already existed between spaces, where the boundaries were already thin.

She walked faster, purpose driving her steps. Kelly would be gone by now, taking with her the last traces of Alyssa's old life. Good. What Alyssa was about to do required her to step fully into her new one, to embrace the strangeness of her heritage instead of running from it.

The earth beneath her feet seemed to pulse in approval, or maybe that was just her imagination. Either way, she was done being passive, done waiting for others to explain her own history to her. If the dead had secrets, she'd ask them directly.

After all, she was a Whenua woman. And Whenua women, as she was learning, had their own ways of finding answers.

# CHAPTER 20

Brendan stood at Alyssa's front door, along with what felt like a horde of spirits. The porch light was off, but music thumped from inside – something angry and female, all grinding guitars and raw vocals that vibrated through the weatherboards. He knocked, knuckles sharp against wood.

Nothing.

He knocked again, harder this time, competing with the bass line that seemed to shake the whole house. Through the door came a loud thud, followed by what might have been cursing. Still no answer.

The doorknob was worn smooth, brass showing through where countless hands had gripped and turned. He pressed his ear against the wood – definitely movement inside, footsteps crossing back and forth with agitated energy. The music continued its assault, lyrics about betrayal and burning bridges. Fitting, given what he'd overheard at the store about Kelly leaving town suddenly.

He tried the handle. Unlocked. The door swung inward on

well-oiled hinges, revealing the dim hallway with its faded runner and family photos climbing the walls like ivy.

"Hello? Alyssa?" He stepped inside, calling over the music. The house smelled different tonight – candle wax and something earthier, like turned soil. "Kelly?"

The music cut off mid-scream. Heavy footsteps pounded down the stairs, and Alyssa appeared like an avenging angel, clutching what looked like an ancient journal to her chest. Her hair was wild, escaping from a messy bun in corkscrews and wisps. Her eyes, when they found his, held a glassy sheen that spoke of tears or alcohol or both.

"Don't say that name again, or I'll banish you from the house." Her voice cracked like a whip, sharp enough to cut. "I'm kind of good at that."

The journal in her arms was leather-bound, the cover worn soft as cloth, pages yellowed and crumbling at the edges. She held it like armour, like a shield between herself and the world. When she looked up fully, meeting his eyes he confirmed that she'd been crying. There was something else in her gaze too, a wildness that made his skin prickle with recognition. Magic.

"Um, okay. Whatcha doing?" He kept his tone deliberately light, following her as she turned and stalked into the lounge.

The moment he crossed the threshold, the hair on his arms stood up. The air felt charged, electric, like the moments before lightning struck. His gift, usually dormant unless he called on it, stirred uneasily in his chest. Whatever she'd been doing, it had left traces in the atmosphere, invisible eddies of power that made his teeth ache.

Then he saw the setup on the floor and his stomach dropped like a stone into deep water.

A Ouija board sat in the centre of what had to be the most meticulously drawn salt circle he'd ever seen. The white granules formed a perfect ring, not a single grain out of place.

Candles marked the cardinal points – north, south, east, west – their flames burning steady and true despite the draft from the open door. The board itself, old and worn with use, rested on what looked like black silk, the fabric pooling around it like dark water.

This wasn't some teenager's slumber party game. This was ritual work, careful and deliberate. The kind of setup that showed intention...and absolutely no idea of the danger involved.

"Okay, I know what you're doing, but why are you doing it?"

"I need answers." She collapsed onto the couch with the boneless grace of exhaustion, tossing the journal aside. It landed spine-up, falling open to reveal pages covered in cramped handwriting, the ink faded to brown. She reached for a beer bottle on the side table – one of several empties clustered there like mourners at a wake. She tilted it hopefully towards her mouth, found it empty, and frowned at it like it had personally betrayed her.

"Well, I can tell you that you won't find them in the bottom of a bottle." He kept his voice light, teasing, even as his pulse quickened. A séance. She was planning an actual séance. His skin crawled at the thought, phantom sensations skittering across his nerves like spider legs. No wonder the dead were gathering here, just waiting for her to open that door and let them in.

He sat down beside her, careful to maintain some distance. The couch sagged under his weight, old springs protesting. She surprised him by swinging her bare feet up onto his lap, toes painted midnight blue, chipped at the edges. She twirled her finger in an imperious gesture, like he was her servant, commanded to attend.

"Can you? It's been a hell of a day, and I just don't know

how much more I can take." She rested her head back on the arm of the couch, though her jaw was still clenched and he could tell that whatever had happened had ripped something away from her, making her both more vulnerable yet blunter, more real than he thought he'd ever seen her. Raw.

Like she had nothing left to lose.

The casual intimacy of the gesture – her feet in his lap, the expectation that he'd simply comply – caught him off guard. He found himself laughing, though it came out strained. "You have a rough day and immediately try to contact the dead? Well, that's a new one. You're one of a kind, Alyssa Whenua."

Her whole body went still, focus sharpening from fuzzy grief to laser precision. "I didn't tell you my surname."

Shit. His mind raced for an explanation. "It's on the letter-box," he lied, the words smooth as silk, "and I did some looking around."

Both things were technically true. The letterbox did say 'Whenua' in faded paint, barely visible beneath years of salt air and weather. And he had done plenty of looking around – just before he'd arrived, not after. Mrs Nolan had been very specific about the family he was to approach, their history, their importance, even though he'd given her that weird warning to stay away from Alyssa initially.

Brendan couldn't figure out what the older woman's game was. He wondered if she even knew, herself.

He rubbed her feet, the gesture automatic, buying time to think. Her skin was warm, soft, with calluses on the balls of her feet that spoke of time spent barefoot. Gardener's feet. Earth-walker's feet.

"Now the truth comes out. You stalking me or something?" She closed her eyes, but tension radiated from every line of her body. She wasn't as relaxed as she was trying to appear.

"Or something. You intrigue me."

It was perhaps the most honest thing he'd said since arriving in Kotahi Bay. She did intrigue him – this woman surrounded by power she didn't want, setting up séances with academic precision while drowning her sorrows in beer. The contradiction of her drew him in despite himself.

A flicker behind her eyelids told him she'd heard more in those words than he'd meant to reveal. "So, who are you trying to contact?" he asked.

She pulled her feet back, tucking them under herself, creating distance. The exhaustion in her eyes aged her, made her look like she'd lived lifetimes in the span of a day. "Whoever the hell will come. Someone from the family, probably. Things just suck right now, and I need some direction."

"Is Kelly going to help?" He asked it carefully, testing the waters of whatever had happened between the friends.

"I killed her and buried her in the backyard. Maybe we should summon her?" The quip was sharp as broken glass, and pain flickered beneath it like fish in dark water.

"Ha ha. We?"

"You're here now, and you know my evil plan, so yes. We. Unless you're scared." She raised an eyebrow, challenge clear in every line of her face.

He laughed again, and this time it came out darker, edged with something he couldn't quite control. With him in the room, she'd definitely bring something through, more than she was prepared for. He'd learned that the hard way – his presence made the veil thin, made crossing easier for things that should stay on their side, even without the ritual Alyssa had set out. The sensation was already building, that familiar crawling feeling at the base of his skull that meant the boundaries were weakening. If he didn't move the energy soon, there was no telling who might appear - to him, at the very least.

"Not scared. I've done this kind of thing before."

"Really?" She leaned forward, interest replacing some of the grief in her eyes. "I thought only teenage girls did this kind of thing."

"Well, I am not a girl, but I am in touch with my feminine side." He batted his lashes, playing up the joke, earning himself a smack on the arm that stung more than it should have.

"Come on then, give me a hand. Fix this for me. I googled it, but who knows if it's right."

He stood, taking the opportunity to properly survey the setup. She'd moved the coffee table against the wall, rolled up the rug to expose the hardwood beneath. The salt circle was even more impressive up close – perfectly round, the width precise. The candles were real beeswax, not the synthetic ones most people used, and they'd been carved with symbols he didn't recognize. Even the board's positioning was correct – aligned with magnetic north, the letters facing the right directions.

"You've actually got it spot on." The approval came out grudging, tinged with unease. For someone claiming igno-rance about magic, her instincts were uncannily accurate. "The only thing missing is... Well, I think you should get me a beer."

She rolled her eyes, but there was something like warmth in it. "Don't worry, I can get it myself."

"Good. We're not living in the dark ages, you know."

While she headed upstairs – for the bathroom, presumably – he escaped to the kitchen, needing a moment to centre himself. His hands shook slightly as he opened the fridge, the fluorescent light harsh after the candlelit dimness of the lounge.

The kitchen still held traces of another presence. A mug with lipstick marks abandoned by the sink, the shade too pink for Alyssa's preferences. The ghost of perfume that wasn't

Alyssa's, something floral and young. Kelly's remnants, not yet erased.

And something else. Someone else. A ghost, lingering, but unwilling to be seen by Brendan.

He grabbed two beers, the bottles cold against his palms, grounding him in the physical world. While it wasn't the best idea to contact the dead while drinking – alcohol lowered defenses, made possession easier – maybe it would help him convince her not to go through with this. He wanted to help her get what she needed, but he didn't think this was going to help in the way she thought it might.

When he returned, she was sitting on the floor in front of the board, legs crossed in lotus position, spine straight. The candlelight did strange things to her face, making her look older one moment, younger the next. Timeless, like all the Whenua women before her, he imagined. Her hands rested on her knees, palms up, receiving.

"You ready to do this?" He settled across from her, the board between them like an accusation, a dare, a bridge to places better left unvisited.

"Sure am." She took a long pull from her beer, then set it carefully outside the salt circle. "Seeing as you're the pro, why don't you take it from here."

"Not a pro, just a little more experienced than you." The understatement tasted bitter. He'd been seeing things since childhood, had learned about séances the hard way when desperate people discovered what he could do.

"Okay, no need to rub it in."

"What do you want to know? Like, who are you trying to contact? You need to have your intentions clear before we do this." Basic séance safety – though with his luck, with his curse, it wouldn't matter. Things found him whether he was looking or not, drawn like moths to his particular flame. The weight of them pressing in was so heavy here that he found himself holding his breath.

She was quiet for a long moment, teeth worrying her bottom lip. When she finally spoke, her words knocked him sideways.

"I want to talk to Magnus, but he's gone. Mostly. I've seen him. But, he might get pissy and come back to haunt me again." She waved a hand, as if it was nothing.

"What?" His eyebrows climbed towards his hairline. There had been mention of a ghost, but he hadn't realised she'd already dealt with a haunting. "Again?"

"Yeah, I thought you asked around?" She gave him a look that was part suspicion, part amusement. "My family's complicated. Gran kept this... spirit, I guess. Magnus. He was a Viking shaman who got tangled up with my family way back. Like, way way back. Medieval times or something." Her eyes went big to emphasis just how far back she was talking.

She took another drink, gathering her thoughts. "My ancestors basically kept him prisoner. For centuries. They bound him to objects – first a sword, then a necklace, then various other things. Dragged him from Scotland to here, keeping him like some kind of supernatural pet. Or slave, more accurately." Her voice was bitter. Pained. As though she were still trying to get her head around this.

Brendan's mind raced, pieces clicking into place. That presence he'd felt around the house since his first visit – the watching weight he'd attributed to standard spiritual residue. Not the crawling wrongness of a trapped spirit, but something older, more patient. Now that she'd pointed it out, he could feel it clearly. Protection. Guardianship. A presence that chose to remain. And remain hidden from Brendan.

He needed to know more.

There was a tension in his gut, not quite jealousy - of a ghost, ridiculous - but something akin.

"This Magnus... he was here? In this house?"

"Until recently, yeah. Gran kept him in an enchanted box. Just like all my other power-mad ancestors, apparently. But he's free now. Finally. Moved on to wherever Viking shamans go when they're released from supernatural slavery after six hundred years. Until he decides to show up with ominous warnings anyway."

She laughed, but it was bitter as burnt coffee. "Just another messed up family tradition. We're collectors, apparently. Spirits, power, obligations. My gran left me a house full of ghosts and a town full of expectations."

"That's... quite a story." Brendan chose his words carefully, all of this information adding to what he knew, creating a better picture of what he'd stepped into.

"Oh, it gets better." She leaned back on her hands, looking up at the ceiling, seance forgotten about as she got into the flow of storytelling. "Apparently one of my ancestors wanted a baby so badly she made one. Out of earth. Like, literal dirt and magic and whatever else goes into making a person from scratch. If that's true, then I'm part dirt too, or something equally insane."

The pieces clicked together with an almost audible snap. Her connection to the land, the way plants seemed to lean towards her like she was the sun. How the very ground beneath the house thrummed with awareness, responding to her presence. Not metaphor but literal truth – she carried the earth in her blood.

Yet she didn't seem to be fully aware of it. Or maybe, she hadn't accepted it.

Part of him was stunned by that, and yet, had he really,

truly accepted his connection with death as Kaipō? No. They were more alike than he had seen.

"According to family legend," she continued as if they were old ladies gossiping, "this ancestor – three, maybe four generations back – couldn't have children the normal way. So she went out to the garden one night, during the new moon, and she... built one. Shaped a baby from soil and clay, breathed life into it with magic I can't even comprehend. And it worked. The baby lived, grew, had children of her own. Had descendants. Had me."

She met his eyes then, and the weight of inherited strangeness sat heavy between them. "So yeah. Viking ghost guardian and earth baby ancestry. That's who I want to contact. My delightful family of supernatural kidnappers and dirt mothers."

"Why?" The question came out rougher than he intended. "Why do you want to talk to them?"

She huffed out a long breath, shoulders sagging, as though all the fun had drained out of the night. "Someone wants me to take over my family's duties. To be the town witch, I guess. Keep the boundaries, help people with supernatural problems, maintain the balance or whatever." She laughed again, sharp and bitter. "Like I'm some kind of mystical janitor, cleaning up everyone else's messes."

"And you don't want to?" He watched her closely, trying to see the truth beneath the sarcasm and bitterness. Trying to understand how she truly felt about all of this.

Sad, he could see. Grieving, for things that had happened long before her, but were still happening to her.

"Would you?" She gestured around the room, at the candles, the salt, the weight of expectation that seemed to press in from the very walls. "My ancestors enslaved a spirit for six centuries. They created life because they could, not because they should. They made bargains and broke them, bound things that should be free, played god with powers they barely understood. And everyone wants me to pick up where they left off."

She pulled her knees to her chest, making herself smaller. "I already hurt someone once, when I was a kid. What happens when I have access to real power? What happens when someone makes me angry and I have centuries of accumulated magical knowledge at my fingertips?"

The fear in her voice was real, visceral. Not of the power itself, but of what she might become. He understood that fear intimately, lived with it every day. But he couldn't tell her that right now. His tongue was bound, his secrets feeling toxic under his skin.

"No one is going to make you do anything you don't want to," he said, hoping it was true, knowing it probably wasn't. People like them – people with gifts, with curses, with power – rarely got to choose their own paths. But if he could help her live the life she wanted, then he would do what it took.

She studied him for a long moment, her gaze uncomfortably penetrating. Evaluating. "You know, for someone new to town, you're taking all this really well. The magic, the ghosts, the earth babies. Most people would be running for the hills by now."

He shrugged, aiming for casual, despite the way his pulse quickened. "It's a strange world. I've seen stranger things." The comment was almost flippant, and yet her gaze sharpened, and he realised too late that he'd revealed more than he'd intended.

"What kind of strange things, Brendan?"

The question hung between them like a blade, sharp and waiting. He could deflect, make a joke, keep his secrets locked away where they couldn't hurt anyone. But something about her – sitting there surrounded by candles and salt, afraid of her own heritage, trusting him enough to share her family's dark history – made him want to offer a piece of truth in return.

"I see things sometimes." The admission felt like pulling teeth, each word dragged from somewhere deep and defended. "Things that haven't happened yet. Sometimes things that happened long ago...those who have passed. It runs in my family." Which was the truth, but not the whole truth by any means.

"Visions? Ghosts?" She leaned forward, interested now, grief temporarily forgotten.

"Something like that." He picked at the label on his beer, peeling it away in careful strips. "It's why your séance makes me... uncomfortable. When I'm around, things tend to come through easier. The boundary gets thin."

Understanding dawned in her eyes. "That's why you looked like you'd seen a ghost when you walked in. You could feel it – what I'd been doing. The magic."

"The whole house is swimming in it. Has been since I got to town. But tonight..." He gestured vaguely at the candles, the circle. "Tonight it's like you lit a beacon. Every spirit for miles can probably feel it."

"So you're psychic?" She quirked an eyebrow.

"I prefer 'cursed with inconvenient foresight.'" The joke fell flat, too much truth bleeding through.

She laughed anyway, a real laugh this time that transformed her face. "God, we're a pair, aren't we? The reluctant witch and the inconvenient psychic. No wonder we found each other."

"When you put it like that..." He waited for her to make a decision about what they would do next.

"Maybe we shouldn't do this tonight." She looked at the

board, then back at him. "I'm too raw, too angry, and if you make ghostly encounters worse..."

"Probably wise." Relief flooded through him, muscles he hadn't realised were tense suddenly relaxing.

They cleaned up together, moving in easy synchronization. She held the dustpan while he swept up the salt, careful not to leave any grains behind. They extinguished the candles one by one, smoke rising in thin streams towards the ceiling. The ordinary actions felt grounding after the electric tension of the almost-séance.

The spirits withdrew a little, the weight lifting off him until it was just the two of them in the house, and this Magnus, his energy hulking and silent, but still there.

"Stay?" she asked suddenly as they boxed up the Ouija board. "Not like that – " she added quickly, biting her lip. He would never have assumed she was propositioning him after the conversation they'd just had though. "It's just... Kelly's gone, the house is too quiet, and I could use the company from someone who gets it. The weird stuff, I mean."

"Okay."

They ended up on opposite ends of the couch, watching some action movie neither paid attention to. The space between them felt charged but comfortable, like the pause between lightning and thunder. On screen, things exploded in brilliant orange blooms while the hero delivered quips, but Brendan found himself watching Alyssa instead. The way she tucked her feet under herself, the way she absently braided a section of her hair, the way grief and exhaustion painted shadows under her eyes.

"I hurt my friend Miri," she said suddenly, not looking at him. The confession came out of nowhere, like she'd been holding it in so long it had to escape. "When I was just a kid. I used my magic and I hurt her with it"

He stayed quiet, sensing that she needed to speak for herself, more than for him.

"I was struggling with keeping it a secret and she was the only one who knew. She was my best friend, and I only saw her in the summer." Her voice dropped to barely above a whisper, the hint of a sad smile playing on her lips.

"What happened?" he asked, keeping his words gentle. He wanted to reach for her, hold her as she relived this memory, but he had a feeling that she just needed to feel her feelings right now.

"We were playing, and she knew about the magic. I mean... I've been trying to deny what this place is for longer than I've been back, but we both know." She tossed a sardonic look his way. He grimaced, nodded, encouraging her to continue.

"Miri, she was so keen to see what I could do, what I'd learned. Gran was outside, and we were alone, and I..." Alyssa swallowed hard, eyes fixed on her hands which gripped her knees. "I knew I wasn't meant to do it alone. There were rules, even with Gran, but I did it anyway. I got some ingredients, and I fucked up, and I lost control. The flames... They were so big, and Miri was screaming and I had this flash of anger. If it wasn't for her, I wouldn't have done magic without Gran. I wouldn't have lost control, and the fire, it jumped to her and she... the smell. Her screams." She wrapped her arms around herself. "She never spoke to me again. Never sent me a letter. Never replied to any of mine. And my mother never let me come back here."

"You were just a kid," he said gently, heart aching for young Alyssa.

"Exactly," she said bitterly. "Just a kid and I burnt my best friend because I got mad. What happens when I'm thirty and someone really pisses me off? What happens when I have access to the kind of power my ancestors wielded?" She finally looked at him, eyes bright with unshed tears. "What if I become them?"

"Alyssa," he said, sliding across the couch to close the distance. She'd let the hurt out, and now he needed to help her put herself back together. As soon as he lifted his arm she practically fell against her chest, finally letting some of her tears free. "The fact that you're worried about it shows that you're not that kind of person," he assured her. "And, we all make mistakes. That doesn't make us bad. It means we get to decide who we want to be." Those last words felt like they were as much for him as her, but he hoped they were of some comfort. He squeezed her tightly, and then loosened his embrace.

"Or it means I'm just not them yet." She swiped at her eyes with the back of her hand. "God, I haven't told anyone that story in years. Sorry for dumping it on you."

"Don't apologize. Magic leaves marks. On everyone it touches. We both know that."

With those words she seemed to relax, leaving her head resting on his chest, his arms still draped around her. It felt... Good. Better than he deserved. Especially considering what Mrs Nolan wanted him to do.

They sat in companionable silence after that, two people carrying unwanted gifts, finding solace in shared understanding. Outside, the Bay whispered its ancient stories against the shore, and in the walls of the Whenua house, an echo of protection lingered – Magnus's final gift to the descendant of his captors, watching over her even in his freedom.

When Alyssa finally dozed off, curled against him, Brendan pulled a throw blanket over her and settled in to keep watch. His phone buzzed in his pocket – Mrs Nolan, no doubt, wanting her progress report – but he ignored it. Tomorrow would bring its own complications. Tonight, he'd guard her sleep and try not to think about how right this felt, sitting in her grandmother's house with its watching walls and patient ghosts, pretending for a few hours that he wasn't here to betray her trust.

The séance materials waited in their box by the door, harmless now but holding potential for later. Soon enough, she'd try again, and he'd have to decide whether to warn her about what his presence might bring through the veil. Whether to tell her the full truth about why he was here, about the child whose life hung in the balance, about the promises he'd made in desperation.

But not tonight. Tonight was for unexpected friendship and the strange comfort of being understood. In a world full of curses and unwanted gifts, that was its own kind of magic.

For now, he was content to sit in the darkness, watching over someone who understood the weight of unwanted sight, the burden of inherited power, the fear of becoming what you were born to be.

He could feel Magnus's presence more clearly now – not threatening but watchful, protective. The Viking shaman might be free, but he hadn't gone far. Like Brendan, he stood guard over Alyssa Whenua, the earth-born heir who wanted nothing more than to be ordinary and would never have that choice.

# CHAPTER 21

Consciousness came slowly, like surfacing from deep water. First, the crick in Alyssa's neck from sleeping at an odd angle. Then the weight across her legs – warm, solid, and rumbling with a purr. Socks. Her eyes fluttered open to find morning light streaming through the curtains, painting golden stripes across the coffee table where empty beer bottles stood like soldiers after a long campaign.

Brendan was sprawled beside her on the couch, one arm flung over his face, the other wrapped around her with unconscious familiarity. He'd stayed. The whole night, apparently, if the throw blanket tucked around her shoulders was any indication. She couldn't remember the last time someone had tucked her in.

His shirt had ridden up in sleep, revealing a strip of skin and the trail of dark hair disappearing into his jeans. His jaw showed the shadow of overnight growth, making him look slightly wild, slightly dangerous.

His breathing was deep and even, punctuated by the slightest hint of a snore. Not the chainsaw variety Grant had subjected her to, but something softer, almost endearing. The thought of Grant gave her a pang of pain, especially after yesterday. But she didn't want to think about that right now; the man beside her was a far more interesting concept.

She extracted herself carefully, not wanting to wake him. Her body protested the movement – couches weren't designed for all-night occupancy, especially not shared occupancy. But there was something about waking up next to another person, even fully clothed and cramped, that made her chest tight with an emotion she didn't want to examine too closely.

Alyssa paused before she left the room, taking in the sight of this man. All the burdens of daylight hours had been stripped away, and he looked younger, more vulnerable, but perhaps not as vulnerable as she had felt after everything she had told him last night. The ache in her head was from bad decisions, one way or another.

But he had stayed. She had told him her worst, the biggest horror stories of her life, and he was still here. If that hadn't sent him running, maybe there was hope.

The floorboards were cold under her bare feet as she padded to the kitchen. Morning sounds filtered through the windows – seagulls arguing over territory, a car down the road, a neighbour's pruning shears.

She put the kettle on, the familiar ritual grounding her in normalcy after yesterday's emotional hurricane. Kelly's betrayal stung like a sharp stone in her stomach, but it had dulled a little in Brendan's company.

"Well, well. Look who finally found herself a proper man."

Alyssa nearly dropped the mug she'd been reaching for. Magnus stood by the window, translucent in the morning light but solid enough that she could make out the intricate braiding in his beard, the amused glint in his eyes.

"Damn, Magnus. A little warning?" She pressed a hand to

her racing heart. "And he's not my man. He's just... a friend who stayed over. And, can I take this to mean that you've decided to return for more than just ominous warnings?"

The Viking ghost snorted. "In my day, when a man spent the night in a woman's home, there were certain expectations. Negotiations with fathers. Exchange of silver. Proper demonstrations of worthiness."

"Well, in my day, sometimes people just fall asleep on couches after emotionally traumatic revelations about psychic visions and family curses." She pulled down two mugs, then hesitated and grabbed a third. Did ghosts drink coffee? Probably not, but it felt rude not to make the gesture.

Magnus drifted closer, his form solidifying slightly. For someone who'd finally gained his freedom after six centuries of imprisonment, he seemed reluctant to move on, but Alyssa was grateful. She had missed him.

"This one has sight," Magnus observed, tilting his head towards the living room. "The veil bends around him like water around a stone. Dangerous, that affliction. Draws things through."

"He mentioned something about that." She spooned coffee into the plunger, the rich aroma filling the kitchen. "He was hesitant about my plan for a seance."

"Smart of him to distract you. Though I could have protected you." Magnus crossed his arms, looking affronted.

"It was you I was trying to summon. Well, you were one of the options." She poured hot water over the grounds, watching them bloom and swirl. "And you don't need to protect me. You're free, remember? You can go where ghosts go. Valhalla or wherever."

Magnus was quiet for a moment, his form flickering like candleflame. When he spoke, his voice carried the weight of centuries. "Freedom is a strange thing, little witch. For so long,

I dreamed of it. Raged against my bonds. Cursed your ancestors with every breath." He moved to stand beside her, close enough that she could feel the chill of his presence. "But now? Now I find I've grown... accustomed to this family. To this place. Your grandmother was kind to me, though not enough to set me free. And you..."

"I'm the one who set you free." She looked up at him, heart warmer from hearing his stilted admission of fondness for her.

"Yes." His smile was surprisingly gentle for a Viking warrior. "And for that, I choose to visit. I will come when you call. You do not need all this...paranormal clutter," He gestured to the seance objects. "I will visit...for now. To see you safely through whatever comes." His expression hardened as he glanced towards the living room again. "Though I'm not entirely certain about this one. He wishes to guard you. Yet he carries secrets like stones in his pockets."

"Don't we all?" She pressed the plunger down slowly, the ritual soothing. "He was honest with me last night. About his visions, his family curse. That's more than most people manage."

"Partial honesty is still partially lies." Magnus leaned against the counter, an interesting feat for someone without corporeal form. "There's more to him. I can smell it. Like iron."

"You're jealous." The realization hit her with surprising clarity. "You're actually jealous that I'm interested in someone."

Magnus drew himself up to his full, imposing height. "I am a warrior, sage and healer of the North Seas. I do not get jealous of whelps who probably can't even swing an axe properly."

"Uh-huh." She poured coffee into two mugs, adding milk to both. "So the fact that you're puffing up like an angry rooster has nothing to do with another man sleeping in your territory?"

"It's not my territory. It's yours." But he looked pleased at the designation. "I simply think you could do better. In my time, a man proved his worth through deeds. What has this one done besides make moon eyes?"

"He stayed." The words came out softer than intended. "When he found out about the magic, about you, about everything my family has done – he stayed. Most people run from the weird stuff. Hell, I want to run from the weird stuff half the time."

Magnus studied her with those ancient eyes. "I suspect that this is what they call low standards. Or settling."

The words stung more than they should have. "Thanks for the pep talk, Magnus. Really helpful."

"I'm not trying to hurt you, child. But you wear your heart like an open wound. Perhaps a little caution..."

Alyssa shook her head, wiping away tears. She had had low standards - with Grant. She had put up with him even though he apparently didn't love her, and had betrayed her with her best friend of all people.

"Who are you talking to?"

Alyssa spun to find Brendan in the kitchen doorway, hair sticking up at odd angles, shirt wrinkled from sleep. His eyes swept the room, narrowing slightly as they paused where Magnus stood, but clearly seeing nothing.

"Magnus," she said simply, watching his reaction. "He was offering relationship advice. Apparently, you haven't proven your worth through sufficient Viking-approved deeds."

Brendan's eyebrows climbed towards his hairline. "I could tell someone was here, but I didn't know it was him. Is that why you look upset?"

"Right there." She pointed to where the ghost stood with

arms crossed, looking supremely unimpressed. Clearly the viking had no intention of letting Brendan see him though. "Being judgmental about modern courtship rituals."

"I can't see him." Brendan moved into the kitchen, accepting the mug she offered. His fingers brushed hers in the exchange, warm and solid and real. "Usually ghosts can't wait to haunt me. This is unusual."

Magnus snorted. "Tell him he's not worth my effort."

"He says you're not worth it," Alyssa relayed, trying not to smile at Magnus's offended expression.

"First time a ghost has ghosted me." Brendan's lips quirked. "I'm almost offended."

"He's gone now anyway." And he was – vanished between one blink and the next, leaving only the faint scent of sea salt and old leather. "He does that. Shows up to offer cryptic warnings or judge my life choices, then disappears when things get interesting."

"Protective. I could feel him last night. Keeping watch" Brendan sipped his coffee, studying her over the rim. "He cares about you."

"He's got a funny way of showing it. Six hundred years of haunting my family, and now he decides to play supernatural bodyguard." She leaned against the counter, matching his posture. In the morning light, she could see the gold flecks in his grey eyes, the way his lashes cast shadows on his cheeks. "How'd you sleep?"

"Better than expected, considering." He rolled his shoulders, working out the kinks. "That couch has seen better days."

"Gran probably bought it in 1987. I keep meaning to replace it, but..." She shrugged. Everything in the house carried memory, history. Even the uncomfortable furniture felt like part of her inheritance.

"But it's hers." He understood without her having to explain.

They stood in comfortable silence, drinking coffee and existing in the same space without need for words. Outside, the pruning shears had gone quiet. The morning felt soft around the edges, protective, like the world was giving them a moment of peace before demanding they face reality again.

"Thank you," she said eventually, locking eyes with him. She inhaled and reached out, placing her hand on his arm. He didn't flinch from her touch; if anything, he moved closer. "For not running screaming when I told you about my supremely messed up family history."

"Thank you for trusting me with it." He set down his mug, expression growing serious as he moved his arm so that they were clasping hands. He gripped her fingers firmly, thumb rubbing circles on her skin. "Alyssa, about what I said last night. About my visions, the curse – "

"You don't owe me explanations." She cut him off, not ready for the moment to get heavy again. Not wanting to know everything, because she knew there was more to it, and right now, she couldn't handle that. She needed his warmth, his scent, and damn, if she didn't think she might need his lips as a distraction sooner rather than later. "We've both got our burdens. I get it."

"Still." He moved closer, close enough that she could smell the sleep-warmth on his skin, the coffee on his breath. "I want to be honest with you. As much as I can be."

"As much as you can be," she repeated, hearing the qualifier, filing it away with all the other small mysteries that made up this man she was beginning to have real feelings for. "That's more than most people offer."

He reached out, fingers ghosting along her jaw, tilting her face up. "You deserve more than most people offer."

The kiss was different from the frantic passion she'd imagined during lonely nights. This was slow, careful, a question asked and answered. His lips were soft against hers, coffee-flavoured and warm. His hand slid to the back of her neck, thumb tracing the knob of her spine, and she melted into him like wax near flame.

When they parted, her breath came shallow and quick. "That's quite a good morning kiss."

"Wait until you see my good evening material." The words rumbled through his chest where she'd pressed her palm, feeling his heartbeat race to match hers.

The kettle whistled – she must have turned it on again without thinking – and they stepped apart, the spell broken but not shattered. She busied herself with toast, needing the normalcy of breakfast rituals to ground herself. He helped without being asked, finding butter and jam, moving around her kitchen with surprising ease.

"I should check my phone," she said, remembering the real world existed beyond this morning bubble. "Make sure the apocalypse hasn't started."

"If it has, I vote we ignore it until after breakfast."

She laughed, but retrieved her phone from where it had been charging. The screen lit up with notifications – twelve missed calls, all from Kelly. Her stomach clenched, the peace of the morning cracking like ice under weight.

"Everything okay?" Brendan noticed her expression, concern creasing his brow.

"Kelly called. A lot." She set the phone face-down, not ready to deal with it. "Probably wanting to explain, or justify, or make me forgive her so she doesn't have to feel guilty about shacking up with my ex."

It came out sharper than intended, slicing through the

morning's softness. Brendan moved closer but didn't touch, offering presence without presumption.

"Hell, Alyssa. That's awful. You don't have to listen to any of it," he said quietly. "You don't owe her absolution."

"I know." She spread butter on toast with perhaps more force than necessary. "It's just – twenty years of friendship, and she threw it away for a guy who couldn't even stick around when I found out I couldn't have kids. What does that say about me? That my best friend would choose him."

"It says nothing about you and everything about them." His voice carried conviction that almost made her believe it. "People who betray trust like that – they're broken in ways that have nothing to do with you."

She wanted to ask if he spoke from experience, but his phone chose that moment to ring. He glanced at the screen and his expression shuttered, professional distance sliding into place.

"I'm sorry, I have to take this." He was already moving towards the door, the phone at his ear. "Hello?"

She couldn't make out the words, just the tone – urgent, demanding. He made agreeable noises while his free hand clenched and unclenched at his side. When he ended the call, the easy warmth of the morning had drained from his face.

"I have to go," he said, apology heavy in every word. "Work thing. But tonight – "

"Bring dinner." She forced lightness she didn't feel. "Seven o'clock. And maybe we can finish that conversation about your good evening material."

He crossed back to her in three quick strides, cupping her face in both hands and kissing her like he was trying to memorize the shape of her mouth. When he pulled away, they were both breathless.

"Seven o'clock," he agreed. "I'll bring takeaways and my best material."

After he left, the house felt too quiet despite Magnus's invisible presence somewhere in the walls. She stood in her kitchen, toast cooling in her hand, and tried to hold onto the warmth of the morning.

But already it was fading, replaced by questions. Who had called him? What had demanded such immediate attention? Why had she let him keep his secrets when, as Magnus suggested, they could be dangerous? Was this just another example of her having low standards? Running from the truth and ignoring things that should be dealt with?

And why had Brendan looked, for just a moment before the mask slipped into place, absolutely terrified?

"He's lying to you." Magnus materialized by the window again, staring out at the street where Brendan's car had disappeared. "Not about his feelings – those are real enough. But about why he's here."

"Everyone lies about something." She took a bitter bite of cold toast. "The question is whether it's a lie I can live with."

Magnus turned to look at her, surprise and something like approval in his ancient eyes. "You're learning wisdom, child. Your grandmother would be proud."

"Yeah, well." She raised her coffee mug in a mock toast. "Here's to wisdom gained through shitty life experiences. May we all be so lucky."

But even as cynicism tried to settle over her like armour, she couldn't forget the feeling of Brendan's hands in her hair, the blanket he'd wrapped around her, the careful honesty in his voice when he'd said he wanted to be as honest as he could be. Maybe that was enough. Maybe, in a world full of complete betrayals, partial honesty was its own kind of gift.

# CHAPTER 22

The garden soil was cool between Alyssa's fingers, grounding her in the present even as her mind kept drifting to the memory of Brendan's mouth on hers. She'd come out here to think, to process, but instead found herself planting sweet peas with unnecessary vigor, each thrust of the trowel punctuated by sense-memories – his hands in her hair, the coffee taste of his kiss, the solid warmth of him beside her all night.

She grabbed her phone, muscle memory already pulling up Kelly's contact before reality crashed back. The half-typed message – *you'll never guess what happened with the hot neighbour* – stared at her accusingly. Delete. There was no one to share this with, no best friend to dissect every moment with squealing excitement.

The loneliness of it sat heavy in her chest. Twenty years of Kelly being her first call for everything, and now... nothing. Just a contact photo of two women grinning at the camera, arms around each other, Alyssa blissfully unaware of the betrayal that may have already started at that point…when did it start? Would it only hurt her more to know?

Loneliness and pain dragged her to a sitting position on the soft, damp earth.

No best friend. She had damaged her first, and her second had broken her heart.

Alyssa sat in silence for a moment. The birds sang and the bees buzzed. The hum of the earth beneath her body soothed her gently until the tears passed.

No best friend. But there was Samantha. Sam who'd stood up to Mrs Nolan on her behalf. Sam, who Alyssa had avoided and told to back off for her trouble. The guilt of it made her stomach twist. Sam was the only person she'd strongly connected with since moving to the Bay - right from the start, she'd offered friendship.

Alyssa needed to apologize. Not just for the sake of their business arrangement, but because she'd been an ass to someone who'd only tried to help.

The shower was lukewarm – the hot water heater had been acting up again – but it served to wash away the garden dirt and cool the heat that kept rising when she thought about tonight. Seven o'clock. Takeaways. And whatever "evening material" Brendan had promised. She wished she had someone to talk to, and maybe she did, if she could repair the damage. Burning words were easier to come back from than raging flames.

She dressed carefully, choosing a sundress that said "I'm approachable and sorry for pushing you away."

The walk to Sam's shop was short but beautiful, the Bay spread out beside her like a postcard. The door of Sage & Salt stood open and she walked in, breath held, apology on her tongue.

Matai stood at the counter, his back to her as he handed a cardboard box to Sam. She recognised him immediately.

" – should last you through the month," he was saying. "But if you need more before then, just call."

"Oh, Alyssa!" Sam's face brightened as she spotted her in the doorway. "Good timing."

Matai turned, and she got her first real look at him without grief clouding her vision. The traditional tā moko tattoos on his forearms told stories she couldn't read, spirals and waves that seemed to move with their own tide. He nodded in recognition.

"Alyssa. Good to see you again," he said with a nod.

"You're the tattoo artist, right?"

"Among other things." When he extended his hand, she felt that familiar tingle of magic, different in flavour to the others. Where Sam's magic felt light and warm, Matai's was dark, somehow. More like Brendan's. Dark, but not bad. "I do traditional tā moko, contemporary work, and supply some of the more specialised inventory for shops like Sam's."

She glanced at the box again. "Specialised how?"

He glanced between her and Sam. "I should let you two talk." But he paused at the door, turning back. "Alyssa, if you ever want to talk about marks of protection, marks of belonging... my door is open."

Then he was gone, flicking the shop sign from 'open' to 'closed' with the casual familiarity of long practice.

"Smooth exit," Alyssa muttered, still feeling the echo of magic where he'd touched her hand.

Sam was already moving towards the back of the shop. "Come on, I'll make coffee. We need to talk."

The kitchen was exactly what Alyssa expected – herbs hanging from the ceiling, crystals on the windowsill catching light, a well-worn table that had seen countless conversations.

Sam moved with practiced ease, pulling mugs from hooks, filling the kettle.

"I'm sorry," Alyssa said before Sam could speak. "For avoiding you... when you were probably just trying to help."

"You were overwhelmed." Sam set a mug in front of her, steam rising in lazy spirals as she settled into a chair opposite.

"Still." Alyssa wrapped her hands around the mug, letting the warmth seep into her palms. "You've been nothing but kind, and I've been..." She searched for the right word as she gazed at Sam. "Difficult."

"Protective," Sam corrected gently. "You've been protective of yourself, which is understandable given everything you're dealing with."

"Actually, I could really do with a friend right now," Alyssa said, setting down her mug.

Sam's expression shifted to concern, though there wasn't the wholehearted buy in that Kelly would have given her. "What's going on?"

"Kelly's gone. Found out she's been shacking up with my ex." The story began to spill out, along with a few tears. The pain was still so raw, and none of it was to do with Grant, which was actually kind of surprising now that she thought about it. The hole in her heart was all to do with Kelly.

"Oh, Alyssa." Sam's hand moved across the table, stopping just short of touching. "That's..."

"So many years of friendship. Gone." She shrugged, aiming for casual, missing by miles. "And now there's this thing with Brendan, and I don't know what I'm doing anymore."

"Brendan? The new guy?" Sam's eyebrow rose, her curiosity obvious. Was that the hint of a smile?

Alyssa nodded. "He's...I don't know what he is..." She paused, searching for words that didn't reveal too much. "He's been kind. But I don't know if I can trust my judgment."

Sam nodded slowly. "It's hard to open up after betrayal."

"Yeah." Alyssa traced the rim of her mug. "Anyway, that's why I needed a friend today. Before all this other stuff crashed down."

"I'm glad you came," Sam said simply. "For what it's worth, you've got people here. Even if it doesn't feel like it right now."

Despite the unspoken words that Alyssa could feel in the air between them—the obvious truth that the town was simply waiting for her to decide she was definitely staying—they sat in comfortable silence for a moment, sipping coffee that tasted of cinnamon and something earthier.

Finally, Alyssa asked, "So what does Mrs Nolan actually want from me? Because she keeps talking about stepping into Gran's shoes, but she's never actually explained what that means. And I know I've been an idiot for ignoring it for so long"

Sam's expression darkened, though Alyssa got the feeling it wasn't because of her. "She wants you to take on your grand-mother's role. All of it. Being the town witch, maintaining the protective barriers, keeping the balance between the mundane and magical." She paused, seeming to weigh her words. "But what she hasn't told you is that those barriers are weakening. Have been since before Sylvie died."

"Weakening how?" Alyssa's brow creased, and her heart hitched.

"You said Kelly found her way here, even though she couldn't before, right?"

"Yeah, she just... showed up." The betrayal still stung, but now there was another layer to it. Pieces of a puzzle coming together. "Last time she tried, she couldn't find the road."

"Exactly." Sam leaned forward. "The Bay has always been hidden, protected. Unless you're from here, or have particular magic, or know exactly what you're looking for, you can't find us. We might as well not exist to most people."

Alyssa felt pieces clicking into place. "That's why the town feels so... separate. Safe."

"But the barriers are failing. More outsiders have been finding their way in, and of course, things become a little more open when the fair comes to town too. Strange things have been washing up on the beaches. The protective wards which have been maintained for decades are unraveling without the support of someone from your line to tend them."

Alyssa gnawed at her bottom lip, guilt threatening to over-whelm her. She'd been so selfish, only thinking of herself, when all of this was going on. She'd have known, if she'd not been so busy avoiding the truth.

"And Mrs Nolan thinks I'm the only one who can fix it?"

Sam's expression grew even more serious. "Here's what she hasn't told you. She's hired someone – a practitioner who specializes in... particular kinds of magic. The kind that deals with death and what comes after."

"A necromancer?" The word tasted foul. But not as foul as the suspicion creeping up her neck. Brendan had dealings with Mrs Nolan, and he was new in town...

"She plans to bring your grandmother back. To bind her spirit and force her to maintain the barriers if you won't." Sam's voice was tight with anger. "It's an abomination. No one should be forced into service after death."

The coffee mug slipped from Alyssa's numb fingers, shat-tering on the floor. Hot liquid splashed across the tiles, but she barely noticed. All she could see was Magnus – centuries of imprisonment, the weight of chains he couldn't break, the resignation in ancient eyes.

"That monster!" The words came out as a snarl. "She wants

to do to Gran what my family did to Magnus. Trap her, use her, make her a slave to the town's needs for eternity."

"Yes." Sam was already kneeling, gathering the broken pieces. "That's exactly what she plans."

And suddenly it all made terrible sense. "That's why she wanted me to keep Magnus in that box. Not because he was dangerous, but because he was part of it. Part of the power that protected the Bay." She helped Sam clean up the mess, her mind racing. "My family used him to strengthen their magic, to maintain the barriers. And now that he's free..."

"The protection is weaker." Sam deposited the shards in the bin, then poured Alyssa a fresh cup. "But Alyssa, you need to know – not everyone agrees with Vivica's methods."

"Vivica?" She quirked an eyebrow.

"Mrs Nolan's first name. And yes, it suits her perfectly." Sam's smile was grim. "For weeks now, some of us have been trying to find another way to strengthen the barriers without forcing you or binding your grandmother's spirit."

"You have?" The surprise in her voice made Sam wince.

"Did you think we'd all just stand by and let her enslave you or Sylvie?" Sam almost looked hurt. "We're not monsters, Alyssa. Most of us understand that times change, that the old ways aren't always the right ways."

"But she's so sure I'm the only option." The words felt hollow as she spoke them, torn between wanting to trust Sam that they would find another way, and yet seeing more clearly than she ever had before just how much help she could be to this place that she was growing to love.

"She's wedded to tradition. In her mind, it's always been a Whenua woman, so it always must be. But magic evolves, just like everything else. We've been exploring alternatives – collective castings, rotating responsibilities, drawing on the town's combined strength rather than one family's sacrifice."

Alyssa felt something ease in her chest. They weren't all like Vivica. They weren't all waiting to chain her to a destiny she'd never chosen. "Why hasn't anyone told me this?"

"Because you've been pretty clear about wanting nothing to do with any of it." Sam's tone was gentle but honest. "You've kept yourself separate, avoided getting to know people, shut down conversations about magic. We've tried to respect that."

The truth of it stung. She had been hiding, running from connection as much as from responsibility. "I just... I'm not a witch. Not really. I haven't been trained, I don't know the rituals or spells or whatever I'm supposed to know."

"And yet you banished June from your house. You freed Magnus after six centuries of binding. You make the most lovely pieces of jewelery through intuition alone. You can feel the magic in others – you felt it in Matai just now, didn't you?"

Alyssa nodded reluctantly.

"So you're not trained. That doesn't mean you're not capable." Sam reached across the table, and when their hands touched, that familiar tingle sparked between them. But this time, Alyssa didn't pull away. She let herself feel it – the connection, the shared power, the recognition of like calling to like.

"It's not about training." Alyssa's voice dropped to almost a whisper. "When I was younger, I hurt someone. Badly. With magic I didn't have full control over."

Sam's fingers tightened around hers but she didn't speak, waiting.

"Her name was Miri. My best friend. She wanted to see my magic, and when I lost control and caused a fire, I got angry and blamed her. The fire... It burned her badly, and that was my fault. My rage did that, and I am so worried that I'll become just like my family."

Sam pursed her lips, as if considering her words carefully.

"People are complicated, and we all have our reasons. Slyvie may have done some questionable things, but she was a good person, Alyssa. She did so much for the Bay, and those who live within it. Don't let that one act change the truth. And your friend? She's still here."

Alyssa's head snapped up. "What?" Her mind flashed back to the fair, where she thought she had seen Miri; decided that her mind was playing tricks on her.

"Miri Castellan. She has a glass-blowing studio about five minutes down the main road from town. Creates the most incredible pieces – vases that seem to hold light, sculptures that look like frozen music." Sam's expression was thoughtful.

"She's here?" Alyssa's stomach clenched. "In the Bay?"

"Thriving, actually. The studio's open to visitors. She does demonstrations on weekends, teaches classes." Sam leaned forward. "What happened when you were young was awful, but Alyssa – she's built a beautiful life. Maybe this is a chance to heal old wounds."

"She probably hates me."

"Maybe. Or maybe she's had years to gain perspective, just like you have." Sam's voice was gentle but firm. "You can't let one mistake you made as a child define your entire relationship with magic. That's letting fear win."

Alyssa inhaled, long and deep, exhaling slowly to try and calm her heart. "What if I do it again? What if I get angry and hurt someone else?"

"Then you'll have learned nothing from what happened with Miri. But I don't think that's true. The fact that you're still carrying this, still afraid of your own power – that tells me you understand the weight of it. That's wisdom, hard-earned."

Alyssa stared at her hands, remembering the feeling of that terrible anger. "I don't know if I can face her."

"You don't have to. But knowing she's here, seeing what

she's made of her life... maybe that's a gift. A chance to see that our worst mistakes don't have to define anyone's story forever."

"What are we?" she asked, giving voice to a question that had been dancing in her mind. "You and me?"

Sam's smile was mysterious. "We're children of this place, in different ways. We're all tied to the gods and spirits that shaped these islands."

"You're being vague again." Alyssa rolled her eyes.

"Some things have to be discovered, not told." Sam squeezed her hand before letting go. "But I will say this – you already know part of it. Whatever way the story might have been distorted, your connection to the earth goddess, Papatūānuku, isn't just family legend. It's real, and it's powerful, and it's yours whether you embrace it or not. You are her child, in the same way that Sylvie was…"

Alyssa felt shivers. "A child of the goddess?"

Sam set down her coffee mug, and when she spoke again, her voice had changed – deeper somehow, resonant with something old.

"Before there was light, before there was sky, Ranginui and Papatūānuku lay locked in eternal embrace, anchored together to the land right here. Their children grew in the darkness between them, yearning for space, for breath, for *being*. When Tāne finally pushed them apart – father sky from mother earth – the world was born. And the place where that first separation happened, where divine tears fell and soaked into the soil, where the gods first walked on solid ground..." Sam's eyes met hers. "This is the anchor point. the birthplace of the Gods."

The words settled into Alyssa's bones like stones dropping into still water. She could feel something stirring beneath her feet, a pulse, slow and vast, like a heartbeat measured in centuries.

"The Gods return here to this sacred land. Sometimes, they fall in love. Sometimes they birth new children into this world. We call ourselves Kuraatua. Children of the Gods."

"Children of the gods," Alyssa repeated, the words feeling strange and enormous in her mouth. "You're serious?"

Sam's smile was wry. "I'm a child of Rehua – the star god, of kindness and summer's warmth. His light runs through my bloodline. It's why I can sense magic in others, why I'm drawn to help, to heal, to illuminate what's hidden in shadow."

As Sam spoke, Alyssa noticed it for the first time – really noticed. The way light seemed to gather around Sam even in the dim shop, the warmth that radiated from her presence, how she'd always felt like sunshine breaking through clouds. Not just metaphor. *Truth.*

"And me?" The question came out barely above a whisper, though she already knew the answer in her bones.

Sam reached across the table, her warm fingers closing around Alyssa's wrist. "You are a child of Papatūānuku herself. The Earth Mother. The foundation upon which all life stands."

The moment the words left Sam's lips, something cracked open inside Alyssa's chest.

She felt it – *her.* Not as a presence, not as a voice, but as a sensation so profound it stole her breath. The weight of mountains pressing against her spine. The patient crawl of roots through dark soil. The slow churn of tectonic plates, continents dancing their million-year waltz. Rivers of magma flowing like blood through stone veins. Every grain of sand on every beach. Every crystal forming in lightless caverns. Every seed splitting its shell to reach for sun.

*Mother,* something in her whispered, and the earth whispered back.

Alyssa gasped, gripping the edge of the table as the kitchen tilted. Tears spilled down her cheeks – she hadn't even felt them forming. "I can feel her," she choked out. "I can feel *everything.*"

"I know." Sam's voice was gentle, anchoring. "It's overwhelming at first. But this is why your family has always had such power, Alyssa. This is why the gardens grow wild around your house, why the land responds to your moods, why you can feel storms coming in your bones. You're not just connected to the earth – you're *of* it. Part of her. Her descendent, in the truest sense."

The sensation ebbed slowly, like a tide retreating, leaving Alyssa trembling and raw. She became aware of her own heartbeat again, her own small human body sitting in a kitchen chair. But something had changed. She could still feel that connection humming beneath her skin, a live wire she'd never known she'd been holding.

"The Kuraatua have always been the guardians of the Bay," Sam said, her expression growing grave. "We maintain the barriers between worlds, keep the old powers in balance, ensure that what sleeps here stays sleeping. For generations, there was a full circle of us – your grandmother Sylvie, Constance, others you never knew."

"What happened to them?"

"Time." The word fell heavy as a stone. "Age. Death."

"Why is Tū making his move *now*?" Alyssa asked. "If he's been out there all this time—"

"Because he's patient." Sam's voice was grim. "War isn't just about violence—it's about strategy. He's waited generations for the right moment. Let the old guardians age. Let us forget why the barrier mattered." She shook her head. "We got complacent. And now Sylvie's gone, Constance is fading, and there are so few of us left..."

"We've been waiting for the new Kuraatua to rise."

"But it's not enough."

"No. The barrier needs an anchor – someone with a direct connection to the land itself. Someone like your grandmother." Sam's gaze was steady, unflinching. "Someone like you."

Alyssa stared at her hands, half-expecting to see dirt beneath her fingernails, vines crawling up her wrists. She felt the weight of it now – not just expectation, but whakapapa… *heritage*. Thousands of years of power, flowing through blood-lines that traced back to the beginning of the world. The earth itself, asking her to stand.

"I'm not ready," she said, but even as the words left her mouth, she felt the ground beneath her feet pulse once, like a heartbeat, like an answer.

*You are*, it seemed to say. *You always have been.*

Those words rolled around in Alyssa's head, the way they put such a different spin on the whole clay baby tale she'd been telling herself. They sat quietly for a moment, Alyssa processing everything. Finally, she asked, "What happens if I say no? If I refuse to take on Gran's role, and they can't bring her back? Not that I want that. She should be able to rest, or move on, or whatever it is she wants to do."

"Then we find another way," Sam said with a shrug. "We have to. The Bay is our home, our responsibility – all of us, not just you." Sam's conviction was clear. "It would be wonderful if you chose to help. Your power could do so much good. But it has to be your choice."

"I need to think." Alyssa stood, feeling overwhelmed again but in a different way. Not trapped, but standing at a cross-roads, poised to take the next step. "Can I ask you something else?"

"Always."

"Matai's tattoos – they're not just decoration, are they?"

Sam grinned. "No, they're not. Tā moko is sacred art, each line and curve carrying meaning, power, protection. Matai is one of the few who still knows the old ways, who can ink more than skin deep. He offered to work with you. That's quite an honour. He doesn't offer his deeper work to just anyone."

"Why me?"

"Maybe because he sees what I see – someone powerful but untethered, carrying strength but no stories to show for it." Sam walked her to the door. "Think about everything, Alyssa. Take your time. Despite what Vivica believes, the sky isn't falling tomorrow."

"Just slowly crumbling over months?"

"We have time. Not infinite, but enough for you to make a real choice rather than a pressured one."

Alyssa paused at the door, then turned and moved back towards the other woman. "Sam? Thank you. For not giving up on me even when I was being an ass."

"That's what friends do." Sam opened her arms, and Alyssa rushed into them, hugging back just as firmly as Sam did. When they pulled apart, Alyssa felt calmer. More centred than she had in a while.

"Thank you," she said, giving a wave and rushing out the door. Sam waved back as she flipped the sign back to 'open.'

Outside, the Bay stretched bright and innocent under the afternoon sun. But now that she was aware, Alyssa could feel it – the thin places where the barriers were weakening, the spaces where the ordinary world pressed against the hidden one. She'd been blind to it before, wrapped in her own grief and denial. In running from reality.

As she walked back to her house, she found herself thinking about marks of protection, marks of belonging. About stories written in skin and magic carried in blood. About choices that defined not just who you were, but who you chose to become.

Her phone buzzed. A text from Brendan that made her smile, even as her stomach churned: *Confirming 7pm. Evening material polished and ready for presentation.*

# CHAPTER 23

The smell of mothballs hit him, with something sweet rotting underneath. Mrs Nolan's office felt colder than the rest of the building, as if the air conditioning worked over-time just for her. Brendan's skin prickled as he stepped inside.

"What do you want?" he asked. She hadn't even bothered to get up from her desk, and the smug smile on her face did nothing to settle his mood.

After seeing Alyssa last night, seeing how upset she'd been, how torn over being forced into something she didn't want to do, it had hardened his resolve even more. There was no reason for him to follow through on this.

"I wanted to see how you were getting on. Any progress?"

"No. I told you, I'm not doing this job for you." He plonked into the seat across from her and put his boots up on the table. The leather creaked, too loud in the quiet office.

"But you can't leave until you do." She gave a pointed glare at his feet. "And I know you've got other things you need to attend to."

His phone seemed to burn in his pocket. Michael. The last photo Esther had sent – tubes and machines and his nephew's face too pale, too still.

Mrs Nolan stood, her chair scraping against the floor. "Actually, I've been reconsidering." She turned back, and something in her expression had shifted – the smugness replaced by calculation. "The girl – Alyssa. She's not up to it."

"What?"

"I'm no longer convinced she can do the job." Her fingers drummed against the windowsill, a nervous tic he'd never seen before. "She lacks the proper foundation. The connection."

A chill ran through him, deeper than the air conditioning could account for. "So what now?"

"Now?" Her smile returned, sharp as broken glass. "Now you'll do the bigger job I brought you here for."

His stomach clenched. He'd known this was coming, somewhere in the back of his mind. The taste of bile rose in his throat. "You said something about binding a spirit, but..."

"Not just any spirit." Mrs Nolan returned to her desk, wood groaning under her weight as she leaned forward. "Sylvia Whenua's spirit. We need her back to do the work her granddaughter is too proud for."

The words hit him like ice. In his mind, he could already see Alyssa's face – the way her eyes would harden, the betrayal that would twist her features. She'd never forgive him.

His hands clenched involuntarily. Binding a spirit without consent went against his values. The magic felt wrong even thinking about it – like oil coating his skin, suffocating. He had done many things before, but he wasn't that person now. Even when Mrs Nolan had first mentioned it, desperate as he'd been, his whole being had recoiled.

There had to be another way.

"Get to work. Your nephew needs you to get the cure."

He shook his head...that twist in his gut. "For the record, this was not the job you told me it would be. You can't expect me to play by your rules when you're playing by a completely different set."

"You will do as you said you would." She was so bloody certain, throwing the words at him as he left her office.

Brendan couldn't pin down what Mrs Nolan was. Not a witch, or a god-child. Not normal though, it tasted wrong — like meat left too long in the sun. He had no idea how she'd managed to trap him here, or what her motivations were.

But none of that mattered because she was the only one who said she could save Michael's life. And that was more important than Alyssa's feelings. Right?

Except that even the thought of it made his skin crawl, his gut churn; his very soul shiver. He'd done some dark stuff in the past, knew his kind were not well loved, but he didn't want to be that guy anymore. The one who forced the dead to do his bidding.

He was so distracted by his thoughts that he shoulder barged another guy entering the offices. The impact jarred him back to reality.

"Sorry mate," Brendan said.

"No worries," the guy replied with a smile. "I know what she's like. Rattles the old brain up a bit."

Brendan laughed, hollow. "You're not wrong. Good luck."

"Thanks." The guy carried on inside.

Outside, the heat hit him like a wall after the frigid office. He typed a message to his sister as he walked to the car, sweat already beading on his forehead.

*How is he?*

*Not good, he took a slide downhill. I don't think we have long. Please come home.*

Damn.

He couldn't give up just yet. But the weight of what Mrs Nolan wanted – betraying Alyssa – pressed down on him like stones.

# CHAPTER 24

Alyssa was pottering around in the garden out back when a shadow fell across her. The late afternoon sun had warmed the soil, and the earthy scent clung to her clothes. She glanced up, squinting at the early evening sunlight that peeked over Brendan's shoulder, golden rays catching the dust motes that danced between them.

"Hey," he said, putting his hand out and pulling her to her feet. His palm was warm and rough against hers. "You ready for dinner?"

"Depends what you brought with you." She raised an eyebrow, brushing dirt from her knees. "Well?"

"I made kebabs. I hope that's okay." He lifted the bag and the aroma escaped – cumin and charred meat, garlic and something tangy.

"Oh god, that smells good. Let me wash up and we'll eat on the deck, okay?"

"Sure." He nodded approval and followed her to the deck, his footsteps heavy on the wooden boards. She left him to unpack the food as she headed inside. She washed her hands in the sink, the cool water a relief against her sun-warmed skin, scraping dirt from beneath her fingernails before grabbing a couple of beers from the fridge. The bottles were slippery with condensation, and she wiped her hands on her shorts before heading outside.

"Thanks for this. I know I can be a little bossy at times, but I appreciate the food." She gave him a wry grin and tapped her bottle against his – the clink sharp in the evening air – before taking a sip. The beer was crisp and cold, bubbles dancing on her tongue. There was a nervous tension between them, as though they both knew what might happen, but felt like they needed to actually eat and talk before taking anything further.

This whole romantic thing was much easier at twenty.

"Well, you did feed me the other night. This was the least I could do." He slid into one of the loungers, and she took the other, though it felt weird to be like this, so she swung her feet around to face him, her bare toes scuffing the grass.

"All the same. Thanks." She felt like he wasn't really hearing what she was saying, or trying to. What she meant was thank you for coming back and not being a jerk. Thanks for potentially ending the months-long drought she'd been experiencing. Thanks for filling the void that Kelly had left behind. But, really, they didn't know each other nearly well enough for that kind of talk. She might have offloaded all of her family secrets on him, but the thoughts she was having were somehow more vulnerable than all of that.

Alyssa grabbed her kebab and peeled back the tinfoil. The scent hit her full force – lamb and spices making her salivate. She closed her eyes and moaned a little. There was no avoiding it. "I didn't even know they had kebabs here. It's not a very big place. Where did you find this?"

Brendan tapped his nose and winked. "I have my sources."

"Spill," she said.

"I made them," he said with a grin. "So if you want more, you'll just have to keep me around." He took a big bite of his kebab, sauce dripping onto his fingers.

Alyssa's stomach grumbled – a hollow, demanding sound – and she bit into hers. The taste was divine, the lamb tender and juicy, the satay sauce coating her tongue with peanut and chili. She bit off another chunk, so big it scraped against the roof of her mouth and chafed her throat as it went down, but she didn't care, she just wanted more.

"So, what if I'd been allergic to peanuts?" she asked, once she'd eaten half of it and satisfied the bulk of her hunger. Her fingers were sticky with sauce, and she licked them clean.

"I saw the peanut butter in your fridge when I was here the other day. Figured it was a safe bet." He shrugged. "Is it?"

"Yes, though right now I'd be happy to eat just about anything. I didn't realise it until now but somehow I totally missed lunch."

"Lucky I made the big size then."

"I don't care what other women might have told you, but size does matter and bigger is always better." The words tumbled out before she could consider them. Her throat constricted and the food stuck, making her cough. Heat crept up her neck, her cheeks burning. She swallowed hard and took a swig of beer, the cold liquid a relief.

"You don't say?"

Not trusting herself to look him in the eye, Alyssa simply nodded and took another bite. The meat was cooling now, the fat congealing slightly.

"I'll file that away for later use then." He chuckled and took a swig of his beer, his Adam's apple bobbing.

"So, how did that work disaster pan out? Things okay?"

Alyssa decided that work was probably a much safer line of conversation for now. Though she could practically feel the air chilling at her words. Brendan's whole being seemed to shudder and twitch, tendrils of magic tinged with shadows leaking from him.

"Yes, and no. For now. I think. Still a few complications, but I have to make some progress sooner rather than later." He took another bite of food, as if it would stop him from saying more, or he needed time to consider his words.

"Sounds tough, and important?" Alyssa raised an eyebrow and assessed his expression. There was more going on here than she wanted to consider, and the food felt heavy in her stomach. Why would she not have just one flirty night with a cute guy who seemed interested in her? She didn't want to think about motivations or manipulations. She didn't want to think at all, just feel something other than pain and guilt and grief.

"Are you fishing for answers about what I'm doing here?" His voice was laced with regret, and he hadn't even told her.

Alyssa couldn't help but think about the fact that Brendan was new in town. And he worked for Mrs Nolan in some capacity. And there was meant to be a necromancer here. A chill ran down her spine despite the warm evening air, goosebumps rising on her arms. She shivered, doing her very best to pretend that Brendan couldn't be that guy.

"Maybe?" She raised an eyebrow and tried to sound her normal, playful self, but her voice came out tight, strained. "I don't really want to talk about that right now though" She turned her attention back to the food, the wrapper now threatening to tear, grease pooling at the bottom. She picked out a piece of cool meat and dangled it between her fingers, watching as Socks stalked across the grass under Brendan's lounger and snatched it from her hand before bolting. Buttons watched with a glare, but whether he was scowling about Socks eating real food, or Alyssa's train of thought, she couldn't be sure.

She just wanted to distract herself. To enjoy something. To enjoy him. Why was this not working the way she wanted it to?

"Well, work is kind of boring." He paused, as if considering his next move, his jaw working as he chewed. Then, because of course he was going to, he asked, "What happened with Kelly? You two seemed close, and then you had that fight and I thought you'd made up, then all of a sudden she's gone and you're not talking about it."

"I'm still not talking about it," Alyssa said, her words sharp, bitter. At least, not with him. She forced her shoulders to drop, and softened her tone. "All I'm willing to say is that she betrayed my trust. I don't forgive that easily." She looked him in the eyes then, searching for something – guilt, recognition that she wasn't just talking about Kelly, anything – but his expression didn't waver. His throat bobbed as he swallowed hard though.

"People always have a reason for doing what they do." He kept his voice kind, considering, full of implied meaning, as though he was trying to make sure she knew that he had reasons too, for when he inevitably smacked her with the true reason for his presence here in the Bay. "Did she tell you hers?"

Alyssa snorted, an ugly sound that cracked between them. "No. I wasn't interested in hearing it. At least, not right now. I have my reasons." She'd hoped that would end the conversation, but he tilted his head to the side, gaze quizzical, brow creased in what almost looked like concern.

"Do you do that much?"

"Excuse me?" She sat up straight, her spine rigid,

discarding the rest of her kebab on the table between them. It landed with a wet thud.

"Not hear people out." Brendan shrugged, as though he wasn't trying to be offensive, but she could feel the heat rising in her chest, anger prickling under her skin. "I'm just curious. I want to understand you."

How dare he? She'd wanted him to deliver on his promise of more kisses, more heat, but here he was trying to have some deep and meaningful conversation about her personal deficits. She knew she had issues, but so did everyone. He had no right to call them out this bluntly.

Alyssa knew what they weren't going to be doing tonight. That was for sure.

"Sometimes people don't deserve to be heard out. And you don't know me or Kelly well enough to be taking her side on this." She grabbed her beer – the bottle was warm now, the label peeling – and got up, her chair scraping against the ground. She dumped her rubbish in the outside bin, the metal lid clanging shut, and headed back to the kitchen, the next words he spoke lost to the noise in her head.

She didn't need this shit. This was meant to be a romantic evening, but it certainly wasn't panning out like that. Who was he to question her like that?

There was a sour taste at the back of her throat though, bile mixing with the lingering spices, because he was right. She didn't wait to hear the reasons why. She never let anyone explain themselves. It was more than a little uncomfortable to have the guy she'd hoped would take her to bed call her out on one of her biggest flaws. Wasn't that stuff meant to happen six months down the track, when things were beginning to sour?

She shrieked as a hand grasped her shoulder – warm, firm, unexpected. She spun to find that Brendan had followed her, his footsteps silent on the kitchen tiles. "Seriously, don't creep up on people. You're lucky I didn't punch you in the nuts."

"Thanks for holding back." He grinned at her, but the smile didn't reach his eyes. His face grew serious, shadows pooling in the hollows of his cheeks. "I'm sorry, really. I wasn't meaning to be a jerk, but I get how it came across. You're allowed to be mad at Kelly, or anyone you want to."

"Then why did you say it?" She put her hands on her hips, the fabric of her shorts rough under her palms, wishing she was a little taller, or a little broader. He dwarfed her, his presence filling the small kitchen, and for a change, that bothered her.

"I guess..." He scrubbed a hand across his chin, the rasp of stubble audible in the quiet room. "I just wanted to know what happened."

"If you must know, I just found out that she'd been sneaking around with my ex, before we'd even broken up. They've moved in together. He told me it was because I couldn't have babies, but now... Well, who the hell knows. That was probably just a lame ass excuse." The words tasted bitter, like ash on her tongue.

Brendan was silent for a full minute, the kitchen clock ticking loudly above them. The pained expression on his face – his brow furrowed, lips pressed thin – said everything. "That was cruel of him. He should never have made you question your validity as a woman. And no, she shouldn't have done that to you either. It was a shitty thing to do."

"And friends shouldn't do shitty things."

"God, if only life was that simple hey?" His lips spread and cracked into a half grin, revealing the slight gap between his front teeth. "People are assholes, even when they aren't trying to be." He gave a little shrug, his shirt rustling with the movement.

"And you?" she asked, her heart thumping against her ribs, a hummingbird trapped in a cage, waiting for him to give her the answer. If he wasn't going to come clean on his own, then it was time she asked some hard questions herself.

"Huh?" He frowned.

"Are you an asshole? Are you trying to be, or is it just on accident?"

# CHAPTER 25

Brendan stood in shock, his mouth suddenly dry. She knew about him. Knew something, anyway. That much was obvious by the glare in her eyes – sharp as broken glass – and the death grip she had on her bare upper arms, firmly crossed over her chest. Her knuckles had gone white with the pressure.

"I don't want to be an asshole. I'm certainly not trying to be," he said, choosing his words carefully, each one feeling heavy on his tongue.

"What are you doing in town? What kind of 'contract' are you here for?" Her voice was tight, controlled, but he could hear the tremor underneath.

She wasn't going to budge, her feet were planted firmly on the kitchen tiles, and if their prior conversation was anything to go by, there was no point lying to her. The air between them crackled with tension. He liked Alyssa and if he ever wanted a chance with her he was going to have to be straight.

"Can we sit down?" he asked, feeling like his legs might

give out on him, like he needed some kind of comfort for this conversation. A cushion to hug, perhaps?

"No."

Brendan nodded. "I got a call from Mrs Nolan, who wanted to use my special skills to help secure the barrier here. She didn't give me the details, but she told me that in return she would give me a powerful healing potion for my nephew. He's dying." The last words scraped his throat raw.

The tension leaked from her face like air from a punctured tire, her arms dropping to her sides with a soft rustle of fabric. "Not an asshole." The words tumbled out in a whisper, barely audible over the hum of the refrigerator.

"So you know why I'm here then?" He reached out to her, his hand trembling slightly in the air, and was thankful when she reached back, twining their fingers together. Their grasp was warm, slightly sticky from the evening heat. "I swear, I didn't know it was you when I met you. In fact, all she told me was that the town witch had recently died, and they needed someone to bring her back."

"Gran?" Her eyes widened, the blue darkening like storm clouds, and then dulled. "You know, I bet she'd have said that was okay. She loved it here."

"And what would you have said?" He traced his fingers up her arm, feeling the fine hairs rise under his touch, trying to keep her grounded. "It wasn't until I got here that she told me I would have to convince you to take your Grandmother's place. That wasn't what I agreed to, but she's trapped me here some-how. I can't leave the Bay until I've completed my task, and the longer I'm gone, the closer Michael gets to death."

"He's really dying?" She looked into his eyes, searching, and hers welled with unshed tears that caught the kitchen light. She pulled away from him, her movement sharp, and swiped at her eyes with the back of her hand. "I can't do anything right, did you know that? I told her I wasn't interested, and she dragged you into this as well. And Michael." She turned back to him, her breath hitching. "How old is he?"

"Six." The word felt like a stone in his mouth.

"So young." Grief lined her face, etching new shadows. "And unless I do this, he's going to die, and it will be all my fault." She buried her face in her hands, her shoulders shaking. "Oh god."

"No. No, Alyssa. The men in our family are cursed. If he passes it's not your fault." He said the words, wanted to believe them, but knowing she was the thing between Michael's life or death made them taste like lies. He swallowed hard, his throat clicking, and then pulled her hands free. They were wet with tears, salt stinging where her nails had dug into his skin. "I don't want to make you do something you don't want to do. That was never my intention. Do you believe that?"

She let out a soft sob that seemed to come from deep in her chest, her bottom lip quivering as she nodded.

"Good. Good. That's something we can work with, right? I'm sorry I didn't tell you why I was here straight away. I wasn't sure what to say, and you were so beautiful and so nice."

Her lips twitched and broke into a smile, a laugh tumbling out – watery but genuine. "Nice? I slapped you in the face!"

"You were just being a good neighbour." He shrugged, the movement pulling at his shirt where sweat had made it stick to his back. "And you did bring me pikelets to apologise."

"I did." She nodded, though the sad look in her eyes hadn't completely dispersed, hovering like morning mist.

"I understand if you don't want there to be anything between us. It's awkward, and awful, and I'd hate for you to think I was only trying to get you into bed because I wanted to manipulate you." The words left a bitter aftertaste.

"Clearly that's your plan, you're just terrible at being the bad guy because you told me first!" She smacked him playfully on the arm, the contact sharp but not unpleasant. "You should know better than that."

"I should," he agreed, relief warming his chest.

She stepped forward and wrapped her arms around him, her body pressing against his, warm and solid. He was so shocked that for a second he didn't respond, his arms hanging uselessly at his sides. But when he folded her in his embrace, it felt good – right. She fit against him perfectly, her head tucked under his chin. He could smell her shampoo, something floral mixed with the lingering scent of garden soil. He squeezed her tightly, feeling her ribs expand with each breath, and almost missed the words whispered against his chest, muffled by his shirt.

"You can bring Gran back?"

He stiffened, his muscles going rigid, and drew back slightly, struggling to find the right words. They stuck in his throat like thorns. "I can, but is that what you really want? She'd be like a ghost, powerful, but bound forever to the Bay."

Alyssa's face paled, the colour draining away like water down a sink, and she shook her head so violently her hair whipped across her face. "No, not like that. That's what they did to Magnus and he hated it. I mean, in some weird way it would be good payback for what my family did to him, but I can't do that, not to Gran."

His shoulders slumped, the weight of disappointment settling on them like lead. He'd thought that maybe this was their way out of the problem, but if it wasn't what she wanted, he had to respect that. "Why don't we ask her?" he suggested, the idea forming as he spoke. "We could do that séance, and, like I said, I know a thing or two about them." He quirked an eyebrow at her, trying for levity. She turned, her bare feet squeaking slightly on the tiles as she walked a few steps away before returning, pacing like a caged animal.

"And you won't influence her?"

He frowned, hurt prickling under his skin. "If I haven't shown by now that my intentions are actually above board, nothing I say here is going to change that. You either believe me, or you don't."

Her pause stretched out, each second feeling like an eternity. The kitchen clock ticked loudly, marking time. He dropped his arms, defeat washing over him, and shook his head, but she reached out and grasped his shoulder, her grip surprisingly tight, fingers digging in. "I do. I do. I'm sorry, it's just that I've been lied to so much. Trusting isn't the easiest thing for me."

"It's hard for everyone. Especially those of us with magic." The admission came easier than he expected.

"I don't have any control over my magic though." Her voice was flat, final.

"You keep saying that, but if you'd just shut up you'd figure out that you do. It's inside you and no amount of verbal denial will change that." He wanted to shake her, make her see. The words came out harsher than intended. Until he saw the look on her face – jaw clenched, eyes narrowing to slits.

Her jaw was tight, the muscles visibly working, and she ground the words out between her teeth. "Never tell me to shut up again. Even if your point is valid." He could feel her magic rising with her emotion, and he had to wonder whether she could feel it too. How she could possibly deny that it ran strong within her veins.

Brendan swallowed hard, his Adam's apple bobbing. "Okay." He licked his lips, suddenly aware of how dry they were, wishing he had another beer, or really, anything to distract himself. The cold bottle in his hand, condensation dripping... but no, that was earlier. Maybe it wasn't a good idea to get her to embrace her magic. She'd be a fierce opponent if ever crossed. Not that he intended to. He hoped she could see that, because he really meant it. As much as he wanted to save Michael, he wouldn't do it at the cost of enslaving Alyssa to the Bay, or her dear old dead Gran.

"So, ah, when do you want to do this?" he asked, his voice cracking slightly on the last word.

She exhaled, the sound long and weary, and the tension seemed to drop from her body like a discarded coat. "Not now. Not tonight. I need to think." She shook her head, hair sway-ing. "I'm really sorry, I know that time is important here and you need me to hurry up and become all magical so that I can boost the barrier and you can skedaddle back home with the cure. But tonight has given me a lot of information to take in, and I don't know what to make of it. I just... I need to clear my head. And I'm sorry if that came out kind of bitchy but I'm just being honest here. And we can be honest. Right?"

"We can. Yeah." Though he'd be lying if he said he wasn't a little disappointed. The feeling sat heavy in his stomach, mixing uncomfortably with the remains of his dinner. He could tell that she wanted to help but there was something holding her back. He had to play his cards right or she was going to shut down on him and he'd never save Michael, let alone get to know her any better than right now. And he wanted that too. Oh, how he wanted it.

With that thought he took the three steps between them – his footsteps loud in the quiet kitchen – and drew her into his arms, planting a gentle kiss on her forehead. Her skin was so soft, salt kissed from the sea breeze. He wanted more, so much more, but now wasn't the right time. He wasn't about to be one of those guys who cashed in on a vulnerable chick. "I'll come back in the morning, okay?"

"Yeah." She gave him a tired smile that didn't quite reach her eyes and brushed a soft kiss on his cheek – her lips barely grazing his skin, leaving a warm impression – before turning away, the scent of her lingering. Flowers and earth and something uniquely Alyssa that made his chest ache.

# CHAPTER 26

She waited until she heard him close the front door behind him before locking it, the deadbolt clicking home with a satisfying thunk. Her hands were still shaking as she rushed to do the same to the back door, checking the handle twice. She hadn't lied when she'd said it was too much to take in for one night, but there was something she needed to do. Right now. Before she lost the nerve.

Alyssa moved to the lounge, her bare feet silent on the cool floorboards. The room still smelled faintly of kebabs and beer from earlier. She pulled the curtains closed, shutting out the world, and stood in the centre of the room. Her heart hammered against her ribs as she took a deep breath.

"Magnus?" Her voice came out smaller than intended, barely disturbing the heavy air. She cleared her throat and tried again, stronger this time. "Magnus, I need to talk to you."

The temperature dropped instantly, goosebumps racing up her arms. A familiar shimmer appeared in the corner of her vision.

"You rang?" His voice held that same dry amusement she'd come to expect.

She spun to face him properly, relief flooding through her. "Thank god you're here. I wasn't sure if – "

"If I'd come?" He materialized more fully, his form clearer than it had been in weeks. "You're getting better at this, you know. Your call was quite strong."

"Yeah, well, having a necromancer hanging around probably helps." The words tasted bitter. "Brendan – he makes the barrier thinner, doesn't he? That's what you said before. Are you talking about the one around the Bay, or between living and dead?"

"Between living and dead. That male of yours has quite the effect on the veil. Your house is becoming a thoroughfare for the departed." Magnus drifted closer, and she could almost feel the chill radiating from him. Buttons walked into the room and she could practically hear his meow of agreement with the Viking ghost.

"He's not my – " She stopped, heat creeping up her neck. "Never mind. Magnus, I need your help. They want Gran to be like you were, contained here, powering the barrier for the Bay. And Brendan... his nephew is dying. A six-year-old kid." Her throat constricted around the words. "If I don't do this, if I don't become the witch they need, that little boy dies."

Magnus studied her, his translucent features serious for once. "And this troubles you."

"Of course it troubles me!" She paced now, unable to stand still. The floor creaked under her weight. "But I can't do to Gran what they did to you. I can't trap her here. Not after seeing what it did to you, how much you hated it." She paused, meeting his gaze. "The women in my family, they took what they wanted regardless of the consequences. One of them literally created a child from the earth itself. What's stopping me from becoming like them?"

"Ah." Magnus's form solidified further, as if he was focusing all his energy on being present. "That's what truly frightens you. What you keep returning to, running from. Not the magic itself, but what you might do with it."

"Yes." The admission came out as a whisper. "I'm terrified I'll become like them. That I'll cross lines I can't come back from. Look at what June did. Look at what happened to her. And part of me..." She swallowed hard. "Part of me thought she deserved it."

"She did harm you, and she manipulated Sylvie, contributed to both her death, and that of Buttons," Magnus pointed out. "Wanting justice isn't the same as being cruel."

"But where's the line?" Alyssa's hands clenched into fists. "How do I know when I've gone too far?"

Magnus was quiet for a long moment, his form flickering slightly. When he spoke, his voice was gentler than she'd ever heard it. "Your fear will protect you, Alyssa. The very fact that you're asking these questions shows you're not like them. Your ancestors took without asking, acted without conscience. You're sitting here, agonizing over the right path. That's the difference."

She sank onto the couch, suddenly exhausted. The cushions still held warmth from the day, and it wasn't long before Socks clawed his way up and onto her lap. Absently she stroked his fur, the life in his body a balm. "But what if I change? What if the power corrupts me?"

"Then you'll have people to pull you back." Magnus moved closer, and she could have sworn she felt something like a hand on her shoulder, though that was impossible. "That necromancer of yours, for one. He seems the stubborn type."

Despite everything, she found herself almost smiling. "He told me to shut up earlier. Can you believe that?" She shook her head in surprise at that whole conversation. Had any man stood up to her the way he did? And she had put up boundaries too, told him what she wasn't okay with.

"Shocking." Magnus's tone was bone dry. "Though I notice you didn't send him away permanently."

"No, I didn't." She rubbed her face, feeling the grit of dried tears. "Magnus, what do I do? How do I save this kid without destroying myself or enslaving Gran?"

"Perhaps," he said slowly, "the answer isn't choosing between extremes. Perhaps there's another way."

"Like what?"

"That is for you to decide. The barriers are thinning," Magnus observed. "Your power is growing, whether you embrace it or not. The question is: will you learn to control it, or let fear control you?"

"I don't know." She kept stroking Socks, amused when Buttons leapt onto the couch as well and settled near them. "I just don't know."

"Then perhaps it's time to talk to someone who might." Magnus began to fade. "Your mother, perhaps?"

Alyssa's stomach clenched. "How did you –"

"I'm a ghost, not an idiot. You were going to the other day and then found yet another excuse not to." He was barely visible now. "Call her, Alyssa. Some truths can only come from family."

"Magnus, wait – "

But he was gone, leaving only Socks and Buttons and a lingering chill in the air. The ghost cat looked up at her with those familiar green eyes, translucent but somehow still full of life.

"Well," she said to the cats, living and dead, "I guess I'm making that call."

Her phone felt like lead in her hand as she scrolled to her mother's number. The screen's blue light was harsh in the dim room. The phone rang three times before her mother picked up.

"My god, I thought you'd dropped off the face of the planet or something," her mother quipped. "Then again, I guess you kind of did, down there in the Bay."

Alyssa could hear the telltale slosh of liquid against glass through the phone, ice cubes clinking. Naturally, her mother was drinking. It was where Alyssa had picked up the habit.

"Look, I know you don't like it here and I know you and Gran had your differences."

Her mother snorted, the sound sharp through the speaker.

"I know you were keeping me away from Gran because you were protecting me. I get that, and, you know, I'm kind of grateful."

The silence stretched out like taffy, thick and uncomfortable. Even the ever-present background noise of her mother's house – TV, dishwasher, life – seemed to pause.

"You are?" Her mother's voice shook, just a little. The ice clinked again, nervously. In their family there was honesty, and then there was honesty, and the second kind almost never showed itself.

"Yeah. I am. I can see why you wouldn't want me to embrace the family magic and all, but I'm a bit out of my depth down here and I need to talk to you about it." Alyssa took a sip of water, the glass trembling against her lips. "They want my help down here, doing what Gran was. Pitching in to help the town out. And I kind of want to help them, but Mum, I'm scared." Her voice cracked on the last word.

"Oh honey, I'm sorry. It's my fault for keeping you away, for not teaching you a single thing. You can feel the pull, can't you? I knew you would. The Bay has a way about it. It's just not what I wanted for myself." Her mother's voice was softer now, the sharp edges worn down, and she was speaking as though she had to get all the words out or swallow them for another decade.

"And that's why you won't come here, right?"

Another pause, another clink of ice. "Yeah. It is."

"Will you still love me if I do it?" The question came out small, childlike.

Her mother laughed, but it was warm, not mocking. "I didn't think that was important to you."

"Mum! Of course it is. I mean, I know we've got our differences but you're my mother."

"That's right. I am your mother, and nothing would ever stop me from loving you. Even if you become a witch, raise the dead, whatever it is that takes your fancy."

"You're not taking this seriously."

"I don't think you're taking it seriously, actually. I've always been here for you, done my best to protect you, but you're an adult now. You have to make your own decisions and take responsibility for them. My love is unconditional, darling. I will even come and visit you, if that will help ease your mind. Now, go and do what you need to do."

The line went dead. Alyssa stared at the phone, her mother's words echoing in the quiet room. She'd never truly doubted her mother's love, but she'd never stopped to think that her actions might make her mother believe it didn't matter.

A cold sensation brushed against her ankle. Buttons was there, translucent whiskers twitching.

She drained her wine glass, the last drops bitter on her tongue, and headed for bed. The house felt less empty now, somehow. Between Socks, Magnus, Buttons's ghostly presence, and her mother's unexpected blessing, maybe – just maybe – she could figure out what came next.

# CHAPTER 27

He couldn't sleep. The moon, all but full, pulled at his senses even through the blackout curtains, making his skin feel too tight, his bones ache with restlessness. The sheets were damp with sweat, twisted around his legs. The tension in his body wasn't just because of Alyssa either. He needed to do something, to move forward and make some kind of progress because while he didn't want to pressure Alyssa, didn't want to force her Gran to do anything, he didn't want to see his nephew die either. And nothing he had found in June's house had felt like a thing that could save his life.

Brendan grabbed his coat from the hook by the door, the leather cool against his fevered skin, and headed out, not bothering to lock it behind him. June had set so many protections on the place that no one was going to get in if they had even the slightest of ill intentions. That woman's paranoia came in handy occasionally.

He knew the urupā was close enough to walk. The town was all that big, and while he didn't need a gravesite in order to call up Alyssa's Gran, he needed to get out of the house and well away from the girl he fancied. There was no way he needed her stumbling in on this.

But hell, what was he even going to say? He shook his head free of that question and focused on the cool night air on his skin. It carried the scent of jasmine from someone's garden, mixed with the salt tang from the bay. Autumn was going to come on soon enough – he could smell it in the crispness, feel it in the way the breeze had teeth. It was his favourite season, that changeover from the vibrancy of summer to the quiet introversion of winter. Fairly fitting, really, being that his magic set him between life and death. He was the autumn of magical folk.

Not the winter. Not like some people would make him out to be. Sure, he'd done some dodgy stuff in the past, but who hadn't? Everyone is young once, and he knew from experience that old age didn't always change a person. June was a good example of that. At least he'd sorted himself out, pulled back from the dark side and made good with his magic. He was torn between wanting to tell Alyssa that, needing her to believe he was a good guy, and just wanting her to see it for herself. Because he was good, now. His history didn't change that, in fact it had made him who he was today.

The gates to the urupā were closed and there was a chain looped between them, padlock securely in place. The metal was cold and rough with rust under his palm as he tested it. It was a token gesture though because the fence was only waist high. He hopped over, the impact jarring up through his knees, and wiped the crumbling brick remnants from his hands onto his pants, leaving dusty streaks. Moonlight flooded the little graveyard, turning everything silver-blue, casting long shadows that seemed to reach for him. Everywhere, shades and spirits pushed in, begging him to notice them, trailing ghostly fingers through his hair for attention. He ignored them all, increasing the strength of his barriers as he meandered past broken and neglected plots, weeds brushing against his ankles with whispers, until he reached the area where things were still pristine and new. The grass here was clipped short, smelling of recent mowing, and it was there that he found the grave of Sylvia Whenua.

"Right then," he muttered to himself, rubbing his hands together. They tingled with anticipation – or maybe fear. He closed his eyes, drawing on the moonlight that felt like cool water on his skin, the life around him pulsing in the earth beneath his feet. The cemetery was never truly quiet – insects chirped, something small rustled in the bushes, and beneath it all, the echo of lives once lived. He focused on the grave before him and everything he knew of the woman. Alyssa kept tugging at his thoughts, her laugh, the way she'd felt in his arms, but he had a feeling that wouldn't detract. He didn't even need to speak the words out loud to call Sylvie; he could feel her nearing, like pressure building before a storm, drawn to the living world from her rest.

"I was wondering if someone would drag me back." Sylvie spoke with a weary voice, her form solidifying before him like mist condensing. Her grey hair was tied in a bun, face lined with age, though her eyes were the same piercing shade of blue as Alyssa's. The air around her dropped several degrees, making his breath fog. "So, what's going on?"

Brendan chuckled, though it came out nervous. Sylvie had that same straight forward attitude as Alyssa did. "We've got a bit of a problem. I'm not calling you back permanently, but I wanted to have a chat."

She eyed him up as if gauging whether he was worth her time, her gaze sharp enough to cut, before shaking her head and tutting. The sound was exactly like Alyssa's. "Out with it then. I was rather enjoying the peace and quiet."

"Mrs Nolan contracted me to come and bring you back to protect the Bay, in the event that Alyssa doesn't step into your position."

"What, the ghost wasn't enough to tempt her into claiming her magic? I was sure that would do the trick. She's contained it at least, hasn't she?" Sylvie's look of consternation bore into him.

"Ah, no. She struck a deal with him and set him free."

"She did what?" Sylvie's form flared brighter, and the temperature plummeted further. Frost began forming on the grass around them. "That ghost was a primary power source for our family, we need him."

"Well, we can't do anything about that," he said. "What is done, is done. She's still resistant to the idea of embracing her magic and I wanted to check in with you and see if you're willing to become a fixture of the town." Before the words had even left his lips, he knew what her response would be.

"I bled for this town," Sylvie hissed, leaning towards him. The icy chill of her power brushed against his skin like frozen knives, making him shiver despite his coat. "I gave my time, and my life for it, and I'm not going to be shackled. It's time for Alyssa to take her place as the head of the family. Time for her to accept her birth-right. She was born of the Bay."

Brendan froze, the words clanging against other snippets of conversation in his head like church bells. His mouth went dry. "She was made of this place, wasn't she? Like the first woman made her baby from the Bay all those years ago."

"You know about that?" Sylvie's brow furrowed, creating deeper shadows in her ghostly face. "Did Nolan tell you?"

"No, but Alyssa knows, and let me tell you, she wasn't pleased to find out that the stories were true. Knowing how the women in your family have manipulated others has put her off accepting what she is."

"It's not like that though," Sylvie uttered, shaking her head in disbelief. Her form flickered like a candle in the wind. "I need to see her, I need to speak to her. Explain. Once she knows the truth, she'll understand, she'll want this."

Brendan shook his head, not so sure of that. The leather of his coat creaked as he crossed his arms. Alyssa was many things, but she wasn't overly forgiving, nor was she inclined to listen to the full story. Yet, she'd heard him out, and they were okay. Weren't they? Maybe she'd listen to her Gran. "Tell me. And then I'll figure out what to do."

"No, this is about family. And you're not family." Her voice had gone cold, colder than her ghostly chill.

"Not yet, but I plan on being around for a while. Alyssa and I are... Well, we're something. I care about her, and I'm not going to let you do anything more to hurt her. Intentionally, or not." His hands clenched into fists, nails biting into his palms.

Sylvie nodded, a slight smile turning her lips up at the corners. "Good. It's about time she met someone, and you seem like you might have the steady hand required to deal with her. The women in our family aren't known for their level-headedness."

"Tell me." He pushed some of his magic into his words, not wanting to force her, just encourage her to proceed.

"Fine, fine." She rolled her eyes, but the smile was still there, making her look younger despite her ghostly state. "When the first of our line came to help with the settlement, she fell in love with the land, and the land fell in love with her. Papatūānuku herself, I speak of. She could see something in our blood, something she respected, and knew that in future times it might come down to the colour of your skin as to whether you could get things done. So she gifted a child to my ancestor. And she grew that child and birthed it, loved it. And when it was her time, she too accepted a child from Papatūānuku."

"Alyssa is a child of Papatūānuku too. Isn't she?" Brendan's brain hurt just thinking about it, a physical ache behind his eyes. That he had almost been prepared to manipulate and control the child of a goddess. Did Mrs Nolan know? His stomach churned.

Sylvie nodded. "She is."

"Alyssa is infertile. Did you know that?" The words tasted like ash.

Sylvie let out a sharp laugh that echoed off the headstones. "We're all infertile. At least until after the goddess blesses us. If it weren't for her longing to be a mother, Bethany would never have conceived a god-child. Alyssa would never have been born."

"Well. Shit." Brendan plonked down hard, felt the dampness of the grass seep through his jeans immediately, cold and clammy against his skin. The earth beneath him felt alive, pulsing with something ancient. "How am I meant to tell Alyssa?"

Sylvie shrugged and Brendan surged to his feet, grass stains on his knees. Willing her form more solid, he grasped her by the shoulder – his hand tingling with cold fire where it made contact. "Don't you shrug. You all just play god with the lives of others. Maybe she's right and she shouldn't do this thing. Don't you care?" He released her, pushing her backwards and letting her form fade out like smoke.

"I do care." Her words were quiet now, filled with pain that resonated in the air between them. "But this is just the way it's always been. We have our duty. We trade our magic for the things we want, and as long as we're not hurting anyone – "

"She's hurting. And you did this. You, and everyone before you." He shook his head and turned away, the gravel crunching under his feet. He cut the connection with Sylvie, feeling the severing like a snapped guitar string, and sent her from this place. The temperature immediately began to rise, the frost melting into dewdrops.

He stood alone among the graves, the moon watching like an accusing eye, not in the least bit comforted by what he'd found out here. His jeans were soaked through at the knees, his hands still trembling from touching a ghost. How the hell was he meant to broach this topic with Alyssa – and on the other hand, was there any way he could not tell her and call himself a decent man?

The walk back seemed longer, each step heavier than the last.

Alyssa was pouring her coffee when there was a knock on the door. The hot liquid splashed over the rim, scalding her thumb. She'd had her phone turned off for days now so it could be anyone – most likely someone she didn't want to see – and she contemplated whether to just ignore it entirely and pretend she wasn't at home.

Hadn't she done that for long enough though? The others were right; she ignored things until it was too late. Pretended that the truth wasn't real. Glossed over the truth that was right in front of her eyes.

She padded barefoot down the hallway, the wooden floorboards cool against her skin, each creak announcing her presence. Her fingers paused before clasping the handle, the metal cold under her palm, and pulled the door open. For a moment she didn't register the fact that there was no one there.

But not nothing. Deja-vu prickled down her spine.

This time it was no strange relic, but the kitten. Socks sat on the front door step, though there was no way he could have made that knock himself. Looking both ways, frowning, Alyssa couldn't spot anyone there, but someone had returned her very new cat to her, despite the fact that she'd had no idea he was out the front. He vibrated against her body as she closed the door, his rumbling purr warming something in her chest.

Buttons appeared further down the hall, slightly hazy as though he wasn't sure whether he wanted to be acquainted with the latest addition to the house. The air around him seemed cooler, charged with static.

"Oh he's just a kitten, Buttons. Seriously. And you're a ghost. If anyone is going to be afraid it should be him."

She gave Socks a kiss on the forehead – he smelled like milk and something indefinably kitten-ish – before plonking him down on the ground. Socks instantly skittered forward, his claws clicking on the floorboards, crashing through the spot where Buttons had been just a second ago. He turned around, tail puffed, as if trying to see where the other cat had disappeared to, and Alyssa laughed.

"Well this should be entertaining at least." She returned to the kitchen to finish making her coffee, the bitter aroma grounding her as she tried to push aside thoughts of Kelly, though she reached for her phone with a sigh and turned it on. The screen lit up with a cascade of notifications: twenty-five missed calls, ten voicemails, and a gazillion text messages. The phone vibrated continuously as they loaded. Alyssa flicked through the notifications, her stomach tightening with each Kelly-related one, pausing when she saw one from Sam and opening it.

*Still waiting to hear from you. Let me know when a good time to talk is.*

Oh yeah.

There were more important things at stake than the fact that her best friend had shacked up with her ex. Like witchcraft and keeping the Bay safe. And figuring out what to do about Mrs Nolan.

And then it hit her like cold water. If she took on Gran's mantle and helped boost the barriers around the Bay, Kelly would never be able to come near her again if that's what she chose.

And she'd be just as bad as everyone else in her family.

*Shit.*

One way or another, she was going to have to resolve their issues, because if she didn't then she'd always know there was a chance she had done magic for the wrong reason. It was okay to be selfish sometimes, but not like this. Not with her magic.

Her magic. Yes, a part of her had already claimed it. Already made that decision. The knowledge sat heavy in her chest, like swallowing a stone. Now she had to go out and make it happen for real.

But first... first she needed to face something else.

The glass-blowing studio sat at the edge of town, where the tourist shops gave way to working studios. Alyssa's hands trembled on the steering wheel as she parked. She'd driven past this place a dozen times since arriving in the Bay, never quite able to stop. The memory of flame and screaming still echoed whenever she thought of Miri.

Through the open doors, she could see the orange glow of the furnace, hear the roar of the flame. The heat hit her as soon as she stepped out of the car, bringing with it the sharp smell of hot glass and propane.

Miri stood at the bench, turning a glowing bubble of molten glass on the end of a long metal pipe. Her movements were fluid, practiced, the pipe spinning constantly to keep the glass from sagging. She wore safety glasses and a leather apron, her arms bare despite the heat. The scars were visible even from the doorway – pale lines tracing up her left arm like a river delta.

Alyssa forced herself forward, gravel crunching under her feet. The heat intensified with each step, making her skin prickle with memory. Thirteen years old, playing with magic she didn't understand, flames leaping from her hands to catch Miri's sleeve...

"Just a sec," Miri called without looking up. She shaped the glass with wooden paddles soaked in water, steam hissing up. The piece was beautiful – a vase with swirls of blue and green trapped in clear glass, like a captured ocean. "Have to get this into the annealer while it's hot."

Alyssa watched, mesmerized despite her nerves, as Miri carried the piece to a large oven and carefully placed it inside. The movements were careful but confident, no hesitation despite working with something that could shatter or burn.

When Miri turned and pulled off her safety glasses, her face broke into a genuine smile that made Alyssa's chest tight. "Alyssa? Oh my god, is that really you?"

"Hi, Miri." The words came out strangled.

"Come here!" Miri crossed the space between them, pulling Alyssa into a hug that smelled of smoke and something sweet – maybe beeswax. Her arms were strong, solid. Real. "I can't believe you're here. I heard you were back in town but..."

"I should have come sooner." Alyssa pulled back, forcing herself to look at the scars properly. They were silver-white against Miri's tanned skin, following the curves of her arm in an almost artistic pattern. "I'm so sorry. About everything. About what I did – "

"Hey." Miri's voice was gentle but firm. "That's all in the past. We were kids. It was an accident."

"But I hurt you." The words scraped out, aged wounds made raw again. "I could have killed you."

"But you didn't." Miri gestured around the studio, at the shelves lined with her work – bowls and vases and sculptures that caught the light like trapped rainbows. "And look where I ended up. I found my calling because of that day. When they were doing the physical therapy for the burns, they had us work with our hands. Clay at first, then I discovered glass." She grinned. "Figured if I could survive magical fire, regular fire wasn't so scary."

Alyssa's laugh came out watery. "That's insane logic." Only Miri would come to that conclusion.

"Maybe." Miri held out her scarred arm, turning it in the light from the furnace. "I'm glad you came, though. I know it haunted you. Your gran told me, years later. Said you never forgave yourself."

"How could I?" Alyssa found herself reaching out, hesitating just before touching. Miri nodded permission, and Alyssa traced one of the larger scars with her fingertip. The skin was smooth, different in texture but not unpleasant.

"These are part of me now," Miri said quietly. "All our scars become seamless parts of us if we heal enough. And you know what? I found my calling from it. Our scars, our wounds, help to shape us."

The furnace roared behind them, a constant hungry sound. Tools hung on the walls – pipes and paddles and jacks, shears and blocks. A bucket of water sat by each bench, and bags of coloured glass frits lined the shelves like jars of candy.

"Want to try?" Miri asked suddenly.

"What? No, I couldn't – " Alyssa took a step backward, but Miri grabbed her hand, tugging her towards the flames.

"Come on. Face your fears and all that." Miri was already moving, pulling a blob of molten glass from the furnace on the end of a pipe. "Here, just hold this. Keep it turning, like a marshmallow over a fire."

The pipe was heavier than Alyssa expected, warm but not hot. The glass on the end glowed orange-white, alive and dangerous and beautiful. She turned it slowly, feeling the weight shift.

"See? You're not afraid of fire," Miri said. "You're afraid of yourself. There's a difference."

Alyssa kept turning the pipe, watching the glass flow and reshape itself with gravity and motion. "When did you get so wise?"

"Somewhere between my thirtieth birthday and my first gallery show." Miri took the pipe back, shaping the glass with practiced movements. "So what's really going on? You didn't just come here to apologize for something that happened when we were teenagers."

"I have to make a choice," Alyssa said, the words coming easier in the heat and roar of the studio. "About magic. About who I'm going to be. And I'm terrified I'll hurt someone again."

Miri nodded, shaping the glass into a small bowl. "You know what the first rule of glass-blowing is? Respect the medium. Glass wants to flow, fire wants to burn. You can't change their nature, but you can learn to work with it. Guide it." She glanced at Alyssa. "Maybe magic's the same."

They worked in companionable silence for a while, Miri finishing the piece while Alyssa watched. When it was safely in the annealer with the others, Miri stripped off her apron.

"Want some water? It's murder in here during summer."

They sat outside on milk crates, bottles of water sweating in their hands. The ocean breeze was a relief after the furnace heat.

"Thank you," Alyssa said finally. "For forgiving me. For... this." She gestured to the space between them, amazed at how it had been transformed. All the guilt and shame she'd been keeping trapped had evaporated from exposure to the truth.

"Nothing to forgive." Miri clinked her water bottle against Alyssa's. "But if you need to hear it – I forgive you. Completely. Now maybe you can work on forgiving yourself?"

Alyssa nodded, throat tight. She thought about Brendan, about Sam, about the choice waiting for her. About scar tissue and strength.

"I should go," she said eventually. "But... can I come back? When all this is over?"

"You better." Miri stood, pulling Alyssa up with her. "I'll teach you to make something beautiful out of fire."

Driving away, Alyssa felt something shift inside her chest. Not quite peace, not yet, but maybe the possibility of it. Her hands were steady on the wheel as she headed for Sam's shop, ready to face what came next.


The door to the shop was open, letting wind into the building where heat pooled under the low ceiling. After the inferno of Miri's studio, this felt almost cool. There was a fan at the counter, spreading the scent of incense across the room – sandalwood and something floral – but not doing a whole lot to actually cool things down. The bell jangled as she moved inside and Sam stepped out from the back, a smile on her face that only wavered slightly on seeing Alyssa.

"Hey," Sam said gently. "How are you?"

"I'm fine, honestly. And I'm ready. I'm going to do this." The words felt more solid now, after Miri. More real.

Samantha frowned. "That wasn't what I expected to hear."

"I know, I know, I run away from things, I never stop and hear people out, I don't trust. Well, I want to change, and I can see that if I do this thing it's going to benefit a lot of people. Benefit me as well. But mostly others. And you said you can keep looking for a way to keep the barrier strong without me needing to prop it up, so it's not like it's going to be forever. Right?"

"Right. You're sure?" Sam moved around the counter and placed a hand on Alyssa's arm. Her touch was cool, grounding. "Do you have a plan?"

"I was kind of hoping you'd have one," Alyssa said. She smiled, though her insides still quivered like molten glass. She had to reassure herself that the speed with which Sam accepted her words was a token of trust, and not a sign that Sam was trying to use her.

"I've been thinking about it a bit." Sam bit her lip. "And, I have an idea. I'm not sure how well it will work, but we'll need all the help we can get. I've got some friends."

Alyssa barely stopped herself from rolling her eyes before reminding herself sternly that she was making herself a fixture here and now was as good a time as any to get out and meet some people.

Which reminded her...

"So, I found out who the necromancer is." She bit her lip, nervous to make this reveal.

"What, who?" Sam looked at her eagerly, leaning forward.

"His name is Brendan, and he prefers the term Kaipō, and we're kind of involved?"

"What on earth, Alyssa? I thought you were all anti-magic." Sam's eyes were blown wide, her frown creased in consternation, as if she'd finally been driven around the bend by Alyssa and her oddities.

"I was, I know, and it's nuts, but he was honest with me, and it's partly because of him that I considered this whole thing. Look, I don't really want to explain it right now, but I think he can help and you said we need all the help we can get." She nodded, as if it was decided. And heck, this was her ritual, her taking on of something big and scary, and if she wanted to have her death-magic romantic interest present, then who was Sam to deny her that?

"I don't know about this, Alyssa." Sam's shoulders slumped a little and she blew out a breath. "I get that you like him but is it smart to trust him? He came here because of Mrs Nolan. He's here to get you to do this, and you're just going to?"

Alyssa's lips pressed tight while she mulled over what Sam had said. The woman wasn't wrong. Brendan was getting what he wanted. Mrs Nolan was getting what she wanted. Even Sam, to some degree, was getting what she wanted. But Alyssa was getting what she wanted now too – a community, a safe home, an interesting man, to save some lives, to reconnect with her oldest friend. And she would find a way to deal with Mrs Nolan after.

"It's not like that, trust me. And, I want this. At least enough to give it a go. Hell, it might not even work." She tossed the words out lightly, but she could feel something heavy in her gut, solid as cooling glass, something which told her it was going to work and that she wasn't at all prepared for the outcome. Alyssa wrapped her arms around herself, wishing they were Brendan's because that would go a long way to comforting her right now. "I'm going to go and fill him in. When should we do this?"

Sam wrinkled her face up, and then reached for her phone, flicking through screens. "Lunar app," she explained. "Can't remember when the new moon is."

"No. Tonight. We can't wait for the perfect moon or astrological phase – if what you said about the Bay not being safe is real then the sooner the better."

"And that gives you less time to reconsider?" Sam gave her a pointed look.

"And that," Alyssa admitted with a half shrug. She needed to get this over and done with. As soon as possible. Like ripping off a bandage, or plunging glass into cold water to shock it into a solid shape.

"If you're sure about this." Sam beamed. "That gives us plenty of time to get things organized. I'll let you know where and when, and you just show up. Okay?" Samantha practically skipped back around to the other side of the counter.

"I guess I'm dismissed?" Alyssa raised an eyebrow, giving Sam a wry smile.

"Sorry, sorry. You don't have to go, but I better make some calls, tell everyone."

Alyssa leaned against the counter, the glass top cool on her elbows. "Who is everyone, anyway?"

"At this point, it's everyone in town who we can trust to help. I'd better make some calls. When I phone you later, actually answer your phone this time, okay?"

"I'll try." Alyssa laughed and headed back out into the sunshine. She wasn't sure she could say she felt good about things, but she did feel somewhat lighter. Stronger, maybe. Like old wounds might finally heal over.

Now to find Brendan.

# CHAPTER 29

"I know. I wish I could be there too." Brendan dragged his fingers through his hair, the strands damp with sweat. His scalp ached from the tension. "I'm literally trapped here. I swear if I could get back I would."

"He's not doing well. You need to see him before..." Esther's voice crackled through the phone, distant and tinny.

He could see her in his mind, the way her shoulders would slump and tears would start to drip from the corners of her eyes. "Don't talk like that. I'm going to find a way to save him."

"I know you're trying."

"I'm going to." His voice came out hard as granite, jaw clenched so tight he could hear his teeth creak. "I mean it, sis. You just be with him, keep him hanging in there and I'll do everything in my power to make him better."

"Okay." Her voice wavered, she was barely holding it together.

He ended the call before she could fall apart completely. The phone screen went dark, his reflection staring back – hollow-eyed and desperate. There was nothing he could say that would make her feel better. The only thing he could do was find a way to stop Michael from dying.

A knock rattled his door – three sharp raps that made him jump. He slipped his phone back into his pocket, the device still warm from the call, and headed towards the sound.

"Coming!"

He swung the door open to find Alyssa standing there. The afternoon sun caught her blonde hair, turning it gold, but it was nothing compared to the determined set of her jaw, the spark in her eyes.

"I'm going to do it. Tonight."

"Do what?" He frowned, hope and disbelief warring in his chest, the last gasps of a dying thing.

"You know, the thing." She raised her eyebrows, impatient. "I'm going to become the town witch! I don't know how it's going to happen, or what they have planned, but I'm going to do it and once I'm done, you can save your nephew! Isn't that great?"

Relief hit him like a physical blow. His knees went weak and he slumped against the doorframe, the wood rough against his shoulder. Tears pricked his eyes but he couldn't release them. "Oh thank god."

Her face fell.

His heart stopped when he realised how that must have sounded. Brendan reached for her, hand hovering in the air between them. "I didn't mean it like that. I just got off the phone with my sister and Michael isn't doing very well. She was begging me to come home and say goodbye. But, well, you know, I can't leave."

Alyssa stepped forward, her palm cool against his cheek. "I'm sorry. I'm sorry it took me so long to decide, and I'm sorry that he's not doing well. I have an idea about that." Delight sparkled in her eyes, a spark he hadn't seen in her before, as if making this decision had released something.

"You do?"

"Yeah. Are you going to invite me inside?"

He swept an arm into the house, attempting levity. "Come on in. Want a coffee?"

"Is it too early for something stronger?"

"Hell no. Not on a day like today. We've got things to talk about, and some things require a little... courage."

She looked him up and down, then nodded. "Yeah, okay."

He led the way inside, the house still smelling of coffee and burnt toast from his attempted breakfast. Once they were seated at the table, hot coffee between them – steam turning the air ethereal – he looked her in the eyes. "You wanna go first?"

"I'm not sure now. But, okay." She took a sip, the coffee spilling a little as she set the mug down. Her hands spread flat on the table, fingers splayed. "Samantha, from the curio shop, has a plan for how we can reconnect me to Papatūānuku. She's going to call together the other magical people, the other god-children or whatever they are called, to help with some kind of ritual. And then, ta-da. Hopefully I'll be all magicky, and you can get Michael healed."

"You don't know anything more about the process?" His mind went blank, the hope abandoning him. There was so much he didn't know and no certainty in the plan that Alyssa was presenting him with.

She rolled her eyes. "Trust me, I know from experience that sometimes it's better not to know in advance. Besides, I'm not even sure they know. Sylvie was the witch for so long it's not like anyone has experience. I might chicken out and we don't want that, do we?" Her words were playful, but she bit the inside of her lip, her nerves leaking through.

"No. No we don't." He frowned, struggling to know how to respond. It was a lot. So much. But he had to trust her when she said that she was doing this for her as well as everyone else. And he still hadn't told her about talking with Sylvie.

"What's your problem?" Her nails dragged across the table, leaving faint scratches in the varnish. "I thought this was what you wanted? This is why you're here isn't it? And I'm giving you what you came for, so the least you can do is look happy about it!" The chair scraped against the floor as she pushed back and stood, stalking towards the hallway.

"Wait, Alyssa!" He caught up with her at the doorway, the floorboards creaking under his rushed steps. His hand on her shoulder was gentle but firm. "I *am* happy. I just... I did something, and I feel like shit about it."

She took a step back, her whole body going rigid. The warmth in her eyes cooled to ice. "What did you do?"

"I spoke to your grandmother."

"You did what?" Her voice pitched higher. "I thought we were going to do that together. I thought you said – "

"We were, yes. I just..." He let out a groan. "After you were so worried about things, I felt like I needed to find out for myself what kind of woman she was, whether she was going to try and manipulate you. You're the one who told me that the women in your family were – "

"Monsters, nasty women, yes," Alyssa snapped. "But not Gran."

"No, not your gran. That said, she did tell me something you should know. I don't know how you're going to react though."

Alyssa marched back to the table, her footsteps sharp and angry. She plonked herself down and chugged back the rest of her coffee, throat working. The empty mug hit the table with a hollow thunk. "Got anything stronger?"

Wordlessly he moved to the fridge. The bottle of rum was sticky when he pulled it from the cupboard, and the cola fizzed as he poured. Ice cracked in the warm liquid. He set one glass in front of Alyssa – the condensation immediately pooling on the table – then dropped into his seat.

"Spill," she said.

"I don't want to." He shook his head, exhaustion weighing on him like lead. He'd barely slept last night after Sylvie's revelation, tossing and turning until the sheets were twisted ropes. "But I know I have to."

She clasped the glass, but didn't take a drink. "Talk."

He took a swig of his drink, though it was only cola. The sweetness couldn't make what he had to say any easier though. "You know how you said your ancestor created a baby from the earth here. From Papatūānuku?"

"Yeah." Her fingers wrapped tighter around the glass but she still didn't lift it.

"Apparently, that's a family thing. Your Gran, your mother, all of the first born women in your family line were created the same way." The words felt like stones in his mouth. He didn't want to say she was as well. Didn't want to be the one to voice it, but he'd said this much and he needed her to know. "You – "

"I'm a bloody clay baby too!?" She picked up her glass and drained it, ice rattling. "All of them? All of us?" The glass hit the table hard enough to make him wince.

"Sylvie said that all the women in your family are infertile, until they bond with Papatūānuku and have a child by her. A magical child who can help protect the Bay."

"But then my mother ran." Alyssa's laugh was bitter as the rum. "She escaped everything. Decided to turn her back on the Bay and leave it to me." Pain flickered across her face before she forced it smooth.

"I hated finding this out, I hate telling you even more, but you needed to know." He reached for her hand across the table. Her skin was cold from the glass.

"You told me anyway. Even though it might change the way I felt." Her face crumpled and tears spilled over, tracking down her cheeks. "Shit." She pulled her hand back, swiping at the tears angrily. "I don't mean to cry. It just hit me that you really are trying to do the right thing here. Even when it's hard."

"Alyssa—"

"No, let me process this." She stood abruptly, pacing to the window. The afternoon light caught the tear tracks on her face. "So I'm not even... I'm not human? Not fully?"

"You're you," he said firmly. "Whatever your origin, you're still Alyssa. Still the woman who freed Magnus, who makes terrible coffee, who throws a mean slap."

That got a watery laugh. "I do make terrible coffee."

"The worst." He moved to stand near her, not touching, just present. "Look, I know this is a lot. And the timing is shit with everything else happening tonight. But I couldn't let you go into this ritual without knowing the truth about yourself."

She turned to face him, eyes red-rimmed but clearer. "The truth." She tested the word like foreign cuisine. "You know what the really messed up part is? It all makes so much sense. Why I could never quite fit in anywhere. Why the magic always felt like it was trying to claw its way out of me." She wrapped her arms around herself. "I'm literally made of this place."

"Does it change your mind? About tonight?" He longed to reach for her, to draw her in, but she was trying so hard to process things, to hold herself together.

A long pause. Outside, a tūī called, its song was complex and mechanical. Finally, she shook her head. "No. If anything, it makes it clearer. I can't run from what I am. Gran knew that. That's probably why she made sure I inherited the house, made sure I'd come back." She laughed again, steadier this time. "Sneaky old woman."

"She loved you," Brendan said quietly. "That came through clear as day when I spoke to her."

"Yeah." Alyssa moved closer to him, close enough that he could smell the rum on her breath, see the gold flecks in her blue eyes. "You know what else is clear?"

"What?" She was so close now and he was struggling to take a full breath. This woman was amazing, so vibrant, so fluid and changeable, and she was his last hope for saving Michael.

"That you told me the truth even when you knew it might push me away." Her hand found his, fingers interlacing. "That matters, Brendan. It matters more than you know."

The air between them shifted, charged with something that made his skin tingle. She rose up on her toes, bringing her face closer to his. Her free hand curved around the back of his neck, fingers warm against his skin.

"Alyssa," he breathed, not sure if it was a warning or a plea.

"After tonight, everything changes," she whispered. Her thumb traced the line of his jaw, leaving fire in its wake. "I become the witch. You save Michael. And then what happens? You leave?"

"I wish I knew." The honest answer hurt to say. "I don't know what happens after."

"Neither do I." She was so close now he could feel her breath on his lips. "But right now, in this moment before everything changes..."

She kissed him. Not the desperate, consuming kiss from before, but something slower, deeper. A kiss that asked questions neither of them could answer. His arms came around her, pulling her against him, and for a moment the world narrowed to just this – her mouth on his, her body pressed close, the afternoon sun warming them both.

When they finally broke apart, they were both breathing hard. Her cheeks were flushed, lips swollen, and she looked at him with eyes that held promises and fears in equal measure.

"I should go," she said, but didn't move away. Her fingers still tangled in his hair, her body still fitted against his like she belonged there.

"You should," he agreed, making no effort to release her.

They stood there, caught between staying and leaving, between now and later, between what they were and what they might become. The moment stretched, fragile as blown glass.

Finally, she stepped back, her hands sliding away slowly, reluctantly. "After tonight – "

"After tonight, we'll figure it out." He caught her hand, pressed a kiss to her palm. "Whatever happens with the ritual, with Michael, with everything – we'll figure it out."

She smiled, soft and uncertain and beautiful. "Promise?"

"I promise."

One more kiss, quick and fierce, and then she was walking away.

But as he watched her go, the ghost of her kiss still burning on his lips, he knew that whatever came after, he wasn't going anywhere if he had to be without her.

# CHAPTER 30

Alyssa paced the kitchen, her bare feet slapping against the tiles. The weight of what she'd just agreed to – the ritual, becoming the witch – didn't feel as heavy as she had expected it too. Now that she'd apologised to Miri, seen that losing control hadn't ruined the girl's life. But there was something else she needed to do first, something that made her stomach churn worse than any magic ritual could.

"I need to call Kelly," she said abruptly. Alyssa needed to put the past behind her; completely. Forgive her friend and wish her luck in her new life, even if that was with Grant. Their relationship had changed since Alyssa had come here, and she knew that closing that door, gently, kindly, would assuage any remaining fear that she might do something bitter and spiteful.

Like others in her family.

Brendan looked up from where he was making coffee, the spoon pausing mid-stir. "What? I thought you weren't talking to her."

"I'm not. But I need to." Alyssa wrapped her arms around

herself, the afternoon air suddenly cold despite the heat outside. "Two reasons. First – your sister needs help. She can't navigate to the Bay on her own, especially not with a sick child and medical equipment. The Bay doesn't show up on GPS all the time, remember? Someone needs to guide them here."

"I could talk her through it – "

"No." Alyssa shook her head. "Phone signals can get wonky near the boundary. They'll need someone with them who knows the way, just to be sure. Kelly knows."

Brendan set down the spoon, his expression careful. "And the second reason?"

Alyssa's fingers twisted together, knuckles white. "I don't want to do this ritual holding onto bitterness. What if it affects the magic? What if my anger at her taints what I'm trying to do?" She forced herself to meet his eyes. "I need to at least try to clear the air before tonight. I don't want to become the town witch for the wrong reasons – like using the barrier to shut her out forever."

Understanding dawned on his face. "You're afraid you'll become like them. Like your ancestors."

"They took what they wanted regardless of consequences." Her voice came out smaller than intended. "What if holding onto this anger is my first step down that path?"

Brendan moved closer, not touching, just present. She appreciated that about him; that he didn't just assume she needed his strength to prop her up. The coffee smell wrapped around them both, comforting like he was.

"Calling her is brave, Alyssa."

"It's practical." She grabbed her phone before she could lose her nerve. "Write down your sister's number. Kelly's resourceful – she'll figure out how to get them there even if Grant has to help."

"Grant?" Brendan's eyebrow raised.

"Her new boyfriend. My ex." The words tasted bitter but not as much as before. "Honestly, he might be useful. He's got that whole 'talk your way past authorities' thing down."

Brendan scribbled the number on a piece of paper, the pen scratching loudly in the quiet kitchen. "You sure about this?"

"No." She took the paper, the numbers blurring slightly. "But Michael needs to get here, and I need to face this. Might as well kill two – " She grimaced. "Wrong phrase. Might as well handle both problems at once."

She stepped out onto the back deck, needing space for this call. The afternoon sun was brutal, making her squint. The phone felt slippery in her sweaty palm as she found Kelly's contact. Her thumb hovered over the call button for a long moment.

The tūī from earlier was back, its call almost mimicking a ring tone.

Before she could overthink it more, she hit call.

Kelly answered on the second ring. "Oh my god, Alyssa, I thought you would never talk to me again. I'm so sorry, this whole thing has made me feel sick – "

"Stop." Alyssa's voice came out harder than intended. "Just stop talking, Kelly."

Silence. For once, Kelly actually listened.

"I'm not calling to hear apologies. I'm not calling to say everything's fine. But I need something from you."

"Anything." Kelly's voice was small, careful.

Alyssa bit back a sarcastic response. "Brendan's nephew is dying. He needs to come to the Bay immediately for... medical treatment. Special kind. But the Bay isn't easy to find, as you know. I need you to contact his sister Esther and help bring them here. Guide them in."

There was a pause on the other end of the line, and Alyssa waited.

"Why can't someone else – "

"Because you know the way. Because they'll need someone who's driven it before when the GPS starts failing at the edge of town. Because there's a six-year-old boy who might die if they get lost trying to find this place." Alyssa's free hand clenched into a fist. "And because you owe me, Kelly. You and Grant started before we were even properly over. You owe me this."

The silence stretched longer this time. When Kelly spoke, her voice was thick. "You're right. I owe you. What's the number?"

Alyssa recited it, listening as Kelly repeated it back. "They'll need to leave as soon as possible. Today. I'll text you more details about where to meet them."

"Consider it done." A pause. "Alyssa? After this, after I help... Do you think you can forgive me?"

The question hung in the air like smoke. Alyssa closed her eyes, feeling the sun burn against her lids. "After this, we can talk. Really talk. You, me, and Grant if you need him there. Though honestly, I don't care about him anymore. It's you who hurt me most."

"I know." Kelly's voice cracked. "I'll call Esther right now. We'll get them here safely, I promise."

"Thank you." The words felt strange but necessary.

"Of course. Anything else?"

"Just... drive carefully. The roads get weird closer to the Bay."

She ended the call before Kelly could respond, staring at the phone screen until it went dark. Her reflection stared back – tired, conflicted, but somehow steadier than before.

Inside, Brendan had finished making coffee. The smell hit her as she entered, rich and grounding. He handed her a mug without comment, the ceramic warm against her palms. His coffee was so much better than hers.

"All set?" he asked quietly.

She nodded, taking a sip. Perfect temperature, perfect strength. How did he already know how she liked it? "Kelly will call your sister. They'll work out the logistics."

"And you?" His eyes searched hers. "You're okay with this?"

"Yes. No?" She managed a small smile. "But I will be. Eventually. First, we need to deal with Mrs Nolan. Make sure she'll actually help Michael when he gets here." Maybe they should have done that before they called Esther, she thought, the realization a stone in her gut that she would have to ignore for now.

Brendan's hand found hers across the counter, warm and steady. "We'll go together. Confront her before the ritual. She wants you to become the witch – she'll have to agree to our terms."

"Our terms." Alyssa squeezed his hand, drawing strength from the contact. "I like the sound of that."

They stood there for a moment, hands linked, coffee cooling between them. In a few hours, everything would change. But right now, she'd taken the first step towards clearing her conscience. Kelly would help save Michael. Alyssa would face the ritual with cleaner hands, if not a lighter heart.

It would have to be enough.

# CHAPTER 31

The Preservation Society building loomed before them, its windows dark despite the afternoon sun. Brendan's shirt stuck to his back with sweat, but as they pushed through the heavy glass doors, the temperature plummeted. The lobby smelled of old paper and something else – something sweet and cloying that made his stomach turn.

Alyssa's hand found his as they climbed the stairs. Her palm was clammy, fingers interlacing with his in a grip that spoke of nerves. At the top, Mrs Nolan's office door stood closed, the brass nameplate gleaming like a warning.

"Ready?" he murmured.

She nodded, jaw set with determination.

He didn't knock. The handle turned smoothly under his hand, and they stepped into Mrs Nolan's domain.

She had her feet up on the desk, phone pressed to her ear. At their entrance, she swung her legs down – heels hitting the floor with twin clicks – and held up one finger. "I'm going to have to call you back. Something has just come up."

The phone met the desk with a deliberate thunk. Mrs

Nolan's smile spread slowly, predatory. "Well, look who the cat dragged in. I take it this means you've been successful." Her gaze swept over them like she was cataloging weaknesses.

"Alyssa has made the decision to take over her grandmother's role in the town. She'll become a witch and help to strengthen the barrier." Brendan kept his voice steady, professional. They were here to negotiate, not to be played with.

"Very good!" Mrs Nolan's enthusiasm rang false as a cracked bell. "You didn't have to drag Sylvie back from beyond the grave after all. Probably a good thing, really. I doubt that would have gone down well with your grandmother anyway."

The words hung in the air like a trap springing shut. Brendan's chest tightened. "Excuse me?"

"What about his grandmother?" Alyssa's voice had gone sharp, suspicious.

"Oh, you remember June, don't you Alyssa?" Mrs Nolan quirked an eyebrow, clearly relishing every second of this tension.

Beside him, Alyssa went completely still. Her breathing stopped. When it resumed, it came in short, shallow gasps. He felt more than saw her jaw drop, could sense the shock radiating from her like heat.

"What about her?" His own voice sounded distant, muffled by the roaring in his ears.

"She's your grandmother?" The words came out of Alyssa as a whisper, then stronger, accusatory. "June is your grandmother?"

"Yeah. Why?" But even as he asked, he knew from the horror dawning on her face that it was something terrible. His stomach dropped like a stone into dark water. What had June done?

"She tried to kill me," Alyssa's voice cracked, pitched high with disbelief.

"Well, not just that." Mrs Nolan leaned back in her chair, leather creaking. She was enjoying this, savouring their pain like wine. "She also quickened your grandmother's demise, put the moves on your house, tried to steal your ghost, too."

The office spun. Brendan gripped the back of a chair to steady himself. "She what? I mean, I knew she was nasty, but that's..." The words tangled in his throat. His grandmother, attempting murder? He forced himself to focus on Alyssa's pale face. "Did you... was it you who hurt her? She was brought back to the city comatose, and she's not much better now."

Alyssa shook her head, violent and quick. "No, that was the ghost. Magnus. And even if it had been me, I was just defending myself." Her voice rose, defensive and hurt. "You heard Mrs Nolan. She tried to kill me!"

The accusation in her eyes cut deeper than any blade. Brendan's face fell, hope crumbling. "I'm so sorry." He reached for her arm, needing to bridge the sudden chasm between them, but she jerked away like his touch burned. The rejection stung worse than a slap.

"Alyssa, I've been straight with you, haven't I?" Desperation leaked into his voice. "I told you who I was, and why I was here. I told you why it was important. You believe me, right?" He couldn't lose her like this. Not over something he'd had no control over, no knowledge of. He'd had no idea their grandmothers had been close, let alone that June had been involved in this much darkness in the town she'd claimed to love.

Alyssa held up a hand, palm out – a barrier between them. "As far as I know, you have. But I just need a little space." Her voice was carefully controlled, but he could hear the tremor underneath. "I'll still do what I said I would, but I'm going to go now."

She shook her head, muttering something that might have

been an apology, and fled. The door slammed behind her with enough force to rattle the framed certificates on the wall.

The silence that followed was deafening.

Brendan rounded on Mrs Nolan, fury replacing shock. His hands clenched into fists. "Now what the hell was that about? We were handing you what you wanted on a silver platter, and you go and throw me under a bus? If this is how you treat those you employ then I'll be damned sure everyone knows it."

Mrs Nolan shrugged, unconcerned. "Think of it as payback."

"What have I ever done to you?" He threw his hands up, the gesture violent. He wanted to punch something – someone – so badly his knuckles ached.

"Well, nothing directly." She examined her nails, red as blood.

"It's June again, isn't it?" Understanding dawned, cold and bitter. "Who else did she piss off in this town? Can I expect any shit from other aggrieved parties?"

Mrs Nolan let out a soft huff of laughter. "There are bound to be a few, but none of them know who you are. You didn't think it was odd that I came to you? There are plenty of necromancers around. Hell, if I dug deep enough I'm sure I could have found someone local to do the job." She leaned forward, elbows on the desk. "And if I'd really wanted, don't you think I could have found someone at the very least to convince Alyssa to go along with what I wanted? I know someone who can do that. It would have been easy."

"But you chose me." The words tasted like ash.

"Yes. Because your grandmother took something from us. Something precious. No matter how strong Alyssa is, she's never going to replace Sylvie, and that poor woman who suffered at the hands of June wouldn't be as strong in death as she was in life. That's just not how it works."

Brendan exhaled slowly, trying to leash his rage. When he spoke again, his voice was dangerously quiet. "And what about Alyssa? You just played around with her, harassing her and getting her riled up for no reason?"

Mrs Nolan licked her lips – a quick, nervous gesture that didn't match her usual predatory confidence. Brendan caught it, filed it away. He took a deep breath, forcing his anger down to a manageable simmer, and waited.

"Things aren't quite what they seem in the Bay." The words came out carefully, like she was picking her way through a minefield.

"When is anything ever what it seems? This is the birth-place of the gods. A town where magical people thrive. A town secluded from the rest of the country, and the world, in order to protect its foundations. What am I missing?"

Mrs Nolan twined her fingers together, steepling them as she rested her wrists on the edge of the desk. The gesture looked practiced, meant to project control. "Change is coming, and we all have to choose a side."

A chill ran down his spine, ice water in his veins. He wanted to protest that he didn't have a side, but the lie died unspoken. He cared about Alyssa – had started falling for her despite himself – and so he was inevitably on her side, which-ever that turned out to be. "And which side are you on?"

She glanced at the door, and for a moment her mask slipped. Terror filled her eyes – real, bone-deep fear. "My own," she whispered.

Her fingers untangled, reaching across the desk with sudden urgency. Paper rustled as she grabbed a notepad, pen scratching frantically. Her handwriting was small, cramped, as if she was afraid of being overheard even in writing. She pushed the paper towards him, sliding it across the polished wood with one finger. A minute nod towards the door.

"Perhaps you should go and see someone down at the curio store. I hear they have excellent trinkets. Pick one up and tell Samantha to charge it to my account. A parting gift." The words were bright, false. Her smile looked painted on, brittle as old paint. "And once the ritual is complete, we can heal your nephew."

Brendan reached down and picked up the paper, the edge sharp against his thumb. He shoved it into his pocket without looking at it and headed for the door. His footsteps seemed too loud on the thin carpet.

Outside, the heat hit him like a physical blow. He exhaled heavily, lungs burning, brow furrowed in confusion. Just what the hell was going on here? Mrs Nolan was all over the place with her behaviour – afraid one moment, vindictive the next.

But perhaps the note would explain. And failing that, a trip to the curio shop. To Samantha – Alyssa's friend.

He had to fix this. Had to make Alyssa understand that June's sins weren't his. That he'd been as much a victim of the old woman's schemes as anyone.

The paper in his pocket felt heavier than it should, pregnant with secrets he wasn't sure he wanted to know.


The curio shop's bell jangled as he pushed through the door, the sound bright and cheerful in stark contrast to his mood. The space smelled of sage and old wood, crystals catching the afternoon light from the window. He surveyed the shop, eyes coming to rest on a slim woman with long blonde hair who was arranging bottles on a shelf in the back corner.

"Samantha?" he asked, moving towards her. His voice came out rougher than intended.

"Yeah, that's me. What can I help you with?" She set down a blue bottle carefully and turned to face him. Her expression was open, friendly, but it shuttered slightly as she took in his appearance – the tension in his shoulders, the grim set of his mouth. "Brendan."

"I was told you could help me out." He tried for casual, missed by a mile. There was definitely a weird energy in the shop, and he couldn't tell if it was because of him, or the pressing issue of the boundary failing around the Bay.

She cocked an eyebrow. "I'll give it a shot."

He pulled the note from his pocket, the paper damp with sweat from his palm, and moved towards the counter. The glass top was cool as he smoothed the note out, Mrs Nolan's cramped handwriting stark against the white. "Mrs Nolan hired me to get Alyssa to help strengthen the barrier, but she's been doing a bunch of random shit that seems to go against that goal. I guess I just figured she was a weird bitch, until today."

Samantha's features closed off completely. Her lips pressed together so tightly they disappeared into a thin line. "Uh huh. And what happened today?"

"Take a look for yourself." He nudged the note forward, remembering its cryptic words.

*Tū's child is coming, and she wants the Bay. Threatened me. Want to help, but been told to stall.*

He knew that Tū probably referred to Tūmatauenga, the god of humans and war, but beyond that... Well, he had no idea what it meant for them all.

"Oh." Samantha's voice pitched high, almost a squeak. "Well, I knew something was off, but I didn't know it was this bad." She looked up sharply. "Where's Alyssa? Is she still going to – "

"Yeah, despite the fact that Mrs Nolan dropped the bombshell that I'm June's grandson."

"You're what?" The words exploded out of her. "Wow.

Yeah, that wouldn't have gone down well." She seemed to realise what she'd said and put a reassuring hand on his arm. Her touch was warm, grounding. "Don't worry. Alyssa's a smart girl and she's been thinking about this for weeks now. She seems to trust you, and while this... Well. She will move past it."

"I bloody well hope so. I'm pretty sure that's the only reason Mrs Nolan hired me." His hands clenched on the counter edge. "What is she, anyway? She told me she could cure my nephew, but now I don't even know if that's true."

"What do you mean 'what is she?'" Samantha's brow furrowed.

"What kind of magical being."

"She's part faery, patupaearehe, but her magic is very weak. Can't you feel it?"

The words hit him like a physical blow. His knees went weak. It felt like he'd swallowed molten lead, burning all the way down. "She was just feeding me lies. She promised access to June's relics and a way to cure my nephew – he's going to die without it." He grabbed the counter for balance, knuckles white. The room tilted slightly. "Whatever they have over her, it must be pretty big."

Samantha looked concerned, but she didn't say anything. The silence stretched between them, heavy with implications.

"What does she mean, about Tū?" He forced the words out past the tightness in his throat. "He's one of the Gods, isn't he, so this is his home too."

Samantha's frown deepened. "He is one of the Gods, yes, but..." She paused, choosing her words carefully.

Sam was quiet for a long moment. When she spoke, her voice was barely above a whisper.

"Most of the atua have faded—sleeping, diminished, content to live through their descendants. But Tū..." She glanced towards the window. "He's different. He's the god of war. Of conquest. Of humanity's *domination* of nature. While his siblings rested, he's been gathering strength. Nursing old grudges."

"What grudges?"

"That's not a story for today." Sam's tone made clear there would be no arguing. "What matters is that he wants Kotahi Bay. He's always wanted it. And now, with the barrier weakening, with the old guardians dying..." She swallowed hard. "His child is coming to take it for him."

"His child? Like, literally?"

"A descendant. Someone carrying his bloodline and his will." Sam met his eyes. "Someone who believes what he believes—that power exists to be taken. That the strong should rule the weak. That everything magical, everything *other*, should bow or burn."

"Bloody hell." Brendan ran a hand through his hair, the strands damp with sweat. "And Mrs Nolan knew?"

"This is worse than I thought it was." Samantha started pacing, her footsteps quick and agitated. "I knew she was behaving strangely, pushing too hard, but I didn't think it mattered because Alyssa was leaning towards it anyway. She can feel the magic in her blood, she feels that connection to the Bay. It was only a matter of time before she made the decision. I was just planning on fending off Mrs Nolan until then."

"But she went and brought me into it..."

Samantha sighed, the sound heavy with regret. "And then Alyssa fell for you. That wasn't something that Mrs Nolan could predict."

His heart clenched, pain that even Samantha could see their connection. That it might have been severed by Mrs Nolan. "So what do we do now? Have you seen Alyssa?"

"Not since earlier, but we're meeting later." Sam chewed

her nail, a nervous habit. She avoided Brendan's gaze, and something about her sudden shifty demeanor set off alarm bells in his head. Then her expression changed, resolve hardening her features. "If Tū has people inside the town working for him, then it's even more important that we get this barrier back up to full strength. Or stronger than before."

He couldn't shake the feeling that she was hiding something about the ceremony. His necromancer instincts, honed by years of reading the dead, told him she was keeping secrets. "Is there something you're not telling me? Or, Alyssa, more importantly. Because no one seems to have told her anything about what's going to go down and if you're holding back – "

"Okay. Yes. Yes there is, but I don't know how to tell her." Sam's shoulders slumped in defeat. "She can't have babies, but I have a feeling that when she goes through this process of change... Maybe she will be. Maybe it's part of the connection."

"Holy shit, and you didn't think to mention this to her earlier?" The darkness at the edges of his vision flickered, responding to his anger.

"I don't know for sure! It's just... it's a theory I have, and I wanted to be more sure before I told her."

The doorbell tinkled, cheerful and discordant. But he couldn't switch his focus, rage building like pressure in his chest. He leaned in, close enough to see her pupils dilate with fear. Parts of his darkness quivered on the edge of his vision, eager to be unleashed. "You say that you care about her, that you're her friend, and yet you're holding on to important information. Were you planning to tell her before tonight?"

"Yes. Of course." Sam shrank back, pressing against the shelves.

"Back off, man. I know you're not from here, but Sam's a good person."

Brendan spun to see Matai standing in the doorway. Tall,

Māori, with traditional tā moko covering his arms. He looked like he could murder someone as he stalked towards them, each step deliberate and threatening.

"Matai. It's okay. Really." Samantha moved between them, hands raised placatingly. "This is Brendan. Alyssa's... friend."

"I know Brendan, and you know I have to keep the Bay's interests first. If he is threatening what we're doing here..." Matai left the rest of the sentence unspoken, but it hung in the air between them.

Brendan forced his shoulders to drop. "I'm sorry if I came over a bit strong, I just... I really care about her and she needs to know. Before tonight." The anger drained away, leaving him feeling hollow.

"I'll see if I can find her now, okay? You're right." She gave him an apologetic smile that didn't quite reach her eyes. "I feel like I've been giving her information she doesn't want to hear ever since she got to town. It's a wonder she still talks to me."

Guilt twisted in his gut. She was obviously feeling fragile herself, carrying the weight of too many secrets. "I can tell that you care, and trust me, she considers you her only friend in town. I don't think you'll see the back of her any time soon."

Samantha sighed, relief softening the tension in her face. "Thanks. I'll go and find her. Matai, can you lock up? And maybe you and Brendan should check in on Mrs Nolan – it seems like she's working with Tū's child, so there's every chance there are others in town doing the same."

"On it," Matai said with a sharp nod.

"Thank you, Samantha, and when you do see Alyssa, let her know I'm worried about her, okay?"

"Of course." Samantha grabbed her bag, bell jangling as she headed through the door, leaving him alone with Matai.

The shop felt smaller with just the two of them in it.

Brendan stuck out his hand, hoping the gesture would ease the tension. "Truce?"

Matai gripped his hand, the shake firm enough to hurt. "Dude, you were sticking up for your girl. I can't hold that against you." He looked Brendan up and down, assessing. "She knows now, huh?"

Brendan shrugged, not sure what the appropriate response was. The tā moko on Matai's arms seemed to shift in the afternoon light, the patterns almost alive.

"Come on, let's get this out of the way. The less time I have to spend thinking about that woman, let alone talking to her, the better."

Brendan couldn't agree more. But as they headed for the door, he couldn't shake the feeling that everything was spiraling out of control. June's legacy, Tū's child, the ritual tonight – and Alyssa, somewhere in town, thinking he'd betrayed her.

He had to fix this. Had to make it right.

Before it was too late.

# CHAPTER 32

Alyssa paced in the front room of her house, her bare feet wearing a path in the old rug. The floorboards creaked with each turn, a rhythmic complaint that matched her racing thoughts. She couldn't believe that Brendan was June's grandson, but it made so much sense! He was living in her bloody house! The walls themselves seemed to mock her – how had she not realised it? Or had she been so intent on pretending that he was just a guy she liked that she'd ignored what was obvious. The same rooms, the same air June had breathed. What was it about his family that attracted the women of hers? This was just ridiculous.

On the one hand, she knew she could trust him. He was right, he *had* been honest with her. He'd told her what he was, and why he was there – it wasn't his fault that he didn't know about the thing between Sylvie and June. And it wasn't like it was something she was keen to think about often – let alone share with potential lovers.

Mrs Nolan was a bloody whack job. She could not figure out what game the woman was playing, but it didn't make any sense. Either way, she needed to calm down before heading out to meet the others. Her stomach churned with nerves, acid rising in her throat.

The air in the room shifted, growing colder. "You're going to wear a hole in that carpet," Magnus observed, his voice dry as autumn leaves.

She spun around to find him leaning against the mantelpiece, more solid than usual. "How long have you been watching?"

"Long enough to see you work yourself into a state." He straightened, drifting closer. "The boy isn't his grandmother, you know."

"I know that." She pressed her palms against her eyes, seeing stars. "It's just... complicated."

"Most worthwhile things are." Magnus studied her with those ancient eyes. "You're more worried about tonight than about him."

He wasn't wrong. Alyssa headed to the bathroom, Socks and Buttons following behind her. The two cats had developed an odd routine – Socks would stalk the ghost cat with predatory intensity, then launch himself forward only to sail through Buttons' translucent form. He'd land in a confused heap, tail puffed, while Buttons watched with what could only be described as feline amusement.

"How long before he figures it out, do you think?" she asked the air.

"The kitten or the necromancer?" Magnus's voice followed her, echoing slightly off the bathroom tiles.

Her phone started ringing before she could answer, vibrating against her hip. Kelly's name lit up the screen. "Hey, how's it going?" The words came out automatically, muscle memory from years of friendship.

"I just wanted to let you know that we're leaving here in an hour."

Relief flooded through her, weakening her knees. "Thank goodness. It was looking a little dire there for a bit, but I'm pleased you've got it sorted."

"I'll always have your back," Kelly replied, her smile audible through the phone.

Alyssa wasn't sure whether she felt relieved or angry about it. The emotions tangled together, impossible to separate. This one deed did not mean she'd forget what had gone on, but at least it would mean she could keep her end of the bargain and help save Michael. "Well, thanks. We'll see you then. Flick me a text when you're on the road."

"Will do! Hey – "

Alyssa hung up, cutting off whatever Kelly had been about to say. She didn't want to talk about anything else right now. She had preparations to make because tonight, like it or not, she was going to meet the mother goddess. The thought made her hands tremble.

She glanced in the mirror above the fireplace, checking her reflection. Her face looked pale, washed out. The dark circles under her eyes had deepened throughout the day.

"You should try the red," Magnus whispered, his breath like winter wind on her neck. The chill crept up her spine, raising goosebumps.

Alyssa whipped around, searching for him, but he'd gone invisible again. Only his laugh remained, bouncing off the walls like marbles in a tin can.

"Red what?"

"Lipstick." His voice came from everywhere and nowhere. "It's powerful, and I think right now you need to look like you're in control. Even if you don't feel it."

"Good thinking. Thanks Mag."

"Mag?" He snorted, the sound surprisingly human. "What am I, an automobile magazine?"

"I'll call you whatever I like! It's a step up from Mr Ghost don't you think?"

"I quite liked that name," his voice faded, growing distant. "Had a certain dignity to it."

She could feel the moment he left the room – the temperature rising by degrees, the air losing that charged quality. But not gone far. Never far these days.

"Well, thanks. Wish me luck."

Silence stretched for a heartbeat, then: "You don't need luck, Alyssa Whenua. You need to remember who you are. Earth-born, god-touched. They should be wishing for YOUR blessing, not the other way around." The words hung in the air like a benediction before fading completely.

She stood there for a moment, letting his words sink in. Then she pulled her red lipstick from her purse, the tube cool and reassuring in her palm. The colour went on smoothly, transforming her face with each swipe. She pressed her lips together, studying the result. Not just red – crimson, like pōhutukawa flowers, like power, like blood.

It would have to do.


The knock on the door was so timid she almost missed it. Three small taps, like a mouse requesting entry. Alyssa frowned, not recognizing the rhythm. She swung the door open to find Sam on the porch, juggling two coffee cups and a brown paper bag that smelled like heaven – butter and sugar and cinnamon.

"What's the occasion?" Alyssa asked, arching an eyebrow

as she rescued one of the cups. The heat seeped through the cardboard, warming her fingers. "I mean, this is nice, thanks, but why do I feel like you've got an ulterior motive – I'm already on board for tonight."

"I'm not very good at being subtle, am I?" Sam's laugh came out strained. She shifted her weight from foot to foot. "Can I come in? We need to sit."

"Sure, but you better talk fast because you're making me nervous."

The coffee was perfect – strong enough to strip paint, just how she needed it. Alyssa claimed her usual spot on the couch, the cushions sighing under her weight. Sam perched on the edge of the opposite chair like she might need to flee at any moment.

"We've got a bit of an issue, well, not really. Maybe? I don't know..." Sam's hands fluttered, coffee threatening to spill. "I was trying to find out for sure before I talked to you about it, but as Brendan pointed out, I'm running out of time."

"Brendan?" Alyssa sat up straighter, tried not to lean forward, eager to hear how he was. "You've seen him?"

"He came to see me after he left Mrs Nolan." Sam's smile looked painful. "He's worried about you."

"Then why isn't he here too?" The question escaped before Alyssa could stop it. She'd half expected him to follow her out of Mrs Nolan's office, despite her telling him she needed space. The absence stung more than it should. But she should have expected it. He always respected her boundaries.

Sam bit her lip, leaving red marks. "I don't know if I'm meant to say anything but it sounds like whatever cure he was promised doesn't exist. His nephew..."

"Oh." Alyssa slumped back, the couch swallowing her. "He was counting on that. Do you think – "

"I think Matai was going back to talk to Mrs Nolan again, see what he can find out. The little boy, he's coming here right? We'll find a way to save him." Sam leaned forward, earnest. "We have healers. Old magic. The power of the atua. Something will work."

"Was that what you came to tell me?" Alyssa sipped her coffee, the bitterness coating her tongue. Today had already stretched like taffy, and there was so much left to do.

"No. I wish it was." Sam set her cup down with shaking hands, coffee sloshing dangerously.

"Come on, out with it." Her old desire to run, to ignore the situation, made her legs twitch. If this wasn't her own house, she might already be on her feet. But she had to stop that. She had decided.

"I think that when the ceremony happens, that's when pregnancy might have occurred in your ancestors."

"Ah. What?" Alyssa shot upright, coffee splashing over her hand. The heat barely registered. "Pregnant. Like, with a baby?"

"Yeah... I think that might be part of the transference of power." Sam's words came out in a rush. "The Whenua women, they've always... Papatūānuku gives as she takes."

A cold presence materialized beside the fireplace. Magnus stood there, solid enough that she could see the concern on his translucent features.

Alyssa threw herself back against the couch, trying to process. Her inability to conceive was so wrapped up in past hurt, in pain, but she felt like she was coming to terms with that. The potential of a baby, gifted from a literal goddess, played with her emotions in dangerous ways. "And we don't know until we do it?"

"I don't think we can."

"She is right," Magnus said quietly. Only Alyssa could hear him. "The goddess works in mystery. Even in my time, the details were kept secret. No one here has done this before. We cannot know."

Alyssa let out a long sigh that seemed to come from her bones. The weight of generations pressed down on her. Then she shrugged, surprising herself. "I guess we just have to wait and see. This won't change my mind, though I'd come to grips with the fact I wasn't going to have a child and now... Now I don't know."

Sam reached across the space between them, squeezing Alyssa's knee. "I'm sorry. I should have told you sooner."

"No, it's okay. Really." And strangely, it was. "Whatever happens, happens."

Because none of that mattered right now. Whatever the goddess decided, Alyssa would deal with it. If she had a baby, she would love it, unquestioningly. Right now, she was more concerned about Michael – six years old and running out of time. About Brendan, who'd come here desperate to save him only to find it might all be for nothing. About the barrier weakening, and the news of Tū's child approaching.

"You're taking this better than I expected," Sam said carefully.

Alyssa glanced at Magnus, who gave her the slightest nod of approval. "I've had good teachers. And honestly? After finding out I'm literally made of earth, that my whole family line was birthed by a goddess... what's one more impossibility?"

Sam's eyes widened. "Brendan told you?"

"About being a clay baby?" Alyssa laughed, the sound only slightly hysterical. "Yeah. Apparently I'm not even human. Not fully."

"You're more human than most," Magnus interjected.

"Humanity isn't about origin – it's about choice. And you keep choosing to help, to protect, to love. Even when it hurts."

Tears pricked her eyes. She blinked them back, not wanting to smudge her war paint lipstick.

"Alyssa?" Sam was watching her with concern. "You okay?"

"Yeah. Just... thinking."

"You're not a clay baby, you know. You're part goddess yourself, one of the Kuraatua."

Alyssa nodded, still trying to align that fact with her reality. Unable to process that very soon, she was going to meet the mother of all the Māori gods herself. She drained her coffee, using the burn to centre herself. "What time tonight?"

"Sunset. We'll meet here." Sam gathered her things, preparing to leave. "The others you met at the fair will be there. Rowan, Hazel, Ursula, Mia. They're good people. They'll help. Matai will be there."

"And Brendan?"

Sam hesitated. "That's up to you."

After Sam left, Alyssa sat in the gathering gloom. Socks had given up chasing Buttons and now lay curled in a patch of dying sunlight. The ghost cat sat nearby, keeping watch.

"You could have told me," she said to the seemingly empty room. "About the pregnancy thing."

Magnus shimmered into view. "I had not connected the dots. Besides, would it have helped?"

"Still."

"Some knowledge is a burden, and you have enough of those." He moved closer, and she could almost feel his hand on her shoulder. Almost. "You're brave, Alyssa Whenua. Braver than you know."

"I'm terrified."

"Good. Only fools feel no fear when approaching gods." He

smiled, an expression that transformed his Viking features. "But you'll face it anyway. That's what courage is."

Her phone buzzed. A text from Kelly: *On the road. ETA 3 hours.*

Alyssa stood, squaring her shoulders. The red lipstick caught the light in the mirror, fierce as flame. Fierce as a child of a goddess.

# CHAPTER 33

"Something's wrong." Matai's eyes were dark, scanning the street behind him as if expecting trouble. "I can sense it – magic gone bad."

"You can sense magic?" Brendan pulled his jacket tighter around him, the leather still warm from the afternoon sun, but it did little to ward off the chill of death in the air.

"Sure, can't you?" Matai was already heading towards his black truck, keys jingling.

"Sometimes." Brendan followed, his Kaipō instincts already stirring, a cold prickle at the base of his skull. "Depends on the type and strength."

They climbed into the truck, the seats hot from the sun. The engine roared to life with an unnerving thunk that made Brendan wonder about its maintenance. As they pulled away from the curb, he found himself gripping the door handle.

"So how strong is Alyssa?" The question had been nagging at him since the confrontation at Mrs Nolan's office.

Matai glanced over, his knuckles white on the steering wheel. "Pretty strong. Strong enough, I think."

"Your words aren't filling me with confidence," Brendan muttered, watching familiar streets blur past.

"Oh lighten up, would you? She's one of us. We're not going to let anything happen to her. And we'll be there to help her adjust to... Well, whatever happens."

Brendan slumped back in the cracked vinyl seat.

"And what about you?" Matai's sidelong glance was sharp. "Are you one of us?"

"I'm not sure I follow."

"Are you going to throw in and help protect the Bay? Or are you heading out once you get what you came for?"

Heat flared in Brendan's chest. "It's not like that! Sure, I came here to save my nephew. I'd do anything to save him, anything not to see my sister suffer. And I've been nothing but up front when it comes to Alyssa. A bloke with ill intentions wouldn't have fessed up like I did, even though it could have cost me a chance with her."

"That's the spirit." Matai nodded, a grin breaking through. "Nice to know you've got some fire in there. Might come in handy."

Brendan shook his head, a surprised laugh escaping. "You asshole."

"Sometimes." Matai's grin widened. "Look, you know I think you're a decent man. Just don't be a dick when it comes to Alyssa. We're family here, and if you want to be a part of it you need to be considerate, and treat people with respect. That's really all we ask."

"Done." Brendan could work with that. Besides, it wasn't like he wanted to go up against this bunch. God children and their partners? Better friends than enemies.

As they turned onto a side street, the wrongness intensi-fied. The air felt heavier, and Brendan's magic stirred uneasily. Death had been here. Recently.

They pulled up in front of a tidy single-story house, which must be Mrs Nolan's. The cottage garden looked normal enough, but lights blazed from every window despite the afternoon sun.

"Looks like she's home," Matai said, though his voice had gone flat. "Come on. Let me take the lead though."

The front door stood ajar. Matai nudged it with his toe, and it swung inward with a long creak. The smell hit them immediately – copper and ozone and something else that made Brendan's necromancer senses flare.

Brendan caught his glare and shrugged. "What? It's not like she's not expecting someone. The door was open." Matai called into the hallway. "We've come to have a word, Mrs Nolan."

The air was still, cloying, the scent of death almost overwhelming.

"What the hell is going on here," Brendan muttered as they moved deeper into the house. The hallway felt too narrow, family photos watching them pass with glassy eyes.

The living room made him stop short. "Shit, something went down here."

Blood pooled on the hardwood floor, dark and congealing. The coffee table lay overturned, magazines scattered. But no corpse or injured party. The air still hummed with the aftershock of violence, and underneath it, the distinctive scent that made his magic surge – souls had been touched here.

"No kidding. I can feel the magic still buzzing in the air. Is she dead?" Matai stood in the doorway, careful not to step in the blood.

"If she's not, then she's close to it." Brendan forced himself to look away from the scene, his darker instincts wanting to dive deeper.

"Let's split up, search the house. Top to bottom. Meet back

at the front door in five minutes, but call out if you find anything. I'll take the upper floor."

Brendan nodded, grateful for the excuse to leave the room. They searched quickly – the kitchen sterile and unused, a medicine cabinet overflowing with prescriptions, a bedroom with sheets that reeked of fear-sweat. He pocketed a few letters with out-of-town postmarks from the bedside table.

Still no Mrs Nolan.

Back at the front door, Matai looked grim. "Find anything?"

"Couple of letters from out of town might be worth a look." He handed them over. "But no sign of her."

"I need you to do your thing." Matai pointed back towards the living room. "Figure out what happened in there."

Brendan's stomach tightened, memories of the past surging to the front. The dead, the hungry, the desperate to be heard. "I'd rather not."

Matai reached out and squeezed his shoulder. "I know you don't like this, but you said you cared. About Alyssa, about the Bay. Prove it."

Brendan shrugged Matai's hand off and shook his head. "I don't need to prove shit, man. Back off."

Matai's hand closed on his arm this time, firm but not threatening. "We need you to do this. You think we like all of the things we do? I know people who have killed to keep the Bay safe. Killed to keep their loved ones safe. All I'm asking is that you man up and figure out what the hell went down."

The weight of it settled on his shoulders. "Fine." He shook off Matai's grip and stalked into the living room, closing the door firmly behind him. He drew the curtains for good measure – this wasn't something for an audience.

Standing in the centre of the room, Brendan took a deep breath and let his defenses drop.

His magic unfurled like smoke, reaching for the echoes of death that clung to the walls. This was the gift that made people fear necromancers – not just speaking to the dead, but reading death itself. Every end left traces, and he could follow them like footprints in snow.

The room shimmered, time peeling back layer by layer. He didn't need chants or circles for this. Death came to him as naturally as breathing – sometimes more so.

The scene rebuilt itself:

Mrs Nolan on her knees in the centre of the room. Alive but terrified, her usually perfect hair disheveled, mascara running. She was speaking, pleading with someone Brendan couldn't quite see – a figure wrapped in shadows that seemed to eat light.

Then another presence entered. A woman, young-looking but with something ancient in her movements. Power radiated from her in controlled waves that made Brendan's reconstructed vision waver. This was magic on a scale he'd rarely encountered.

The woman reached out casually, almost gently, and placed her hand on Mrs Nolan's chest. What happened next made Brendan's own magic recoil.

She pulled something free. Not physically – Mrs Nolan's body remained intact – but something essential came loose in the woman's grip. A soul, but traumatized, twisted by the violent extraction. Mrs Nolan's body crumpled, not dead but empty. A fate worse than death.

"Weak," the woman said, her voice carrying even through the echo. "But sufficient for a down payment."

The vision began to fade, but not before the woman glanced towards where Brendan would eventually stand. A coincidence, surely, but it sent ice through his veins.

He pulled back, slamming his mental walls into place. Sweat beaded on his forehead as he opened his eyes to the present. The blood on the floor looked darker now, and he could still feel the resonance of that stolen soul.

His hands shook slightly as he processed what he'd seen. Someone had torn out Mrs Nolan's soul. Not killed her – that would have been kinder. They'd hollowed her out and taken the essence for... what? Payment? Power?

Brendan wiped his palms on his jeans and opened the door. Matai took one look at his face and stepped back.

"That bad?"

"Someone ripped out her soul." The words came out flat, matter-of-fact. "Not killed – took her soul and left the body breathing somewhere. There was a woman, powerful. Maybe Tū's child, based on what Mrs Nolan wrote." He swallowed hard. "She called the soul a down payment."

Matai's face went pale. "Shit. We need to warn the others. If she's collecting souls – "

"Then the barrier might not be enough." Brendan finished the thought that neither wanted to voice. "We need to tell Alyssa. Tell all of them. Tonight's ritual just became a lot more urgent."

As they hurried to the truck, Brendan couldn't shake the memory of that casual violence. The way the woman had just plucked out Mrs Nolan's soul. Like picking fruit.

Whatever was coming for the Bay, it had already begun its harvest.

"That woman," Brendan said as they reached the truck. "The way she just... took what she wanted. No hesitation."

Matai's jaw tightened. "That's Tū's way. Domination. Conquest. His followers don't negotiate – they take. They believe strength is the only virtue that matters."

"And we're supposed to stop people like that?"

Matai turned the key in the ignition, the engine growling to life. "We don't have a choice, bro. Because if we don't, there won't be anyone left to try."

# CHAPTER 34

They came to her door in small groups: Samantha and Matai first. Rowan, Ursula, Hazel and Mia, witches from the market, not long after. Sunlight streamed into the house still, but she knew that it would fade along with this day and her current existence.

Inside, the house felt different. Charged. Even Socks seemed to sense it, watching from his perch on the stairs with eyes that reflected more than just the light.

The house felt crowded with so many people in it. Until now there had been one, maybe two at a time, but this was kind of nice. Magic buzzed in the air, as though the auras around each individually were mingling, and the different scents they brought with them from the world outside seemed to blend together seamlessly.

Brendan leaned against a wall, his presence both distracting and comforting her. Alyssa longed to collapse into his arms, but for right now she needed to stay strong and keep herself together. Whole. So that she could go into this ritual and do what she must.

Finally, Constance entered the house, moving with more purpose than her years should allow.

"We don't have much time." Constance's weathered hands gripped her walking stick. "The barrier weakens with every passing moment. I can feel it fraying."

"The cards have been warning me," Mia said, even now shuffling the same tarot deck she'd done Alyssa's reading with. "Enemies approach."

"Tū's followers," Sam added. "They sense the vulnerability."

Brendan pushed off from the wall where he'd been silently waiting. "So where do we do this?"

Constance turned those knowing eyes on Alyssa. "Child, you know where. You've always known."

Alyssa's stomach dropped, her eyes going to the door that led down to the place she had been avoiding. "The basement."

"Your ancestors built this house for a reason. Right over the heart of her power, sealed and waiting for the day it would be needed." Constance's expression softened. "The day you would be ready."

"I'm not ready," Alyssa said automatically.

"No one ever is." Ursula spoke for the first time, her voice carrying emotional undertones that made everyone turn. "But the earth chooses its own time. I can feel it calling to you – it's probably been calling ever since you arrived."

Sam moved to Alyssa's side, and gripped her hand. "We'll all be with you. You won't do this alone."

She appreciated the support, and gave her friend a gentle squeeze before withdrawing. She couldn't touch the others right now. It was too much. "The basement," Alyssa whispered. The locked room. The one place in the house she'd avoided even after reclaiming everything else.

Alyssa could feel it now – the pulse beneath the foundation, the power that had always been there, thrumming like a heartbeat.

"Sam, help me walk," Constance instructed. "The rest of you, gather what we need. Salt, water from the kitchen – the tap's connected to the well, it's pure enough. Candles if you can find them."

"What about me?" Brendan asked.

Constance studied him for a long moment. "You carry death's mark, boy. We'll need that before this is over. Stay close to Alyssa."

The basement door had never looked more forbidding. Alyssa's hand trembled as she reached for the handle. It opened into the secret room with its chest of journals and grimoires, where she'd first truly understood what Gran had kept from her all these years.

The earth beneath their feet began to tremble.

"Stay calm," Constance commanded, though her own voice held a note of awe.

The tremor intensified, dust cascading from the ceiling, and then with a grinding sound like continents shifting, the floor split open. Not violently, not destructively, but with deliberate purpose – stone and earth peeling back like curtains to reveal ancient rock, as the wall opened into a cavern that stole Alyssa's breath. It was vast, impossibly vast, the ceiling disappearing into darkness. In the centre lay a perfectly circular pool of water.

"The heart of Kotahi Bay," Constance said, her voice echoing in the space. "Where the first ancestors found the gods' footprints. Where your bloodline accepted the responsibility of guardianship."

"It's beautiful," Hazel said.

"It's power," Matai corrected, but not unkindly. "Raw, ancient power."

"And – it feels like someone is coming," said Mia.

Sam nodded. "Tū's followers can sense magic. They'll be moving faster now, summoning whatever power they can."

The sound of footsteps echoed from above, urgent and uneven. Brendan was already moving towards the stairs. Moments later, Kelly appeared at the cavern entrance, her face pale with exertion and fear. Grant was right behind her, and between them they carried Michael, the boy's small body limp in their arms. Esther followed, her hands fluttering helplessly, tears streaming down her face.

"Where – " Kelly started, then stopped, her eyes widening as she took in the impossible cavern, the glowing pool, the assembled group. "Damn, Lysie. What is this place?"

"No time," Alyssa said, pushing aside the complicated knot of emotions at seeing Kelly here, in this sacred space. "Bring him to the pool. Carefully."

They descended the ancient steps, Michael's labored breathing echoing off the stone walls. The boy's skin had taken on a greyish cast, and dark veins spider-webbed across his temples. Whatever poison or curse was killing him, it was accelerating.

"Here," Constance directed, gesturing to a smooth patch of stone beside the pool. "Lay him down gently. He needs to be within the circle but not in the water – not yet."

Grant had already left. No one stopped him. Whatever this was, whatever was about to happen in this impossible cavern beneath his ex-girlfriend's house – he wanted no part of it. Alyssa felt a flicker of grim satisfaction. At least he had the sense to know when he didn't belong.

Kelly stood awkwardly at the edge of the gathering, uncertainty written across her face. Alyssa met her eyes for a brief moment – there would be time for their reckoning later. Right now, all that mattered was the dying child at the centre of their circle.

As they settled Michael on the ground, his eyes fluttered open for just a moment. "Mum?" he whispered, his voice barely audible. "It's so cold."

"I'm here, baby," Esther dropped to her knees beside him, smoothing his hair back from his fevered forehead. "These people are going to help you. You're going to be okay."

Esther looked up then, her eyes finding Alyssa's across the cavern with a mother's raw, unfiltered hope. Alyssa crossed to her, kneeling on the ancient stone. Up close, she could see the grey hollows beneath Esther's eyes, the way her hands trembled as they smoothed Michael's hair.

Alyssa reached for her hand. "We're going to do everything we can."

Esther's hand found hers - cold, desperate, clutching. "I don't understand any of this. The magic, this place, what you're about to do. But I can feel it. Something in the earth here. It's... alive."

"It's been waiting," Alyssa said softly. "For a long time. For someone who needed it enough."

"He's all I have." Esther's voice cracked. "His father left when Michael got sick. Said he couldn't watch him die. So it's just been us."

Alyssa thought of all the futures she'd imagined - the family she'd planned with Grant. Different wounds, but she understood the ache of being left to carry something alone.

"You're not alone now." She squeezed Esther's hand. "Whatever happens next—you're not alone."

Esther held her gaze for a long moment. "Save him," she said simply. "Please."

Alyssa rose, that single word settling into her bones like a vow.

"Let's begin with a karakia," Constance said. She moved to the pool's edge with surprising grace, beginning to chant in a language older than memory. Sam and Matai joined her, their voices weaving together in haunting harmonies. It made her feel more in sync with this moment, as though the energy of the earth was reaching up to join them.

"Form the circle," Alyssa said, the words coming from somewhere beyond her conscious mind. "Samantha – take the west. Rowan – east. Matai, south. Hazel, north." She didn't know why, but intuition was guiding her, or perhaps it was her grandmother, Alyssa could feel her presence now, soft, calm, stable, and far too strong to mess with. Brendan joined the circle as well, adding to the strength of the ritual.

The karakia rose and fell, Constance's voice carrying the weight of generations. She sprinkled salt in a circle around the pool, dropped herbs into the glowing water – kawakawa for protection, harakeke for binding, mānuka for healing. The scent rose with the steam, filling the cavern with sacred purpose.

"Now," Constance said. "Call to her, child. Call to your mother."

Alyssa stepped to the pool's edge, her reflection wavering in the dark water. She could feel the others channeling their power. Ursula stood steady, reading and balancing the emotional currents, keeping them stable. She could feel each of the others, the specific tingle of their magic flowing into the conduit of the pool.

"I don't know what to say," Alyssa admitted.

"Speak from your heart," Brendan said, moving to stand beside her.

Alyssa closed her eyes, feeling for words that weren't words, for the language that existed before speech.

"Papatūānuku," she began, her voice stronger than she'd

expected. "Mother Earth, Mother of All. I am Alyssa, daughter of your daughters, blood of your blood. I come not as a stranger but as a child returning home after too long away."

The water began to churn, slowly at first, then faster. The temperature in the cavern dropped, then rose, as if the earth itself was breathing.

"I've been afraid," Alyssa continued, tears flowing freely now. "Afraid of what I am, what I might become. But there's a child dying, and a town that needs protection, and I can't be afraid anymore."

The pool erupted.

Water shot upward in a column that should have hit the ceiling but instead seemed to pierce through stone and earth and house to touch the sky itself. And in that water, forming from droplets and light, came a figure of such terrible beauty that everyone except Alyssa fell to their knees.

Papatūānuku was every woman and no woman, young and ancient, fertile and barren, creator and destroyer. Her hair was rivers and roots, her skin was rich soil and solid stone, her eyes held the depth of every chasm and the height of every mountain.

As the goddess's presence filled the cavern, Alyssa felt a memory surface unbidden – Mia's crimson tent at the fair, the scent of vanilla and dried herbs, those knowing dark eyes. Three cards laid out on velvet: The Empress, Temperance, Death.

"Something significant is shifting in your life. Old patterns falling away to make room for new growth."

She'd been walking towards this moment ever since. Maybe longer. Maybe her whole life.

"Daughter," Papatūānuku said, her voice earthquake and whisper, volcano and breeze. "You call me Mother, but do you understand what that means?"

"I'm learning," Alyssa said honestly.

And then the goddess's power began to flow into her.

It wasn't like anything she could have prepared for. The energy rose through her feet, through the ancient stone, through every root and rock of Kotahi Bay—and as it filled her, it found all the empty spaces she'd been carrying.

"Please – help us. Help me save them."

The goddess studied her with eyes that had watched continents drift. "To save a life marked for death requires permission from my sister. Will you call her too? Will you stand between earth and ending? Will you let go of what needs to be relinquished?"

Alyssa felt Brendan's hand slip into hers, cool and steady and right.

"I will," Alyssa vowed. Brendan's words mirrored her own.

"Then call her. Call Hine-nui-te-pō, and we shall see what death may offer to life in exchange for your sacrifice."

The temperature plummeted. Frost spread across the pool's surface despite the spring's warmth, and shadows gathered in the corners like living things. Brendan's grip on her hand was the only warm thing in a world gone cold.

"Goddess of Death," Brendan said, his voice carrying an authority Alyssa had never heard before. "Keeper of the final threshold, guardian of the last journey. I am Brendan. My blood has carried your blessing and your burden for generations. We call you now not to take a life but to spare one."

The shadows coalesced, and she was there.

Hine-nui-te-pō was beautiful in the way winter was beautiful, in the way endings could be merciful. Half her face was that of a young woman, lovely and serene. The other half was bone and shadow, neither cruel nor kind but simply final.

"My marked child," she said, focusing on Brendan with something almost maternal. "How long your family has misunderstood my gift. Death is not a curse, boy. Death is the rhythm that makes life precious. Without endings, there are no beginnings. Your family's connection to me – it's not a burden. It's a responsibility. To help others cross when their time comes. To ensure the cycle continues."

"But Michael's time – it doesn't have to be now," Alyssa interjected. "He's just a child. He's done nothing wrong."

Both goddesses turned to her, and the weight of their combined attention nearly drove her to her knees.

"To interfere with death's pattern requires a price," Hine-nui-te-pō added. "What do you offer?"

Alyssa straightened, feeling power flow through her from the earth below and the others around her. The power was all here, but to let it flow through her completely, a sacrifice was required. She had to let go of what was blocking its path. She had to let all the old dreams die – the future she'd once longed for that no longer fit – maybe it was all social conditioning, anyway. She'd longed for family, for connection...But now, she needed to clear space for whatever came next.

This energy of the earth was the very lifeforce that had allowed her ancestors to birth their babies, and yet something else was more important now. She had to let go. She opened up to her grief, letting the old emotion pour out of her.

"I offer you my old dreams so that they may return to the earth and feed new life," Alyssa said as the tears burst forth and long-buried pain bloomed in her chest – not just grieving for her future, but for her childhood self who never felt truly loved by her own mother, who never fit in her childhood, who had felt so abandoned.

The goddesses both nodded, receiving the flow of energy as a gift, but they wanted more.

"What else?"

Alyssa reached deep inside her heart for the answer. "Service. Not just mine – ours. We'll be your hands in this world. Guardians of the balance. Protectors of the boundary between life and death, earth and void. Use us."

The goddesses exchanged a look that spanned eternities.

"The new guardians offer themselves freely," Papatūānuku mused. "Not from fear or obligation, but from love."

"Love for a place, for people, for life itself," Hine-nui-te-pō agreed. "Few mortals understand that service and freedom are not opposites."

"Warning!" Mia's voice cracked like a whip from the stairs. "They're here! We can't hold them much longer!"

"Very well," Papatūānuku said with something that might have been amusement. "Your offer is accepted. But remember – power given freely can be freely taken if you prove unworthy."

Both goddesses moved at once. Papatūānuku flowed forward like an avalanche in reverse, entering Alyssa with the force of continental drift. Every cell in her body screamed and sang as earth-power filled her, old as mountains, patient as erosion, strong as bedrock.

Hine-nui-te-pō touched Brendan's forehead with one bone-white finger. He gasped, shadows wreathing him like armour, but there was no fear in his eyes. Only understanding.

"Now," Constance commanded, her voice cutting through divine transformation. "All of you – lend them your power! Weave it together!"

The circle erupted as all their magic pooled together.

But it was Alyssa who had to direct it all.

She felt herself fracturing, not breaking but multiplying. Part of her stood in the cavern, hands linked with Brendan, channeling divine power. But part of her rose, swift and sudden, her consciousness taking the form of a tiny bird.

A fantail. Of course.

She burst from her body like a soul set free, darting upward through stone and soil as if they were mist. In an instant she was above the house, wings beating frantically, seeing Kotahi Bay spread below in the dying light.

The attackers were spirits of war and conflict, pressing against the town's failing barrier with claws of smoke and teeth of night, eager to reclaim this place for humankind only. They whispered promises of blood and conquest, of a world remade in Tū's image – all war, all rage, all the time.

*No*, Alyssa thought, and her fantail form burst into light.

She saw the pattern as it formed – not a wall this time, not a rigid barrier that could crack and fall. Instead, a web, flexible and strong, able to bend without breaking. Every strand connected to every other strand, creating redundancies, creating resilience. The old barrier had been a fortress. This was a living thing.

The spirits howled their frustration as the web solidified, golden strands becoming harder than steel, brighter than starlight. Where they touched the web, they burned. Where they tried to break through, the web simply flexed, absorbed the blow, and snapped back stronger.

*More*, whispered Papatūānuku through her. *Show them the earth's true power.*

Alyssa poured everything into the web – the love she'd rediscovered for this place, the friendships she'd begun to forge, the connections she'd made. Every strand hummed with purpose, with the combined will of the new guardians.

The spirits recoiled as if struck. She felt their master's rage – Tū's daughter, child of war, furious at being denied her prize. But also... was that fear? Yes. They feared what Kotahi Bay had become, what she and the others had become.

*Good*, she thought fiercely, and sent one last pulse of power through the web.

It lit up like a sunrise, every strand blazing with light that could be seen only by those with eyes to see. The spirits fled, streaming away like smoke before a hurricane, leaving only clean night behind.

But the effort had cost her.

The world spun, tilted, fractured. She slammed back into her physical form with enough force to shatter stone.

Back in her body, her knees buckled. Blood filled her mouth, tasting of copper and spent magic. The cavern whirled around her, and she would have fallen if Brendan hadn't caught her.

"Alyssa!" His voice seemed to come from very far away. "No, stay with me. Stay here."

She tried to speak, to say she was fine, but only blood came out. The divine power had been too much, the channeling too intense. She'd burned herself out like a candle in a hurricane, all light and fury and then –

Nothing.

# CHAPTER 35

The darkness reached for her, but it wasn't Hine-nui-te-pō's shadow. This was the void, the nothing, the place between heartbeats that might stretch forever.

Brendan's hands found her shoulders, cool and steady against her burning skin. "No," he said firmly, and she felt his power flow into her – not death this time, but life. His life force, freely given, pouring into her like cool water into a parched riverbed.

"Brendan, don't – " Alyssa started, but he was already deep in the working, his face set with determination.

The transfer was visible to those with eyes to see – silvery threads of energy flowing from him to her, each one carrying memories, emotions, pieces of his very essence. She felt his love, his grief, his fierce protectiveness, and underlying it all, his growing feelings for her.

"That's enough!" Sam moved to pull him back, but Ursula caught her arm.

"Wait," Mia said softly. "Look."

Because something else was happening. As Brendan poured his life into Alyssa, Papatūānuku's presence rose from the earth itself, adding her ancient strength to his modern sacrifice. The goddess's power flowed up through the stone, through the pool, weaving itself with Brendan's offering until the two energies merged into something new.

Alyssa gasped, her back arching as the combined forces flooded through her. The taste of copper faded from her mouth, replaced by something like spring rain and deep earth. Her eyes flew open, meeting Brendan's for one perfect moment before he swayed and Sam yanked him backward, breaking the connection.

Brendan lay on the cavern floor, blinking up at the ceiling. But he was smiling.

"What have you done to yourself?" Alyssa said, softly.

"Worth it," he mumbled.

A soft cry from beside the pool drew their attention. Michael's eyes fluttered open, the dark veins fading from his temples like morning mist. Colour seeped back into his grey skin, and his breathing deepened from those terrible shallow gasps to something normal, healthy.

"Mum?" His voice was weak but clear. "What... where are we?"

Esther let out a sob that echoed off the cavern walls, gathering him close. "It's okay, baby. You're okay. These people helped you."

Behind them, there was a soft thud. They turned to see Constance crumpled on the stone floor, Sam already moving towards her.

"She pushed too hard," Sam said, checking the elder's pulse. "The karakia, the ritual — it was too much."

Hazel was there in an instant, her hands glowing faintly as

she assessed Constance's condition. "She's stable, but exhausted. Her energy is completely depleted."

"We need to get her upstairs," Ursula said, Rowan and Matai moving to help even before she'd finished speaking.

"Go on..." Alyssa managed, trying to sit up. The world tilted alarmingly.

"Slow down," Brendan said, though he wasn't doing much better. "You just channeled two goddesses and rebuilt the entire town's defenses."

"And you just gave me part of your life," she countered, still feeling all of the memories and emotions he had flooded her with. "So maybe we're both idiots."

A weak laugh surprised them both. It was Constance, her eyes cracked open. "The young," she whispered. "Always so dramatic. Help me up, would you?"

It took all of them to get everyone mobile. Matai and Rowan supported Constance between them, the elder's feet barely touching the ground. Mia helped Esther with Michael, who insisted he felt fine but accepted the support when his legs wobbled.

Kelly was waiting in the basement room, pacing between the stored furniture and old boxes. When she saw them emerge – Alyssa with her darkened hair, Brendan with his silver streak, Constance barely conscious, Michael walking but fragile – her face went through a series of expressions too complex to read.

"Lysie," she started, then stopped. "Your hair..."

"Not now, Kel." Alyssa couldn't handle this conversation, not when she could barely stand.

Upstairs, Alyssa sank into a kitchen chair. Everything felt heavier now, as if the earth's power had added density to her bones. The kitchen felt impossibly normal after the cavern's ancient power. Socks sat on the table, tail twitching with disapproval at the invasion of his domain.

"Michael needs water," Esther said, hovering over her son. "And food. He hasn't eaten in days."

"I'll handle it," Mia offered, already moving to the cupboards. "Sam, you should check on Constance. I've got this."

The house filled with quiet activity. Footsteps as they settled Constance in the spare room. The whistle of the kettle. Michael's quiet voice asking his mother why everyone looked so strange. Normal sounds that felt surreal after what they'd just experienced.

"We did it," Alyssa mumbled. "We actually did it." She was looking at her hands, cupped together on the table. They looked exactly the same. She felt the same, and yet changed as well, more connected to everything inside the Bay, especially the earth beneath them.

"We did," Sam agreed. She was perched on the next chair over, an ethereal glow about her.

"How's Constance?" Alyssa asked, looking up and around at the other faces. Just Matai and Samantha now, as Brendan was checking over his whānau - his family, and the other witches were giving them space.

"Sleeping. She'll pull through. But Alyssa..."

She looked up at Sam's tone – serious, worried.

"What you did today, channeling both goddesses, rebuilding the barrier that way... it's changed you. Permanently. You need to understand that."

Alyssa thought of the fantail flights, of seeing Kotahi Bay from above, of feeling every thread of power that protected this place. "I know," she said quietly. "I can feel it. I'm not just Alyssa anymore."

"You're still you," Brendan said firmly, re-entering the room. He crossed the kitchen and sank to his knees before her, one arm looping around her waist, the other hand reaching for hers. His skin was warm, grounding, full of awe. "Just... more."

"More." She tasted the word, found it fitting. "I suppose we all are now."

# CHAPTER 36

Sunlight streamed through the kitchen windows. Alyssa stood at the counter, watching steam curl from two mugs of tea – nothing stronger, not this morning. Her body still hummed with the earth's power, a constant thrum beneath her skin that felt both foreign and perfectly right.

Kelly was asleep on the couch where she'd crashed last night, too stubborn to leave. It had seemed cruel to send her away after she'd helped guide Esther and Michael to Kotahi Bay, after she'd witnessed magic that must have shattered her understanding of the world.

Kelly stirred at her approach, mascara smudged beneath her eyes, hair a tangled mess that reminded Alyssa of countless sleepovers from their youth.

"Morning," Alyssa said softly, holding out a mug.

Kelly sat up slowly, accepting the tea with hands that trembled slightly. "Was that all real, then?"

"Not a dream." Alyssa settled into the armchair across from her, cradling her own mug. "Though I understand the feeling."

"You really are magic..." Kelly sipped the tea as if it might restore her view of the world. "The earth... your basement... I..." She closed her mouth, clearly unable to form the right words to express what she was thinking or feeling.

They sat in silence for a moment, years of friendship and recent betrayal hanging between them like morning mist.

"I need to tell you something," Kelly said suddenly, the words tumbling out as if they'd been building pressure. "About Grant. About everything."

Alyssa waited, watching her friend's face crumple and rebuild itself.

"I fell in love with him years ago," Kelly whispered. "Before you two ever met. We had a class together, and he used to make me laugh, and I... God, Lysie, I was such a coward. I never said anything. And then you met him at that party, and watching you two fall in love..." She pressed her free hand to her chest. "It broke my heart. Every day, watching my best friend with the man I loved, it was like dying inside."

"Kelly – "

"No, please, let me finish." Tears tracked down Kelly's cheeks. "I know there's nothing that can excuse it. I tried so hard to be happy for you. All those years...it felt like I was dying inside. And when your relationship started drifting apart, part of me came back to life. I'm so ashamed of that. When he started showing interest in me, I avoided him at first. I swear I did. But eventually, I betrayed myself and you, and I'm so, so sorry."

Alyssa set down her mug, processing this new version of their history. "Why didn't you tell me you loved him?"

"I didn't want to hurt you." Kelly laughed bitterly. "Turns out I hurt you a lot worse by not saying anything. Love is hard, Lysie. Heartbreak is hard. And I made it so much worse for both of us."

Looking at her friend – really looking at her – Alyssa saw

the years of pain Kelly had carried. The weight of unspoken love, of watching from the sidelines, of finally grasping what she'd wanted only to lose her best friend in the process.

"I want to forgive you," Alyssa said, and meant it. The words came from somewhere deeper than hurt, from the part of her that had touched divine understanding. "What you did wasn't okay, but I don't hate you for it. Or him."

Kelly's sob was half relief, half disbelief. "How can you just —"

"Because none of it really matters anymore." Alyssa stood, crossing to sit beside Kelly on the couch. "I don't want anything to do with Grant. I'm so different now, Kel. So far from who I was. I know you better than anyone. I know you wouldn't have tried to hurt me on purpose. I know you suffered."

Kelly pulled her into a fierce hug. "I love you, Lysie. I've missed you so much."

"I've missed you too," Alyssa said, though the words held different weight now. There was no going back to what they'd been. But perhaps they could build something new.

A door opened upstairs, and the thud of Constance and her walking stick moved carefully but steadily. As she rounded the door into the living room, Alyssa could see that the exhaustion had lifted from her face, replaced by something that might have been satisfaction.

"Good morning," she called out. "I trust the tea is on?"

"Always," Alyssa called back, then to Kelly: "Come on. Let's get some breakfast."

---

The garden welcomed her like an old friend. Alyssa knelt in the rich soil, her hands pressed to the earth, feeling the pulse of life beneath her palms. Around her, the plants seemed to lean in, as if drawn to the power that flowed through her now.

"Showing off?" Brendan's voice came from behind her, warm with amusement.

She smiled without turning.

He settled beside her on the grass. "Do you think the barrier will hold now?"

She closed her eyes, reaching down through soil and stone to the heart of Kotahi Bay's power. "Long enough."

"Long enough for what?"

"To learn. To grow stronger. To find the others who'll help protect this place." She turned to face him. "To figure out what we are now."

"And what are we?" He lifted a hand, thumb tracing the line of her jaw.

"Different," she said. "Changed. But still us."

He kissed her then, soft and certain, and she tasted promise in it. Not of easy happiness or simple answers, but of partnership in whatever came next.

"So," he said, "what happens now?"

Alyssa looked around the garden – at the house her ancestors had built over sacred ground, at the plants that grew in impossible abundance, at the town spread below them that she'd sworn to protect. She thought of Constance, carrying the old wisdom. Of Sam and all the others who'd stood with her. Of Michael, alive and laughing.

"Now?" She stood, pulling him up with her. "Now we have coffee, and maybe watch a movie." She smiled, feeling the earth's contentment echo through her. "After all, the barrier's not going anywhere. And neither am I."

"Alyssa?" he said, drawing her towards him. "I'm not going anywhere either, if that's alright with you."

She pursed her lips as if she was considering whether she wanted him around, but when a line of tension creased his forehead she laughed and kissed him. "Yeah, I think that's a good plan. You do give a good foot massage after all, and Magnus tolerates you, so you must be okay."

He laughed then too, swatting her backside playfully.

As they walked back to the house hand in hand, Alyssa felt something settle in her chest. Not an ending, but a beginning. The first day of whatever came next. And out of the corner of her eye, Magnus's face appeared in the reflection of the window. He smiled and winked at her, then vanished.

That night, Alyssa dreamed.

She hovered above the Bay, the barrier rippling around the sleeping town.

A wind rose then, lightning and thunder crashed, sweeping through the barrier, bringing something with it. Something new was coming. Something born on the air.

# EPOLOGUE: MELODY

*The wind used to love me. It used to twist its fingers through my hair and kiss my cheek. It used to wrap around my body and respond to my whims. But here in this city, within the confines of this barren concrete cage, I cannot hear it sing.*

Melody looked up from her writing, out the window to the park. Nothing moved, it was dull and lifeless – just the way she felt.

An odd sensation crept over her, as if the air itself thickened, touching something hidden…a longing for a freedom she couldn't quite place.

Melody's fingertips grazed the cold glass of the window, a shiver running over her arm, not from the chill but from a fleeting sense of connection, like a half-remembered dream of being one with the wind. The sensation was gone as quickly as it came, leaving her more aware of the empty void inside her.

She pursed her lips. "I want to go out, Robbie." She spoke loudly so that her boyfriend could hear her from his studio in the room next door, but there was no response. "Robbie?" Still nothing.

She picked up the notebook, holding it for a moment before letting it fall. It hit the floor with a soft thud, more a surrender than a statement. Melody's fingers lingered on the pen as her frustration grew. It wasn't just the lack of response from Robbie that irked her; it was the growing realization that she was missing something.

No response.

Melody rolled her eyes and pushed up from the chair, slipping her feet into her comfortable old skate shoes. Spring might be here, but it didn't feel warm enough yet to go barefoot.

As she moved through the apartment, a sense of isolation wrapped around her, tighter with each step. In the muted light, Melody's reflection caught her eye briefly as she passed the mirror. Her long, wavy dark blonde hair hung listlessly around her shoulders today as though it felt the weight of the still musty air. She barely recognized the woman staring back at her. The light that once danced in her eyes had dimmed, her skin was pale under the artificial lights.

She padded her way to the studio door, pushed it open and leaned against the frame.

"Robbbieeeee..."

He faced away, bent over his table, focused intently on the piece of jewellery he was crafting, his back and neck taut as he worked. She imagined his expression, his brow furrowed in concentration, the delicate dance of his fingers over the metal and stone.

She hadn't been allowed to look at it yet. 'Not until it's ready,' he would always say.

She clutched the necklace he'd made her, the silver still felt jagged under her fingertips, though he'd said it would wear smooth after a while. She tugged at the chain around her neck as she watched Robbie, completely engrossed in his craft.

A silent sigh escaped her. There was a time when his dedication would draw her in, sparking warmth. Now, it only highlighted the distance between them, a gulf filled with the echoes of conversations they no longer had.

His heavy-duty headphones blocked out all sound and she didn't dare break his concentration. The smallest upset during these moments of focus could cause him to go into an artistic rage for a week, and she couldn't be bothered with that.

The shadows in the room seemed to shift subtly, reacting to her mood. Melody paused, a chill running through her despite the lack of breeze. It was as if the plain beige walls whispered of secrets. She felt it then, a nudge, towards the door. It was a silent call, a reminder that the answers she sought must lie beyond the confines of these boring walls.

She waited another few minutes, feeling her own rage build. Surely he could sense her presence, feel the change in air pressure the open door created.

He was ignoring her.

Turning away from the studio door in frustration, Melody felt something else – a pull toward the outside world, a whisper in her heart urging her to seek out the answers that seemed to dance just beyond her grasp. It was a call from the part of her that yearned for the wind's caress.

She clenched her jaw and tightened her fists, sick of being ignored. She glanced around the apartment, at Robbie's things, his collection of video games, his work on display, his car magazines. Nothing here reflected her at all. It was his place and she was just another object here. Another item to be collected. The notepad on the fridge caught her eye like a beacon in the dim kitchen. Melody shut the door and stomped to the fridge. With a few quick strokes of the pen, she left a message for Robbie, scrawling *gone to the park* on the notepad.

Melody's hand paused. He would hate this. The act felt like

defiance, but it was rebellion she craved now - reclaiming a part of herself long buried beneath the weight of everyday life. With each step towards the door, she felt a stirring, a sense of anticipation for what lay beyond the confines of the concrete and glass that had become her world.

She grabbed her coat.

The door slammed behind her as she headed for the stairs.


A PERSONAL MESSAGE FROM IRIS:

Hello lovelies. Thank you so much for joining Nova and I for the second book in our co-written series. It's wonderful to share another magical New Zealand-based story with you, drawing on local mythology and nature.

If you enjoyed this book, please leave a rating or review to help other people find it! You can pre-order book 3: The Way the Sky Curves, the next Kotahi Bay book on Kindle.

If you're interested in my real magic books and courses, see my website www.irisbeaglehole.com

If you haven't yet read our interconnected books, The Witches of Holloway Road, Hexes & Vexes by Nova Blake, feel free to check them out.

If this is your first time reading my books, you might also want to check out the Myrtlewood Mysteries series, starting with Accidental Magic or the Myrtlewood Crones. If you're looking for more books set in New Zealand, you might want to take a look at my Dreamrealm Mysteries series too.

We absolutely loved writing this book and hope you enjoyed it too. Feel free to join my reader newsletter and Nova's and follow us on social media to keep up to date with our various witchy and writerly adventures.

. . .

Many blessings, Iris xx


P.S. You can also subscribe to my Patreon account for extra Myrtlewood stories and new chapters of my books before they're published, as well as real magical content like meditations and spells, and access to my Myrtlewood Discord community. Subscribing supports my writing and other creative work! For more information, see: **www.patreon.com/ IrisBeaglehole**

# HEXES AND VEXES
## CHAPTER 1

Mia stared out at the rain through the window of Lucy, her house bus. Mia firmly believed that all vehicles needed a name, and a vehicle that was also your home, even more so.

That said, she had no idea where the name Lucy had come from. The bus itself, most likely.

The rain had been coming down hard all night, leaving pools of water on the field that the travelling fair had set up camp. That always kept the customers away, and seeing as it was the last day of the fair, she figured the whole day was a washout for most of the crew. Other people were already starting to pack up their tents and displays – not many visitors came in for hula hoops and fire poi when the weather was this bad, but it didn't always deter Mia's tarot clients.

She glanced at her clock and sighed, downing the dregs of her tea and looking at the leaves in the bottom of the cup. They didn't tell her anything good. It was just going to be that kind of day. She rinsed her mug out and set it to dry on the small kitchen counter. Rufus, her foundling magpie, walked towards her and then hopped onto her shoulder, burrowing into her hair.

"I know, not the best day for a fly around the park. Sorry, bud." She ruffled his feathers, then gently removed him. He tugged on a few strands of hair in protest, then hopped away in a huff when she put him back down on the bench. "Be like that," she called after him. "I'm going to work!"

And with that, she opened the door and went down the steps into her 'office'.

It was a small bell tent – they always had the best atmosphere, and half of her job was atmosphere. One entrance led to her bus, the other to a small awning where the clients normally waited for their appointments. She lit the candles on the round card table, the warm scent of vanilla hitting her nostrils quickly, and then switched on the fairy lights and adjusted her headscarf. Finally, she picked a few tarot decks from the wooden box under her seat and scattered the table with her gems. She was ready.

Mia braced herself as she approached the door. The tarot card reading wasn't taxing, but sometimes the people were, and she could never be sure who she'd find on the other side of the tent flap. With a final exhale, and a quick call for strength to the goddess, she opened the door.

And saw her little sister, Poppy, drenched from head to toe, water running from her black hair in rivulets.

"Poppy! What—"

The teen pushed inside the tent, and Mia noticed that Poppy was shivering badly. "What are you doing here?" Mia asked again. "Why? How?" She frowned, a million thoughts rushing through her head, and then pushed through into the bus and grabbed a blanket, before returning and draping it around the girl.

"Hi," Poppy said, and then sneezed.

All the sisterly instincts Mia thought she'd left behind rushed back in. "How long have you been out in the rain? Let me make you a hot drink or something." Mia spun back to the bus, and then stopped and turned around. "Wait. Why are you here, in the rain? Where's Camilla?"

Poppy finally looked up at Mia. Her face fell and her shoulders sagged even further, if that was possible. She must be, what, fifteen by now? A geeky looking kid that reminded Mia more of herself than she'd have liked.

"She's why I'm here," Poppy said. "Something's going on."

"Something that meant you couldn't pick up the phone and call me?" Mia raised an eyebrow. "You know I'm only a message away."

"And I know that you never come to Okato. And you need to come. Now."

Mia leaned back, surprised by the vehemence in the girl's voice. "Um—"

"No. Camilla needs you," she said. "I need you." Her voice broke, and Mia realized that Poppy was crying. She closed the distance between them and wrapped the girl in her arms. Hell, they were basically the same height now. When had that happened?

"Are you old enough to drink coffee?" Mia asked.

"I'm not a baby," Poppy said with a sniff.

"Got it. Come on." She led her little sister through the bell tent and up the steps of the bus. The girl had never been in there before; Mia had been on the road now for about six years, and they'd never managed to cross paths. AKA: their older sister refused to come and visit the travelling fair. It reeked of all the things that Camilla hated, including Mia. If they caught up it was in a café or fast food joint.

Poppy slid herself into the bench seat at the small table, while Mia put the kettle on the cooktop, then turned and leaned against the counter and eyed the teen up. The mascara on her lashes had streaked in the rain, and her freckles were barely concealed beneath a fine layer of foundation. Her thick black glasses frames gave her a librarian chic look, but underneath it all she was a girl, struggling with something.

"So, what's going on, kiddo?" Mia tried to keep her voice light. "And where is Camilla? You're not here alone, are you?"

"I hitchhiked."

Mia opened her mouth to protest, but Poppy shook her head.

"Don't say it. It's not like I've got a driver's licence. Come on, Mia."

"Fine, continue," she said with a wave of her hand. The kettle boiled and she turned away, preparing the drinks and giving Poppy the space to explain what the hell made her do such a silly thing. At her age!

To be fair, at her age, Mia had been up to all kinds of things, so she couldn't really judge.

"Cam's...changed."

"Menopause? Hormonal changes can really mess with your system. Mum went into it early," Mia said over her shoulder, pouring the milk into the mug before topping it off with boiling water and stirring.

"She's not that old." Poppy let out a big sigh. "It's hard to explain. But you need to come."

Mia slid the mugs onto the table and then frowned. "I forgot to ask if you take milk."

"It's fine. Sit."

"I'm the adult here. Aren't I meant to be giving the orders?" Mia sat anyway. "Look, if Cam has a problem, then she should be asking me for help, don't you think? It's not your job—"

"That's the thing. It is my job, because she can't... Won't... I don't know." Poppy shook her head. She wrapped her hands around the mug and sighed, her eyes closing for an instant. "It's complicated."

Mia didn't really know what to do with kids, or even teens, who were kind of like mini adults without all the wear and tear of an actual adult. But she could do this. She could.

"Okay. I'm going to need a little bit more information. Because I'd like to think you traipsed halfway across the island to find me, on your own, getting into cars with strangers, for a really good reason."

"I think..." Poppy looked into her mug, and then up into Mia's eyes. Her voice came out in a whisper. "She's different now. Cold. Erratic. I think she might have what Mum did. Or it's drugs."

Mia snorted coffee out her nose, tried to catch some of the mess in her hands, but ended up spilling the contents of her mug even further.

"What?" She dragged her headscarf off and wiped her face with it, then dabbed at her chest, her legs, but the coffee was already soaking in. "Why would you think that?"

"Have you seen her lately?" Poppy fired the accusation back. She crossed her arms and scowled. "I came here because you're the only adult I trust. The only one that might be able to help her. To help me."

"Oh, hon." Mia reached towards her, hoping her sister would forgive the outburst, but Poppy leaned back against the seat, just out of reach. "I'm sorry. I just— Cam was always the most together girl. Organized, driven, kind." Apart from when it came to Mia, anyway. Camilla had hated Mia, for being different, for being hard, for what had happened with Chris and Georgia, and the stares from everyone in the village; which was why Poppy had come here rather than just called, Mia assumed.

She could hardly just put her on a bus and send her back to

their sister if she thought Camilla was on drugs, could she? Even if that was exactly what she'd like to do.

"Yeah, well, things have changed. Big time. And I need her, so you need to come home because I'm just some dumb kid who's figured it out, so it must be really bad."

Poppy glared at Mia, and for a second she saw the echo of Camilla's rage at her. But this was the sister who loved her, who thought she was cool. Who thought her life, travelling around the country, doing readings for clients, was badass.

Right? Or had she blown it with this one too?

"Okay." Mia nodded as she stood up. "I'll come, but you owe me for this, kiddo. You know I can't stand that place, so you have to have my back. Got it?" She dumped her coffee in the sink and rinsed out the mug, putting it next to her tea cup from earlier. "Now, I have clients, and you need to get out of those wet clothes. If you're smart enough to find your way to me, you're smart enough to find some dry ones."

And with that, Mia swept from the bus, back to her bell tent and her first actual customer of the day. Any problem they threw at her had to be better than wondering if her big sister was a drug addict, or heading into early onset dementia like their mother.

# WITCHES OF HOLLOWAY RD
# PROLOGUE AND CHAPTER 1

The light of the waxing harvest moon slipped silkily over the ivy that clung to the weatherboard of the cottage near the end of Holloway Road.

Light flickered through the windows.

Inside, Sorrel and Esme Cauldwell braced themselves as they leaned over the small cauldron, their white hair tied back in scarves, and their wrinkles deepened by the low light of candles.

Esme threw a bundle of mugwort, sage and thyme, into the cauldron. The smoke rose in plumes, forming intricate patterns, as the herbs burned aromatic against the hot charcoal. Esme squinted into the smoke, allowing her mind to relax and let the patterns reveal themselves. "It's time, Sorrel," she said to her sister.

"I know the energy has been building for a while, but she's still young," Sorrel said. "She's not going to listen to a couple of old biddies like us."

"It's her Saturn Return," said Esme. "She needs to come back here for her powers to set in."

"That was the exact thing that sent her mother packing, remember," Sorrel replied. "That girl hasn't been back here in twenty years, despite all our visits. What makes you think she'll come back now?"

"She'll come back," Esme said, assuredly. "Because we're going to need her to housesit for us."

"We are?"

Esme raised her eyebrow, cunningly. "Oh yes, and you know, she's a sweet thing with nowhere else to go right now, how could she refuse a request like this from her dear old grandmother?"

"Where are you expecting us to go, then?" Sorrel asked.

"It's time for another trip to Bermuda, don't you think?" Esme strode over to the oak armoire and pulled out a tattered scroll of paper. "My list of questions for the Arch Magistrate is getting rather long, after all."

Sorrel laughed. "Of course you do! And what will you tell Ursula? That we've gone to lobby the witching parliament?"

Esme narrowed her eyes at her sister. "Of course not. It will be a while until she's ready for all that, but it will come in time. You know she has to connect with the witching world, it's in her destiny. Even old Galdie Thorn foretold it, may her spirit rest in peace."

Sorrel chortled. "You know as well as I that Galdie will be as busy in the spirit world as she was in this realm, not to mention keeping an eye on her descendants. I hear the Thorn girls are getting themselves into quite some trouble over in Myrtlewood and I'm sure they're just getting started."

Esme couldn't help but smile at that and then turned her attention back to the scrying smoke. "Oh, Sorrel! Look what you've done to the magic – you've sent it all over the place with your mischievous mind – as usual!"

Sorrel grinned and watched the smoke for a moment. "All that passes is surely meant to be."

Esme let out a grumble. "You always say that, and yet you know we believe in the power of will, especially where a witch is concerned."

"Destiny, will and chaos!" Sorrel crowed. "The three strands woven by the fates themselves. And from what the herbs are telling me, Ursula's destiny may well be entwined with Myrtlewood too – if she can ever connect with her magic."

"It's settled then," said Esme. "I'll call her tomorrow."

Sorrel tutted. "Always so hard-headed. Are you sure we can't stick around to help her figure things out?"

Esme shook her head. "You know as well as I do that she has to do this on her own. We can cast extra protections on the cottage to keep her safe." Esme's expression hardened.

"Oh..." said Sorrel, suddenly solemn. "Oh, I see. Ursula's powers coming in will open up more than just her own magic. It will—"

"It can't be helped," said Esme.

"But she doesn't know anything. She'll be completely vulnerable. No. We mustn't."

Esme smiled sadly. "It's the only way, Sister. Ursula will have to come into her powers, one way or another, and Holloway Road is the best place. She'll simply have to face whatever may come with it."

## CHAPTER 1

Ursula Cauldwell stepped off the bus and into the Wellington wind. She pushed her dark hair out of her face and shivered, partly from the cold and partly from an un-named thrill that ran through her.

*I'm finally back in the Aro Valley...after so many years.*

Ursula buttoned her red woollen coat. Auckland had been much warmer, though she hadn't noticed the temperature when she'd caught the bus from the airport.

Exhausted and still burdened from the life she's left behind, she dragged her luggage down a more gentrified Aro Street than the one she vaguely remembered. Most of the old villas and cottages had clearly been painted and refurbished, with newer houses cropping up in between them in faux old-fashioned styles.

Though there was still daylight in the last minutes of the late afternoon, the streetlights had already turned on.

As she neared the corner that took her closer to Holloway Road, Ursula felt a renewed energy. Some of the weariness she'd been carrying with her from the breakup and the betrayal and the anguish of the past few weeks melted away as new a sensation shimmered through her torso and down her limbs.

The streetlight above her flickered.

At first, Ursula thought nothing of it, but by and by she recalled walking down the same street twenty years before with her grandmother, Esme, who had stared up the flickering light and said, "Oh, bother."

"What is it?" the child Ursula had asked.

"Another surge," Gran replied.

"Surge of what?"

"Oh, don't you worry. It's nothing for us to be afraid of. Just the energy doing its thing."

The now-grown Ursula shook her head and walked on, trying to dislodge the memory. It had surfaced, raw in a way she couldn't quite explain.

Leaving this place as a child had felt wrong, even though she'd had no choice. After they'd left—well, Violet made sure they never returned to visit. Something precious had been torn from her; now all the memories carried that ache with them.

She continued walking, right to the beginning of Holloway Road. The streetlight above her flickered as well.

*...Must be something up with the grid.*

There was a certain sense of stillness at the entrance to Holloway Road, where the quirky suburbia of Aro Street gave way to hints of native forest at the periphery of the reserve, as if the land was taking a breath. A stranger to this place might think there was no more to see, but Ursula knew there was always a new level of depth within this part of the world, feeling it as she took her next steps into Holloway Road—a valley within a valley, almost an island of its own.

Ursula looked up at the familiar sight of the forested hill to her right, and then towards the small park to her left. She, too, took a breath, before being flooded with memories: bright red boots, the yellow bucket she'd carried everywhere she went as a child, gathering herbs and stones to make charms and spells as she played her favourite games.

She stopped in the middle of the path to inhale the scent of moss and lichen, mulched leaves and cut grass, reminding her she was finally coming home. Auckland had never felt like this. It irked Ursula that she'd been kept away from this place for so long, despite never belonging anywhere else.

Here there were few houses under a hundred years old, and though some of them now looked much nicer than the dreary run-down shacks she remembered from her childhood, the history of the place hung, syrupy, in the air.

A dark jewelled gleam caught her eye in the low light.

*Blackberries.* Perfectly plump and just waiting to be foraged. She couldn't help but reach out and pluck them, mindful of avoiding the thorns. Their juice stained her hands like blood, and taste exploded in her mouth, complex and tangy. It sent an unexpected shiver through her body. Tingles ran down her arms and spine in a way that reminded Ursula of the old saying...*someone's walking on my grave...*

A streetlight flickered again. Ursula glanced back towards it to see a glimpse of someone. A stocky man in a white suit, his oily dark hair slicked back.

She blinked and he was gone. Ursula felt a chill that was nothing to do with the cold wind.

*Surely I just imagined that...I must be tired.*

It wasn't that she didn't believe in apparitions or spirits or psychic phenomena, *per se*; they just never happened for her.

There were certainly ghosts here, with so much history.

Ursula vaguely recalled old stories of a murder, of police raids, activism, and even a mysterious disappearance: a young woman who went missing long ago, never to be seen again.

The place was almost a living thing, all knitted together into a rich tapestry of wilderness and potlucks, intrinsically connected to the real power holding the whole place together.

But that man didn't belong here. No, he was more the stuff of nightmares—of her imagination running wild on a dark night—than of anything truly mystical, she decided.

It was just before dusk, and the starlings were congregating as they always did, murmuring themselves into a fervour. In Ursula's imagination they asked each other, *is it time yet? Is it time?* And then the oldest, wisest one, with a streak of grey at her temples called, *NOW!*

They all took flight.

# Acknowledgments

A big thank you to all my wonderful Patreon supporters, especially:

Renate Gase

Linnea Johnson

Cheryl Gawel

Cindy

Shari Yates Farrell

Dawn Dexter

John Stephenson

Danielle Kinghorn

Ricky Manthey

Rachel

and William Winnichuk

# About Iris Beaglehole

Iris Beaglehole

Iris Beaglehole is many peculiar things, a writer, researcher, analyst, druid, witch, parent, and would-be astrologer. She loves tea, cats, herbs, and writing quirky characters.

facebook.com/IrisBeaglehole
x.com/IrisBeaglehole
instagram.com/irisbeaglehole

# About Nova Blake

Nova Blake is a Māori/Pākehā speculative fiction author from Aotearoa New Zealand. She enjoys coffee (and lots of it), devouring good stories (in any format), and sleep (though she never gets enough).

**f X ⊙**

www.ingramcontent.com/pod-product-compliance
Lightning Source LLC
Chambersburg PA
CBHW021220310726
48971CB00006B/1629